American GAUNTLET

ALLIE LEWIS

ISBN: 979-8-9863796-2-3 (paperback), 979-8-9863796-3-0 (ebook)

prologue

ONE question.

It had all come down to one question.

Everything I had worked for over the last seven months. Everything I planned to do with the prize money. Everything I had endured in this grueling competition, this excruciating Gauntlet. The physical strain. The mental toll. The pain and the struggle and the perseverance.

I never imagined it would come down to seven words with a question mark at the end.

One, simple question.

And the worst part is I'm not the one answering it.

one

MY MUSCLES are howling at me in misery. They're well past the phase of gentle pleading, the dance of deft negotiation. They've officially moved on to undignified begging, and yet, I still force them to lower the bar to my chest for one more rep, even as they begin to shake in one final act of rebellion.

Of course, when I say my muscles are howling at me, I really mean my brain is. In fact, my muscles will perform until they literally collapse from exhaustion, but far before I reach that point, my brain will try to convince me they're on the cusp of failure. That if I do one more rep, they'll surely give out. That I simply have nothing left to give, not a single drop of energy left in the tank. *Liar*, I say as I press the bar up and heave it back onto the rack.

I sit up on the bench a little too quickly and dizziness hits me in a wave—a sign of fatigue, no doubt—but it subsides as I blink the black spots away from my vision. I snatch my water bottle off the gym floor and take a graceless gulp, relishing the way I can feel the ice-cold liquid running down my throat. Wiping a stray drop of water from the corners of my mouth, I snap the cap back on and steal a glance at myself in the condensation-ridden gym mirror, fogged up from excessive body heat and the stifling Houston humidity.

Strands of my straight brown hair have begun escaping from the elastics holding the high space buns I always wear when I work out. The sweat from my chest has seeped through my charcoal gray crop, a dark, T-shaped sweat blot growing by the second. The excess sticky moisture on my face has smeared my mascara to where it's running a little from both eyes. I look like a mess.

I absolutely love it.

That feeling when you finish a workout and reek of sweat and hard work and sheer force of will—I crave it. I savor it. To think I avoided exercise at all costs only a few years ago seems so wild to me, considering now my love affair with the gym is dangerously bordering on an addiction.

I lie back down on the bench to tackle my last set, my gym playlist blasting at an ungodly level through my headphones. But just as I go to grab the bar, my music cuts off abruptly, replaced instead by my ringtone that comes exploding through my headphones so loud I jump up and nearly smack my head on the barbell, my pulse skyrocketing in the process. I'm on the receiving end of a few concerned looks from the two guys on the bench press next to mine, but I toss them a clipped smile to let them know I'm fine and promptly seat myself back down.

Before I grab the barbell, though, I pause. I'm inclined to ignore whoever is calling me—I almost never check my phone when I'm at the gym—but every time my phone rings, my heart beats a little faster of its own volition, waiting for a call I know will probably never come.

I fight the hope and anxious desire that flutters through my stomach, but in the back of my mind, I admit it's kind of nice to hope for something, even if it's probably not going to happen. I haven't had anything to really hope for in a long time, and it feels…invigorating. Like that feeling when you were listening to the radio as a kid and you beg for your mom's phone to call into the station, desperately hoping you'll be caller number seven, so you can win whatever it is they're giving away. Concert tickets or backstage passes or tickets to see *Disney on Ice*. In the very back of your mind, you know you probably won't be caller number seven, but it feels so exhilarating to try in the moment. It feels like you've never wanted something more in your life.

Giving into the hope-fueled desire, I seize my phone from where I've haphazardly tossed it next to my bench and quickly glance at the caller ID. It's a number I don't recognize, and as I catch a glimpse of the location below the number, I freeze. *Burbank, CA*. My arms, already wobbly from my upper body session, start trembling more, even as that little seed of hope begins putting down roots in the pit of my stomach. It's a tiny runt of a root, but it's a root nonetheless.

Is this it? I think to myself. *Is it my time to be caller number seven? This type of stuff…it doesn't happen. Not to me.*

As I stand pinned in place, I realize I'm losing precious seconds, and I really don't want to let this call go to voicemail. I dash out the nearby back door of my obnoxiously loud gym and press the green button at the bottom of the screen with a shaky finger.

"Hello?" I wince at how out of breath I sound. I can hear my own pulse as it wages war behind my eardrums.

"Hi!" A cheery voice exclaims from the other end of the line. "Is this Dani?"

My voice runs even more breathless as I immediately recognize the voice and picture the four-foot, eleven-inch blonde ball of energy that it belongs to.

"Oh, hi. Yes, it's me," I answer, trying to simultaneously sound hopeful but not overeager.

Why am I overthinking this? Just be normal.

"Dani, it's Kelly, one of the producers from *American Gauntlet*. We video chatted a little while back."

"Hi, Kelly. Yes, of course I remember," I say, even as I'm dying to know if she's delivering good or bad news for me. I nibble at the hangnail on my thumb before I yank my hand away, praying she couldn't hear the obnoxious sound of my teeth clicking. I need to get a grip. Quickly.

"Well, I'm sure you'd love to know why I'm calling," she says, and I can practically hear the smile that her tone tells me is currently spread across her face. "I just wanted to let you know that you and Lana are in! You've been chosen for the show!"

I gasp, sucking in a breath so sharp it knocks me back a step.

The next sound I hear is my phone smacking against the gravelly pavement beneath me, skidding over the tiny rocks upon impact. I apparently let it slip from my grasp, unable to contain the overwhelming joy and triumph and pure elation that accompanies the words Kelly just spoke to me.

I scramble to pick my phone up, just as Kelly asks, "Oh, um, Dani? Did I lose you?"

"I'm here!" I probably scream at her. I pause, filling my lungs with a deliberate breath before I say, "I'm here, sorry. I just can't believe it. You have no idea what this means to me, Kelly. This… this is everything for me. I don't know what else to say, except thank you." I fight back the urge to ramble on about how life-changing this opportunity is, about how some of my favorite memories are ones where I was glued to the TV, unable to peel my eyes away from the competitors on *American Gauntlet*. "Just—thank you."

"The whole team of producers fell in love with your family's story when we watched your audition video, and you and Lana really sealed the deal when we did the video chat interview. So you better believe it, Dani—you and Lana are going to be on season 23 of American Gauntlet in six short months!"

The rest of the conversation is a blur as Kelly continues reassuring me that no, this is not a prank, and yes, Lana and I will actually be going on the number one reality competition in the whole freaking country. She says she'll be in touch with all of the details soon before she bids me a bubbly goodbye.

Just before I hit the button to end the call, I hear Kelly murmur to herself, "Man…I love this job." Because who wouldn't want to be the person to call contestants and let them know they have a shot at winning $300,000?

I'm high on excitement and adrenaline and pure, unadulterated happiness. All I want to do is go shout the news to my offensively noisy gym, but I refrain, remembering the cast is top secret—there's a non-disclosure agreement currently making its way to my inbox, per Kelly—and we can't tell anyone other than immediate family, which just leaves my mom and my two sisters, Penny and Lana.

Wait—Lana!

I'm not surprised when she doesn't pick up my phone call. Lana takes personal offense to anyone who calls instead of texts her.

ME: CALL ME NOW

Lana responds to my text immediately, confirming my suspicion that she could've answered my call, but simply chose not to.

LANA: What do you need?

ME: Are you serious? Answer your phone, you muppet.

LANA: Muppet? Who are you?

I grin down at my phone, laughing at the term I picked up from watching too much British reality TV. It's definitely one of the more polite terms, so she should be grateful. I shoot Lana another text begging her to call me so I can give her the news.

After several anxious moments, my phone screen lights up with Lana's picture. It's a goofy one that I took of her when we stayed up all night right before she left for college. She's elbow-deep in a half gallon of mint chocolate chip ice cream, the sticky wreckage smeared across her lips and chin. She looks entirely disheveled and delirious from sleep deprivation, and she'd die if she knew I used it as her contact photo, but it perfectly portrays her chaotic personality, and I can't make myself part with it. Maybe I'll change it to a photo of us holding a $300K check at the end of *American Gauntlet*. I grin at the thought.

Lana sounds exasperated as she sarcastically asks, "Who died?"

I roll my eyes and wish she were here with me to see it. "Aw hi, sis. I missed you too," I reply with feigned sweetness. "Do you want the news or not?"

She relents and I want to give her more grief for being so dramatic about phone calls, but I'm so amped, I end up blurting the news out to her, half-screaming from excitement, in one convoluted mess of a sentence.

"Are you serious? It's really happening?" she squeals at me.

"Oh, I'm serious," I say to her, still high on the endorphins flooding through my body. It's a dangerous mixture of excitement and disbelief with a healthy dose of nerves. It feels exhilarating all the same, and I'm not sure if my heart rate will ever return to a healthy level.

We go back and forth squealing and exchanging the same *"I can't even believe this"* statements over and over again until I'm able to calm down enough to focus.

"On a real note, Lana," I say to her, trying to rein in her rambling excitement, "you've seen the show. You know how absolutely grueling and competitive it is, even for a college athlete."

Lana had been beside me as I obsessed over every episode of *American Gauntlet* in high school, our necks craned up at the television screen, both of us absorbing every second of the show like little sponges. (I'd like to say I'm not quite as infatuated with it now as a newly minted adult, but that would be a blatant lie.) Lana and I had always wondered what it might be like to be a competitor. How it might feel to get the call that we've been selected. What we would do to prepare for it. What it would be like to see the show behind the scenes. Is it all real? Are any of the competitions staged? Is the show's infamous host really as intimidating as he seems on TV? My mind still can't wrap itself around the fact that I'll get answers to every one of these questions in six months' time.

Having watched so many seasons of *American Gauntlet*, Lana knows how intense it is, how people have walked away with concussions or broken bones. Even worse, maybe, are those that leave the show with broken wills, their spirits so thoroughly obliterated that it's difficult to imagine how they recover.

"You know how much I train with all of my track practices.

I think I'll be fine." There's a subtle air of cockiness to her tone. She would probably just call it *confidence.*

"I know, sis, but you're going to have to add in different types of training. Obviously, your cardio is unmatched, and you've got a lot of lower body strength, but you'll need to work on your upper body."

Lana groans from the other end of the line, the sound so grating I have to pull the phone back from my ear for fear of bursting an eardrum. "Dani, you know how much I *loathe* lifting weights."

I laugh at the dramatics because they're so typically Lana. "I know, I know," I reply, attempting to soothe her despite my giggle. "But at least you have a boyfriend who can train with you. Graham can be your accountability partner."

I'm convinced Lana wouldn't still have her track scholarship at UNC if it weren't for Graham keeping her schedule straight, reminding her to get to practice, prompting her to eat more than half a banana and a spoonful of peanut butter as a meal. Lana operates in the moment and simply can't be bothered to, I don't know, plan ahead. Ever. She finds it hilarious that I use the Reminders app on my phone and map out my meals for the week, which, I often remind her, is a very normal thing that people do. The organization gene apparently skipped her over… or maybe it's the fact that I simply necessitated it more than she did growing up. Shouldering the responsibility of a family does that to a person.

"Yeah, yeah. We'll see," she replies, and just like Kelly's grin, I can practically hear Lana's eye roll. I picture her bored expression, her shoulders sagging in exasperation.

In a blink, I've suddenly had enough of her lackadaisical attitude. I stifle the urge to snap at her, an angry hive of irritation threatening to breach the protective emotional wall I've spent years carefully constructing. Setting the fact that Lana and I are literal superfans of *American Gauntlet* aside, she must understand what this prize money means. For us. For Mom. For our sister Penny most of all.

I inhale deeply, holding it for a moment before expelling every drop of oxygen from my lungs. The familiar action instantly calms me, awarding me a level head, as I pull out my amiable but authoritative big sister voice; it's one I save for when I really need it.

"There's no '*we'll see*,' Lana. You're going to lift weights and train and watch film and do everything else you need to do to properly prepare for the show because we only have one shot to win this money. And we're not going to waste it."

[THREE MONTHS OUT]

THE gym at 8:45 p.m. on a weeknight is absolute insanity, filled with an interesting mix of bodybuilders, swarms of high school boys, and people dragging their feet in a zombie-like state who are working out before they head to their graveyard shift. I've been at the gym, quite literally, all day long, starting with my front desk shift, then to a full afternoon of personal training clients, then to my own two hours of lifting and cardio. I'm exhausted and I smell and all I want is a hot shower for my aching muscles.

When I'm almost through the maze of weight racks and machines and gym bags left in the middle of the narrow walkways, I hear steps behind me. I glance back and see it's a newer member of the gym—Aiden, I think—as he jogs to catch up with me. He has a bashful smile on his face, as if I've just caught him doing something he shouldn't. He joined the gym while I was working the front desk a couple weeks ago; I helped him get all of his paperwork squared away.

"Hey, it's Dani, right?"

"Yeah," I say. "Aiden, if I remember correctly?"

His eyes light up, the corners of his mouth lifting into a smile. "Yeah. I didn't know if you'd remember. I'm sure you see a lot of people in and out of here every day."

"I do my best," I reply, smiling back at him. I always try to remember people's names; it's something my sister Penny is passionate about. I can practically hear her in the back of my mind as she tuts, *Remembering someone's name is a small kindness that makes a big difference.*

I'm still making my way toward the door, food and a hot shower beckoning me home like a siren's call, when Aiden clears his throat, pausing beside me. "Hey, so listen," he begins.

Oh no.

"I know we just met not too long ago, but I'd really like to get to know you better," he says, running a hand through his light brown hair, already slick with sweat. "Would you want to go out sometime?"

I look him in the eyes, trying my best to soften the blow. "Aiden, I'm flattered, honestly. But I, um…I just can't."

Trust me, Aiden, I think to myself. *You don't want to go down this road.*

His brown eyes pinch together, confusion overtaking his features. "Oh, is there—"

"It's not you," I cut in. I want to finish with "It's me, really," but the *"It's not you, it's me"* line seems like a cop out. Although in this case, it's the truth.

Suddenly, a huge, muscley arm makes its way around me from behind. I don't need to look at the man behind me to know who it belongs to. "You ready to go, babe?" Ford asks.

I look at Ford and roll my eyes where Aiden can't see. "Yep, all set," I reply, all exaggerated sweetness. When I turn back to Aiden, I find his face has turned an ashy gray color as he takes in the sheer size of Ford.

He darts his eyes back to me. "Sorry, Dani." To his credit,

he's recovered impressively quickly. "I didn't realize you have a boyfriend."

So many responses come to mind, but I say none of them. Instead, I say, "No worries, seriously." I toss him a genuine smile as I head out the door, Ford's arm still securely around me. "I'll see you around!"

As soon as the gym doors shut behind us, Ford bursts into laughter.

"Gross, you're so sweaty," I tell him as I wiggle out from under his *very large* arm.

"Oh yeah? How do you like this?"

I squeal as Ford rubs his disgusting, smelly arm sweat all over me. Between my average height and his above average stature, my head comes right to his armpit, so I shove him away before he can put me in a death hold under his pits.

"*Gah*, you're disgusting," I say, even as we both continue cracking up at each other. "Also, you've got to stop scaring guys off with the fake boyfriend bit."

"Oh come on," he snorts. "I did you a favor. You weren't going to go out with him."

"You don't know that!"

He turns to me, a skeptical eyebrow lowered in my direction. "Were you?" he asks.

I groan. "No."

That makes him cackle, apparently. "See, I did you a favor," he declares. His tone is all self-assured confidence. "*That's* not the guy for my Dani. Whenever you do finally fall for someone, he'll be…" his voice trails off as he tries to pinpoint the right word. "Spectacular. A knock-your-socks-off kind of guy."

"Oh, is that so?" I snort, quirking an eyebrow at him. "*Spectacular?*"

"That's right."

"How will I be able to tell who's so 'spectacular' when you scare them all off in the first place?" I ask with a laugh.

"You'll just…" he says, trailing off again. "You'll just know, okay? It's not Adam."

"First of all, it's *Aiden*. Second of all, I can't wait to find this mythical guy who can get the elusive Ford Peterson seal of approval," I tease. I lurch out of reach of Ford's sweaty arm as he moves to pin me under it again before we dissolve into laughter.

As we walk toward Ford's car, I can't help but appreciate the vision of perfection that is Ford Peterson. He's tall, dark, and handsome in every sense of the word. He's built like a bodybuilder, but he's a warm, gooey cinnamon roll on the inside, one that also has a fiercely protective side. A cinnamon roll with the exterior of The Terminator, more like.

He's perfect in pretty much every way.

It's a shame we feel absolutely no attraction for each other whatsoever.

I always say that Ford is simultaneously God's greatest gift to me, as well as his greatest prank. Like, here this absolute specimen gets dropped into my life—someone who checks every box that any girl could ever ask for—and yet, nothing. Not one measly sizzle of attraction, on either end.

In a lot of ways, though, I'm grateful for it. Ford came into my life right after I graduated high school and went through my first and only breakup, a breakup that absolutely crushed my soul into hundreds of teeny tiny bits. It was the kind of breakup that left gaping emotional scars. They're healed now, but you can still see them; you can still run your finger over the pinkish-white skin, raised like permanent speed bumps on my body. With no stable male role model really ever in my life, my self-worth was at an all time low, and then Ford walked right in and gave me the stability I so desperately craved. He also introduced me to the gym, and that pretty much transformed my life and gave me the greatest gift: confidence.

Even though I joke about it, I'm actually relieved that Ford and I have never and will never date. His love for me is so sacred, so unconditional, so stable; it's the ultimate comfort knowing Ford will never be taken away from me for the sake of romantic feelings.

Romance. I struggle to even think about what that would look like for me. Part of me is convinced that part of my life has a permanent rain cloud over it, one that lingers long past its welcome. That's why it's so easy to joke about my dating life with Ford—said dating life is nonexistent.

After my breakup, I was so broken, so hollow, I swore I'd never put myself in that position again. I promised myself the next person I dated would be worth the risk of getting my heart shattered into a million tiny pieces once more. I haven't met that person yet, and to be completely honest, I'm not sure they exist. I give Ford a hard time about never letting guys get close to me, but in reality, I don't let them get close enough either. A relationship means opening yourself up to someone, and when you do that…there's always the possibility they'll leave.

The thought terrifies me.

"Do you want to talk about it?" Ford asks from the driver's seat, pulling me from my thoughts. I probably have the same grimace on my face that always magically appears when I think about the breakup. I'd rather let all my memories of him die in the deepest chasms of my mind.

"I don't know…" I say, unsure if I want to open this can of worms. I never discuss my one and only disastrous relationship with anyone, but Ford is the one exception to that rule. I've already divulged every grisly detail in one of the countless heart-to-hearts we've had over the last four years. "Thinking about dating again always dredges up the past. It's embarrassing," I say with a pitiful laugh. "I lost myself all over a guy named Justin who didn't know how to do his own laundry and listened to Nickelback unironically."

Ford scowls, always upset when I blame myself for everything that happened with Justin, but whether I was ready to go down this path or not, there's no going back now. The painful cache of memories consumes me in full force.

I met Justin my junior year of high school. There wasn't anything particularly alluring about him, but he gave me attention, and I guess that was all it took for a girl who never had it from her dad. We dated for almost two years, and I spent every moment I could with him, looking to him for guidance, for validation, for approval on everything I did. Looking back, I see how much he took advantage of me, how much he manipulated me into caring for him, just because he knew I had pretty much raised my two younger sisters when my dad was gone and my mom wasn't able to. He knew what heartstrings to tug on to get me to do his laundry and cook him food and do his school projects for him. To sacrifice my own happiness and wellbeing and autonomy for him.

I nearly vomit just thinking about it.

When Justin and I graduated, we spent every single day of the summer together and then he tried to break off our relationship right before he went to college. I didn't have the money to go to college, nor the grades to get scholarships, and what financial assistance I could receive still would've left me in an uncomfortable amount of debt, so I stayed in our little Houston suburb while Justin and everyone else from our giant high school went off to big universities. Justin said it would be too hard to do long distance, but I begged him to just try. Begged him to not leave me alone, to not abandon me.

"Please," I begged, grasping his hands so tightly in mine that he winced in pain. I couldn't let them go; I knew if I did, if I let this moment pass, I'd lose him forever. "We can do long distance. It's not even that far. You'll be less than two hours away."

"Dani…"

I took his hands and forced them around me, threading my arms around his neck and clutching him so tightly, my knuckles turned white. Tears began leaking from my eyes like a faulty faucet, but I blinked them back, wiped them on my arm before he saw, because I knew how much he hated it when I cried. *So emotional,* he'd say.

"I'll come visit," I pleaded. "I'll…I'll transfer after a year or two of community college so we can be together." The words tasted like acid as they left my lips, but I didn't care. "Please, Justin. Just *try.*"

So, he "tried."

He came home some weekends, bringing his dirty laundry for me to do for him, since, it turns out, he didn't know how to do it himself. (I partially blame his parents, who had spoon-fed him since birth, for that one.) We'd hang out for a couple days, and I'd send him back with clean clothes and handwritten love letters, only to find out a few months into the semester that he had been cheating on me the whole time.

The memory is clear as day in my mind. Me, bored, opening up Instagram to mindlessly scroll. Seeing a message request from a girl I didn't know. Clicking it, thinking it's probably nothing, but quickly realizing she's not connecting with me on social media because she wants to be friends. No; suddenly my DMs were a confessional, and this girl—Madi Ryling, I'll never forget her name—was breaking the news to me that she and Justin had hooked up at a party the previous night. *I didn't know he had a girlfriend,* she'd said. I swear. *I didn't know until I found his Instagram this morning.* That's all I read before I threw my phone across the room and stumbled to my bathroom to empty the contents of my stomach into my toilet.

I drove to Justin's dorm that night to confront him, to wait for him to tell me it was all some big mix-up, some case of mistaken identity. But he didn't. He not only admitted to cheating on me, but he made it sound like it was *my fault*. I was the one who begged him to stay in the relationship after all, he'd said. But it wasn't just what he said, it was the way he said it, the way he looked at me without a single ounce of remorse. I wished he'd looked at me with guilt or sorrow or even anger, but his expression was so much worse. He gazed at me with a look of unmistakable pity.

And the worst part of it all was that I believed him. I believed his cheating *was* my fault. I shouldered the blame and ended up being more angry at myself than I was at him.

I've since filed that time in my life away in my brain as "rock bottom."

Thankfully, I didn't beg him to stay with me. That was the only shred of dignity I could still grasp like a lifeline. Justin and I were done. But I was a mere shell of a human.

Cue: Ford, four years older than me, moving into the same apartment complex as me, Mom, Lana and Penny. He quickly endeared himself to me (and my whole little misfit family) and hauled me off to the gym with him. The rest is history, really.

With every weight I lifted, my confidence built itself up, brick by painstaking brick. I not only felt confident, but also strong. Empowered. I knew I wanted to make fitness a huge part of my life, to help other people feel confident too, so after two years of working out almost every day (and working at the gym's front desk to get a free membership), I became a certified personal trainer and, well, here we are.

"That garbage can of a human doesn't deserve a single second more of your thoughts," Ford says vehemently as we both step out of his Honda Accord. Seeing Ford next to his car is almost comical. The sheer size of his body makes it look like a clown car.

"I know," I say. "But when I think about him, it always leads me to you. I stinkin' love you, Ford Peterson. Even though you actually stink."

Ford wraps me under his arm as we climb the steps to our neighboring apartments and presses a kiss to my temple. The scruff on his jaw is like sandpaper against my skin.

"I love you," he says as heads into his apartment. "And just FYI, you stink, too."

three

MY back thuds against the mat for what feels like the millionth time. The wind is knocked clean out of me. Again.

I pick myself off the mat with my heavily chalked hands and move back to the climbing wall, ready to tackle it for round one-million-and-one.

"Hey! You okay over there? You've, uh…well, you've fallen quite a few times," the gym manager calls over to me. He's wearing a look of concern mixed with mild amusement that I'm sure he's trying to cover up.

I do my best to smile, although it probably appears more like a grimace. "All good!" I call back. I can't blame the guy for nearly laughing at me because, let's be honest, I would be doing the same thing.

Luckily, I am one of the only people in the obstacle course gym that I've dropped into for a couple days this week. I could only afford to buy a three-day pass to this gym, which has a plethora of different training tools that my regular weight lifting gym doesn't have, so I've got to make efficient use of my time. The space is covered with all sorts of multifaceted obstacles and challenges, often used by people who practice parkour and ninja and other unique sports. There are monkey bars and moving obstacles and colorful floor-to-ceiling climbing walls all around me, and I currently find myself near one of the larger climbing walls with nasty overhangs that test every ounce of grip strength—and mental strength—I have.

I climb up a few feet and begin to make the transition to the handhold on the nearest overhang, which requires me to push off a tiny foothold and launch myself toward the steep cliff. I've tried to get this transition no less than twenty-five times, but I'm determined to nail it before I move on.

I hurl myself toward the handhold and grip with everything I have, my fingers screaming from the pressure and exhaustion. I keep my elbows bent and biceps flexed to minimize the swing from the jump so I don't slip off, and I unwittingly close my eyes to brace myself for the impact I know is coming when my back inevitably drops to the mat.

Except it doesn't come.

I throw open my eyes and see myself hanging off the minuscule rock the gym owners apparently think is sufficient for a handhold. I get so excited that I drop to the ground with a huge grin on my face, not even minding when I thud against the mat again, a cloud of chalk engulfing the air around me.

"There you go!" the manager shouts.

I've started adding in any and all types of athletic training that I can to prepare for *American Gauntlet.* There's always some type of climbing-related competition sometime during the season, so I've been working to build up my grip strength and climbing techniques these last few months. I have a lot of upper body strength from lifting weights, but pushing a bench press or curling dumbbells doesn't directly translate to holding the weight of your own body and manipulating it to your advantage.

I shake the chalk from my clothes as I try to come to terms with the fact that I'll actually be going on *American Gauntlet,* the most popular reality competition show in the United States and the obsession of pretty much everyone I know, myself included. It's not some far-off dream anymore, some fantasy I had as a high schooler who was desperate to escape her reality. It's *really happening,* and the craziest part is I actually feel confident in my abilities. In myself. I'm not the insecure high school girl I once was. I may have a long way to go when it comes to becoming the person I'm meant to be, but I'm confident in this rough draft version of myself.

And I can't shake this feeling that Lana and I…we could really win this thing.

Each season, contestants go on the show and compete in absolutely insane physical challenges, all in the hopes of winning the grand prize of $300,000 at the end. The thing is, though, there's no way to *really* know what you're in for. The only thing you can expect about each season of *American Gauntlet* is that you have *no idea* what to expect.

To put it plainly, *American Gauntlet* is known for the plot twists of the century.

When Lana and I head off to the show, we'll compete in four phases, each phase represented by a gold star in the show's logo: *Strength, Endurance, Strategy, and Grit.* If we make it through each phase—as if that isn't already an accomplishment in and of itself—we'll face the Gauntlet, an agonizing final competition that puts all four phases together and tests every bit of physical and mental toughness we have. If we complete the Gauntlet first, we'll be $300,000 (and an eternity of bragging rights) richer.

Some seasons, contestants compete as individuals, while other times they compete in duos or even teams. This season, though, everyone will be competing as a duo—with a family member. All the pairs this year will be related to each other, so I imagine things could get interesting. And messy. *American Gauntlet* is undoubtedly a display of physical fortitude, but it's also a reality show, so viewers can always expect drama. And when you put family members through intensely stressful situations like those in *American Gauntlet*…I imagine things will escalate quickly.

To be honest, though, I'm not too worried about Lana and myself. We have been through so many challenges in real life, and we've made it out the other side stronger than ever, so I know we can make it through the show in one piece. Lana is twenty-one, only two years younger than me, but I practically raised her throughout some of her most formative years. We have a connection unlike any other pair of sisters. As long as she follows the training plan and protocols I sent her, we'll be golden.

As I catch my breath and take a sip of water from the water bottle I carry with me everywhere, I quickly look at my phone and see I missed a text from Graham.

GRAHAM: Just left the gym with Lana. She's doing great with the training plan you sent!

I sigh in relief as I reread Graham's text. *She knows how important this opportunity is. There's nothing to worry about,* I think to myself. I immediately feel a little guilty for being so concerned that Lana isn't training or taking this opportunity as seriously as I am, but Lana has always been a bit more of a free spirit (and careless at times), so it's hard for my brain *not* to go there. I am the eldest sibling after all.

Since Lana is halfway across the country, I'm relying on Graham to make sure she follows through with her training. Lana is a hard worker, but I know she has a lot going on between track and keeping her grades up to hang on to her scholarship, so a little extra motivation from Graham can't hurt.

Since we haven't been able to train together, we both let ourselves tell one person outside of the immediate family that we're going on the show. Naturally, she told Graham and I told Ford. Being able to plan and strategize and rely on Ford to push me through all of this intense training has been a huge asset. It's helped me feel not so alone, but then again, Ford has always helped me feel that way.

I shoot a quick text to Lana.

ME: Graham said your training is going really well. I'm so proud of you, sis. I know you have a lot going on, so thank you for making this a priority. It'll all be worth it when we win – promise.

I toss my phone back in my gym bag and head toward the door leading to the outside obstacle course. I gaze outdoors and don't see a single other person, which isn't surprising considering it's currently pouring rain, the raindrops beating against the metal roof of the gym like little tin drums. As I study the dark, cloudy sky and the flood of water coming from it, I smile. While I wouldn't typically consider a downpour the best time for outdoor training, I'm actually grateful for it. There's no way to know what kind of conditions we'll be competing in when we're on the show, so I've been using the frequent rain to get comfortable with less-than-ideal weather conditions.

I tuck the stray pieces of my hair back into my space buns and take a deep breath before jogging out the door and into the pouring rain. The thick droplets instantly cool me off as I step into the drizzle. I close my eyes and tilt my face up to the sky for just a moment, soaking in the feeling of the fresh, cool water on my skin.

Get comfortable with it, I tell myself. *Any conditions are your ideal conditions.*

My eyes shoot open, and I take off running to the military-style obstacle course awaiting me. I relish the feeling of my leg muscles working a little harder as they trudge through the mud and throw myself right into it, taking to my elbows. I work my way under a net that is so low to the ground I have to crawl under it.

When I get to the other side of the net, I'm met by a ten-foot wooden wall. I grab the rope, frayed from use, and climb my way up, throwing my legs over the top as I reach it and jumping down into more mud. I stopped training with my headphones—*you won't get to listen to music to pump you up when you run the Gauntlet*, I keep telling myself—so I've grown used to the silence. I've learned to welcome it. Even the smallest factors at the *American Gauntlet* camp can mess with the psyche of its victims, and I want to be prepared in every way possible.

The training may sound extreme, but $300,000 is on the line. (Well, actually it'll be $150,000, since Lana will take half of it, and even less when taxes are taken out.) Regardless, the prize money is a life-changing amount of money for me.

And I've got big plans for it.

WHEN I stop to pick Ford up on my way home, his eyes go wide as soon as he gets into my beat-up old clunker of a pickup truck, the linen scented Febreze car freshener doing nothing to mask the musty stench of mud and sweat on my body. The truck sinks a little as Ford eases himself into the passenger seat.

"Do I even want to know what you've been up to?" he asks.

I roll my eyes at him. "You already know what I've been up to," I reply dryly.

"Dani, I know you were training for the show, but did you, like, roll around in the mud afterward just for the fun of it?"

I glance over at him, a deadpan look on my face.

"Oh wait, no—you fell, didn't you?" he asks, cracking himself up. "You were walking to your car or something and totally ate it in the mud?"

"No, you brat," I say, punching him in the arm and leaving a fist print of semi-dry mud on his shoulder. "That obstacle course gym I was at had an outdoor training course, and it was my last day training there, so I just ran it in the rain."

"Of course you did," he says, shaking his head and eyeing me from the seat beside me. "I'm proud of you—have I mentioned that?"

"Once or twice, or, like, a hundred times."

"There's no way you don't win it, Dani."

I smile at him, even as my stomach drops at the mere thought of winning the show. It's almost too overwhelming to think about. There's still so much I feel like I need to do to prepare in the next three weeks.

"Penny's excited to see you," I say, changing the subject.

He grins. "You know I'm always excited to see the youngest Di Laurentis."

I UNLOCK the door of my apartment with a pronounced *click* and open it for Ford to step inside while I remove my mud-caked training shoes. I already know Penny is waiting for him on the other side of the door; she's probably been waiting there since the moment I told her Ford was coming over for dinner.

"Ford, darling! It's so good to see you! I'm so tickled you could join us for dinner," she coos as soon as he steps across the threshold of our apartment.

If I could describe Penny's energy, it would be a mix between a 1950s housewife and a doting Texas grandma. She's 18 going on 80 and gathered most of her speech patterns from black and white TV sitcoms from 70 years ago.

"How's my girl?" Ford asks with an ear-to-ear grin. The next second, he's in front of her, smothering her in a giant bear hug. He stands practically a foot taller than her and completely engulfs her as she wraps her arms around him with a huge smile of her own.

As I stand in the doorway of our apartment, something hitches in my throat as I look at my best friend and my youngest sister before me. I've seen this scene play out hundreds of times, but warmth still floods through my veins as I see the admiration in Penny's eyes, the authentic kindness in Ford's.

Penny has Williams syndrome, and it's always been a bit of a struggle for her to make genuine connections with other people her age, many of whom have difficulty looking past her perceived differences. Williams syndrome isn't a super well-known genetic disorder, so when kids her age saw her growing up, many of them didn't understand her. As kids, unfamiliar things can seem scary, so they often shy away from people who look different, or they simply act like they don't see them.

The problem is those kids grow up to be the same scared adults.

Penny's appearance makes her differences obvious at first glance, but once anyone gets to know her, they see how kind and caring and passionate she is. I always say she's like a warm hug in human form.

There are so many things about Penny that I wish I had. Her ability to see the best parts of people, always. Her vocabulary, which is extensive and impressive. Her superpower of meeting someone one time, even in passing, and remembering their name. Her ability to be in social situations and never get burnt out. She's a social powerhouse, but she hasn't always had the opportunity to use her incredible gifts.

Ford unwraps himself from Penny, and as soon as she sees me stepping through the doorway, caked in mud from head to toe, she gasps.

"Dani! What's happened to you?"

"I'm fine," I laugh. "Just some extra training in the rain today."

"Well, let's get you cleaned up," she says, motioning for me to follow her toward the bathroom. "Ford, we'll be right out. There's iced tea on the counter in the kitchen. Please help yourself." She's such a picture perfect host for guests that she could teach a class on hospitality. I should honestly start taking notes.

I let Penny usher me into the bathroom, muttering under her breath about tracking mud through the living room. She turns on a hot shower for me, and even though we're sisters, she turns around to give me privacy, as I strip off my muddy clothes. She's extremely modest that way.

"Just leave them in a pile," she says. "I'll take care of them. You don't need to worry about a thing."

"You're the best." I could do my muddy laundry myself, but I let her handle this situation because I know how much she genuinely *enjoys* caring for people and serving them. If letting her usher me around tonight brings her joy, who am I to stop it?

As I step into the shower, a sigh escapes me as the scalding water hits my skin, loosening and releasing the caked mud from my body. Dark brown water races toward the drain, eventually running clear. I wash the mud out of every nook and cranny of my body before throwing on a t-shirt and shorts and heading to the kitchen, where I find Ford and Penny drinking iced tea and gabbing at the table like old ladies on a Southern wraparound front porch. All they need are two rocking chairs and knitting needles, and the image would be complete.

I look around the kitchen, and my eyes turn to slits as I scowl at Ford.

"I didn't invite you over for dinner so you could cook for us, Ford."

"Oh, please," he says, pushing a plate loaded with chicken breast, rice, and veggies in front of me. "You've cooked for me plenty of times."

"Mhmm," I finally murmur, the hunger quickly dissolving my resistance like the sugar in Ford's tea. "Well, thank you. This smells amazing."

"Yes, thank you for this fantastic and nutritious meal, Ford. We are so thrilled to have you here with us this evening," Penny says, as she digs into the plate he prepared for her.

He looks at her with a little gleam in his eye and metaphorically tips his hat at her. "Anything for my favorite girls," he says. "Is your mom working tonight?"

"Yeah, she's working nights now," I reply, swallowing a mouthful of broccoli that somehow tastes good when he makes it. "I'm going to watch some old *American Gauntlet* episodes tonight to study up for the show if you want to join me."

"I don't know. I'm pretty busy…"

"Liar," I snort.

"Yeah, you're right," he says, laughing. "I'm down to study

up with you. Although, you know they never repeat any of the competitions."

"I know. It just helps me visualize actually being there on the show. I feel like half of winning *American Gauntlet* is the mental game. So many of the contestants break from the pressure, even though they're doing okay physically."

"Good point. Let's watch season eighteen. That's the best one."

I dramatically halt the forkful of food that's already halfway in my mouth. "Absolutely not," I scoff. "Season twelve is objectively the best."

Ford and I snipe across the table at each other as we debate the merits of each season. I notice Penny observing us with a smile, her eyes popping back and forth between us like she's watching a tennis match.

"Hey, Penny," I say, grabbing her attention. "I was thinking you could start working on the application for that program we talked about?"

She drops her fork on her plate, flinging a piece of rice into the air. Her eyes go wide as she looks up at me. "But I…I couldn't possibly ask that of—"

I hold my hand up to stop her. "We talked about this. I'm going to win the prize money and we're using it to pay for the program. And I don't want any ifs, ands, or buts about it," I say to her, pulling out my most authoritative voice for the occasion. "Plus, I'm ninety-nine percent sure that the only reason Lana and I were selected for the show was because you were in our audition video."

I couldn't submit my and Lana's audition video without Penny. It's always been the three of us, and it didn't feel right to not have her in it. She loves the spotlight and absolutely ate up being able to talk about her sisters and how much we deserved a spot on the show. I'm pretty sure Penny sealed the deal for us; she helped us stick out among the thousands of other audition videos.

"Dani…" she says.

"Hey, I'm serious. No complaints. Look at the website and see what you need to do to apply, okay?"

"Yes. Okay," she relents.

Now that Penny has aged out of her high school program, we've had trouble finding her a job. She wants to work and would without a doubt be the hardest worker (and friendliest!) wherever she's employed, but the problem is getting her employed in the first place. It's hard to even get her an interview with the proper accommodations.

So the good news is I found a program at the large university in the city that provides education and training to individuals with intellectual and developmental disabilities like Penny. It's a four year program, and she would graduate with a certificate and tons of marketable experience. The program providers also have a ton of connections with employers, so it would be easier to get Penny's foot in the door. She'd get to live on campus, eat her meals at the dining hall, and get paired with a student who would help her navigate campus life. She would get the college experience that she deserves.

The bad news is the program is $25,000 a year.

Between my paychecks from the gym and personal training, coupled with my mom's paychecks, we're doing okay, but $100K for a four-year program is a *mountain* for us. Mom's already in debt as it is.

My plan is for me to take home my half of the prize money, which might not even be a full $100,000 after taxes are taken out, and put it towards Penny's program. Even if the prize is a little short of the $100K mark, I can make the ends meet. It might be tight, but it'd be doable. And it is absolutely worth it for Penny to have a life that is fulfilling, one where she feels included and valued in society.

Lana already has big plans for her half of the money that involve finally getting herself a car and taking a lengthy summer vacation to all the places none of us have ever been able to visit because we haven't had the means. Even if she offered her half of the winnings to pay for part of Penny's program, I wouldn't take it. Since mom doesn't have a partner to help with these things, I've always stepped in to fill that role, and this program for Penny is my and my mom's responsibility to bear. I want Lana to have the things she wants, just like I want that for Penny.

Lana worked her butt off to get her full-ride track scholarship, and she's worked even harder to keep it. She really needs a car so she doesn't have to rely on Graham all the time, and she deserves to have some fun, too.

Now if I could just get Penny squared away, I think I would finally feel like we've made it. All three Di Laurentis daughters would be on the road to the lives we've all dreamed of, the lives our dad never thought would amount to anything.

So winning *American Gauntlet* isn't just something I'd like to do. It's something I have to do.

[THREE DAYS OUT]

"COME on, Dani. Give it all you've got. Right here."

I throw a jab, followed by a right hook, and finish with a powerful kick to the body.

"That's it! Thirty seconds left. Finish strong," Mateo commands. He's holding up boxing mitts and is covered in padded protective gear from head to toe.

My arms feel like they have nothing left in them, and I'm breathing heavily, mouth wide open to get as much oxygen as possible, but I drain my energy reserves in the final seconds of our training session and finish with a front kick to Mateo's (pad-protected) abdomen that knocks him to the ground.

"Yes, Dani!" Ford yells from outside the boxing ring.

"I felt that way more than I should have through these pads," Mateo grunts. Even so, he beams with pride as he stands back up off the canvas floor of the ring. "Good work."

"Thanks," I say, as I collapse onto the ground, trying my best to slow my heart rate with deep, deliberate breaths. I can feel the heat radiating off my skin, sweat streaming down my neck.

Mateo's wife, Mariana, is one of my personal training clients, and he was kind enough to bring me in for a free session in his kickboxing gym today. My clients don't know where exactly

I'm headed for a little over a month while I'm filming *American Gauntlet*; I just told them I had an amazing opportunity and that I'd be training hard for it up until I left. When Mateo offered a free session to me, I couldn't turn it down.

I don't necessarily think I'll be punching people in the face while I'm competing on *American Gauntlet*, but kickboxing is a killer workout, and Mateo said he'd also show me a few hand-to-hand combat moves, which could actually come in handy. I don't foresee a situation where I'm going to be throwing punches and roundhouse kicks, but these competitions get physical, and there's almost guaranteed to be a situation where I'll need to be fending people off or when I'll be on the attack myself. My mind drifts to a competition during season sixteen when contestants had to race across sand dunes trying to reach a flag before their fellow competitors by any means necessary. One contestant had been yanked back so hard by another that her shoulder came clean out of its socket. I shudder as the image of her shoulder hanging loosely a good six inches below where it should be floods my mind. The more I think about it, the more I'm convinced a few MMA takedown tactics wouldn't be the worst thing to have in my back pocket.

Mateo has stripped off his protective gear, and I admire the tattoos that cover every inch of his arms. He's one of the most fit middle-aged men I've ever seen.

"Gloves off, Dani," he instructs. "And Ford—get in here."

Ford looks a little surprised at first, but his expression quickly liquefies into excitement. Like any brotherly figure, he's probably elated at the possibility of putting me on my butt without consequence.

"Are you sure, Mateo? Wouldn't want to hurt my Dani here before she heads off on her *opportunity*," he says, stepping under the ropes and onto the ring floor. He's putting his shoulder-length brown, wavy hair into a bun with a wicked gleam in his eye as he stalks toward me.

"No one's scared of you, Ford," I say with a challenge.

He leans down and puts his face inches from mine. "We'll see about that."

Mateo ushers me off to the side and whispers instructions to me so Ford can't hear what I'll be doing. Ford is a giant—he's literally the size of a fridge—but Mateo assures me that this tactic will work despite our size difference.

"Okay, you got it *mija*?" Mateo asks, the term of endearment filling me with warm affection.

"Got it," I say as I stare down my target. My fingers twitch at my sides, and I feel the adrenaline build in my veins, replenishing the energy I had just emptied. I'm practically chomping at the bit, a racehorse ready to be released from the starting gates.

"Speed is your friend," Mateo instructs as I stalk toward the center of the ring where Ford is standing. "He's stronger than you, so don't give him enough time to figure out what you're doing and fight you off. Get in and get out."

I nod my head, visualizing what Mateo told me to do before I make a move for Ford.

"Ready?" I ask.

Ford's face is full of a distinct cockiness that makes me want to wipe it clean off.

"You bet. Do your worst, Dani."

Challenge accepted.

In an instant, I feint to one side, causing Ford to move that direction, but then I actually make my move to the other side, wrapping one arm under his armpit and the other over the top of his opposite shoulder. I immediately clinch my hands together behind his back, locking in my arm placement, and before Ford can figure out what my next move is, I stick my leg out behind him and throw all of my body weight into him. The move works like a charm. Ford doesn't know my leg is there behind him and as he steps backward, he trips over it, falling on his back with a loud thud.

I wish I could take a snapshot of the look on his face and tuck it in my back pocket as a keepsake because, yeah, it's gold.

"*Excelente!*" Mateo yells from the side of the ring.

"How—how did you *do* that?" Ford asks from his position on the ground.

"What can I say? I'm a natural," I tease, even as I stick my hand out to help him up.

He reaches for my hand, but yanks me down onto the mat next to him.

"Aw Ford, don't be a bad sport." I push him in the chest, knocking him onto his back as I stand myself back up.

"His pride is hurt, Dani. Give him some time," Mateo says with a mocking tone that makes me burst into laughter.

Mateo teaches me a few more moves, and I continue putting Ford on his butt, much to his bewilderment. I won't deny it; it feels good to be able to do that to a man who can deadlift nearly five hundred pounds.

"Had enough yet?" I tease as I help Ford back up to his feet toward the end of the session.

Ford rolls his eyes in response.

"I'll take that as a yes," I smirk.

"Good work today, Dani," Mateo says, lifting the ring ropes up for me to step through. "You're welcome at my gym anytime."

I'm breathing heavily as I put my things in my gym bag. "I'm dead, Mateo. Thank you for the session."

"Of course. Best of luck on your adventure. Whatever it is, you'll crush it," he says with a smile. "Mariana and I are always in your corner, *mija*."

I grin at the "in your corner" reference and give him a sweaty hug, then I throw my things at Ford.

"Can you take my bag home with you?" I ask him after he catches it without so much as a bobble.

He looks at me like I've lost my mind. "We rode here together, remember?"

"I know. I'm just not riding back with you."

He looks around at the empty gym. "Who exactly are you riding with then?"

"No one. I'm running home."

His bewildered look only grows. "Dani, it's like seven miles back, and in case you haven't noticed," he says, gesturing toward the door, "it's pouring rain outside."

I laugh and give him a peck on the cheek. "See you at home!"

I race out the door before he can get another word out and run the sevenish miles back to the apartment complex. As my feet pound against the pavement, splashing the little puddles of water that stand in my way, I feel more alive with every stride. Even as the rain picks up, pelting me in the face, I can't help but feel at home in the drizzle.

My life has always been a bit of a rainstorm and something about running in the rain makes me feel seen. Known. Like it's the only thing that truly understands me. It masks the thought that always seems to be present in the back of my mind: *You're not worthy.* Not worthy of stability. Of happiness. Of love. My failed relationship with Justin made that thought pound loudly in my head, but he's not the root of the notion. No, it's been there, lurking like a wraith, ever since I was a kid. I can trace it like a line on a map, all the way back to my father.

Today, though, the steady thrum of the rain drowns out any doubts I have about what's to come. I'm strong—physically and mentally—but I know I'm not bulletproof. I'm nervous about the show, about the potential outcomes, but although my mind wants to view this anxiety as a weakness, I don't think it has to be; it can be a strength, as long as I don't let the doubts and nerves overwhelm me.

As I sprint the last half mile home, pushing my body to the absolute limit, I feel ready. Six months of training for *American Gauntlet* and I finally feel like I'm prepared. The time has come, and I can't help but feel like it's mine for the taking.

five

HOUSTON'S rainiest spring on record. That's what the meteorologists have been saying.

I ring the now-cold rainwater out of my hair, listening as it splashes against the concrete, and step through the threshold of our dated apartment, beelining for the shower I know is waiting for me.

All of Houston has been complaining about the incessant rain for months now. At first, everyone was grateful for it, grateful for lush lawns and cozy Sunday afternoons and the promise of spring flowers and post-drizzle rainbows. But when the rain didn't stop, when it kept draining from the skies as if from an endless tap, it all became too much. Green lawns turned to brown mud and flooded streets. Cozy afternoons turned to ruined plans and canceled ballgames. The promise of a beautiful spring quickly faded to one humid, dreary, gray day after the other. The entire city has been begging for even an ounce of sunshine.

But while the city has hung its head in mourning, the unending rain, coupled with Houston's heat and torturous humidity, have made my outdoor training conditions about as tough as they come: unideal for most, but absolutely perfect for me.

The harsh conditions have only made my confidence grow more as *American Gauntlet* approaches. I've become used to adversity, to thriving under less-than-favorable conditions. With each training session, I've worked on growing stronger mentally, on not getting thrown off when things don't go as I expect. Strength and endurance and strategy and grit are all things you need to win *American Gauntlet*, sure, but you also need adaptability, a willingness to shift your game plan when things don't go your way.

American Gauntlet is known for its surprises, its game twists. Just when contestants think they know what direction the show is moving, the producers throw them a complete 180. That's what keeps the viewers coming back season after season.

I think the trick isn't to try to predict the twists. The trick is to adapt to them.

I rush through my shower so I have enough time to spend on my hair and makeup before Ford picks me up in less than an hour. He insisted on taking me out for a celebration dinner before I leave for the show in just two days.

"What, exactly, are we celebrating?" I had asked him.

"You winning the show, duh," he'd replied, like it should've been obvious.

That's how much faith Ford has in me and Lana to win.

I quickly blow dry my hair and run a straightener through it, although it's naturally straight as a board. I almost never wear it down, so I take the opportunity to wear it loose tonight. My hair brushes against my collarbones as I start my makeup routine, and I take my time as I apply my foundation and powder and highlighter, savoring the feeling of the smooth brushes as they glide across my skin. After I've finished, I take a Q-tip and clean the makeup off my tiny nose stud so it's shiny again.

I slip on my favorite baby blue dress that I've worn countless times. As the fabric slides over my body, a subtle grin works its way onto my face, taking in my reflection in the full-length mirror in my bedroom. I love the juxtaposition of grinding out an intense training session then putting on a full face of makeup and a pretty dress that makes me feel feminine. Soft. Pretty.

Frankly, my body is not the kind you see in outdated ads for bougie yoga brands. I'm muscular. I have visible biceps and quads and delts that I've worked hard to build, supplementing my weight training with a diet that has helped me foster muscle growth, not minimize it. I'm confident in my skin and proud of the progress I've made during my fitness journey over the last four years. I know that the "well-intentioned" men at the gym who have called me "bulky" or have said I need to "stop lifting so much weight" are really just insecure and fragile themselves. The time a man approached me at the gym and told me that if I stuck to cardio and light weights with high reps, my body would look more like the hourglass figure I was probably going for is etched into my mind forever.

I laughed in his face.

Just because I love shredding my muscles apart at the gym, though, doesn't mean I don't love putting on my favorite heels and glamorous makeup and feeling downright beautiful. You can be both. You can be the sporty gym girl and the wears-a-dress-and-heels-and-lipstick girl, and anyone who says otherwise clearly doesn't know what they're talking about.

I hear a hard rap on the door and swing it open to see Ford standing on the other side, dressed in a nice pair of jeans and a plain black shirt that clings to his prominent pectoral muscles. He has his hair shoved in a bun on the back of his head, and it's the perfect amount of tidy and tousled, like he tried to make it neat but not *too neat*. He has a five o'clock shadow that I think is also intentional (trimmed but not entirely clean shaven) and I know if I were to run my hand along his jawline, it would feel a lot like sandpaper.

Ford gives me a quick once-over, his gaze not lingering anywhere too long. "You look great, Dani," he says with a smile. "Ready to go?"

"Ready," I say, giving him a quick hug and locking up my front door.

Ford, ever the gentleman, opens his car door for me and drives us to our favorite upscale-casual restaurant with a gorgeous covered patio in the back, one that I'm hoping will be available for us since the rain has stopped, at least for this evening. In the interest of saving money, I don't eat out often, so this dinner with Ford is a treat.

Ford leads the way into the familiar restaurant, and he breezes right past the host.

"Uh, Ford? What are you--"

The question drops from my lips as soon as Ford guides me to the back patio where all of my favorite people are waiting for me.

"Surprise!" everyone yells in unison. I can't even choke out a response as I look at all of the people gathered in my honor: my mom and Penny, my coworkers from the gym, Mateo and Mariana, and a whole slew of my personal training clients. The only person missing is Lana because she'll be flying straight to LA from North Carolina, right as she finishes up her semester. I'm not one for big displays of emotion—those died long ago— but even so, I feel a warmth begin to drift through me like warm, golden honey.

As soon as the tender emotions are there, they're gone again, replaced by excitement and joy, and soon I'm not just in my favorite dress and heels—I'm also wearing an ear-to-ear grin.

I turn to Ford and see he's already looking at me with a smile to match mine.

"You did this?"

"Yes," he says, throwing an arm around me and guiding me toward the group of people awaiting me. "And Penny, of course."

I make my way through my little crowd of people, greeting them and hugging them and thanking them for being there to support me, even though they don't know where I'm going. They don't ask me to tell them where I'll be for a month, they don't pry; they simply say how much they're rooting for me on my "adventure."

Although now that I think of it, I might not be gone for a month. If Lana and I get eliminated from the competition early, I'll be headed right back here to Houston. It's funny that the thought is only just now crossing my mind—I'd told everyone I'd be gone a month because the thought of *not* winning *American Gauntlet* simply never occurred to me.

I bury the thought immediately. I *will* be gone for a month because Lana and I *will* win. End of story.

After I've chatted with everyone, I make my way over to my mom. As soon as I'm in front of her, she engulfs me in a hug that is surprisingly tight. I breathe in a wave of her favorite perfume that smells of lilac with subtle notes of vanilla, savoring it as the scent washes over me. She's had the same bottle of perfume for as long as I can remember, and she only wears it on special occasions. I smile and breathe deeper, wanting to tether this contented moment to her scent.

Mom pulls away, and as I look into her eyes, I see the tears are already flowing. She hugs me again, resting her chin on top of my shoulder.

"I'm so, so proud of you, Dani," she says through more tears. "Not just for this opportunity you have, but because of the young woman you are. Lord knows your sisters wouldn't have made it without you. I—I'm sorry I wasn't there when you needed me—"

I pull back from Mom's hug, cutting her off.

"Mom, you've got to stop apologizing. Look at you. You made it, Mom. You're here now. That's all that matters."

There's no stopping the floodgates that have unleashed from her tear ducts. "I know," she hiccups through ragged breaths. "I just—"

"*Rebecca*," I say, my voice hard and stern. It's the voice that makes me feel like the matriarch of our family, the one that I spent years perfecting.

"Fine, fine!" she says, breaking into a laugh and wiping away tears. I can always pull a laugh out of her when I call her by her first name. "Just know how proud I am of you. And Lana, of course. And Penny," she adds. "I don't know how I got so lucky with the three of you."

I smile, even as the souvenirs of years past tiptoe into the corners of my mind. I don't know if Mom will ever forgive herself for abandoning us when we so desperately needed her. After my father walked out on us when I was thirteen, Mom went into a deep, dark depression and instead of focusing on us, her daughters that were still very much with her, she picked up a bottle instead. Then she picked up another one. And another. Eviction notices and empty bottles and even emptier stomachs became markers of my adolescence. It was the stringent smell of whisky, the putrid stench of vomit. It was freezing cold water when I dragged my mom into the shower to wake her up, praying she wasn't dead. My feelings for her were a confusing mixture of despair and hope, hatred and love, all at the same time.

From that point on, I practically raised my sisters—getting them up and to the bus stop for school, signing their permission slips, making their Instant Ramen every night, giving them a shoulder to cry on when girls at school were mean. Most days Mom was so out of it, she had no idea what was going on with the three of us. Luckily, my father kept sending us money—most times after I *begged* him for it—so we could stay afloat, even though Mom blew a lot of it on alcohol. I learned to pilfer it, to tuck it away when she wasn't conscious. But when I was old enough to get a job, the monetary support (and all communication from him) eventually stopped too. Mom was too out of it to take him to court for child support, so we scraped by without it, and Dad got off scot-free, finally able to wash his hands of us—his mistakes.

I'd begged and pleaded with Mom to get some help, to check herself into rehab, but it always fell on deaf ears until one afternoon when I was eighteen and nearly done with high school. I was at work and Lana was at track practice, which left Penny alone at home with mom. This wasn't usually cause for alarm—Penny had grown to be very self-sufficient—but that afternoon, she was chopping up an apple and the knife slipped, slashing clean across her palm. She screamed for Mom's help, but Mom was already drunk, passed out for the rest of the day. As soon as she saw how much blood was streaming out of her hand, Penny passed out on the kitchen floor.

I still vividly remember walking through the doors of our apartment. The distinct sound of the deadbolt as I locked the door behind me. The *clink* of my keys as I tossed them haphazardly onto the coffee table.

"Penny, I'm home!" I yelled to her, my voice tired and strained from fatigue.

Silence.

"Penny?" I called again. She was usually waiting by the door for me to get home from work, always ready to ask about my day. When she didn't respond, I had a gut feeling that something was off, and cold dread began slithering through my mind. "Pen—"

Blood. There was so much blood, spreading across the white kitchen tile like spilled paint. The blood-curdling scream I let out was enough to wake the dead, enough even for Mom to come stumbling out of her bedroom.

The day after Penny's incident, Mom checked herself into rehab, and she's been sober ever since. I'm grateful to have my mom back, but it was too late for me to have any sort of "normal" adolescent years. I went from a child to an adult in the time it took my father to walk out the door and never look back. I didn't have Friday night football games or homecoming dances or high school parties. But I have Mom back. And I have Lana and Penny. And we're all okay. We're better than okay, actually. And we'll be even better after Lana and I win *American Gauntlet*.

"I'm proud of you too, Mom," I say, giving her one more squeeze for good measure.

FORD eases his car into his parking space at our apartment complex, and we sit in comfortable silence as we finish our

Wendy's Frosties. It's sort of our thing. I leave for Los Angeles in less than two days, so after the dinner-slash-surprise-party Ford insisted we pull through the drive thru for one last Frosty.

"You're ready, Dani," he says after inhaling a giant spoonful of chocolate soft serve. "You feel it, don't you? You know you're ready."

"Hmmm…" I flip my plastic spoon upside down as I drag the ice cream off of it, pondering his question. "I mean, I would love more time to prepare. But I also think you could spend years training for *American Gauntlet* and still be thrown off by one of its twists. I guess that's the point. But all things considered, I feel ready. As ready as I'll ever be."

"And what about Lana?" he asks. "How does she feel?"

My phone vibrates with a text alert.

"Speaking of," I say, opening the text message. "I think she's ready too." I show Ford my phone, the text I just received from Graham illuminating the dark car.

GRAHAM: Lana just finished up the last session you sent over. She killed it!! Definitely ready to take on the Gauntlet.

"Well, that sounds like good news," Ford says.

"I don't think I've ever heard Graham use the term 'killed it' or one, much less two, exclamation points, so it must be a good sign," I say with a laugh.

"You two have worked hard for this, Dani. You're going to win. I know it." Ford has repeated this phrase so many times, I think he's convinced himself that if he says it enough, it'll come true.

I look over at Ford, both of us scraping the bottom of our

Wendy's cups for the last remnants of our Frosties, and I can't help but feel that Ford and I are two sides of the same coin. Maybe that's why we grew so close so fast. We always have the same line of thinking, same thought processes, same reactions to situations. Looking at him is like looking in a soul-deep mirror.

"Gah, Ford. I'm going to miss you. I wish you could come with us…I honestly don't know what I'm going to do without you there." I hadn't spent much time thinking about what it would be like without Ford there. Truthfully, the thought is a little scary.

He takes one last bite of ice cream before he sets the empty cup in his cup holder. He meets my gaze and doesn't blink as he says, "Win, Dani. You're going to win."

[ONE DAY OUT]

"OKAY, now put everything in the suitcase."

Lana lets out a whimper that I feel to my core, even through a FaceTime call.

"But that's the worst part," she whines.

"Well it's not going to pack itself. Your flight is in less than twenty-four hours, Lana."

She groans before she reluctantly begins taking items of clothing from the giant pile on her bed and haphazardly folding them.

"You're already packed aren't you?" she asks mid-fold, a look of annoyance on her face.

I flash a smug smile. "Yep. Penny could hardly contain her excitement to help me. I was all packed up a week ago."

Lana goes on and on about how unfair it is that I had Penny to help me pack, and I placate her with a few half-hearted "*mhmms*" until an email notification pops up on my phone. When I see who it's from, my heart starts beating a little bit faster, anticipation and nerves quickly fluttering through my body.

"…I mean, if I had Penny to help me, I would have been packed by now, too. And also—"

"Lana," I cut in.

"What? I'm just saying, you can hardly blame me that—"

"*Lana.*"

"What?"

"I just got an email from Kelly. Do you want to know the subject line?"

"Well, obviously."

"The subject is…" I pause just a moment to keep her on the edge of her seat. "…*Meet Your Competition.*"

"*WHAT?*" she exclaims, her voice blaring through my phone's speakers.

"Pull it up on your laptop," I say. "You should've gotten it too."

"It's dead right now," she says. *Why am I not surprised?* "Just read it to me!"

I pull my clunky second-hand laptop in front of me. Both of us have been dying to know who the other competitors are, but the producers have kept it top secret. It's not lost on me that they've waited until anxiety and pre-show tension is at an all-time high the night before we all fly out to Los Angeles.

The mind games are already starting, I think to myself.

"Holy moly," I say as I see the contents of the email. I look up to see Lana pacing the floor, stepping over the largely empty suitcase in the middle of her floor. "It's pretty bare bones. There's just pictures attached with first names only."

There's seven photos attached to the email, which I assume means there are seven teams competing this season, including Lana and myself. I click on the familiar photo of Lana and me that I had submitted to Kelly a while back. At the time, I had assumed it was for internal purposes, like they would use the photos so the crew members could memorize each of this season's competitors. The attachment is simply named "*Dani-*

Lana."

"That's it?" she asks, incredulous. "No bios or anything?"

"Yeah, that's it," I say. "But that doesn't mean we can't find out a little bit more." A sneaky grin worms its way onto my face as Lana eyes me, one eyebrow quirked with interest.

"Spill," she says.

"Well, I'm willing to bet these photos that everyone submitted are on the internet somewhere. I can reverse image search them, where you drop an image in and it pulls up websites featuring that photo. Maybe their social media profiles will pop up or something."

She pauses, her foot hovering halfway over her suitcase. "Sis, you're a genius."

"I would like to personally thank MTV's *Catfish* for this little trick," I joke as I download the six other images from the email.

Lana laughs and picks up a shirt from the pile on her bed before tossing it into her suitcase. The messy pile in her bag is a stark contrast to the neat rows of clothes that Penny and I packed, both of us working with organized precision.

"Okay, here's our first one," I say, angling my laptop to where she can see the photo over our FaceTime call. I doubt she can see it very well, but I try nonetheless. "It looks like this is Naji and AJ, if the file name is to be trusted."

The picture I'm attempting to show Lana shows two very muscular guys, probably in their early twenties like Lana and me, each with an arm around the other's shoulder. They're flashing huge, brilliantly white smiles, their teeth contrasting brightly against their deep tawny skin and jet black hair. Both of them have the sides of their heads shaved but have kept it long on the top. The one on the left, Naji, has placed his in a neat bun just below the crown of his head, while AJ wears his in a tight ponytail.

I drop the photo into the reverse image search and *bingo*. Naji's Instagram profile pulls up almost immediately. I scroll through his profile—being *extremely* careful not to accidentally like an old post—and give Lana the rundown as I go. This season, all the duos will be related in some capacity, so I'm not surprised to see that Naji and AJ are brothers. They're apparently of Malaysian heritage, if the Malaysian flag next to the American flag in Naji's bio is any indication, and the brothers apparently work as stuntmen. The profile is flooded with insane videos of them doing backflips off of various risky places, and they've also posted a ton of hilarious fails and videos of them pranking each other.

I pull up the next photo, "*Kyler-Chase*," and it's a picture of two buff guys wearing stringer tank tops, flexing in a gym mirror. *Classic.* A quick reverse image search reveals the two are cousins. Their social media accounts consist of lifting videos and *a lot* of photos of them flexing.

"They seem…confident," Lana remarks.

"Looks that way," I snort. Having worked at a gym for so long, I know the type.

The next team, "*Tris-Benji*," features a woman, probably in her thirties, with raven black hair closely shorn on the sides and a little longer on the top. In the photo, she stands with a guy who looks to be just barely over the show's eighteen-year-old age limit. He's thin with black hair in a style that matches Tris's. I'm unsure of their relation, until I find Tris's Facebook page and discover they are aunt and nephew—one of those big-age-gaps-between-siblings situations where the aunt and nephew end up being closeish in age. There's not much else to be discovered on Tris's page other than the fact that she and Benji are serious climbers. There's photo after photo of them scaling sheer rock faces, adorning intense rock climbing gear. *That'll come in handy*, I think to myself.

Next is "*Ivy-Blaire*," a photo of two girls who look so much alike, they have to be identical twins. They are the same height (relatively short if my gauge is right), have fiery red hair, smatterings of freckles across their faces, and curves for days. I keep giving Lana the rundown as I find and pull up a joint Instagram account for both of them.

"Oh, this is interesting," I say to Lana as I scroll through their account.

"What's interesting?"

"They, like, have a name for themselves. They call themselves the 'Twisted Twins.' See?" I show her their Instagram. "Apparently they're gymnasts, so the name makes a little more sense now. But does that name seem sort of, I don't know, eerie?"

"It definitely has a certain…vibe," Lana responds, still working on shoving clothes in her suitcase. Her waist-length, deep mahogany hair—almost the exact same color as mine—has worked its way out of her braid and into her face.

"Interesting…I'm sure they're great though. I'm glad there's at least one other all-female team," I say, as I close out their profile and pull up the next photo.

Lana is nearing the end of her packing when I pull up the second to last team, "*Sarge-Junior*." Before I even do the reverse image search, I know this pair is a father-son duo, as Junior, with his rich ebony skin, shaved head, and taut muscles, looks like the spitting image of his father, just twenty-five or so years younger. I also take back what I said about Mateo—*Sarge* is, in fact, the most fit middle-aged man I've ever seen. In the photo, they're both wearing military fatigues, and they look intimidating. But then again, all of these teams look intimidating. I suppose that's the point.

"Okay, last team," I say.

"Lay it on me," Lana replies, doing her best to shove another pair of trainers in her suitcase.

I click on the photo named "*Ryder-Joss*," but the picture is extremely grainy—*When was this photo taken?*—and it's hard to make out any distinguishing features on either of the two guys pictured. One seems to have a bigger build, like that of a football or hockey player, while the other is taller and more lean with blonde hair. That's truly all I can make out about the two, thanks to the quality of the picture.

I pop it into the reverse image search and yield no results.

"Why would they submit an old, grainy photo like this?" I muse aloud. "It makes no sense, unless it was a part of some strategy…I can't imagine how that would be any advantage, though."

"It's weird," Lana replies, "but at least we got some intel on the rest of the teams. Can you run through the teams again? I honestly can't keep them all straight."

"Okay, so it's Naji and AJ, the stuntmen. Kyler and Chase, the gym bros. Ivy and Blaire, the so-called 'Twisted Twins.' Tris and Benji, the climbers. Sarge and Junior, the veterans. And Ryder and Joss, nickname to be determined thanks to their inadequate photo."

"I'm impressed you memorized them already," Lana laughs. "The nicknames are definitely helpful."

"I feel like the producers sending this email the night before we leave is like our first test. Anyone who can utilize it to their advantage gets a leg up," I say. "I'll take any advantage we can get."

"Yeah, I mean, it looks like the producers definitely found some steep competition…it's too bad they have nothing on us," she says with a grin that makes me all the more excited to take on this competition with her.

"Exactly," I beam. "I can't wait to see you in LA." According to Kelly, who arranged our travel, Lana and I will be meeting up at the Los Angeles airport before we're transported to wherever the competition is taking place, somewhere they've kept, unsurprisingly, top secret. Past seasons have been shot all across the United States. Season fifteen was somewhere in the Rocky Mountains, which looked incredible. Season twelve was in Alaska. Season eighteen was in Hawaii, which looked like a dream. A flash of excitement shoots through me at the possibilities that await; my family hasn't taken a single vacation since my dad left, so no matter where this season takes place, it'll be a new experience for me.

Lana grunts as she practically body slams her suitcase, trying to get it to shut around her haphazard heap of clothing and toiletries. "Can't wait to see you!" she huffs, smashing her bag down with one foot while forcing its zipper together.

"I'll leave you to it, then," I laugh. "See you soon."

"Love you, bye!"

As soon as the call ends, I jump in bed, but the evening's discoveries and the general buzz of anticipation for *American Gauntlet* have me wide awake, kicking at my sheets for what feels like hours. The six other teams we'll be competing against play on a loop in my mind like flashcards. I bind each of them to memory, repeating what little I know about them like a chant in my head.

Six teams. There are six teams standing in our way to get to that $300K.

And I intend to take each of them down one by one.

seven

AS FORD inches forward toward the departures lane, I
can't form a single coherent thought. It's as if there are so
many potential outcomes to consider after this flight to LA
that they've jumbled together to form one giant cloud that has
commandeered my brain. It's not necessarily good or bad; it's
just, well, nothing. Right now, *American Gauntlet* is a blank
canvas, an empty journal page just waiting to be filled.

To think of winning *or* losing *or* being eliminated first *or*
coming in second *or* getting so severely injured in a competition
that I can't continue is simply too much to wrap my brain
around as we slowly make our way to the airport in the Houston
traffic. So I just don't.

Ford has remained uncharacteristically silent beside me.
Based on his stoic demeanor, I'd think he were almost bored if it
weren't for the quick, nearly panicked dart of his eyes over to me
in the passenger seat every so often or the way he's clenched the
steering wheel so tight that he has to flex his fingers back and
forth when he releases it. He's what I imagine a nervous dad is
like as he drops his first-born off at college. Leave it to Ford to
give me the father figure experiences I never got to have.

The airport roads are congested with anxious travelers doing their best to make it to their flights on time, but the honking of horns (coupled with the occasional road rage expletives from passersby) and the roar of planes taking off just overhead fill the empty void in my mind, and for that, I'm grateful.

We finally make it up to the departure dropoff zone, and Ford squeezes his car in between two others. He won't have long before other drivers will need his spot, so our goodbye needs to be quick, which is definitely for the best. Suddenly, a rush of nerves overcomes me at the thought of leaving Ford. He and I have been nearly inseparable for the last four years. In fact, we haven't spent more than a week apart.

Ford places the gearshift in park, and as soon as the car settles in place, I know it's time to face the music. Wordlessly, Ford and I open our doors and meet each other around the back of his silver Accord. The Houston humidity feels like I'm suffocating on hot air, making the already weighty goodbye all the heavier.

I throw my backpack over my shoulder, while Ford grabs the matte black, hard-shell suitcase I borrowed from him out of the trunk, placing it in front of me with a gentle thud. Having taken all of two vacations in my life, both of which were short term, I'd never had a need for a huge suitcase until this trip, and when I looked into buying one, I realized they're *expensive*. Like ridiculously pricey. Luckily, Ford loaned me his without so much as a second thought.

I stare at the mammoth suitcase at my feet for a few moments before I finally drag my eyes up to meet Ford's. As I do, all the heaviness in my chest dissolves like cotton candy on my tongue. Ford's lips that had been pressed into a statuesque line only moments before have now turned up into the makings of a grin. There's a little gleam in his eyes and a knowing expression that somehow instills the utmost confidence in me.

Ford believes in me. I believe in myself. *I can do this.* And I'll do it without the personal safety crutch that this man has become for me.

"You're ready," he says, his small grin blossoming into a full Ford Peterson smile.

"I'm ready," I repeat with a smile of my own. "You'll take care of my mom and Penny while I'm gone?" I ask, even though I already know the answer.

"I'm offended you even have to ask," he teases. As someone honks their horn behind us, Ford looks down at me, grabbing me and pulling me into a bear hug. "I'm so proud of you," I hear him say from where my face is buried in what I now realize is his armpit.

"*Gah*, how do I always end up in your freaking pits?"

Ford lets out a belly-deep rumble of laughter before pressing a kiss to the top of my head, strands of my hair catching in his dark stubble.

"Love you," I say to him, and I mean it.

"Love you," he says back. "Now go get it, Dani."

My smile liquefies into a wicked grin. "Oh, I intend to."

THE protocols involved in airport travel are keeping my mind safely off of *American Gauntlet* and all of the possibilities (and potential disasters) that await me once I step foot off the plane in California. It's like driving down a densely foggy road; you can only see what's right in front of you, and you're not exactly sure what lies beyond that. You can't floor it, so you focus on doing what you know to do, creeping forward, slowly making progress as safely as possible.

I've traveled via airplane two times in my life, once when we took a family vacation to Florida when I was nine and once last year when I flew to visit Lana at UNC. Despite being a relatively inexperienced air traveler, I'm not anxious. Airports are literally made for ushering uncertain people to the right places, getting them to their proper destinations. I feel a little like herded cattle among the airport crowd as I walk through the airport doors and begin robotically shuffling through the motions.

Pull up boarding pass on phone. Check bag. Find security line. Wait in said line. Get out ID. Show said ID to TSA. Put backpack and shoes on security belt. Stand on yellow foot marks. Put hands above head. Get scanned. Hope you don't have to get a full pat-down for no reason.

It's simple. It's mindless. It's just what I need this morning.

I don't get flagged for a pat-down—*bless*—so I grab my backpack and shoes off the security belt and make my way to one of the nearby benches to put my sneakers back on and organize my things. The airport is packed, but I'm focused on the task at hand and don't so much as look around before seating myself between two people and getting to work on my belongings.

I'm just about finished tying my shoes when the person sitting next to me stands up, their knee brushing against mine, and begins walking away, dropping their boarding pass in the process. *Who prints their boarding pass these days?* I shoot my gaze up to see if this mystery person has noticed, only to see him—a very tall him—striding away, oblivious.

"Hey!" I yell, but not so loudly as to attract too much attention. I'm definitely not trying to cause a scene in the middle of the Houston airport. He hasn't gotten too far thanks to the heavy foot traffic, but he still didn't hear me.

I quickly glance down at the boarding pass to get his name. "Kellan!"

From behind, I see Mystery Guy—or Kellan, apparently—whip his head around with a confused look on his face, his eyes scanning across the crowd.

"Kellan?" I question loudly again, wondering if it is, in fact, the guy who's turned around.

When his gaze finally meets mine, I find myself rooted in place, unable to tear my eyes away from his. He has the most beautiful blue eyes I've ever seen in real life, a blue so light, they could be carved from glaciers. They're my exact favorite color.

Kellan holds my gaze, the look of confusion still plastered to his face, before dropping it to my hand where he finds his boarding pass. I still haven't fully recovered from whatever has overtaken my body in this moment, but as he starts walking towards me, something feels…familiar. But I'm almost certain I've never met this guy before because I'm *absolutely* certain I would have remembered him. You don't have such a strong physical reaction to a pair of eyes like his and forget it.

Still, I can't shake the feeling.

"*Oi!*" he calls out to me in an accent that is so distinctly *Australian*. And just like that, it's confirmed that I have never, in fact, met this Kellan guy in my life because I would have never forgotten not only the most arresting pair of blue eyes, but that accent to go with them.

I've watched a couple seasons of *Love Island: Australia* and as he's walking towards me, I wonder if he was on the show, if maybe that's why he seems familiar, but I quickly dismiss it after doing a rapid recall of all the men from past seasons. He doesn't match any of them, but if he wasn't on *Love Island*, he definitely could be with his dreamy eyes and perfect hair and attractive…

everything.

He stalks toward me, running a hand through his tousled golden hair, and as he gets closer, I realize he has to be at least six-foot three, maybe taller. He's all long limbs and lean muscle, accompanied by tan skin that is so perfectly bronzed, I think he could be the poster child for Australia's Gold Coast.

What is it about strangers in airports that automatically makes them hot? This guy is beautiful; objectively speaking, there is absolutely zero doubt about that. But I wonder if this odd and, quite frankly, out-of-character physiological reaction I'm having to him is just because he's a guy in an airport, someone whom I know nothing about. And maybe that's just it, isn't it? Airport hot guys are mysteries. You see them in passing and all you have is this idyllic, picture-perfect image of them. They could be downright jerks or straight up weirdos, but you don't know that, do you? You don't know them, and there's not really the potential to get to know them. You're going your way, and he's going his. He's a mystery, one that you won't get to uncover, and that's what makes him next-level attractive.

"I reckon I dropped this?"

I'm ripped from my internal hot-guys-in-airports tangent by Kellan's heavily accented voice that has that classic Australian lighthearted note to it. I crane my neck up and catch his eyes, the color of *Toy Story* skies, before I shoot my gaze down to his boarding pass.

"Oh, um, yes," I say, unable to keep my eyes off of his as I glance back up at him again. "Here you go."

I hand the boarding pass to him and notice how a small smile has worked its way onto his face, a shine in his eye to accompany it.

"Thank you," he says, but he doesn't turn around to leave just yet. Like maybe he's not ready for this conversation to be over.

And apparently, neither am I, as I say, "I didn't know anyone under the age of forty still printed their boarding pass these days."

His smile widens. "Maybe I'm old-fashioned," he says. "Or maybe I have my reasons."

I can't help but find his accent extremely charming, but I'm suddenly hauled out of our short conversation when the alarm on my watch goes off, telling me I need to get to my gate. The airport traffic made me later than I would've liked this morning, so I don't have a lot of time to kill in conversations with strangers.

"I better get going," I say, silencing the vibrating alarm on my watch with a tap of my finger. "Nice to meet you, Kellan."

The corners of his mouth curl up again, as if there's some inside joke I'm not in on. But it eventually turns into a full, easy smile, as he says, "Have a good one."

I steal one last glance at him before picking up my backpack and heading on my way. I'm actually grateful to be running a little later than usual because it keeps my mind safely away from *American Gauntlet*. I've thought of almost nothing other than the show for the last six months, but now that I can't go for a run or climb obstacles or hit a punching bag to prepare, I'm avoiding the thoughts and hypothetical scenarios the same way I avoid over-confident men at the gym: like the plague.

I beeline it to my gate, and once I see it, I quickly turn around and head to the restroom. I have no idea why I need to double check that the gate is, in fact, there and hasn't somehow spontaneously combusted, but it's a thing, and I can't explain it. I stop in one of the little airport convenience stores to buy an unbelievably overpriced water and bottled protein shake, which outs me a whopping $11.19. *Good grief.* I'm suddenly very thankful I'll be paying for nothing while I'm on the show. I make it back to the gate to find boarding has started, and the gate agent is already on the final boarding group. I stick myself at the back of the long line of passengers, stretching my legs while I wait.

My phone buzzes in my pocket. I click the notification and see it's an email from Penny, who, of course, prefers email to texting.

Wishing you all the best on your wonderful adventure, Dani. Remember what we talked about and you'll do great. I love you to the moon and back!
Warm regards,
Penny

My mind immediately drifts to the conversation Penny and I had last night as I said my goodbye to her, not wanting to wake her up on my way out this morning.

"Any last minute advice?" I asked her, knowing she loves giving words of wisdom whenever she can.

Her eyes lit up at the question, before she immediately answered, "Remember what I always say, Dani. Even when the rainiest day seems to be at its darkest, the sun is always there, even if you can't see it behind the clouds. It'll come back out eventually."

Sweet Penny. Thankful for her wise words, I brought her in for a hug, and when I pulled away, there were soft, warm tears in her eyes.

She shook them off and then stood up, motioning for me to get up as well. "Now let's get you off to bed," she tutted. "You'll need as much sleep as you can get."

I smile as I pull myself from the tender memory and open my boarding pass on my phone. I scan my mobile pass and head down the jet bridge, only to look behind me and realize I'm the very last person to board.

I step onto the plane, greeted by faint buzzing and the smell that is so distinctly "airplane," a strange concoction of antiseptic and stale, recycled air. I glance down at my boarding pass to check my seat. Left aisle seat, row twenty-three. As I'm walking through the narrow aisle, doing my best not to hit any unsuspecting passengers with my backpack, I see one remaining seat on the aisle—my seat—awaiting me.

And that's when I realize that for the next three hours, I'll be sitting next to Kellan.

eight

MY eyes shoot up to the little numbers above each row, double checking that the seat next to Kellan is, in fact, my seat, but I already know it is. With no one shuffling onto the plane behind me, I am almost certainly the last person to board.

My stomach somersaults as I see Kellan's sun-kissed blonde hair over the rows of seats, and I'm instantly annoyed that this guy's mere existence has caused such pronounced physical reactions in me today. *When was the last time my stomach fluttered at the* sight *of someone?* He's looking down at something, probably his phone, and he hasn't seen me yet. As I get closer, I realize how ridiculous it is for me to be so clearly hung up on one two-minute interaction with him this morning, but I chalk it up to the airport-hot-guy effect. If he happens to be a chatty seat neighbor, I guess I'll find out if he really is a jerk or a weirdo, and the effect will have worn off by the end of our three-hour journey.

Still unnoticed by him as I get closer to my seat, I notice Kellan is seated in the middle seat (next to a woman who already has her neck pillow secured, AirPods in, and eye mask firmly in place) and he looks very uncomfortable. His unfairly long legs are crowded in the teeny space that is the reality in economy, his knees solidly pressed against the seat in front of him. The flight from Houston to LA isn't exactly short, and he'll likely have indentations in his knees from the seatback by the time we land in California. I imagine LAX is just a layover for him to get back to Australia, so he's got a marathon journey ahead of him.

I finally make it to row twenty-three and find that Kellan isn't looking down at his phone. He's reading a book.

Hot, I immediately think, before shaking the thought off just as quickly.

"I think you're in my seat," I say to him.

He shoots his gaze up at me, his eyebrows furrowed together in a mixture of confusion and worry, before recognition hits him. Even when a brief smile meets his eyes, his concerned expression returns, no doubt wondering if he did actually take my seat. He looks down at his boarding pass and then back at me.

"I dunno about that actually," he says to me, his brows still creased. "I think I'm in the proper seat."

"Mmm, I don't think so. I'm pretty sure you've got the aisle seat," I say with a pointed look to his knees pressed against the seatback in front of him.

The doubt instantly vanishes, understanding washing over him. It appears he's finally picked up on what I'm doing, what I'm offering him.

"You really don't have to do that," he says, securing his seatbelt even tighter around his lap to signal he doesn't intend on accepting my seat-swap proposal.

"I know," I reply. "But also, it doesn't make a difference to me if I'm in the middle, whereas it clearly will make a difference for you. Do it for your knees at the very least."

Kellan appears riddled with indecision as we find ourselves in a standoff. I'm not making any move to sit in the aisle seat, and soon enough, we hear the boarding doors close at the front of the plane.

"Ma'am, please take your seat," a flight attendant says as she tries to scoot by me, loudly smashing all the overhead compartments closed in her wake.

"Of course!" I quickly respond. "Just waiting to get into my seat in the middle here." I suppress a grin. *Checkmate.*

"Sir, can you please—"

Before she can finish her request, Kellan shakes his head as he undoes his seatbelt, muttering something like "*stubborn*" under his breath, but I see the smile, even as he looks down, trying his best to hide it. He puts his boarding pass in his book to hold his place and steps out of the row, ducking his head so he doesn't smack it on the overhead compartment above. I slide into the row, slipping my backpack off and placing it underneath the seat. The woman by the window hasn't so much as stirred during our game of musical chairs.

Kellan sits in his new seat beside me and immediately angles his body toward the aisle, stretching out his legs, flexing each knee as he does. He already has red marks on his skin from where the seatback was pressed against his legs. I try not to look at the relief on his face, even as a smirk makes its way onto mine.

As if he caught it in his peripheral vision, he inclines his head to me. "My knees thank you."

Before I can respond, the flight attendants take to the aisles and the intercom to begin their safety instruction. I hear the jet bridge pull away, and the plane lurches into motion. But as soon as it does, the *American Gauntlet* mental blockade that had been safely in place all morning is obliterated, and the nerves hit me like a tidal wave from a dam, freshly broken.

The what ifs. The disastrous scenarios. The myriad of potential outcomes other than winning. They all come flooding into my head, washing over every level-headed, rational line of thinking that I would typically use to combat them. I'm a bundle of anxiety, which feels so unfamiliar to me now. My seatbelt suddenly feels too tight. The airplane feels like a prison, my seat like a cell. I'm half-wondering if an oxygen mask is about to pop out of the ceiling for me to hyperventilate into.

I look down and notice my leg has begun to shake, my foot *tap-tap-tapping* as if it has a mind of its own. I can feel little beads of sweat forming along my hairline. I know if I look in a mirror my typically olive-toned skin will undoubtedly look pale.

"First time?"

The question surprises me, and I turn my head to Kellan to find a slightly uneasy look on his face as he stares at my shaking leg, noting my obvious discomfort.

"Sorry, what?" I ask. I can barely break through the wall of nerves that has constructed a fortress in my brain.

"Is it your first time flying?" he asks again. "Or do you just hate flying?"

"I'm not usually a nervous flier," I reply, looking straight ahead at the seat in front of me, hands gripped to the armrests, sweat seeping from my palms. Even though I've flown only twice, I haven't been anxious either time. "Just this particular flight."

"Did you see the pilot having a coldie at the bar before this? Or notice a fuel leak when you were boarding? Should I be worried as well?"

I turn to him, ripped from my mini meltdown, and see a smile has broken out over his face. That's when I pick up on the joke.

"Oh yeah, the pilot and I were slamming back—What did

you call them? *Coldies?*—in the airport lounge before this. He's completely plastered," I reply, trying to keep my expression serious, but failing. "You don't happen to have any pilot experience, do you? Just in case, you know, someone needs to take over?"

"I used to fly remote-control helicopters on the beach all the time as a kid. That's relevant experience, I reckon. Aerodynamics and all," he replies.

"Oh, thank goodness. And here I was, nervous for nothing."

The moment of levity kept the onslaught of nerves at bay, but as soon as a brief pause takes hold, they return with a vengeance. My leg begins moving again, my foot thudding against the floor. I'm not usually super talkative with strangers, but Kellan hasn't reopened his book and doesn't have earbuds in, so I take the opportunity to distract myself with whatever I can. Since my seat neighbor to the other side is already sleeping like the dead…Kellan it is.

"It's your bookmark," I say to him, dipping my head in his direction.

He turns toward me. "What was that?"

"That's why you printed your boarding pass," I say. "You use it as a bookmark."

"Right," he says, looking down at where he carefully placed his boarding pass in his book, repositioning it to where it's perfectly straight. "I mean, it's the perfect height, the perfect width." He's laughing a little as he says it, but I can tell he truly thinks boarding passes are the ideal bookmarks. "I always save them and use them as bookmarks, but I also like being able to look back on everywhere I went."

"Where's your favorite place you've traveled?" I ask.

"Thailand," he says with absolutely no hesitation. "But if I'm being honest, my favorite place in the world is where I live in Sydney. I practically grew up on Bondi Beach."

You're kidding. Bondi Beach? He really could've been plucked out of an Australia tourism ad.

"Don't tell me," I say with the makings of a grin. "You're a lifeguard on Bondi Beach who spends all of his free time surfing?"

He laughs so hard it draws the attention of our neighbors across the aisle. He lowers his voice, inclining his head a couple inches closer to mine.

"I'm really that easy to read, ay?"

"I think if I were to Google 'Australian surfer aesthetic,' your picture would be the first to pop up."

He lets out a low laugh before resting his head back on the headrest. "I'll take that, I reckon. And by the way, you don't have me entirely pegged."

I lift an eyebrow at him, waiting for him to fill me in on where exactly I went wrong.

"I'm a lifeguard in the summer, during the busy season," he says, grinning, "but not year-round."

"Man, I was way off base," I joke. He eyes me from the side, tilting his head down toward me from where it still rests against his seat. "What do you do the rest of the year then?"

"I'm a tradie."

"I'm going to need a little more assistance with the Australian slang." I'd picked up on some of the terminology from *Love Island: Australia,* but I have a feeling I've barely scratched the surface. Aussie slang is its own beast.

"Sorry," he says, laughing. "We tend to shorten everything. Tradie means tradesman. I'm actually a brickie."

I laugh because he's completely unaware he just did it again.

"Oh," he says, his cheeks rising a hair higher when the realization hits him. "I'm a bricklayer."

"I gathered as much," I reply, a relieved breath escaping me. I'd been waiting for him to say he's trying to make it as a model or an influencer, which is fine enough, but there's something about a guy who understands the toil of physical labor that I find exceedingly attractive. Maybe it's the fact that Justin was so lazy he couldn't be bothered to even help me haul my family's groceries up the stairs to my apartment when we were dating or maybe it's that I know how exhausting it is picking heavy things up over and over again, but either way, it's hot.

Not that it matters, I add to myself.

"Do you like it? Being a *brickie?*" I ask, the word feeling funny on my tongue.

"I do. I mean, it's hard work, but I like getting to be active all the time—I definitely couldn't sit at a desk all day—and it pays the bills and gives me a lot of free time…which I spend surfing, as you so aptly guessed," he adds, grinning. "What about yourself? Are you from Houston?"

"Born and raised," I say. "I've spent a lot of time at the beach too, though. Maybe you've heard of it? Galveston Island? World famous."

He barks out another larger-than-life laugh that has multiple rows turning their heads to us. "Ah yes," he says, trying his best to keep his voice low. "I'm familiar with it."

Galveston is the closest beach to Houston, and the water is notoriously murky. Thanks to its location right at the mouth of the Mississippi River, all of the sediment gets deposited in the water surrounding our beaches for us to…*enjoy*. But "dirty" or not, a beach is a beach in my eyes, and Galveston holds some of my dearest memories. We were always strapped for cash, and, well, the beach was always free. During some of the darkest times in high school, when Mom was in the depths of her drinking and my dad was long gone, I would drive Lana and Penny to Galveston to spend our Saturday there, just the three of us, fighting the sticky Gulf Coast heat with the cloudy Galveston water.

"Is this water sanitary?" one of us would always ask.

"It looks questionable to me!" the other two would yell before the three of us dashed into the waves.

It may not be the prettiest beach, but it holds some of my prettiest memories. I envision Lana wiping out on a boogie board we'd borrowed from someone, water spraying her in the face, and Penny running around with a bucket, saving hermit crabs from obnoxious seagulls.

Still, I can get why someone who's used to Australia's picturesque beaches would enjoy a good Galveston joke because even though I love it, I also enjoy a good Galveston joke.

"My favorite part is how you can't see where you're walking in the water because it's so murky," I continue. "It's a fun game of *did I just step on garbage, a sting ray, or a dead body?*"

Kellan literally bursts out laughing, which makes me laugh, and soon enough, we're causing a scene on the plane. The woman beside me jolts awake and levels us with a threatening scowl. Some nearby passengers share in her annoyance, while others chuckle to themselves because it's the kind of laughter that feels contagious.

And before I realize it, Kellan and I have spent the entire three-hour flight talking, which has kept my mind thoroughly off *American Gauntlet.* We had asked each other all sorts of questions, discussing random bits and pieces of our very different lives. He'd told me about his travels, his family, his

favorite things to do in Australia (or *'Straya*, as he called it).
I'd asked about his experiences lifeguarding, and he'd talked at
length about all of it—about treating nasty Bluebottle stings and
caring for people with sun poisoning and executing the water
rescues themselves.

"Tourists don't understand how dangerous the rips at Bondi
are. They'll be in knee-deep water one second and swept out
to sea the next. A lot of them don't even know the first thing
about swimming," he'd said, his voice a mixture of anxiety and
exasperation. "It's…it's terrifying to watch a person's head dip
below the surface and not know if I'll make it to them in time."

In return, Kellan had asked me all about my life but not in a
way that felt obligatory or like he was simply being polite. He
nodded encouragingly, even when I rambled without direction,
and his face lit up when something I'd said prompted him to
think of another question. I couldn't remember the last time
I'd felt so engaged in a conversation with someone I'd just
met. Emboldened by his demeanor, I'd let Kellan into so many
different compartments of my life, covering everything from my
personal training clients to what high school in America was
like, funny moments I'd witnessed at the gym to future places I'd
like to travel.

When I named off Australia on my future vacations list,
Kellan's eyes lit up. *"Oi, you fancy a trip Down Unda?"* he'd
asked, exaggerating his Aussie accent even more.

I laughed, my cheeks hurting from the permanent smile glued
to my face. "I don't know…the people there just don't seem that
friendly," I'd teased.

He'd nudged my shoulder playfully before saying, "Well, you're
welcome to visit me at Bondi Beach anytime. Well, as long as
you stay out of the rips." An image of him battling the surf on

a lifeguard board, effortlessly heaving me from the water in a movie-like rescue entered my mind. I shook it off, hating the way my face had heated at the mere thought. *Plus, you're a good swimmer, you muppet,* I told myself. *He wouldn't need to save you anyway.*

"Tell me about your family," he prompted later.

My family is my most prized possession. I'm always instinctively protective when it comes to them, and I don't often talk about them to people outside of our little circle; it's like my mind raises warning flags that I should give as little information as possible about them to avoid…I don't even know what. Judgment, maybe. Or maybe it's the fact that I can't do them justice in a quick conversation. They're multifaceted and there's so many things I could say about each of them; it's hard to explain just how much they mean to me in the amount of time that's appropriate in a conversation with someone else.

But when I looked at Kellan, something about him—his demeanor, maybe, or the way his eyes danced with what felt like genuine interest—made me *want* to talk about my family, the thing that I treasure the most in this life. It made me want to help him understand.

So, it was decided. And I hoped I wouldn't come to regret that decision. I pulled my phone out of the seatback pocket in front of me and showed him my screensaver, a photo of me, Lana, Penny, my mom, and Ford, all of our faces squished together, cheeks smushed against one another, as we huddled in for the picture. We look incredibly happy, all of us equally obsessed with each other.

"My mom," I said, pointing her out in the photo. "She's one of the strongest people I know. She's…um, she's been through a lot, and she made it out the other side like a champ." Kellan smiled and nodded, encouraging me to keep going. "My sister, Lana. She's just fun. There's no other way to put it. She's fun and bright and bubbly and people just adore her. This is Penny. She's warm and welcoming and kind and basically every good thing under the sun." I couldn't help but beam as I talked about them. Kellan grinned along with me. "They're my world. Everything I do is for them."

"And who's this?" he asked, pointing to Ford.

I smiled again. "That's Ford. He's basically my brother."

"Basically your brother?" he repeated. "So not your boyfriend then?"

I laughed. If only he knew the utter lack of romance that has been my post-Justin reality. "No, none of those."

"Righto," he said, eyeing me from his seat next to mine. "What about your dad? Taking the photo, ay?" he asked, glancing back down at the photo, a smile still plastered to his features.

"Oh, um, no. None of those either," I replied. "He didn't pass away or anything," I immediately added, which is usually the follow up question. "He's just not…in the picture."

I waited for the classic pitying look that I absolutely hate—the one that says, *Oh, bless your heart*. I've gotten it too many times to count from friends and teachers and classmates whenever the dad subject was brought up over the years.

But the look didn't come. Instead, Kellan looked directly in my eyes and said, "The picture's full anyway. He wouldn't fit."

A tingle shot up my spine at the accuracy of his words, at the way he said them with both tenderness and ferocity, at the way he seemed to pluck the very thought from my head. I felt…seen. It was scary the way this guy had made it so easy to open up to him in such a short amount of time.

I'm usually guarded, an iron-clad closed door with a couple

extra locks and deadbolts for good measure. I wouldn't usually be so open with someone I've just met, but I chalk it up to the fact that Kellan lives on the other side of the world, and I will literally never see him again. I will, however, be eternally grateful to him for giving me a *very* welcome distraction from the meltdown that threatened my sanity at the beginning of this flight.

Soon enough, we've landed in Los Angeles, and it's time for me and airport-hot-guy Kellan to go our separate ways. And after three hours with him, I can confirm that he's neither a jerk nor a weirdo…from what I can tell, at least. Anyone can put a mask on for three hours, I suppose.

He looks at me with those baby blue eyes of his and runs a hand through his sandy blonde hair, naturally highlighted with sun-kissed streaks.

"I'm sorry—we've just chatted for an entire flight and I didn't even ask your name," he says, looking genuinely embarrassed.

I give him a reassuring smile. "Dani."

"Dani?" he asks, his blue eyes widening so slightly I feel like I'm imagining it. Which, like, I get it. It's not a super common name for girls. It wouldn't be the first time someone thought they heard me wrong.

"Yep—Dani." I stick my hand out to him. "It was really nice to meet you, Kellan."

He takes it in his, and I notice he doesn't react to how rough and calloused my hands are from hours at the gym. His are exactly the same, the hands of a brickie.

"I hope to see you again, Dani."

Not likely, I think.

Nonetheless, I give him one last smile and say, "Yeah. Maybe someday I'll make it to Bondi."

nine

I TAKE my time heading to baggage claim, stopping first to use the restroom, refill my bottle at a water fountain, and grab a burrito, which ends up taking forever. I shoot a quick text to the family group text to let them know I arrived safely, and I wonder at what age I'll stop texting my sisters (and Ford) to tell them every detail of my travel day. *Probably never.* By the time I finally make it down to baggage claim, Ford's suitcase is riding solo around the baggage carousel. I snag it off the belt and look down at my watch. I've killed thirty minutes, which means I'll be waiting another hour before Lana's flight gets in from North Carolina.

I'm literally a ball of energy, the nerves having made way for new emotions: excitement and pure *readiness*. I'm pretty sure if someone touched me, I'd make their hair stand on end like one of those static electricity generators at science museums.

There's absolutely no way I'll be able to just sit around waiting for Lana, so I pace around the roomy baggage claim area, sure that airport security is probably eyeing me suspiciously, doing my best to focus my thoughts and prepare myself mentally for what's to come. Easier said than done, I'll say that much. At one point, I settle against a wall and start stretching, wanting to keep my muscles loose and ready, ignoring the wary glances I get from middle-aged women with severe bob haircuts.

Finally—*finally*—I hear a squeal from behind me before turning around just in time for my sister to spring off the escalator and launch herself into my arms. I catch her, even as I match the screech coming from her, our obnoxious screams radiating off the tile floor.

She plants her feet back on the ground, an ear-to-ear grin on her face. "Nice catch."

"I don't lift all those weights for nothing," I tease.

Lana looks radiant. She's all hazel eyes and brown hair to her waist and lean muscle and pearly white teeth. She looks like she has as much energy radiating off of her as I do, something that only instills more confidence in the pit of my belly. She's ready for this. And so am I.

"How was your flight?" I ask, collecting my bags to go wait at the right baggage carousel with her.

"Honestly? Incredible. I slept the whole time," she says. *How did she manage to sleep on the way here?* I couldn't have slept even if I wanted to. She either isn't nervous at all about *American Gauntlet* or the end of her semester left her energy tank on empty. "What about you?" she asks.

A quick flash of indecision hits me as I wonder if I should mention airport-hot-guy Kellan, but I refrain. Lana lives for stuff like that, and she would no doubt go down a long, insufferable tangent about how I probably met my soulmate, how tragic it is that I'll never see him again since he lives on the other side of the world, and so on. The more I ponder it, the more confident I am that I should not mention Kellan to my sister. I'm trying to keep her as focused as possible from here on out.

"It was fine" is all I reply.

I see Lana struggling to grab her very large suitcase off the carousel when a text from the producer, Kelly, pops up on my phone. My sister drags her suitcase over to me when she's done wrestling it off the belt.

"Kelly said there's a van waiting outside of baggage claim for us. You have everything?"

"Yep," Lana huffs, slightly out of breath. She brushes the loose hair from her face. "Let's do this."

We walk outside to the busyness that is LAX and try to spot our ride. Soon enough, I see a tiny blonde woman waving her arm excitedly in our direction. *That would be Kelly.*

We hurry over to her and she embraces us both, trying her best to fit her arms around me and my sister simultaneously.

"Hi girls!" she screeches from deep within our welcome hug. "It's so nice to meet you two in person!"

The large, muscular man standing near Kelly grabs our bags and loads them in the back of the inconspicuous black van. The windows have been completely blacked out like a limo. Kelly grabs a bag out of the passenger seat and hands it to me and Lana.

"Okay girls, these are your uniforms. You'll receive more uniform options and branded clothing when you get there, but as soon as we arrive at the location, you'll be filmed, so we'd like you to be ready to go. Sergey and I will wait here while you change in the van."

Lana and I thank Kelly and jump in the roomy vehicle. There's a row of seats toward the front, but the other rows have been laid down, so there's plenty of room to change. I wonder for a moment why we can't just go change in the airport restroom, but I realize they don't want to draw any attention to us. The uniforms are all branded, provided by the same clothing sponsor, and they're a tight, spandex-like material. We're each given a tank top and form-fitting shorts in a matching purple color, which will be the color we wear all season, I presume. Smack dab on the front of the tank tops is the *American Gauntlet* logo, with the show's name in its signature fonts and a row of four gold stars beneath it, each representing one of the four phases of the show: strength, endurance, strategy, and grit.

"I'm digging the purple," Lana says as she puts her trainers back on after changing. We both stuff our airplane clothes in our backpacks, then we slide the van door open slightly to let Kelly and Sergey know we're ready to go.

With our luggage already loaded in the back before hopping back in the van, Kelly and Sergey hop back in with Sergey at the wheel. We pull away from the curb, and we're off on our adventure, albeit at a snail's pace. The LAX traffic is horrendous. Kelly tells us how thrilled she was that she was the producer assigned to riding with our team and then begins asking us all kinds of questions about how our flights were, how excited we are, how proud our parents must be.

One of them is proud, I think. *We wouldn't know about the other one.*

Still, Lana and I both politely nod and ask her a few questions of our own. Kelly could teach a master class on letting us down easy. In fact, she's so polite in refusing to answer our questions that you almost want to thank her afterwards. Regardless of her cheery tone, she doesn't budge. She won't tell us where we're going or how long it's going to take or basically anything about what lies ahead of us. Sergey could be driving us to a smaller private airport for us to hop on a private charter somewhere or he could be driving us to the actual filming location. We have absolutely no way of knowing.

The chatter has died down the further we've gotten, but I don't know how long it's actually been. Kelly took our phones and my watch from us after we changed, as we won't have access to them at all when we get to wherever it is we're going, so I have no idea how long we've been driving. It could be three hours at this point. It could be four or five. It *feels* like it's taking forever, but I'm also so ready to get there that it might be a trick my mind is playing on me.

At one point, Sergey exited the highway to refuel, but he hopped right back on the road afterwards. He exits the highway once more now, but this time, he doesn't pull off into a gas station. He starts taking roads that are getting progressively smaller and more obscure, and if Kelly wasn't sitting in the front seat with him, I would definitely be concerned that Lana and I are about to get murdered out here in the middle of nowhere.

Soon enough, Sergey brings the van to a stop on what appears to be the side of the road, and as he does, panic begins to set in. My heart beats so quickly, I'm sure the vein that sometimes protrudes from my temple is visible. I feel my body heat rising from the stress, and I'm suddenly thankful sweat doesn't easily show through the material of these uniforms.

"Is there something wrong with the van?" I ask. I look over to find Lana has drifted off to sleep, her head resting gently against the window. I nudge her, and her eyes flash open. She looks disoriented, her eyes widening and then slowly narrowing as if she's trying to remember where she is. *Seriously, how is she able to sleep at a time like this?*

Sergey doesn't answer my question, but Kelly turns around in the passenger seat to face us.

"Alrighty, girls! This is your stop!" she chirps, all smiles.

"Wait, what?" Lana asks groggily, wiping her eyes. She's careful not to ruin her mascara. "Where are we?"

Kelly gives her a look that I can only describe as a let-you-down-easy look. There's a little bit of pity mixed with that same cheerfulness Kelly seems to always exude. It's like an "it's not you, it's me" breakup.

"Sorry girls, I can't tell you anything else."

As she says this, Sergey slides our van door open and ushers me and Lana out of the vehicle, Kelly hopping out of the front seat in the process. As Lana and I stand there on the side of the road, utterly speechless, Kelly hands me what appears to be a GPS. She also gives Lana a small, sponsor-branded backpack, which is filled with water and two drinking spigots.

Adrenaline has begun coursing through my veins, honing my mind and heightening my senses. I look at Lana who still appears half-awake and dazed.

"Hey," I say, squeezing her shoulder to get her attention. "Are you with me?"

The small gesture seems to whip her back into the present moment just in time for another identical black van to pull onto the side of the road behind us. The doors burst open and out pops a camera crew followed by someone I didn't expect to see until the first competition. Dax Philipps, the *American Gauntlet* host.

Dax slides coolly out of the van, black aviator sunglasses shielding his eyes and only adding to his intimidating demeanor. He's wearing black jeans and a crisp white, short-sleeved button up shirt, showing off his two full arm sleeves of tattoos. There's a smug smirk on his face that makes me feel like he's about to say *"gotcha!"* Dax prowls over to us with the grace of a panther, and I bask in the air of confidence that surrounds the legendary MMA fighter who has hosted *American Gauntlet* since it began. He's sort of a legend.

And one thing's for sure: he's definitely as intimidating in person as he seems on TV.

A mob of crew members quickly swarms us, sliding wires up our backs and clipping tiny microphones onto our clothing, several of them muttering apologies at the intrusion into our more intimate spaces. It's suddenly very real that everything we say and do during our time on the show will be recorded and shown to the whole world. A shiver involuntarily works its way up my spine right along with the mic wire.

After our microphones are tested and the camera crew has settled in place, Dax finally speaks. "Dani, Lana. Welcome to *American Gauntlet.*"

Shaking off the starstruck feeling that has accompanied meeting my favorite TV show host and understanding there are cameras surrounding us that will undoubtedly zoom in on our shocked expressions, I mask my face into a confident guise that would give Dax's a run for its money.

"We're happy to be here," I reply, all cool assurance and poise, even as nerves pound in my belly like the incessant beating of a drum.

"I wouldn't get too comfortable yet," he responds, and the sharp edge of his tone tells me there would be a challenge in his eyes if I were to get a glimpse behind his opaque sunglasses. "You didn't think making it to the camp this season would be so easy, I hope. Anyone who thinks they've got what it takes to take on the Gauntlet is going to need to earn their way there in what I like to call, The Trial.

"Dani, in your hands is a GPS tracker that will guide your team to the camp. You will encounter a few roadblocks along the way—I'm sure that won't be a problem for the two of you." There's that smug look again. "Fail to complete a roadblock or make it to camp, and your time on *American Gauntlet* will be over before it even starts. Best of luck, ladies," he says, offering a brief smile before he turns and begins walking back toward the van he came in.

"Oh, and by the way," he adds. "Be sure to hydrate with the water you've been provided. I'm afraid it does seem like a hot one today, doesn't it?" He emphasizes the word *hot* like we can't already feel the sun burning into our skin.

With Dax inside, the van peels off, burning rubber in the process for dramatic effect, I'm sure. Sergey and Kelly have returned to their van and watch us from the front seat. Now, it's just me and Lana and a small camera crew who will document our journey during "The Trial" as Dax called it.

I turn to my sister. "Are you with me, Lana?"

"I'm with you," she says, squeezing my hand.

"Then let's get to it," I reply. "*American Gauntlet* has officially begun."

ten

THE sun is shining so brightly it's almost obnoxious. Like a
pageant queen who refuses to be upstaged, the heat of the sun
commands our attention, drowning out all thoughts other than
those consumed with the blistering temperature. I squint my
eyes as I tilt my face up toward the sky, placing a hand above my
brows like a visor, only to find there isn't a single cloud to offer
reprieve. As the rays beat relentlessly against my skin, I already
feel the first droplets of sweat sneaking down the nape of my
neck, tracing the dip of my spine.

But that's the beauty of training in Houston. The temperature
here—wherever *here* is—might rival the highs we get at home,
but nothing compares to the Houston humidity. The air here is
hot, yes, but far drier.

As Lana throws her hair in a ponytail, I study the landscape
around us, taking stock of what we'll be up against. I toe the
ground with my sneaker, my foot sliding easily over the dusty
terrain. It's all dry grass and wiry shrubs and loose rocks that
could easily pull our footing out from under us. I shudder at
the thought of suffering a sprained ankle before we've even
really begun the competition. A few football fields away, the flat
terrain gives way to low, rolling mountains, and while they're
not necessarily fourteeners, they're big enough to send nerves

roiling through my belly. *Did we train hard enough?* I ask myself. Doubt instantly sinks its jagged teeth into my flesh, but I force the thought from my mind, shedding the anxiety like a discarded jacket. There's no more room for panic, not when there's $300K on the line.

It's not a hypothetical situation anymore. *American Gauntlet* is here. And I intend to win.

There's no question as to who will be navigating; Lana can barely make her way around her college campus, much less the sprawling wilderness around us, and poor sense of direction aside, it's also natural for Lana to follow my lead; she's been doing it for most of her life, so we slide into our usual dynamic like a key in its lock. A perfect fit. What *doesn't* feel natural is the camera crew surrounding us, documenting our every move. A swarm of intrusive thoughts angrily congregates in my mind, taking every available braincell hostage. *Does my face look weird from the side? Gah, I'm going to hate hearing my voice when this airs. Exactly how much of our day-to-day will they be capturing? Are there going to be cameras in our rooms?*

Good grief. I'd prepared for this competition in nearly every way possible, but I'd grossly underestimated what it would feel like to have a dozen cameras in my face, their lenses like one-eyed monsters waiting to pounce. Regardless of my discomfort, which I have a nasty feeling is clear from the grimace on my face, Lana and I need to get going.

My eyes find Lana's. "We need to get there as fast as possible. We don't know if there's a time limit, so we need to go for speed, just in case."

"Got it," she says. The moment we've taken to mentally prepare ourselves has done wonders for Lana, noticeably bolstering her mood and confidence. She's pulled herself from her sleep-induced haze, a competitive edge making its way into her voice. That's one thing I love about her—she's an athlete, a competitor. She doesn't like to lose. And neither do I.

With the GPS guiding our every step, Lana and I embark on our journey, jogging through the grass and rocks and brush, heading in the general direction of the mountains. We quickly find ourselves in a moderate jog; we don't want to expend all of our energy too quickly while still trying to keep a decent tempo. Strategy is a key component of this game, and the smallest mistake, like tiring ourselves out too quickly or taking a wrong turn, can be the difference between going home with a full bank account or leaving empty-handed. I'm keeping a pace that we can sustain for miles on end, since we have absolutely no idea what lies ahead. This is the first season of *American Gauntlet* where teams are forced to complete a task before even stepping foot onto the camp.

The competition has barely begun and they're already throwing curveballs at us.

My eyes stay glued to the GPS, following the route as it takes us toward the foothills until we veer right, running adjacent to the rolling mountains beside us, not up them. A small blessing. We jog for what feels to be almost a mile until we arrive at a skinny lake, the length of it stretching far beyond its width. An American Gauntlet-branded sign tells us we've arrived at our first roadblock. "Swim," it commands.

Challenge accepted. Lana and I have years of neighborhood swim team under our belts from the years when Dad was still around and we still lived in our happy little home in our cute little neighborhood with its preppy little swim team. Swim meets at the crack of dawn on summer Saturdays didn't feel much like a luxury to my twelve-year-old self. I nearly laugh.

If only that little girl knew how much her life would change in under a year. We lost the house. We lost the luxury of costly extracurricular activities. But I continued swimming wherever I could—public swimming pools, nearby lakes, friends' houses— as if I could hold onto any semblance of what my life was like before it got turned upside down.

I included a healthy dose of swimming in Lana's training plan and kicked my own training up a notch with open water swimming in Galveston Bay, so the lake doesn't intimidate me. In fact, I'm thrilled to see it, ready to welcome any reprieve from the dry heat that has made it feel frighteningly close to roasting in an oven.

As we reach the lake's edge, I realize there's no rustling grass around us, no tumbleweeds rolling languidly by; the day is utterly windless. I squint, shielding my eyes against the placid lake, the bright rays of the sun reflecting off its pristine surface like a mirror.

I stick the GPS in its waterproof case and shove it into the small backpack Lana has been carrying.

"Do we have to keep pushing the pace?" she asks, her breathing quickly growing ragged. "We don't even know if it matters how fast we finish. It just matters that we *finish*."

Irritation prickles at my skin as if a dozen tiny needles are pressing against my nerves, prodding my frustration. Goading it. With a measured breath, I tamp the unwelcome emotions down, a gesture I've done so many times before, it's as easy as flipping a switch. I hate getting angry with my sister. We've had so much darkness in our lives that I just want to be the light for her. A safe haven.

"That's the thing, Lana—we *don't know* if time matters," I say, my tone warm. No one would ever be able to tell I'd been seconds from snapping at her. "It's better to finish quickly than regret it later. If we get the fastest time, we might get some sort of advantage in the first competition. It could be worth it." I give her shoulder an encouraging squeeze. "And if it doesn't matter how fast we finish, then this was a great workout," I add with a wink.

She stifles a groan; it escapes as a sharp breath devoid of a voice to give it life.

"Here," I say, gesturing to the backpack Lana's been carrying. "I'll carry it during the swim." The subtle brightening of Lana's eyes tells me she's grateful to be rid of the extra weight, but her energy still feels off. I imagine it's a mixture of the exhaustion of travel, the sweltering heat, and the fact that she doesn't feel the need to push our pace as much as I do, but as I absorb the dejection on her face, I suddenly know exactly what to do to propel my sister forward.

"Race you there!" I yell, sprinting full force toward the water, reenergized by the promise of cool water against my hot, sticky skin. Lana's eyes burst open with renewed vitality, and she races after me. Like the sprinter she is, she's nipping at my heels before I"ve even hit the water. I smother my self-satisfied grin. I can always count on a little healthy competition to get Lana motivated.

The dirt and dust vanish from my legs as the first spatter of water hits my skin in brisk splashes. The lake feels utterly glorious, and I can't help the ragged gasp that escapes me through heaving breaths. I dive in headfirst and torpedo toward the other side, Lana at my heels. Caught up in the excitement of doing something other than jogging through the oppressive heat, I quickly realize I'm pushing our pace too much to maintain, so I gradually slow us down, envisioning a shiny black line of tiles, just like the neighborhood pool used to have, in an effort to avoid veering off to the side. It feels like neighborhood swim meets all over again, except this time, the stakes are far higher than a gold ribbon at the end of the day.

I turn my head to one side to get a gulp of air and nearly scream at the figure I see in the water a few yards away from me. *Is someone…scuba diving right now?* My brain tries to make sense of what I'm seeing, and realization hits me quickly. It's a safety diver, an expert the producers hired to come to our rescue should anything go awry while we're underwater. Relief hits me where the shock was only moments before, and I almost want to laugh, even though my lungs would riot if I expended my precious oxygen on something so trivial at a time like this.

The viewers won't see them, of course. I've watched every season of *American Gauntlet*, and yet I've never given a second thought to things like camera crews and divers and medics. I don't know how to feel about it. It's somewhat disenchanting to see how the sausage gets made, but it also feels…exclusive. Like I'm a part of a bougie airport lounge that only *American Gauntlet* competitors get to be a part of.

Once Lana and I dredge our soaking wet bodies to the opposite shore, I pull the GPS out, thankful that not even a drop of water has somehow snuck its way into the case. Breathing a little heavier from the swim, we keep trekking through the wilderness, stirring up dust and loose gravel with every step. I don't know how many miles we've run, but I *do* know that we've run enough to where breathing feels like hard labor. By the time we reach the next checkpoint, we're forcing the oxygen into our lungs in rough gulps.

The checkpoint is marked by a sign, like before, and a bistro table with what appears to be two skewers sitting atop it. Upon closer inspection, I see what's on the skewers: giant…*creatures*. I struggle to call them bugs; the word isn't large enough to encompass the monsters impaled on the thin wooden sticks before us.

"Eat," the sign demands.

Lana's eyes widen as she reads the directive and sees what, exactly, it is we'll be eating. I immediately stab her with a look that wordlessly says, *"I already prepared you for this."* Before coming to the show, I had a lengthy discussion with Lana about the fact that, if past seasons were any indication, we would have to eat some things we're not accustomed to, things like Rocky Mountain oysters or sweetbreads or cow brains. But discussing it and staring it directly in the face—literally—are two very different things.

There are two skewers before us on the table, one of which has a sizable scorpion impaled upon it. The arachnid's jet black exoskeleton is nearly luminescent in the sunlight, its sheen so glossy we can nearly see our reflections. The other skewer has two mammoth cockroaches affixed to it, each at least four inches in length. I pick up the thin, wooden skewer with the roaches and flip it over, inspecting it. On one side, the roaches look almost like cocoons, light brown crescents descending down their backs, contrasting against the woody, hickory brown of the rest of their bodies; their wings lay nearly translucent across them. At a quick glance, it isn't necessarily unappetizing. On the other side, however, their legs are visible, each leg protruding from their bodies like thin tree branches. When I take a closer look, I see the minute, hair-like prongs jutting out from their long legs and quickly glance away, suddenly not wanting to inspect my potential meal too closely.

Lana looks like she's going to be sick.

"It's just protein," I tell her. "Lots of people eat things like this every day. We're just not used to it," I remind her.

A memory shoots to the forefront of my mind, and I'm transported back to sophomore year of high school. I'm seated next to Katy, one of my best friends at the time, as we dine at her family's dinner table, a Lazy Susan filled with steaming food in front of us. I fumble around with two chopsticks, while her parents, first-generation immigrants from China, give me encouraging smiles. I should feel embarrassed, but they've somehow put me at ease, and I follow their lead as they pluck food from various dishes and place it in their bowls. I was used to surviving off of Easy Mac and instant ramen, so a meal like this? It was a luxury I didn't have. Ever.

Katy's father retreats to the kitchen only to return minutes later with the centerpiece of the meal, a fish. Only it's not a *filet* of fish; it's the entire thing, its head and tail still on. I see its dead, bulbous eye, and it feels like it's watching me, staring me down, as the platter is set on the table. A moment later, Katy's father digs the eyeball out of the fish's socket with a squish and turns to me with a genuine smile. I realize then that he's offering it to me. It was a sign, I later learned, that I was the most honored guest of the evening.

"You don't have to eat it if you don't want to," Katy whispers from beside me, but I just smile back and pop the eyeball into my mouth. The gooey orb slides around my mouth before I bite into it with a subtle *pop*. It tasted like the ocean.

The scorpions and roaches in front of me right now are no different. People eat them all the time.

Thinking of the precious time we're losing with every second that passes, I look at Lana who is still staring uneasily at the skewers.

"Which one do you want?" I ask. She doesn't respond. I would eat both the scorpion and the roaches, but I know we're each intended to eat one skewer. I'm not trying to get us kicked off the show by skirting the rules.

"Lana," I say again with urgency. "Which one?"

"The scorpion," she grits out.

Finally. I pick up the scorpion skewer and hand it to her, while taking the roaches in my other hand.

"Okay, Lana," I say, grasping her hand to stop the subtle tremble. "Together."

I raise the skewer to my mouth and slide one of the colossal cockroaches off. I want to swallow it whole, but it's too big, and I don't want to risk choking on it. I bite into it, its shell and guts spilling out onto my tongue and between my teeth with a series of *crunches*, before I quickly swallow. I suddenly realize my mouth is as dry as the soil in this arid wilderness, and I feel little pieces of the roach floating around in my mouth, snagging on my parched tongue. It takes every ounce of willpower to keep myself from scraping out the pieces with my finger like a makeshift toothbrush. Before I can talk myself out of it, I slide the other roach off the skewer, quickly chew and swallow, doing my best to gulp down all of the crusty bits that are lingering on my tongue and making a home in between my teeth. I grab the water spigot and wash it down before opening my mouth and sticking out my tongue to show the producer standing next to one of the camera operators that I'm completely finished.

To be honest, the roach tasted a little bit like gamey chicken; it's the texture that would take a little getting used to.

Nevertheless, the whole ordeal with the roaches is over in forty-five seconds, but Lana hasn't made a lick of progress. She opted to take a series of smaller bites, starting with tearing off each of the scorpion's tiny legs, one at a time, and at this rate, we'll be here until nightfall, any chance of an advantage slipping away with the day.

"Just do it all at once, Lana. It'll be easier." *And faster*, I think to myself.

She gawks at me, her eyes pleading, but I don't give her reprieve. Instead, I toss her an encouraging nod and ready her water spigot. "Do it now, Lana," I say to her, my tone gentle and supportive, even as my shoulders tense from unease.

Lana slides the rest of the scorpion off the skewer like the last bite of a Popsicle. She chews twice and swallows, heaving a gag that she quickly drowns with water.

"Good job, sis," I say, before we pull the GPS up again and return to the route, jogging at a consistent tempo until we reach our next roadblock at the foothills of the rolling mountains beside us. I catch sight of a gravelly path that winds up the mountainside, two black and red mountain bikes with extra thick tires awaiting us at the bottom. "Ride," the sign instructs.

Without a word to each other, the bleary exhaustion having arrived like enemy forces, we toss on the provided helmets and hurl our legs over the bikes to mount them. As we begin pedaling, it becomes clear that every inch up the hill will be a chore. The incline rapidly becomes more intense, and we have to stand and ride out of the saddle to propel ourselves up at a painstakingly slow pace. With each movement, flames lick at my quads, and my brain has begun the dance of trying to convince me to quit, persuading me that there's no possible way I'll make it up the hill. *Ah, I've been expecting you*, I say, ignoring its pleas for reprieve.

As Lana and I toil up the mountain, each breath is as laborious as the pedaling, my lungs screaming for more, more,

more oxygen. I can't seem to placate their cries for air, no matter what breathing technique I employ, and despite our efforts, I can't help but feel like our pace feels entirely too slow. I just hope the other teams, wherever they may be, struggle in the same way we are.

"Just a little further to the top," I huff out as the peak (slowly) gets closer. Lana simply grunts from where she's fallen behind me.

And just as I feel like my quads will give out on me at any moment, I finally make it to the top of the hill, Lana following behind a minute later. As we survey the horizon, we see it.

We've arrived at the *American Gauntlet* camp.

eleven

GIFTED with a fresh burst of energy upon seeing the *American Gauntlet* camp, Lana and I sprint down the hill as fast as we can without throwing ourselves off our mountain bikes. It's almost humorous to see the camera crew racing down on ATVs beside us, their cameras thrown over their shoulders and strapped to their bodies. There's a finish line chalked in white at the bottom of the hill, and Lana and I race each other to it, not letting up until both our tires have crossed.

There's not a single other competitor to be seen, but behind the finish line, Dax Philipps awaits us.

"Congratulations, ladies. You've made it to camp," he says with a brilliant smile, his teeth almost too white to be real. He gestures to the sprawling compound behind him. "Find your cabin and get settled."

Lana collapses right onto the ground after we've walked no more than twenty yards past Dax. "We made it," she says, her tone tinged with both relief and fatigue. "A triathlon. They literally just made us complete a triathlon."

"I guess they did, didn't they?" I laugh. Now that my leg muscles aren't pushing me up a hill on a mountain bike, I take stock of my condition. I'm tired, for sure, but not completely exhausted. Another little seed of confidence drops into the well in the pit of my stomach.

"The thing is," I add, "something tells me that was the easiest thing we'll do all season."

Lana momentarily lifts her head off the ground to give me a terrified look. She opens her mouth to say something, but ends up settling on a pained grunt instead.

"Come on," I say, extending my hand to help her up off the ground. "Let's go find our cabin."

"Just go ahead without me. I'll catch up," she says, dramatic as ever. Although Dax hasn't turned around to look at us, I hear him chuckle under his breath, clearly listening in on every word that passes between us.

"Yeah, not likely," I say, grabbing her forearm and hoisting her to her feet. "Hop on."

Lana knows what I mean as soon as the words come out of my mouth. As her smile finally meets her eyes, I hand her the backpack, and just like when we were kids, Lana hops on for a piggyback ride. From her spot on my back, she shoves the water spigot in my mouth so I can get a drink.

As we draw closer to the camp, a sense of wonder overtakes the edges of my mind. From the vantage point at the top of the hill, it looked like there was a large, white warehouse-like structure in the middle of camp, with what appeared to be a series of disjointed black shipping containers surrounding it in a larger circle. From above, the camp almost resembled a sun, with each of the structures surrounding the larger one in the middle like black rays. As we get closer to the outskirts of the camp, sure enough—they're double-wide shipping containers. Each one is made of matte black corrugated metal with the show's signature four gold stars plastered on the sides.

Because this is *American Gauntlet* and they never repeat *anything*, every year the "camp" looks different, so we really had no idea what to expect. Past seasons have included everything from a luxury villa to an underground bunker to a string of treehouses in the jungle, but I have to admit, this year's accommodations are unmatched. Seeing the stark black and white contrast, the creativity in which the show's crew made this unique vision come to life, is sort of mind boggling. They took an arid piece of land in the middle of nowhere and turned it into a fully functioning, livable space that also looks…cool. Like we're the last survivors in some future dystopian society and we've trekked through dangerous wilderness and finally made it to safety. It's another part of what keeps viewers watching the show year after year. They love to see what the producers come up with next.

Lana hops off my back as we reach the camp, her childlike curiosity suddenly curing her fatigue, as the rocky, grassy terrain gives way to smooth gravel that has been placed, well, everywhere. The ground surrounding the compound is full of tiny white and gray pebbles, our feet making little waves in the stones as we walk. Lana reaches her hand out to touch one of the structures, almost as if making sure it's real and not a mirage in this wilderness.

"Huh," she says, her tone disbelieving. "Fancy…shipping containers."

We get to the front of the container and see a door labeled "CREW ONLY." We follow the wooden sidewalk that's been placed as a walkway on the inside of the circle of containers, passing a few labeled "Crew" or "Security" or "Medical" before finding one that says, "Naji & AJ."

"That's one of the other teams," I say. I had labeled them the *stunt brothers.* "Our container—er, cabin?—is probably around here."

We pass another team's cabin, until we find the door with our name on it.

"Do you want to do the honors?" I ask.

"Duh," she says before bursting through the door, a cameraman following us inside.

I'm not sure what I expected the inside of one of these double-wide containers to look like, but as I look around, the only word I have to describe it is *pristine.* The walls are black as the night, the floor and ceiling a crisp, eggshell white. There are the show's four gold stars painted on one of the walls, with gold accents in little places around the small space. Even though it's double its usual width, the cabin is still a shipping container, so it's longer than it is wide, which leaves enough space for two twin beds with bright white sheets and black pillows, as well as a white nightstand with gold accents in between them. There's a small wardrobe that, when opened, reveals a closet full of sponsor-branded uniforms and athleisure clothing. There's a mirror on the inside of one of the doors that I quickly close after catching a glimpse of what I look like right now after the day's triathlon. How does Lana still look perfect, even after getting soaked and then air dried via mountain bike? I also notice our suitcases and backpacks have been placed next to the wardrobe. The whole room has a futuristic vibe, like we're passengers aboard a spaceship.

As far as shipping containers go, this one would definitely fall in the "luxury" category, meaning it has air conditioning and electricity. The quarters are tight; there's no doubt about that. But overall, I definitely won't mind spending a month here with Lana.

Lana flops on one of the beds, her arms and legs splayed wide, as she says, "This feels so…"

"Unreal?" I offer.

"*Un-freaking-real,*" she says. "I can't believe we're actually here. Have I thanked you for submitting that audition tape for us? Because if not, let the record show: *thank you.*"

"Did you get that?" I ask the camera operator. "Make sure that's included in the final edit. Actually, you know what—just send me the clip so I can play it on a loop whenever I feel underappreciated by my younger sister here."

The cameraman laughs, and I'm suddenly worried I'll get him in trouble by speaking to him. How am I supposed to act when there's someone following us around everywhere? It seems rude to just ignore him, but that's probably what I'm supposed to do. "Act like we're not even here," they'd said.

A rap at the door interrupts my runaway tangent.

I only need to take a few steps to get to the door—again, tight quarters—and I open it to find Kelly beaming at me on the other side of the threshold.

"You girls made it!" she chirps. "I'm so thrilled. I just stopped by to let you know that the bathroom is a few doors down that way," she says, pointing. "Feel free to freshen up, but otherwise stay here in your cabin. We'll come round everyone up later."

"Okay, thanks Kelly," I smile. It's hard not to smile at her when she has a permanent one plastered to her face at all times.

"Of course! So happy for you both!" She starts to turn around but pauses, adding, "Also, keep your mics on at all times. We've also got microphones and cameras across the camp, so, you know, just be aware."

I grimace.

"I mean, not in the bathrooms or anything!" she amends, as

if that simple fact alone will placate my obvious discomfort. I mean, I'm glad there aren't cameras in the bathrooms, but having nearly every second of the day documented for the world to see (and judge) will take some getting used to. In fact, I'm almost positive they have our cabins rigged with cameras and microphones, having seen footage on past seasons that takes place in the sleeping quarters. I shudder. I suppose if I ever need a moment to myself, I'll just go hide in the bathrooms.

With her spiel over, Kelly heads on her way, her blonde ponytail bouncing up and down with every step. I grab my makeup and a few other essentials and head to the bathroom to do something about the state I'm currently in after a swim, bike, and run through the outdoors. I get to the bathroom, which looks like a few containers that have been morphed together. There's a series of bathroom and shower stalls, sinks, and mirrors. I still don't see anyone else, aside from crew members milling around camp.

Lana finds the bathroom and we both freshen up before camping out in our room for what feels like a few hours. Kelly dropped a meal off for us, which we devoured in seconds, the scorpion and cockroaches apparently not doing a lot to stave off our appetites. The next time I peek out our door, night has begun to fall, and a cool breeze gently rustles the fallen wispy pieces of my hair before I push the door closed again.

Just when I begin to doubt we'll leave the cabin that night, Kelly returns, a grin on her face. "Ready girls?"

My stomach somersaults as I mentally prepare to meet the other contestants. Seeing photos and stalking them on social media has done a lot to take the mental intimidation out of this first meeting, but now that the time is here, I still feel a hum running through my veins, a nervous energy drenching the evening air.

Kelly looks at her watch, waits another thirty seconds, then says, "Alrighty, it's time!"

Lana and I follow her out of our little cabin. Night has fully fallen, but the compound is aglow with small street lamp-like lights to guide our path on the wooden sidewalk. We walk past the other teams' cabins and then hang a right off of the pathway and onto the pebbles, where we head to the outskirts of the camp. As we round the corner, we're met by a fire pit, Dax Philipps on one side, his face radiantly lit up by the fire, and five teams standing in a semicircle on the other side, each team looking like a mere silhouette against the night from behind. Thirty yards in front of us, another team is being led to the semicircle. The producer walking with them peels off before the duo finds their place around the fire pit.

Lana and I are the last pair to arrive, and at one point, Kelly stops walking beside us and we take the final spot on the contestant side, bringing the semicircle of competitors to completion. Including me and Lana, there are seven teams, which means every team made it through the trial this morning, I assume. I keep my eyes focused ahead on Dax, not yet willing myself to look at our competition too closely. The sole light is coming from the fire, and the whole scene feels…*intense*.

"Welcome, competitors," Dax says, his face a mask carved of granite. "You've made it—"

"*CUT!*"

A producer runs from behind one of the cameras and approaches Dax. "Sorry, we need to adjust your mic. Give us a second everyone!" he yells to both the teams and the crew surrounding us.

And just like that, the harsh, eerie atmosphere has evaporated, replaced by something much lighter and almost comedic, as a crew member starts fussing with Dax's mic and a makeup crew member runs over to powder his nose. These are the things the viewers never get to see, and the thought Lana and I had earlier resurfaces: this whole experience feels surreal. I can't believe that we are lucky enough to be here, to experience this once-in-a-lifetime opportunity.

"Hey," a voice to my right says. I look over to see two muscular guys, both with mousy brown hair, standing beside us. *The gym bros.* Kyler and Chase. One of them extends their hand to me. "What's up," he says. "I'm Kyler. This is Chase."

Kyler's voice sounds exactly like what I imagined—unnaturally low and rumbly, like he's trying to make it deeper than it actually is. The once-over he gives me makes me feel like I'm being rushed at a fraternity party.

"Nice to meet you," I say, shaking each of their hands. "This is my sister, Lana." She smiles.

"So, are you two in college?" Chase asks. He's looking at me, so I feel pressured to answer first.

"No, I'm not."

"Oh, so you graduated already?"

"No," I say, tamping down the little flare of insecurity that tends to rise up when people press me on the subject. "I didn't go to college."

Chase's brow furrows, as if the thought of someone not going to college is an entirely new concept to him. "Oh" is all he says, before turning to Lana. "What about you?"

The corners of her mouth lower into a scowl at his obvious dismissal of me. I give her hand a squeeze to let her know I'm fine. "I'm at UNC," she answers.

"Yeah, on a track scholarship," I add, always proud of my little sister.

"Sick," Chase and Kyler say at the same time, their eyes lighting up in obvious appraisal. It's been thirty seconds, but the gym bros are already giving me a gross feeling. Talking to them makes me want to take a shower.

"What about you guys?" Lana asks out of obligation.

"Yeah, we're both going to be seniors at Stratford U in Oklahoma," Kyler says. "You know, where that murder and all the stuff with the administration went down last year? Yeah, we had front row seats to all of it," he says, his eyes glossing over as if reminiscing on it all.

I remember keeping up with that whole story last year. It was pretty crazy, but the fact that Kyler says they had "front row seats" when referring to a girl getting murdered only reinforces the gross vibes.

"Oh, wow," Lana says, and her tone indicates she and I are clearly on the same page about these two.

"Yeah, it was—"

Kyler is cut off by the producers running back to their spots and yelling, "Okay everyone, we're ready. Go ahead Dax!"

A hush settles over the cast of competitors again, and in a matter of seconds, the intensity from before has returned with renewed fervor.

"Welcome, competitors," Dax begins. "You've made it to the *American Gauntlet* camp. Each of your teams was chosen for a reason. You all have a different set of skills, and you'll need these skills—and more—if you think you have a chance at running the Gauntlet at the end of this season."

My mind darts to the words Dax delivers to competitors who make it to the Gauntlet at the end of each season. You do have what it takes to face the Gauntlet. Ever since we'd been chosen for the show, I'd envisioned Dax Philipps delivering those exact words to me and Lana, playing it on repeat like a song I can't get out of my head. Now that Dax is standing mere feet from us, it feels all the more real.

Dax flicks his gaze to Lana and me.

"Dani and Lana. Welcome," he says, before shooting his eyes to the gym bros beside us.

"Kyler and Chase. Welcome." And so he goes down the line, my gaze following his, as he names off each of the competitors, the bright light of the fire shining on each of their faces. I silently repeat the nicknames I've given each team to try to keep them all straight. Tris and Benji, *the climbers*. Sarge and Junior, *the veterans*. Naji and AJ, *the stunt brothers*. Ivy and Blaire, the self-proclaimed "Twisted Twins."

Dax gets to the last team on the opposite end of the semicircle, the team I don't have a name for thanks to the terrible picture they submitted to production. I quickly glance at the one closest to me, before my eyes bolt to his partner standing beside him. The flames of the bonfire are dancing, casting highlights and shadows that illuminate only portions of his face at one time, but as each new feature comes to light, my stomach begins to churn.

I squint. I look closer. I cock my head ever so slightly to the side because it can't be. It's impossible, really.

Dax's voice cuts through my confusion. "Ryder, Joss. Welcome."

But it's not "Joss." It's Kellan. *Airport-hot-guy Kellan.* The same guy who I told *my entire life story* to for three freaking hours on the plane ride here. The one who made it so easy to open up to, who made my anxiety evaporate into thin air.

My mind is in a full sprint, running through the possibilities of how this could be possible. Is that why he—*Kellan or Joss or whatever his name is*—looked familiar for that split second when I first saw him at the airport? Recognizing whatever I saw in the grainy photo I'd seen the day before?

That doesn't explain the name, though. Was it not really his boarding pass? Did he just take some random guy's boarding pass from me? But, like…for what reason?

No, that can't possibly be right. He's *Australian*. That's one of the reasons it never even crossed my mind that he could be an *American Gauntlet* contestant. It was clear as day in the submission rules—you have to be an American citizen to be on the show.

Which brings me to my next thought—was he *faking* it? Did he fake an accent and a whole Australian-surfer-Bondi-Beach-lifeguard-brickie life story? *Anyone can wear a mask for three hours,* I had thought at the time.

I'm wondering now if he recognized me from the photo that Lana and I had submitted when he saw me at the airport and decided to, what? Get in my head before the competition even started? What kind of person does that? And *gah*, was I really that naive? *Of course,* I think. Our interactions, that instant easy connection, felt good. *Too good.* I should've freaking known.

When your life has largely been a rainstorm, the sunshine feels too good to be true. Like you're always waiting for the punchline, for the other shoe to drop.

I don't have time to unwind my thoughts, to soothe the confusion and apprehension racing through my mind, because Dax's voice cuts through my thoughts like a freshly sharpened machete.

"Now that you're all here, I hope you didn't get too comfortable in your cabins," he says, his voice taking on a sinister tone in a register that sounds nearly otherworldly. "Because one team will be back on a flight home. *Tonight.*"

twelve

O N E *team will be back on a flight home tonight.*

Of course. *Of course.* I'm starting to believe the producers are being extra cruel this year, forcing us to not only run a mini-Gauntlet to even get to the camp, but sending one team home immediately, ripping their dreams away, right as they've given them hope. They're purging the weakest ones, right off the rip.

"Hope you gave The Trial this morning all you had," Dax says, "because the team with the slowest time is packing their bags this evening."

As soon as the words leave Dax's mouth, the other teams become unsettled. From beside us, I hear Kyler and Chase mutter something under their breath that will definitely need to be bleeped out in post production. One of the Twisted Twins, red hair nearly glowing from the light of the fire, has a sour look on her face as she says, "You've got to be kidding me."

Naji—I think?—just bursts out laughing.

Internally, I'm a mess. Externally, I'm a statue. I watch Lana out of my peripheral vision beside me; her eyes have gone wide, but otherwise, she has no reaction. I'm pleased. Assuming we don't get sent home on a flight tonight, I want the other teams to remember how confident and unconcerned we were that we weren't going home.

Of course, I would be stupid not to be worried. Every person standing beside us is an athlete, and although I was pushing our tempo this morning, every little detail from The Trial is playing over in my head. How many minutes did we waste as Lana struggled with the scorpion? Could we have swam faster? Pushed harder?

The group settles and awaits the verdict from Dax, each of us hanging on his every word. He lets the silence dangle over us, knowing he's got us right where he wants us. We're the puppets, and he's pulling every one of the strings.

"We intentionally staggered your start times so you wouldn't know what you were up against, and I've got to say, I'm impressed with a lot of you." Dax's mouth turns to a grimace. "And not so impressed with some of you.

"The team with the fastest time today was…" Dax pauses a beat, and I feel myself lurching forward, anxiously anticipating his response. "Joss and Ryder. Congratulations, fellas," Dax says. Joss—Kellan?—puts his arm around Ryder and they briefly celebrate together, clamping hands on each other's shoulders, broad smiles taking residence on their faces.

"The second fastest team was Sarge and Junior. Coming in third were…Dani and Lana." I allow myself to breathe again. "Next were Naji and AJ, followed by Tris and Benji."

Although I don't let it show, a huge sigh of relief engulfs me. Third place. I'm elated with this finish because it puts us right in the middle of the pack; it doesn't put a target on our backs yet, but it also doesn't make us look like one of the weaker teams. Now knowing there's no advantage given to the first place team, third place is absolutely ideal.

"Congrats to all five of you. And to our remaining teams—

Ivy and Blaire and Kyler and Chase—I gotta say…I'm, well, unimpressed." I didn't know it was possible for a word to be spoken with so much disdain. I shudder, thankful his sentiments aren't directed at me.

Kyler and Chase look like they might be sick. The Twisted Twins, on the other hand, are having very different reactions. Blaire, wearing a "B" necklace around her neck, looks angry, while Ivy, adorning the same necklace but with an "I," still has a smile plastered to her face, although it doesn't quite reach her eyes.

"It's called energy conservation," Blaire spits at him, her tone dripping with acid. "It's a long competition—we didn't want to tire ourselves out on the first day."

Dax raises his eyebrows at her, clearly unfamiliar with being spoken to in that way. In every season I've watched, the competitors treat Dax like he's some sort of demi-god. Blaire clearly has other plans.

"Strategy is a huge component of this game," Dax replies coolly. "We'll see how that one worked out for you."

With no snarky comment to return it with, Blaire falls silent, her arms crossed across her chest like armor.

"The team leaving us this evening is…"

Dax lets the silence linger, keeping the two remaining teams in purgatory. I can practically hear the dramatic music the post production team will edit in before they cut to a commercial, leaving the audience hanging in the balance.

"…Kyler and Chase," Dax says with a tone of finality.

Chase hangs his head, while Kyler turns around and actually vomits. I grimace, taking a small step to the left, as I hear it splatter against the pebbly ground beside us.

"It looks like all those muscles did nothing to help your lack of cardio," Dax adds.

Brutal, I think. But also…good riddance.

Then Dax delivers his signature line, the words I hope to never hear during my time on American Gauntlet.

"Kyler and Chase, you do not have what it takes to face the Gauntlet."

Without another word, the gym bros leave the competitor semicircle, ushered in the right direction by a production assistant. The rest of us are silently rooted in place, no doubt basking in gratitude that it's not us catching a flight home tonight.

"Remember," Dax says after the gym bros have made their exit. "This is only the beginning."

DISMISSED for the evening, the teams begin trudging back to camp, each of us giving the adjacent pairs a wide berth. It's as if none of us have the energy to make proper introductions, the whirlwind of our first day clearly taking its toll on everyone.

The only thing I can focus on, however, is Joss. Or Kellan. Or whoever he is.

I keep peering over my shoulder, trying to catch a glimpse of him, but he and his partner are too far away in the near-darkness, and I can't get a good look.

"What's your deal?" Lana asks. "Why do you keep looking over your shoulder? You look paranoid."

"What?" I meet her eyes and find concern…and mild amusement. "Oh, sorry."

"Aren't you, like, ecstatic? What if we had made it all the way here just to get sent home? Can you imagine?" I look at her and wait. As soon as she sees the deadpan expression on my face, she rolls her eyes. "And I guess a 'thank you' is in order."

Ah, there it is. I don't directly say I told you so, but it's most definitely implied.

"Seriously," she adds. "Thank you for pushing me today."

"That's what I'm here for, right?"

We make it back to our new home for the next month, and I immediately collapse on my immaculately made bed, but while my body is winding down, my mind is whirring in turbo mode. I can't stop thinking about Joss/Kellan and just the fact that I can't stop thinking about him makes me angry, almost irrationally so. It's distracting. And the last thing I need is a distraction.

Once I get to the bottom of this whole situation, I'll be more clear-headed. I just need to know what his deal is. Did he lie to me? Actually, I'm almost positive he lied to me. The real question is: how much?

I'm abruptly pitched from my unbridled thoughts as a loud knock comes at the door.

"Do you think it's Kelly again?" Lana asks.

"Probably," I respond, crossing the expanse of our room in a few steps to answer it.

But instead of a four-foot-eleven blonde, I find a six-foot-three one standing before me. Holy moly.

The door is cracked, and I shield the opening with my body so Lana can't see who stands on the other side.

"Who is it?" she asks.

"Kelly!" I blurt. "Be right back, Lana."

I shut the door before she can ask anymore questions and then find myself standing mere inches from Joss/Kellan.

"Kelly? Is that your new nickname for me?" he teases, his

voice still very much Australian. "Care to go for a chat?"

The last thing I expected was to find Kellan standing at our door, wanting to speak to me no less, but at least after I "go for a chat" with him, I'll be able to get my freaking questions answered.

"Yes," I say. "But not where anyone can see us."

His eyes light up, amused. "Oh, so it's that kind of chat? At least take me on a date first, Dani. Or are we counting our flight here as a date?"

I groan, but he just laughs, a low rumble of a thing. "I don't want any of the other teams to see us, you muppet," I snarl. "The last thing I need is anyone thinking we have some sort of alliance going on. The alliances always get targeted first."

"Muppet?" he asks, his eyes dancing. "Spoken like a true resident of the Commonwealth."

"Gah, you're worse than a muppet. You're a—" I struggle to find the word before my brain lands on one. "A menace."

"Whatever you say," he chuckles and follows me as I snake my way past the security and crew cabins to the outskirts of camp. We come to a stop behind one of the containers, and luckily, no cameras have followed us, although I have no doubt the whole place is rigged with them.

Kellan/Joss stands just a few feet in front of me, his back to the cabin and a devilish smirk on his face.

"You have some explaining to do," I say, attempting to poke him hard in the chest. He intercepts my hand, holding it there for a second, before he lets it drop.

"Cheeky," he says. "I like it."

"Good grief," I groan, eyes rolling. "Just explain yourself."

"What, exactly, do I need to explain?" His tone indicates that he thinks this whole thing is a joke, but I don't find it funny in the slightest. I feel like—like I've been played. Like I was taken advantage of. Deeply buried feelings from when I was so thoroughly humiliated and manipulated by Justin bubble to the surface, and I just don't have the mental capacity to deal with them right now. American Gauntlet is not the time to confront my trust issues.

"Well, let's start with your name, Kellan. Or is it Joss?" I ask, combatting the emotions that have risen with every word.

Finally, he wipes the amused look off his face, his expression giving way to something more serious.

"Kellan is my name," he replies, "but I've never really cared for it, so I go by Joss."

I'm not sure what I expected him to say, but it wasn't that. I mull over his response, turning it over in my brain, before asking, "Well, where does Joss even come from?"

"If you had looked at my last name when you found my boarding pass, you'd have seen it's Josskowski. And, well, I'm an Aussie. We shorten everything. So I go by Joss."

So I suppose that answers one question out of the fifty I have for him.

"Okay, well how are you even competing on the show? The rules say you have to be an American citizen."

"Ah, but I am."

"You are?" My brow furrows. I feel the subtle dip of it, my forehead creasing together from bemusement. My mind drifts to everything he told me about growing up in Australia, how he practically grew up on Bondi Beach. How could he be a U.S. citizen?

"I was born in the States—Houston, actually—but my parents moved us to Australia when I was three," he says. "So I'm actually a United States citizen by birth. And that's why I was in

Houston. I came over a few weeks early to visit my gran."

Okay, two questions answered. I'm annoyed that it makes total sense. But there's one question that has been looming over the others ever since I saw him at the fire pit. The one that's been causing the uneasy rock in my stomach.

"Did you know?" I ask. "Did you know I was going to be on the show?"

His face softens in the barely-there light around us. "I didn't, I swear. Not at first, at least. Not until you told me your name after we'd gotten off the plane and were going our separate ways. I didn't read the email the producers apparently sent, but Ryder had called me and talked to me about all of the contestants the day before," he says. "When you told me your name, it's like all the pieces clicked into place. Your name—a bit of a unique one, yeah? The nervousness, but not because of flying. The fact that you're absolutely ripped, a personal trainer, no less. It all started making sense. But I swear I didn't realize it until we were parting ways, and you sort of rushed off."

Relief washes over me that he wasn't intentionally asking me all those questions on the flight just to dig at information that he might be able to somehow use against me later. Heat rises to my neck as I replay everything I told him. I can't contain my wince. We talked about my dad for crying out loud. But his perfect response to that exact discussion is what keeps rebounding around in my head.

"I'm sorry," he continues. "I could've said something when you were walking off, but I didn't know it'd make a difference, really."

"It's…fine," I say. "But what's with the lousy photo you submitted to the producers? It's the worst picture I've ever seen."

He laughs. "Ryder lives in Georgia, and we only see each other every few years. That photo was taken, like, years ago on Ryder's old phone that he refuses to upgrade. It's one of the only pictures we have together. When we did our submission video, I just filmed my part from 'Straya and he did his from the States."

I hate how every answer he has makes sense, and I especially hate that I don't hate him. It would have been so much easier to compete against him if I hated him. An enemy is easy to take down. Easy to eliminate. Easy to not care about, to not give a second thought to.

As soon as you start forming friendships with these people, it can impact your decision-making in the game. If you're friends with a certain team, all of sudden you're not gunning for them in competitions. And I had seen way too many people make stupid decisions because they decided to trust the wrong people or form some false sense of friendship. Or worse, romantic relationships.

At the end of the day, everyone is here for the same purpose: to take out every other team, win, and take home the money. And it isn't something I'll soon forget.

Joss is looking at me, and I suddenly realize how close I'm standing to him, how I've stepped nearer to him, backed him up against the cabin. How I can hear him breathing. How I can feel his Bondi blue eyes on me, searching. I take a step back, putting a safe distance between us.

He holds my gaze for a moment before the light mask of amusement returns to his.

"Friends?" he asks, sticking his hand out.

I take it.

"Competitors."

PHASE ONE

★★★★

strength

thirteen

WHERE *am I?* I wake up in a blitz of confusion, and my body involuntarily shoots upright as I do my best to blink away the haze. I whip my head around to find a snoring Lana beside me, and that's when I realize I'm in the shipping-container-turned-cabin for the show. *American Gauntlet.* The words settle over me like a weighted blanket. I can't believe I'm actually here.

I throw my pillow at Lana. "Wake up, goof."

A flash of emotions crosses her face in under two seconds. Confusion then rage then the smallest hint of a smile, as if she, too, just remembered where we are and how lucky we are to be here.

She gradually eases herself out of bed with a moan. "I'm dead tired from yesterday."

"You know the best way to work out that lactic acid buildup in your muscles, right?" I say with a grin. "Time for a run!"

"You're kidding," she deadpans.

"For your sake, I wish I was."

Lana reluctantly joins me for a light, easy jog, then we freshen up and get ready for the day in the bathroom, not yet running into a single other team. The fact that one team—a mildly unpleasant one, at that—is already gone brings a smile to my face.

One down, five to go.

It's mid-morning by the time Lana and I are ready, and we head to the large, white structure called "The Commons" in the middle of the compound to eat. The Commons is made of the same corrugated metal as the shipping containers, but it's probably ten times as big with an almost barn-like shape. Kelly told us that's where the kitchen is located, as well as a large lounge area. I imagine some of the other teams will be in there this morning eating breakfast and getting to know the competition.

I take a deep breath before opening the door. I know these first interactions with the other teams will set the tone for the rest of our time here, and the nerves hit me deep in my belly, although I refuse to let it show on my face. Just as I'm about to reach for the door, a voice from behind me says, "Allow me, ladies."

I turn around to see Naji doing a little jog to grab the door before me, his brother AJ closely in tow.

"I'm Naji," he says, flashing a huge grin and extending his hand to me, then Lana.

AJ follows suit. "I'm Ajiad," he says with a smile to match his brother's. "But you can call me AJ."

Lana and I beam back at them. "It's really nice to meet you both."

Naji opens the door and steps aside for us to walk in. "After you," he says with a wave of his hand.

We have a split second before the other teams notice we've walked in. In the expansive kitchen that looks way too luxurious for the warehouse-like structure, I see Sarge and Junior, the vets, prepping omelets behind a frying pan. Tris and Benji, the climbers, seem to be preparing some sort of salad for themselves. I'm questioning what kind of person craves a giant salad for breakfast, but to each their own, I suppose.

There's a sleek, black banquet-style table just off the kitchen where the other teams are sitting. Ryder is sitting on one side, while Joss sits across, a Twisted Twin on each side of him. My stomach twists itself into a knot when I realize I'm not exactly sure how to act around him. I don't want anyone else to know that we met beforehand, even if it was only for a brief period. Joss and Ryder have an illuminated sign that screams *"bullseye!"* on their backs since they were the first place team yesterday, and I'm not trying to inherit one bit of it. Ideally, I'd like to fly in the middle of the pack until it's absolutely necessary to rise to the top.

My eyes flash to his, and I regret it as soon as it happens. His eyes—two bottomless swells of cerulean blue—meet mine and they light up, if only for a moment. Ivy, who hasn't taken *her* eyes off of him, I notice, follows his gaze to me. A brief scowl forms on her face, but it just as quickly recedes as she plasters an over-the-top smile on and waves me and the rest of the group over to the table.

"You guys finally made it! What took you so long?" she asks as the four of us head their direction. I deliberately keep my eyes away from Joss. "Oh my gosh, look at you two, a full face of makeup on already!" she says pointedly to me and Lana. Her voice is saccharine sweet, but there's just a touch of acid to it, like sweet tea laced with arsenic. "Good for you. Blaire and I are *so* lazy and hardly ever wear makeup," she adds, even though I can see the mascara on her lashes.

I stifle an eye roll. Lana and I share a quick glance, but Naji jumps in before the silence hangs too long in the air.

"AJ and I slept in. I had to get my beauty sleep in, obviously,"

Naji says, pulling a laugh from the group at the table.

As Naji and AJ jump into conversation with the two teams already seated, my stomach growls, and I realize how desperate I am for sustenance.

"You get the coffee, I'll get our breakfast?" I ask, turning to Lana.

"Sounds good to me," she says before hanging a left to go around the giant white kitchen island toward the coffee maker. I have my eyes set on the fridge straight ahead as I walk away from the table.

"Good morning," Joss says from where he's seated, and I freeze for a moment. I don't look his way, but I can feel his eyes searing holes into my profile, and I know he's pulled the entire table's attention toward me. *So much for avoiding an interaction with him.*

"Morning," I say back over my shoulder, and it's admittedly lackluster. I want him to ignore me. I want to build a wall up between us. Or I suppose I want to *rebuild* the wall, since he's already torn it down once. My game plan was to be *friendly* with everyone, not *friends.* I never would've shared so much with him on that plane had I known we'd be competing against each other.

To his credit, he doesn't react in the slightest, but when I get a few more steps from the table, I hear Blaire snark, *"She* seems fun."

Ivy giggles in response, but Joss only replies with a cool tone, "I'll bet she is when we're not all competing for three hundred thousand dollars."

I nearly choke.

As I start prepping Greek yogurt bowls for me and Lana, I meet Sarge and Junior and Tris and Benji, all four of whom are pleasant enough to interact with. Sarge and Junior are stoic and intimidating, and I get the idea that they want to keep a healthy distance from everyone. Fair enough, considering I want to do the same. Tris and Benji seem very chill in the way that many Coloradans are. They're the kind of people you picture living in a van, periodically traveling between various national parks. They're both smaller and leaner in stature, and at first thought, it seems like that would be a huge disadvantage; however, it all depends on the competition. That's the beauty of the Gauntlet— it can turn perceived weaknesses into the greatest strengths, all depending on the game.

Lana and I sit down near the other teams at the huge table, closest to Naji and AJ. It also happens to be as far away from Joss as I can manage.

Naji immediately turns to grill us. "So where are you two from?"

"Houston," Lana and I say in unison in almost the exact same tone; it's an annoying habit we picked up over the years.

"What? You guys are from Texas? Where's the accent?"

We both laugh, again almost in the same exact tone. "We're from the Houston suburbs, Naji," I say. "It's not exactly the wild west of Texas."

"Yeah, but I just expected something…I don't know, more like his accent!" he says, jabbing a finger at Ryder.

"Me? You think *I* have an accent?" he jokes through his thick, Georgia drawl. Everyone melts into laughter, even Sarge and Junior from where they've separated themselves from the group at the opposite end of the table.

"What? Did y'all actually think we, like, rode horses to school or something?" Lana chimes in.

"Ah, there it is," AJ says. "You might not have a thick accent like our Georgia boy here, but the *y'all* gives it away," he laughs.

In the five minutes I've known them, it's easy to see how charming the stunt brothers are. They're like magnets, drawing the group together in a way we might not have otherwise. I'm starting to think it might be more difficult than I anticipated to keep everyone at arm's length. But even though everyone seems friendly enough, Lana and I are in the middle of the lion's den, and I won't soon forget it.

"So anyway," Ivy cuts in, standing up and making sure everyone's attention is squarely on her, "Blaire and I are off to explore. I heard there's a lake nearby that we get to use. Anyone care to join us?" she asks, with a pointed look at Joss that I—and probably everyone else at the table—pick up on. *Interesting.*

I look from Ivy to Blaire, evaluating their dynamic. In the short period I've interacted with them, they appear to be opposites—Blaire is all biting retorts and snarky humor, whereas Ivy is all fake smiles and passive aggressive remarks. I get the strong feeling that Blaire wants to come off as threatening, while Ivy intends to endear herself to all the other teams. And if her eye batting and touchiness are any indicator, she's especially interested in the men here. Not exactly my strategy, but to each her own, I suppose. I'm hoping the Twisted Twins will pay so much attention to the guys that Lana and I fly right under their radar.

Until it's too late for them, of course.

After no one takes the twins up on their offer, Blaire and Ivy head out, while the rest of us finish breakfast, clean up, and eventually go our separate ways. I make a pointed effort to avoid any further interactions with Joss at all costs, even as I feel his presence like a looming shadow. It's the subtle whiff of coconut as he passes, the lightest graze of his elbow against mine, that seems to follow wherever I go. I chalk it up to close quarters in the kitchen.

KELLY informed us there would be no competition today, as the powers-that-be are still getting everything prepared for it, so we largely have the day to ourselves. When Lana dozes off for an afternoon nap, I sneak out, sponsored workout gear on, to find the gym Kelly had mentioned to us at one point or another.

My feet thump against the wooden sidewalk of the camp, bringing back memories of long walks along the Galveston boardwalks with Penny and Lana at my side. I trek across the full perimeter of the camp before finding a covered space on its outskirts. As I approach, I see the outdoor gym covered overhead by a black metal pavilion, the same metal as practically everything else around this compound. Under the pavilion is a full set of state-of-the-art workout equipment, including free weights, squat racks, cables, and cardio machines.

I find Ryder under the open-air pavilion squatting an insane amount of weight. At breakfast, I learned he's a football player at the University of Georgia, and yeah…that much is evident. He's a formidable guy with a body type similar to Ford's.

Ford.

A pang of sadness sinks its teeth into me. It's barely been a couple days, and I already miss him, but knowing he's taking care of Penny and my mom while I'm away allows me to really focus on being present. That's what I tell myself, at least. To be honest, I felt guilty for leaving Penny. She was "just tickled" for me and Lana to have this opportunity, but her excitement did nothing to ease my conscience. It doesn't feel right that Lana and I get to have this grand adventure while she's stuck at home, but the only way I've been able to turn the volume of my guilt down to a manageable level is by convincing myself I'll win. That I'll take home this money so she can finally have *her* adventure.

As I make my way to the weights and benches, Ryder and I wave and smile at each other but otherwise, we coexist in silence. He eventually finishes his workout, leaving me alone in the gym. Just how I like it.

An hour later, I'm dripping sweat and trying to pound out the last few reps of my workout, when a voice startles me from behind.

"Fancy seeing you here," Joss says, and I can already hear the smirk on his face before I even turn around to see it for myself.

"And that's my cue to go," I reply, half-serious.

He summons a mock-wounded expression. "Aren't you just a ray of sunshine today?" he asks sarcastically. "Why exactly is my presence a cue for you to leave?"

"I just don't think it's a good idea to spend more time together than we have to," I say, already starting to make my way out of the pavilion. "And I was finished with my workout anyway."

"Just because we're competitors, as you so aptly reminded me last night," he says, following me step for step, "that doesn't mean we have to avoid each other."

"It would be better for both of us if we did."

He runs a hand through his hair, blonde and slightly unkempt and sunkissed in all the right places. "And why is that?"

"You don't quit, do you?" I groan. He looks like he has the quit of a golden retriever, which is to say absolutely no quit in him. "Listen, I just don't want to get distracted by…anything. I'm here to compete. To win. Not to make friends."

"That wasn't the case at the airport," he challenges with a smirk.

"*That* was before I knew we were directly competing against each other for three hundred grand," I retort. "At the airport, you were just a random airport hot guy that I was never going to see again. Here, you're the person I'm trying to eliminate from the game. Don't you see how spending *even more* time together than we already have could be detrimental for both of us?"

"All I got from that explanation, Dani, is that you think I'm hot," he says, a cheeky grin smothering his features.

"Menace," I say, even as I fight back a laugh because…yeah. I *did* just call him hot, albeit unintentionally. But also, objectively speaking, it's the truth, and I have absolutely zero doubt he knows how attractive he is. If he's trying to embarrass me by pointing out what I said, I won't give him the satisfaction. "Go find Ivy. I'm sure she'll hang out with you. Seemed that way this morning, at least," I blurt, the words escaping my mouth as if they grew legs and let themselves out the front door without so much as asking permission. *Good grief, why did I say that?* I'd wince if I wasn't actively schooling my face into an emotionless mask in front of Joss.

"Oh, Dani," he tuts. "Jealousy is a good look on you."

I roll my eyes. "The expression is jealousy *isn't* a good look on you."

"I know what I said."

"Not jealous," I say, fighting the flush of heat clawing up my neck. "Just offering solutions since you seem so desperate for companionship."

"Whatever you say, sunshine," he says.

"Oh, don't tell me you have a nickname for me now."

"After how pleasant these run-ins with you have been today?" he asks, sarcasm dripping from his tone like languid honey. "I'd say you've earned it."

"Call me whatever you want. It won't make a difference when Lana and I take you and Ryder out of this competition sooner or later."

"Yeah, we'll see about that, sunshine," he says, his eyes dancing at the challenge. "You want to be competitors? Have it your way then," he says, stalking back toward the gym. "Fair warning, though. You better be ready for that first competition tomorrow—because I'll be gunning for you now."

fourteen

DAY three on the compound is here, and a nervous energy has suspended itself in the air, tingeing every breath with flustered anticipation. It's a dangerous concoction of the excitement you feel on Christmas morning and the anxiety you feel before a root canal appointment. Exhilaration and suspense, eagerness and a healthy dose of dread.

We know the first competition is taking place today—we just don't know exactly when today. Lana and I are lying on our beds, our legs strewn up vertically against the wall for no reason whatsoever, doing our best to pass the time.

"Do you think Graham would still love me if I was a worm?"

I sigh. "Yes, Lana."

"Okay," she says, pausing. "What if I didn't have eyebrows?"

And that's how it's been for the last hour or so, both of us slowly losing our minds as the minutes crawl away with the urgency of a long-suffering DMV employee.

Suddenly, sirens begin blaring from speakers I didn't know existed until this very moment. My stomach drops to the floor, my heart pounding in my ears, and I accidentally kick Lana in the shin in an effort to scurry to my feet. My mind is racing, wondering if World War III has broken out and a nuclear bomb is headed our way. The feeling that we're living in some alternate dystopian reality has increased tenfold. I cross the distance to the door in record time, throwing the cabin door open only to hear the sirens screaming even louder outside. I find the teams in the neighboring cabins gaping around with the same look, a cocktail of shock and confusion.

A team of producers approaches from the crew cabins. "That's your signal, everyone!" one of them says. "You've got thirty minutes to get ready and head to the vans on the north side of the compound."

Well, that was horrifying, I think to myself, but I'm thankful there isn't a bomb or a tornado currently en route. I shouldn't be surprised, I suppose. *American Gauntlet* is known for upping its dramatics each season. I can picture the production meetings prior to shooting this year. "Why simply notify them that it's time to compete," a producer might have mused, "when we can scare them half to death first?"

"We need to do our signature hairstyles," Lana says as we frantically throw on our uniforms.

"It's only appropriate," I reply, jumping on one foot as I shove a sock on. "Sit."

Lana sits on the ground in front of my bed while I pull her long brown locks into a tight ponytail on the top of her head. After I've secured it, I take a few tiny clear rubber bands and begin placing them about an inch apart down her ponytail, loosening each little tuft of hair a bit as I go. When I finish, her hair looks like a horse's mane, thick and beautiful, with her natural highlights streaking down the length of it.

When I'm finished with Lana's hair, I open the wardrobe door and place myself in front of its mirror. I part my hair down the middle and begin French braiding the very top of one side. After I've reached the crown of my head, I gather all of my hair and put it into a neat little bun. I repeat the same process on the other side until I have two perfectly symmetrical space buns— my signature. I grin at my reflection. Having pulled my hair into this exact style countless times before, it's nice to feel a drop of familiarity in an ocean of novelty here at *American Gauntlet*.

"We look dang good," Lana smiles, as we head out and speed walk to the Commons for a pre-competition pit stop.

Most of the other teams are already at the Commons, scarfing down some last minute fuel before the games begin. I head straight to the coffee maker to do just that.

"I like your hair," Naji comments as I squeeze past him.

"Hey, thanks," I smile.

As the coffee begins streaming into my cup, Ryder heaves me a look from where he's eating a peanut butter and jelly sandwich across from me in the kitchen. "Are you seriously making coffee right now?" he asks, an eyebrow raised. "It's the middle of the afternoon."

"It's like a natural pre-workout," I say, chuckling a little at his expression. "The caffeine gives me an extra kick."

I've apparently caught the attention of Joss, who flings a smirk my way as he brushes past me. "You're gonna need it, sunshine," he says under his breath.

I ignore him, even as goosebumps rise on my neck in the place where I could feel his breath against my neck. I guess we're past the point of being on friendly terms, but it's better this way, I remind myself. It's exactly what I asked for, and this animosity from him is only going to make it easier to eliminate him.

The sooner, the better.

With my to-go coffee in hand, I load up in the van with the rest of the teams. Sergey drives, while Kelly rides in the passenger seat, a couple other vans full of crew members following in separate vehicles behind us. We speed down a dirt road that leads us out of the camp, a cloud of dust flying in the air around us, but, of course, we have no idea where we're going or how long it'll take, something I've now come to expect. My mind has run amuck with the possibilities of the first competition. *Will it involve water? Has my body fully recovered from The Trial? Is it going to be timed or objective-oriented?* The only thing I know for sure is that it will have a strength focus.

"Okay, everyone," Kelly says. "I know you're all excited, but I just wanted to go over a couple things real quick. Remember what we discussed last night—this will be a physical competition, but you are not to intentionally hurt anyone. And no playing dirty," she adds.

Everyone collectively laughs, half at what Kelly has said and half at her overall adorable demeanor. She has fully taken on the mom role, and she is thriving in it. As Kelly finishes up her spiel, we arrive at the second location, not more than ten or fifteen minutes from the compound.

Unsurprisingly, Dax is there waiting for us, but it's what is behind Dax that catches my attention.

I gawk as I take in the giant pit of mud, about the size of a backyard swimming pool, with slanted muddy walls on all sides. Outside the pit are six contraptions, evenly spaced around the pit perimeter. The contraptions are unlike anything I've ever seen before, each one appearing to have a platform, about six feet long by four feet wide, that is rigged via a cable to a giant barrel suspended overhead. And my first question of many is: what is in those barrels? There's also a small trash can-sized bin next to each platform.

At the directive of the production crew, each team lines up in front of Dax, awaiting his instructions. Prompted by production, he begins.

"Welcome, contestants, to your first competition in phase one of *American Gauntlet:* the Strength Phase. Physical *and* mental strength are essential if you think you've got a chance at running the Gauntlet at the end of the season, so I hope you're ready to show what you've got.

"Behind me, you will find six platforms, one for each of your teams. Your team's platform is the one with your corresponding uniform color." I quickly spot the platform with streaks of purple on its sides to match my and Lana's uniforms. Next to ours is Joss sand Ryder's platform, painted an icy blue that exactly matches the color of Joss's eyes, now that I think of it. I shed the thought, annoyed that I lost focus for even a second.

"In the bins next to each platform," Dax continues, "are dozens of one-pound weights. Each team will designate one team member as offense and one as defense. Those playing offense will grab one weight at a time out of your bin and traverse through the pit to place that weight on another team's platform. As weights get placed on the platform, making it heavier with each added weight, the tension on the cable connected to the barrel above it will increase. If too much weight is added to your team's platform, the cable will cause the barrel to topple over, spilling gallons upon gallons of water into the pit…making it even muddier than before. Once your barrel spills, you're out.

"The teammate playing defense will defend your platform against the other teams by whatever means necessary. If you strip the weight from an opposing team member, you can deposit it in your bin for your offensive teammate to use against the other teams. The last team standing will win first place and will have both immunity and power this week. The second place team will have immunity this week. And the rest of you…well, you won't be so lucky." Dax pauses for dramatic effect. "Now's the time to decide who will play offense and who will play defense. Take a few minutes to discuss it with your partner."

Lana and I put our heads together.

"You're way faster than me," I say. "You should be offense."

"That's exactly what I was thinking," she says, nodding her head, all business. Then she smiles, a wicked gleam in her eye. "You heard him, Dani. Defend our platform by whatever means necessary."

"Oh, I plan on it."

After the producers make sure no one has any questions and remind us once again that although this will be a physical competition, we should *not* intentionally hurt the other contestants by way of (including but not limited to) biting, scratching, hair pulling, choking, or eye gouging, the defensive players take our spot in the pit, each of us a little ways in front of our own platforms.

I peer down at the mud beneath my running shoes. Quickly, I plant a foot in the ground and pivot, trying to test how much traction I'll be working with. It sticks slightly, but it doesn't slide, doesn't force me to lose my footing. There's a faint musty smell emanating from the earthy pit, and I take a few heaving breaths through my nose, trying to acclimate my nostrils to the distinct odor.

"On my whistle!" Dax yells from where he stands safely outside of the muddy abyss. I look at the offensive players standing next to their platforms, quickly shooting past Joss and landing on Lana. I give her a look that says, *You've got this.* She nods in return. *Go get 'em, sis,* I urge her wordlessly.

As Dax allows the tension to build, I feel my heart beating through my chest, my pulse pounding as the blood rushes through my veins. The caffeine from my coffee has given me an extra boost, but the adrenaline coursing through my body has me soaring.

Finally, a whistle.

And then all mayhem breaks loose.

fifteen

CHAOS is unleashed as Dax's shrill whistle pierces my ears. The noise is downright offensive, and I half-wonder how the crew managed to secure the most disrespectful whistle on the planet for our very own Dax Philipps.

The offensive players—Lana, Naji, Joss, Ivy, Benji, and Junior—dive into their bins and pull out a weight, quickly making a mad dash for the pit. The majority of the players make it to the middle of the pit in a quick wave, but as they come to stand in its center, indecision seems to loom for a split second. It's as if no one wants to make the first move in fear of being targeted by the other teams.

Benji is the last to make it to the middle of the pit, and he clearly doesn't take notice of the political bulwark unfolding before everyone. He doesn't hesitate, immediately aiming for Naji and AJ's platform, and suddenly everyone simultaneously decides that Tris and Benji need to be the first to go. All of the remaining offensive players make quick work toward Benji's platform; Tris doesn't stand a chance at defending against all five of them. In the meantime, AJ has stripped the weight from Benji, so he's forced to return to his bin to get a new one.

It only takes the rest of the offensive players a handful of trips before we hear an ominous *creaaak* and gallons of water from Tris and Benji's barrel are unloaded into the pit. The water gushes over my feet, soaking my shoes clean down to my socks. I take a step, testing the new consistency of the mud. My shoe sticks in the moist, cushy marshmallow of mud beneath my feet for a half-second longer than before, but it's still maneuverable.

With the easiest targets out of the way, Lana kicks into high gear, sprinting to grab a weight before beelining it back toward me.

"Who should I target next?" she asks, her tone clipped with intensity.

Sarge appears momentarily distracted by Naji, who decided to make his move on him and Junior, so the door to target them is open. "Sarge and Junior. Then just think on the fly and go for whoever you can. Go, sis!" I yell, nudging her along. "You've got this."

She sprints away, and that's when I realize Ivy snuck past me and is currently making her way up the incline behind me toward our platform. *Not today,* I think.

I dash toward her and grab her ankle, yanking it back down and causing her to face plant into the muddy incline. Knowing I only have a couple seconds of distraction thanks to that quick maneuver, I tear the weight from her hands and don't take a second glance back as I place it in the bin for Lana to use later, even as I hear a shriek of frustration from Ivy.

It looks like Naji, Lana, and Joss teamed up to target Sarge and Junior, so before long, another tidal wave washes into the pit, transforming the mud into a thick mire beneath our feet. It's as if the mud is magnetic, pulling my feet, my ankles, down with every step. My shoes, now filled with wet sludge, have become like cinder blocks in the heavy mud, so I ditch them, along with my socks, and I'm immediately able to move more efficiently.

With fewer teams left, it's almost impossible to completely defend our platform. It's every team for themselves now, and as soon as I turn my back to defend another attack from Ivy, Joss has placed a weight on my platform. He tosses an overconfident smirk over his shoulder at me, as if to say, *You asked for this.* A moment of unexplainable weakness allows the slightest inkling of hurt to flash through my mind, before I discard it in the corners of my brain. Hurt feelings aren't going to help me win this game. So instead, I swap them for something that will: anger. I let it seep into my bones, fueling me to my core. The anger quickly warps into determination, to resolution and resolve. I use it to heighten my senses, to strip a weight from Naji, to defend yet another attack from Ivy.

In a moment of inaction, I search for Lana, who is, quite frankly, killing it. She's probably the fastest offensive player left, and she has scored on every team innumerable times. I watch as she places a weight on Naji and AJ's platform. Turns out, that weight is the one to break the dam, and another wave of water washes into the pit. Everyone is covered in mud from head to toe, but lucky for me, I've been here before. Running that obstacle course in the mud was a *fantastic* idea, now that I think of it.

You're prepared for this, I repeat to myself over and over again. *You're ready for every situation.*

The game continues at a breakneck pace, each team scoring on one another with abandon, players tripping and tackling and heaving weights from the others. I take stock of my and Lana's current situation, and it appears our platform is pretty evenly weighted with Joss and Ryder's and Blaire and Ivy's. Any weight could be the one to topple the barrel and our chances of winning. I'm aiming for second place, which would give us immunity but not power. Power means decisions. And decisions mean blood on your hands. I'm not trying to make any waves among the teams just yet.

Strategy. This competition is about strategy. And as much as I'd love to barrel through everyone, guns blazing, I just don't believe that's the plan that will keep us here the longest.

I turn to see Ivy headed up toward our platform again, and I've got to hand it to her: she's nothing if not relentless in her pursuit to bring me and Lana down. In fact, I'm almost positive she's only targeted our team this entire game. I run up behind her, but she sees me coming this time, and she throws her elbow back directly into my eye. In a surge of pain, I plunge backward and splat into the mud, my eye already pulsing in pain. She'll say the move was unintentional, but I'll remember the way her eyes met mine in the split second before she shoved her elbow directly into my eye socket.

She places the weight on our platform, and the cable's tension tightens precariously, the contraption emitting a noise that sounds scarily close to a groan. I know it can't handle many more weights. *Hang in there, buddy,* I think to myself, clearly not above silently encouraging inanimate objects. I don't have time to nurse my throbbing eye, as I look up to find Joss dashing my way. The thick, thick mud oozing beneath him has slowed him down, and I know this is my opportunity.

Moving as rapidly and nimbly as I can manage, I bolt toward him. He sees me coming, and his face looks both fierce and intrigued, mud streaked across his brow and down his cheeks. His eyes are darting quickly back and forth between me and my platform behind me, and it's clear he's trying to determine what my move will be, but I've been here before; I've practiced this exact maneuver.

I feint to one side before I slam my body into him, quickly hooking one arm beneath his armpit, throwing the other one over his shoulder, and hitching my inside leg behind his. He grabs onto me, and as we tumble to the ground, I hear the distinct sound of fabric shredding.

In our tumble, it takes me a second to realize what happened, but I'm suddenly very aware that my body has landed on top of his, both of us slick with sweat and mud, and my head is lying on his very bare chest. I sit up, and to my horror, I find I'm fully straddling him. I quickly realize the shredding sound I heard was his shirt as it ripped right down the center, now giving me a glimpse of abs that look like they've been chiseled from stone and that lead to the most insane Adonis Belt I have ever seen. I can't help but follow the V-shaped muscles, tracking them as they lead down to—

And that's when I realize what I'm doing. *Holy moly.* I shoot my eyes up to see the cockiest grin I've ever seen greased across Joss's face.

"Enjoying the view, sunshine?"

I feel the heat rush to my neck, and I start scrambling to try to get off of him, but he grabs me and rolls his body over mine, caging me into the muddied ground beneath him.

"Now where'd you learn that little trick?" he asks, and I assume he's referring to the takedown move I flawlessly executed to get him to the ground, which gives me a glorious kick of confidence.

I loop a leg around him and throw my body weight up and over, rolling him to where he's back underneath me.

"Wouldn't you like to know," I say, a self-satisfied grin at my lips, before I press a hand to his chest and push up to my feet.

As I do, though, I see Ivy and Lana scrambling up the muddy incline toward the platforms, Lana toward Joss's and Ivy toward ours. Lana has slipped past Ryder, who is now struggling with the mud, and as I watch Lana sprinting toward the platform in front of her, I'm positive she's got the speed to beat Ivy. I can't help the huge smile that forms on my face, ecstatic that Lana and I will not only have safety this week, but that Ivy won't have the satisfaction of taking it away from us. Lana takes her final steps toward the platform, but the mud beneath her suddenly gives. My stomach plummets as Lana slips, falling to the muddy ground beneath her, giving Ivy the opening to reach our platform first. I start sprinting toward Ivy, even though I know there's no possible way I'll reach her in time. The scene unfolds before me in agonizing slow motion. Ivy reaching the platform. The slow creaking of the barrel. The impossibly powerful cascade of water upon us. I wouldn't be surprised if post-production actually edits this scene in slow motion for dramatic effect.

I'm brought back to the present when I see Joss and Ryder's barrel overturn no less than three seconds later, Lana having placed the final weight there. The only barrel still upright is Ivy and Blaire's.

As the water rushes over my feet, turning the mud pit into a swamp, only one thought crosses my mind: we lost. Actually, not only did we lose—we got *third*, which doesn't guarantee our immunity this week.

And it was all because I let myself get distracted. Had I eliminated Joss as a threat and immediately turned my attention back to our platform, I could've stopped Ivy. I could've locked in our safety this week. Instead, I was too busy making a fool of myself with Joss, trying to prove that I wasn't someone he should mess with in this game.

No part of me blames Lana, who practically killed herself sprinting those weights to the platforms, and I don't even blame Joss for his part in our little roll in the mud. The only person to blame is myself. Before I can stop it, my chest feels tight and my breathing becomes labored, like every breath takes too much effort. I start to panic, to hyperventilate, my lungs suddenly working in triple time.

It's crushing me, I think. *The pressure is crushing me.*

"Hey," Lana says, patting me on the back. I draw my gaze up from where it's been focused on the mud beneath me. Lana's touch coaxes me back to reality, and I slow my breathing, doing my best to take deep, oxygen-filled breaths. "We did great. Third place is great, Dani."

Her words ring hollow in my ears. "I'm sorry," I mutter.

"Dani, you don't have to be sorry; it's not your fault," she assures me. "We got beat. That's it. It happens"

"You did great," I say. My voice is still deflated but it's doing its best to sound upbeat. "Better than great. You were amazing, practically flying out there."

She smiles and opens her mouth to say something, but Dax blows his whistle and gathers all of the teams back outside of the pit before she can finish.

"Well, I'd say that was exciting," Dax says, a severe smile on his face. Everything about him is intense, even his grins. "Joss and Ryder, congratulations. You came in second and are safe from elimination this week. Ivy and Blaire, well done. I'd say you definitely redeemed your first performance."

I want to wipe the self-satisfied looks right off their faces.

"So, why are you here, ladies?" Dax asks. He usually gives the winners a chance to talk about their motivation for coming on the show, a little something extra for the viewers. "Why'd you decide to try your hand at *American Gauntlet?*"

"We're winners," Blaire blurts out. "We came to win. This is just another trophy on our shelf."

Dax cocks an eyebrow. "Confidence is good. Cockiness is… dangerous."

Blaire opens her mouth to speak again, but Ivy nudges her sister's arm, silencing her with a single touch.

"I think what Blaire meant is that we're *competitors.* We love to compete," Ivy responds almost automatically, as if she's already memorized her response. She sounds like she's answering a question in a beauty pageant and she knows she has center stage. "We're gymnasts, so competition is a part of us. We're always looking for new challenges."

Dax purses his lips together before replying, unceremoniously, "Congratulations on your win. You are safe from elimination *and* you'll have the power this week. I'll get there in a second.

"For the rest of you, I hope you're not tired yet," he continues, a sinister expression quickly surfacing. He pauses, letting the anticipation linger. "Because part two of the Strength Phase is happening *now*…and it'll determine your fate in this game."

sixteen

OF COURSE, I think. Of course the next part of the Strength phase is happening now, after we've completely depleted all of our energy on the first part of it.

Dax's announcement receives mixed reactions. Sarge and Junior are like statues, stoic and unmoving, practically standing at attention in front of our host. Lana lets out a quiet whimper that she quickly kills when I flash her a death glare. Tris and Benji simply look exhausted. And beside me, Naji tightens his bun, sighs, and lets out a long, exaggerated expletive that will need to be bleeped out in post production.

"Sarge and Junior, Dani and Lana, Benji and Tris, and AJ and Naji," Dax bellows, drawing our attention back. "You all are *not* safe from elimination and will be competing in the next part of the competition. Right now."

I glance over at the Twisted Twins and find a set of matching grins on their faces, streaks of their bright red hair shining through the mud that's caked everyone from head to toe.

"To begin, each of your teams will lift your platforms using the handles on each side," Dax instructs. I look over and notice the crew has disconnected the cable from each platform, freeing it from the overturned barrels above. "You'll then carry it a hundred yards away to that finish line," he says, pointing across the gravelly field next to us. We all turn that direction to where the producers have placed white flags a football field away to indicate the finish line. "Easy enough, right? Oh, and you'll be keeping all of those weights on your platform. This is the Strength phase, after all.

"The last team to cross the finish line will be thrown into elimination this week. And the other three teams—you *might* be the ones joining them. Blaire and Ivy, as the winners from today, you will be able to choose which of the remaining teams goes into the elim. Got it?"

"You look absolutely knackered," a very Australian voice near my ear murmurs. I glance beside me to find a smug Joss leaning toward me, his breath tickling my ear. "And that platform looks *heavy*," he remarks, drawing the word out with a grin.

I paint my face in ten shades of nonchalance. "Your concern is touching," I bite. "But it's going to take a little more than that to get under my skin, menace."

"We'll see about that, sunshine," he winks.

Ignoring him, I turn to Lana to quietly strategize. "Okay, we just need to focus on not being last. I think Sarge and Junior and Naji and AJ are bigger targets than us, so as long as we're not last, I don't think the twins will throw us into the elimination."

"Okay," she says, nodding intently. "How heavy do you think the platform is?" Her voice is stained with apprehension.

"Hard to tell," I sigh, eyeing the platforms that look to be made of solid iron. "They look pretty heavy…plus they've got all that extra weight on top. It won't be fun, but we'll make it."

Lana nods then shoots her gaze down, seemingly noticing something on the ground. "Sis, what about your shoes?"

I drop my eyes to my feet, instantly realizing what she's staring at: my bare feet. I stare into the muddy abyss, and my heart drops. I don't catch sight of my shoes anywhere. They're probably lost forever to the opaque bog.

"I guess I'm going barefoot," I wince. My eyes drift across the grassy field, its terrain similar to what we slogged through during The Trial. It's all sandy dirt and tiny rocks and dry grass, and I know in my soul that the trek across this gravel-ridden field is going to hurt, but there's nothing I can do about it. I don't have time to go digging around for my shoes as Dax instructs each team to stand next to their fully-weighted platform. He doesn't want to give us any extra time to rest before we're forced to become pack mules for this second part of the competition. I take another glance at Dax, noting the lifted corners of his smile, the sparkle in his eye. I have no doubt he's enjoying every bit of pain he inflicts on us. The viewers eat it up.

"On my whistle…" Dax says. Another shrill bleat pierces the air, and we're off to the races, my ears ringing and my heart thudding out of my chest.

Lana and I lift the handles of the metal platform simultaneously, and the weight catches me off guard. It's *heavy*, much heavier than I anticipated. And if it's heavy for me, I know it's really pushing it for Lana. She grunts with effort as she struggles to hold onto her side of the platform. To my dismay, we only make it a few yards before she has to set it down.

"Sorry, I just need to readjust my grip," she says, grimacing.

Precious seconds tick away, and I watch as Sarge and Junior steadily move past us in perfect unison, like their life depends on their flawlessly timed and executed movements. They're not even breathing heavily. I don't have time to take a look at the other teams; I just know that Lana and I need to get moving.

Quickly.

We lift again, and as we begin moving further down the field, pain ambushes my brain, my nerves rioting at the tiny rocks pressing into my bare skin. It feels like I'm trudging through a field of Legos, not to mention the extra weight from the platform that amplifies the pressure on my feet. They'll be absolutely shredded by the end of this, and for once, I wish my feet were just as calloused as my hands.

Suddenly, the right side of our platform hits the ground, and I realize Lana has dropped her side again, causing a few weights to slip off.

"Sorry, Dani. I'm really trying, but I—it's just so heavy." Lana scrambles to pick up the weights that have toppled from their positions atop the heavy platform.

"It's okay. We've got this," I say, making sure my tone comes off as encouraging and not at all irritated, although I feel it stirring deep within me. "We just can't be last. That's it."

We keep at it, and every step is a struggle, a grind. We're only moving five or so yards at a time before Lana has to drop it again, but I bury the frustration I feel at her because I single handedly could have avoided this if I had just done my job earlier.

Sarge and Junior smoothly reach the finish line within a few minutes. Naji and AJ aren't far behind them, and they both collapse into a heap once they're safely on the other side. I haven't looked back at Tris and Benji yet; I'm just relieved they're behind us. I do my best to focus on anything besides my bare feet and the jagged rubble that feels like it'll be permanently embedded in my skin.

With each step, I'm practically dragging Lana along, physically and mentally. She looks both defeated and disappointed in herself by the time we lug our platform across the finish line. The weight plummets to the ground, and Lana immediately begins massaging her aching arms, wincing as she eyes the fresh blisters on her hands. The searing pain I'd felt suddenly subsides, replaced instead by pure relief. *We're not last. That's all that matters right now.*

I turn around, expecting to see Benji and Tris a few yards behind us, but instead I find them barely halfway across the field. It looks like they can't even pick up their platform any longer, and even though they're my competition and I should be happy to see them struggling, my heart still sinks, a weighty stone drifting to the pit of my stomach. The duo is doing their best to drag the stubborn platform along the ground, but it doesn't budge. It's impossible to watch, like watching one of those nature documentaries where a whale gets beached and can't get free, no matter how hard it tries. Despite it all, Benji and Tris haven't stopped, even though they know they're last; they know they're headed to elimination, but they want to see it through to the end, and I respect that.

I look around and find the other teams doing their best to avoid watching the climbers struggle through the task. And I don't necessarily blame them because it's…hard to watch. They are pulling with every bit of strength they have, but their lean bodies that are perfect for climbing up rock faces and repelling down cliffs are not made for this type of challenge.

Even though my feet are raw and every step feels like walking across burning coals, I trek the fifty yards to Tris and Benji. They look up at me with surprise in their eyes, but I say nothing as I stand next to Tris and lift. Our side of the platform rises, but we quickly realize Benji can't hold up his side by himself. But before I can think through how to get this wretched platform to the finish line, Joss jogs over from where he was following along with the competition on the edge of the field and helps Benji lift. I try not to stare as Joss's arm muscles bulge from the strain, his veins pulsing as they snake up his forearms.

We make it a few yards before Sarge and Junior join us and each lift from the front and the back of the platform, making the rest of the journey feel like a light stroll on the beach compared to what it was originally. When we reach the finish line and finally set the platform down together, Tris turns to me, an earnest look in her eyes.

"Thank you," she says, sweat dripping from her closely-shorn black hair. "Seriously, thank you. We wouldn't have made it otherwise. Before we came, Benji and I swore we'd finish every competition, even if we were last. You helped us keep that promise." She grabs my shoulder and squeezes. "*Geez,* I need some of these," she adds, clutching my delt again for good measure.

"Happy to help," I laugh.

Tris walks away to check on Benji, and I turn around to find Joss staring at me, an unreadable look on his face.

I raise an eyebrow. "Enjoying the view?" I ask, using the same line he used on me earlier.

He cracks a smile. "Wouldn't you like to know."

The slightest hint of something warm and unfamiliar begins blooming in my chest, but I don't have time to unpack it as the producers summon us back to the pit where we started the first stage of the competition. I wince, already dreading the walk across the burning Lego minefield before me. The adrenaline from the competition has worn off, and the pain is in full effect, white hot fire licking at the bottoms of my feet. I pick my foot up to check the damage, and I'm greeted by nothing but dried mud and pink wounds. I immediately regret sneaking a peek at them. The sight of my muddy, raw feet makes me want to gag.

Still, the hundred yards back aren't going to walk themselves, so I slowly start heading toward the pit, lagging well behind the rest of the group. With no one watching except, of course, a camera or two, I allow myself to hobble, exposing my weakness for a brief moment. After a few steps in agony, I consider crawling because the idea of tearing up my knees sounds like a better alternative to ripping my feet to shreds even more. Suddenly, panic begins to set in. *Are these wounds going to be healed by the next competition? Is this going to set me back during—*

A voice cuts through my thoughts.

"Oi, you alright there, sunshine?"

I shoot my eyes up, realizing that Joss has turned around and taken notice of my current (disastrous) state. He's standing a few yards ahead of me, his brows creased together in concern.

"I'm fine," I say, but it admittedly comes off as more of a wince. Joss looks down, his eyes widening.

"Are you *barefoot?"*

In a split second, he's kneeling in front of me, inspecting my mud-caked and bloody feet that look absolutely repulsive. I feel the heat rush to the back of my neck, embarrassed by the state of the foot in his hand. And I'm not exactly sure what happens next, but one second Joss is kneeling in front of me and the next second, he's hoisting me over his shoulder, carrying me like a sack of potatoes.

"Joss!" I scream in my loudest whisper, not wanting the other teams ahead of us to take notice. "Put me *down.* I can walk."

"Nah, that's not happening."

His arm is secured steadily around the backs of my thighs,

and from where I'm positioned over his shoulder, I see his back muscles brace with every step. They're on full display before me since he's currently shirtless, his shirt having been ripped—by me—in the pit. *Oh no,* I think. *Production is going to edit this episode to make it look like I got him half-naked on purpose. I just know they are. America eats that stuff up.* Plus, semi-fake episode edits aside, I'm concerned about what this might look like to our fellow competitors.

"*Joss,*" I hiss, quieter this time, although I have no doubt we've already captured the attention of the other teams. I can't confirm that assumption, though, since I'm momentarily incapacitated while strapped to Joss's body like a giant sloth. "Everyone's going to think we're, like, working together or something. I'm your *competition,* you menace."

"To be honest with you sunshine, I don't really care what they think. You can't walk on these rocks without shoes, so I'm helping you out," he says, his tone matter-of-fact. "Why would you go out of your way to help Tris and Benji like you did, even though *they're* your competition?"

"Because it was the right thing to do," I snipe back.

"Exactly, Dani."

I snap my mouth shut, understanding washing over me. Joss really just used my own logic against me, and I both respect and resent him for it.

"Don't worry, sunshine—this doesn't change anything. I'll go back to gunning for you in the next competition, not to worry," he says, his usual light-hearted demeanor having made its full return. And as much as I'm worried about what it might look like to the other teams, deep down, I'm extremely grateful not to have to walk across this field again.

All of a sudden, he stops, and I feel him craning his head back toward me, a wave of coconut-scented shampoo enveloping me.

"Do you really want me to put you down?" he asks, entirely serious.

A quick pause. "No," I finally relent so quietly I'm not sure Joss can even hear it. But as soon as the word leaves my mouth, he begins walking again, muttering something about "stubborn" to himself.

We make it to where the teams, crew, and Dax are awaiting us, and as Joss brings me down from my perch over his shoulder, I find Ryder and Lana peering at us with the same curious look on their faces. Their expressions linger somewhere between confusion and intrigue.

"Dang, Joss, showing off for the cameras already," Naji teases.

"You're just mad he beat you to it," AJ retorts, nudging him in the shoulder.

Ivy, who showed the barest hint of a petulant frown only moments before, suddenly plasters an exaggerated look of concern on her face. "Are you okay, Dani? It must be pretty bad if you couldn't even walk back on your own." Something about her tone instantly irritates me, grating against my patience like nails on a chalkboard.

"I'm fine," I reply, my tone neutral thanks to a great deal of internal effort on my part. "I ditched my shoes in the pit and couldn't find them before the second stage of the competition. Joss helped me out."

As if on cue, Kelly emerges from the pit looking like a swamp creature, her previously white shirt and khaki shorts stained a dingy brown hue. She's caked in mud, and her outfit will need to be dry cleaned if it's not ruined entirely.

And in her hands, I see, are both of my shoes.

"I couldn't find the socks, but at least I got the shoes!" she chirps, her voice as upbeat as ever.

"Oh my gosh, you're my hero," I gush, slipping the shoes back on my feet. The sloshy mud on the inside of my running shoes actually feels kind of nice, naturally cooling off my stinging wounds. It's definitely not sanitary, but at the moment, I truly couldn't care less.

Shoe drama aside, the producers arrange all the teams in our typical semicircle around Dax, and we jump right back into the *real* drama of the day.

"To everyone who competed in stage two, nice job today. I liked what I saw out there," he says, and we all smile a little to ourselves, satisfied to have Dax Philipps's rare seal of approval. "Tris and Benji—you came in last place, which means you will be up for elimination. You might be at risk of going home, but you didn't quit, even when you knew you were last. That's the kind of stuff I like to see here at *American Gauntlet*."

Tris looks at me from where she and Benji are standing on the other side of the semicircle, giving me a small nod of respect.

"Blaire and Ivy, as I mentioned earlier, you've got the power this week. Which team would you like to send into elimination with Tris and Benji?"

The Twisted Twins put their heads together, taking a few moments to strategize, although I imagine they've already thought through their pick. My stomach drops at the thought of being sent into elimination this early, but I hold onto the hope they'll select another team like Sarge and Junior, who are quickly solidifying themselves as huge threats in this competition. It might seem like Tris and Benji wouldn't be able to beat them, but again, it all depends on what the elimination challenge is.

"What'll it be, ladies?" Dax prompts.

They turn to him, matching grins on their faces. They look

simultaneously beautiful and cruel.

"This was *such* a hard decision, but we're just going to go with our gut," Ivy says. "The team we'd like to send into elimination is—"

Ivy doesn't finish her sentence, as Blaire cuts her off at the last second, apparently wanting to deal the blow herself. I'd been confident we were safe, but there's something about the way Ivy's gaze flicks my direction for a split that tips me off.

Before her twin says the words, I already know they're coming.

"Dani and Lana."

seventeen

IT'S TAKEN five nights at the *American Gauntlet* camp for me to finally wake up and not spiral into a panic attack, immediately questioning where I am.

I sit up in bed, Lana still snoring loudly beside me, and I immediately throw off the covers to inspect my feet. *Bless.* The blisters and lesions have dried out and are on their way to being fully healed. Fortunately, they're also free of infection thanks to the care I received from Steph, the lead medic this season, who sent me on my way with delicately swathed feet in gauze and antibiotics, plus a tongue lashing about the importance of wearing shoes in the wilderness.

I'm grateful to have had a few days since our first competition to heal up. When watching the fully-edited show, everything seems to happen so quickly, but in reality, they squeeze almost seven days into one or two hour-long episodes. It takes a lot of time to tear down and set up each of these complicated competitions, many of them taking place at different locations, so thankfully, the break in production gave me some much-needed recovery time.

The relief that hit me upon seeing my nearly healed feet is washed out like rain down a gutter as anticipation rapidly takes over. Tomorrow is the elimination. Tomorrow could be the day

Lana and I are sent packing.

As soon as the thought enters my head, I envision myself crumpling it up and tossing it into a garbage can in the recesses of my mind. I can't think that way. I'm going to win our elim, and Lana and I will live to fight another day in this competition.

After the Twisted Twins announced that Lana and I would be sent into elimination, Dax so generously threw another curveball at us. "You'll need to choose *one* team member to compete in the elimination," he had told us. "Oh, and you'll need to choose right now."

"We don't get to know what the elimination challenge is before we choose?" Benji had asked. I'm pretty sure it was the first thing he'd said to Dax this whole time.

"Now where's the fun in that?" Dax replied with a grin. "You've got thirty seconds to decide."

"You," Lana said, turning to me, a heated fervor in her eyes. "It has to be you."

"Wait, let's just think about this for a second," I replied. "If it's any sort of speed challenge, you kick my butt every time. You're like the fastest person here. You're also better at anything having to do with a ball. You inherited the good hand-eye coordination genes."

"I can't do it, Dani. It's too much pressure. It has to be—"

"Time's up!" Dax shouted, loving the fact that we were still clearly in the middle of the discussion like the sadist he is. "Dani, Lana—who will it be?"

"Dani!" Lana blurted my name out like it was on fire.

And so that was that.

The climbers chose Benji to compete, so I know the elimination tomorrow will be some sort of head-to-head challenge: me versus Benji. I've been praying the competition plays to my strength—literally and figuratively—and that I wouldn't get to the makeshift arena where all of the elims are held to see some sort of climbing challenge. That would be the nail in our *American Gauntlet* coffin. I wouldn't stand a chance against him.

I throw on my workout gear and running shoes, not feeling even a whisper of pain in my feet this morning, and head out for a jog. I let Lana sleep, knowing she could use the extra recovery time.

The past few days have passed in a bit of a blur. Time on the compound feels warped. As we await the next competition, the seconds seem to tick away at half speed, which leaves far too much time for me to overthink, well, *everything* here. The impending elimination. The next phase of the competition. The way that I interact with the other teams. All of it. Lana and I had seen the other teams in passing, especially around meal times at the Commons, but we'd spent a lot of time to ourselves, focusing on stretching and mobility workouts to recover from the first week of tough challenges and to stay limber and prepared for the competitions to come.

Naji, boredom getting the best of him, had resorted to pulling pranks on everyone around the camp. Other teams, producers, crew members…no one was safe. He had looped me into a prank he pulled on Ivy, having me distract her while he put a fake spider he'd brought with him under the piece of toast she was having for breakfast. When she picked the bread up, she screamed and nearly jumped across the table before realizing it was fake. Naji and I disintegrated into laughter, but Ivy was anything but amused. For a moment, she was livid, her fists clenching at her sides, redness rising up her neck like a thermometer, but realizing that everyone in the Commons was laughing at the harmless prank, she gritted out a burst of forced giggles, before embarking on a spiel about how she pulls pranks like that *all the time* and just *loves* them.

Yeah, I wasn't buying it. But my part in the prank didn't seem to help the disdain she seems to carry toward me at all times, the annoyance and contempt always simmering just below the surface. If we both stayed in this competition long enough, it was bound to boil over sooner or later.

Lana and Naji aside, the other person I'd seen a lot of— probably *too much* of—was Joss. We seemed to gravitate to the same places at the same time, and I wasn't sure if it was just a coincidence or if he was intentionally trying to get under my skin before the next competition. When I was in the Commons making coffee, he was there grabbing a snack. When I went for a run around the nearby lake, he was there swimming. I couldn't escape him. Even when I was trying to build up my mental and emotional fortress around him, though, we typically ended up laughing and joking around, a competitive edge added to all of our interactions. And here at the camp, minutes easily turned into hours when you had nothing else to do. Without any distractions—no phones, no internet, no Netflix—one day here feels like the equivalent of one full week in the normal world. By the end of the show, we'll have been here, like, six months in *American Gauntlet* time.

But just as soon as I started getting comfortable with Joss, I'd always remember how detrimental getting close with *any* competitor could be, and I shut things down. I shut him out. I'd quickly cut off conversations or feign an excuse and remove myself from the situation entirely. I closed myself off because it was better that way, even if watching Joss's smile fall from his face when I did felt lousy.

Now heavily focused on the elimination ahead, I start to jog, focusing on controlling my breathing and heart rate with deliberate breaths. I break away from the wooden sidewalk around the camp and head toward the nearby lake. Thanks to the varying elevation surrounding us, it's not directly visible from camp, but as I crest the top of the hill on the northwest side of the compound, I find it waiting for me, tucked away like a hidden gift, a present, just for me. The water is pristine. It's so clear I can see the smooth, dark stones that have made a home on its floor. It's definitely an upgrade from the sediment-filled Galveston water I'm used to.

As I trot toward the lake, the surface appears like a mirror, perfectly reflecting the picturesque terrain and panoramic, cloud-filled sky above, the sun peeking just above the horizon. I picture putting on ice skates and gliding across its surface, smooth as ice.

My mind is pulled away from the scenery around me when I hear footsteps in a steady jogging cadence behind me. Before I can turn around to see who it is, Joss is beside me, looking ahead and pretending not to see me. As I watch his arms pump with every step, my mind flashes to him throwing me over his shoulder with ease. To what it felt like for his arms to be wrapped around me.

Before I let myself wander too far down *that* line of thinking, I push the thought away with a subtle shake of my head. Then Joss looks down at me, mock surprise on his face.

"Oh, didn't see you there, sunshine," he says with a wink.

I stop, intent on running in the opposite direction around the lake. I need to focus on getting my mind right with the upcoming elimination that seems to be looming over me like a storm cloud, and I've already let my guard down too many times with Joss. Every conversation, every joke passed between us is another chink in my armor, and I already messed up once with him during the first competition; I can't let myself slip up again.

But being the menace he is, Joss stops with me.

"You know," I say, "I'm beginning to think you're following me."

"Maybe it's just a happy accident," he replies. "Or," he says, closing the distance between us in a single step, "maybe I am following you."

"Well, don't," I say, taking a step back.

He steps forward, closing it again. It's a challenge. A dare. "Why not?"

I don't step away, don't back down to his challenge. "You know why."

He looks out at the water beside us, his lips pressed in a thin line; it's an expression that looks entirely out of place on his face. I'm used to a smile, a cheeky grin, a smirk.

The way he looks sends a pang of sadness through me because the fact of the matter is I like Joss as a person. I liked him when I thought he was airport-hot-guy Kellan, easily taking my mind off of the anxious thoughts that consumed me, and I like him now. He's light and fun and energizing and even when he's egging me on, pressing buttons he knows he shouldn't, it only motivates me more.

But I can't let a new friendship jeopardize everything I've worked for. This prize money is literally *life-changing,* and Joss clearly doesn't get that.

"Joss," I say, drawing his attention back to me. His eyes are so intense as they meet mine, I feel like I'm under a microscope. "If we weren't here directly competing for three hundred thousand dollars, things would be different. I'd be open to getting to know you, to being friends. I'm not usually like *this*—this closed-off, stone-hearted version of myself." *Or maybe I am,* I think to myself. "But I can't risk messing this opportunity up. This competition, this prize money—it's everything for me…and for my family."

When he's not joking around, Joss is unreadable. Trying to understand the smallest softening of his eyes, the tiniest movement of his lips, the nearly soundless sigh that escapes him, is like trying to read a book in a language I've never seen before. Still, he says nothing, so I take that as my cue to leave.

Before I get even a couple steps, though, Joss grabs my arm gently, his calloused hands feeling surprisingly tender against my skin.

"Listen, I just wanted to wish you luck," he says, then adds, "Not that you'll need it." And his tone is back to what I'm used to, back to being light and easy. A much safer territory.

"Aw, don't tell me you're going soft on me," I tease. "I like you better when you're a menace."

"Don't get it twisted, sunshine," he says, the challenge back in his voice that I've grown used to already. "I want you to win the elimination against Benji just so I can take you out of this competition myself."

eighteen

THE treadmill rolls to a stop like a train having finally arrived at its station. I step off and sit back against a nearby weight bench, feeling the sweat dripping from my neck all the way down my spine but not caring enough to dab it with my shirt. Even though I only did a quick cardio session, not wanting to exhaust myself too much before the elim tonight, I'm dripping in sweat from the heat of the outdoor gym.

I welcome it. The sweat feels cleansing, renewing. The elimination is the difference between a life-altering amount of money for the Di Laurentis women, and I can't lose. I won't lose.

I close my eyes and lean my head back against the bench, focusing on letting the oxygen fill my lungs completely before I breathe it out with intent.

It might be the most relaxed I've felt since getting to the *American Gauntlet* camp, but a high-pitched, nasally voice pulls me from my trance. I open my eyes to find Ivy in front of me, and although she's smiling, the way she looks down her nose at me feels smug. Condescending.

"Hey girl! Oh my gosh, you look *exhausted*. I've got this cream that will work wonders on the bags under your eyes if you ever want to borrow it!" Her voice is chipper, but it doesn't do anything to mask the less-than-subtle insult.

It's a shame her opinion of me is the absolute last item on my list of things to worry about today.

"Yeah these bags do look pretty brutal, huh?" I respond, relishing the way she stiffens at my response. "I may need to take you up on that offer."

"Of course," she says, scrambling to recover. She's wearing red leggings with a matching sports bra that are so bright, they're nearly the exact shade of her hair, which is pulled into a voluminous, wavy ponytail on top of her head. She opens her mouth then decides against whatever she was going to say. "Anyway," she lands on, "just wanted to say I hope there's no hard feelings about putting you up for elimination."

"Yeah, no worries. It's a competition. You and Blaire have to do what's best for your game," I reply, and I mean every word. I don't want or expect an explanation as to why they chose us. It was a strategic move, even if it wasn't the one I would've pulled.

Ivy, however, seems intent on continuing this conversation, despite my dismissal of it.

"It was just *such* a tough decision on who to choose, but I'm so hoping you win so you and Lana can stay in the competition." The way she emphasizes her words irks me almost as much as the way she crinkles her nose like some sort of doe-eyed woodland creature when she's trying to seem sweet and harmless. I don't buy it. "Blaire and I would *hate* to be the only female team left."

I mentally pat myself on the back at the way I'm able to freeze my face just before my eyes unleash the biggest eyeroll of my life. "Yeah, I guess we'll just see what happens at the elim tonight."

"I guess so," she says with another nose crinkle, her smile

never quite reaching her eyes. They maintain that same purposeful disdain. "Anyway, I'm off for a walk. If I don't see you before we all head to the arena, best of luck!"

After Ivy leaves, I'm in a mood. I can see through her mind games like a freshly-cleaned window pane, but the fact that I practically gifted Ivy this power over me and Lana makes me sick. The notion that I allowed Lana and myself to be put in jeopardy is making the familiar mixture of disappointment and frustration bubble to the surface again. Feeling drained, I drop my elbows to my knees and start kneading the back of my neck the way my mom used to back before she ever picked up a bottle.

When mom lost her way after dad left, I started massaging my own neck, pretending. Pretending it was her hands instead of mine. Pretending everything wasn't a complete mess.

"Oi. You alright there, sunshine?"

I groan, even as I lift my head up to see a glacier blue pair of eyes staring back at me.

"I'm fine. Just…thinking."

"It doesn't look like you're thinking, it looks like you're *brooding*," Joss replies. "If it's about the elim tonight, the brooding stops here. You're ready for it, whatever it is."

"What if it's a climbing challenge?" I ask, flicking my gaze up toward him. "Or one that involves puzzles or math problems like they have sometimes? That immediately evens the playing field between Benji and me."

"Something tells me you'll find a way to win regardless of what it is."

"Mhmm," I reply half-heartedly. I don't have the energy to go head-to-head with him right now.

"You need to cheer up, sunshine," he says, reaching down and lifting my chin up. I don't reply; I just stare back at him, not wanting to "cheer up" in the slightest. He watches my expression before he suddenly looks at me with all the seriousness in the world. "Dani," he breathes.

Something in my stomach plummets to the floor at the low breathiness of his voice. "Um," I say, trying to clear my throat. "Yes?" I can't stop thinking about the way his finger feels where he's so gently placed beneath my chin. Tender. Warm.

His eyes are locked on mine, and I couldn't rip them away if I tried. He tilts my chin up to him and pulls his face close to mine. My breath hitches, even as I beg it not to. I have no idea what Joss is doing, but I can't stop it. I don't *want* to stop it. He lowers his mouth close to my ear and whispers, "Did you know that the little blob of toothpaste you put on the end of your toothbrush has a name? It's called a nurdle."

It takes a full two seconds for my brain to comprehend what he said before I pull back from him and punch him hard in the bicep. I do my best to calm my breathing and act like what he did had absolutely no effect on me, but in the meantime, he bursts out laughing, and it's the type that's impossible to witness without laughing yourself. So soon enough—and against my better judgment—we're both melting into laughter on the gym floor.

"Is that true?" I ask, finally catching my breath. "Is it really called a nurdle?"

"I'm many things, but I'm not a liar, sunshine," he says, still grinning at himself in the most self-satisfied way. I have no doubt he knows *exactly* what he was doing.

"Not a liar," I reply, "but a menace to society."

Joss lets out another laugh. "A hot menace, if I'm quoting you right," he says with a wink.

"Don't push it."

WHEN I walk back into our cabin, I still can't get rid of the smile on my face, hard as I try. And it's then that I realize Joss's little joke tactic worked—I haven't thought about the elimination (and the pressure that goes along with it) since.

"What are you smiling about?" Lana asks, lifting an eyebrow from where she's lying on her bed, a letter that Graham had written and hidden in her suitcase before the show in her hand.

"It's nothing."

"Hmm, if I had to guess, it has something to do with the hot, seven-foot Australian who is obsessed with you?"

Lana's statement catches me entirely off guard. "Don't," I grit out.

"Oh, Dani," she grins.

"There's nothing going on between me and Joss," I say, my voice stern, leaving absolutely no room for argument. I debate whether I should tell her the only reason we're somewhat friendly—I avoid the word *friends*, even in my own mind—is because we met on the plane here, but I ultimately decide against it. She doesn't need any more encouragement in this department.

"Yeah, not *yet* maybe. I saw the way he threw you over his shoulder the other day, and more importantly, the way you *let* him," she says, heading over to the wardrobe mirror to brush some mascara on her lashes.

I scoff at her. "I'm not about to be the girl that gets in a showmance, Lana." Every season of *American Gauntlet,* it seems that two players get in a "showmance"—a romance while filming the show—that always ends in disaster either during or after filming. They never last. Ever. In fact, they usually blow up in spectacular fashion, flooding social media and gossip sites and Reddit threads with every grisly detail. Superfans of the show pick sides on who was right or wrong in the breakup, and the guilty party can get cyberbullied into oblivion. I've heard rumors of death threats. *Death threats!* Yeah…no thanks.

"Who cares, Dani? He's fine. Like *fine* fine. And you haven't liked anyone since what's-his-face." Lana has so much disdain for Justin that she exclusively refers to him as *what's-his-face*. She never liked him, even at the very beginning of our relationship. She was always droning on and on about how much better I deserved. Of course, at the time, I just thought she was just being an annoying little sister, but it turns out, Lana is a far better judge of character than I am.

"Now how is Graham going to react when he hears you refer to Joss as '*fine* fine' on national television?" I ask, desperately trying to change the subject. I have no doubt this fun little conversation will make its way into the final edit of the show. The producers live for anything that adds a little bit of intrigue to the show outside of the competitions themselves.

"He would agree that Joss is hot and that you should let yourself have a little bit of fun with the nice, funny, good-looking Australian surfer, Dani Di Laurentis."

I groan. "I hate to break it to you, but this little *showmance* you're rooting for isn't going to matter if I don't win the elimination tonight."

Lana's eyes meet mine in the reflection of the wardrobe mirror. "I'm not worried," she says with confidence. "You've got this."

Easy for her to say. She's not the one competing.

Then, sirens begin to blare and I know it's time to face the music.

nineteen

I DOWN my pre-competition coffee even though I'm pretty sure it's almost eight o'clock at night and everyone has commented about how unhinged it is to drink coffee this late. I don't care. I need the caffeine kick. The van is quiet and tense as Benji and I mentally prepare to go head-to-head in whatever insane competition the producers and Dax Philipps have cooked up.

The arena where the elims take place is a quick five minute drive through wherever we are in the middle of the wilderness. We all unload from the van and are met by a makeshift stadium made of the same black and white corrugated metal as the compound, harsh stadium lights shining down and illuminating the area. There's a set of bleachers for the other teams to watch the game unfold.

As we enter the arena, it feels like entering the Colosseum. Like this is life or death. And in a way, I suppose it is. This is to give Penny the life she deserves. It may not be life or *death*, per se, but it's a matter of surviving or thriving for Penny. This is to give her a better life. To help others understand her value and what she brings to the table as an equal.

To put it plainly, this is everything.

As I walk further into the arena, Lana by my side, I catch sight of what this elimination will entail. There's a pit of sand in the center of the space with a ring of rope around it, forming a circle about twenty-five feet or so in diameter, if I had to guess. There's a metal horseshoe stuck in the sand in the middle of the circle. I don't know what the competition will be, but I'm just glad I don't see anything to climb. Benji would win with ease if that were the case.

The producers send everyone else to the bleachers, while Benji and I join Dax in the middle of the circle.

"Benji, Dani—welcome to the first elimination," he says. Everything he says has a foreboding edge to it, and it makes the already high stakes feel unbearable. "If you win tonight's elim, you and your partner stay in the competition. Lose? You and your partner will be sent home. Immediately."

Instead of running from it, I let Dax's intensity fuel me. I feel ready. I feel nervous, too, but nerves are healthy to a certain extent. They sharpen your senses; they pump adrenaline into your system. I can already feel it building in my veins.

"Before I explain what the competition is," Dax continues, "we're going to have you suit up."

At the direction of the producers, Benji and I each put on a harness with a carabiner on the back. We are then positioned on opposite sides of the circle, and I watch as they attach a cable to Benji's carabiner on his back, run the cable through the center of the horseshoe, and attach the opposite end to my back. Benji and I are essentially bound together on opposite sides of a cord with the horseshoe serving as a pivot point in the middle. If I move a few feet in one direction on my side, Benji is forced to give up slack on his side, and vice versa.

On the outside of the rope ring, there's a small metal pole, only about a foot high, sticking out of the sand on each side of the circle, one on my side and one on his.

When we're in our harnesses and attached via cable, Dax continues his instructions.

"As you can see, you two are bound together by this cable on your backs. On my whistle, you will begin digging through the sand on your half of the circle, looking for three metal rings that are buried beneath the sand. Once you find a ring, you will then place it on the pole on your side of the ring. Once you find and place all three rings on the pole, you win.

"Oh, and as you can probably already tell, there's not that much slack in the cable for you both, so you'll be pulling against the force of your opponent the entire time. Hope you've got the strength to get where you need to go."

Okay, I think to myself. *Find the rings. Put them on the pole. Don't let Benji do it first.*

The producers line Benji and I up on opposite sides of the circle. At this point, the cable is pulled tight and equally dispersed on either side of the sandy ring.

My blood is pumping. I've come up with my strategy. I tuck a little piece of hair back into my space buns. I'm ready.

"Remember, you lose, you go home. You win, you stay," Dax says. He brings the whistle to his lips, and it's as if time slows. My fingers twitch at my sides in anticipation, my breath growing shallow. I feel like a horse stamping at the ground, anxious to get out of the starting gate, but just as the buildup makes my heart want to explode out of my chest, I'm jolted back into the moment, the shrill sound of Dax's whistle piercing my ears.

I immediately run to the middle of the circle, intent on starting my dig closest to the center in case I need to keep Benji away from his pole later. I drop to my knees and begin scooping the sand with both arms like a one-woman wrecking crew, sending tiny grains flying into my eyes, my hair, my shoes. I've barely begun and sand is already coating me from head to toe, but I pay it no mind as I methodically move through the circle, digging and searching, making sure I don't accidentally miss a metal ring as I rush.

Digging through the deep sand is exhausting, the thick sand providing a healthy dose of resistance. But I've got a full gas tank of energy, and I'm prepared to leave it on empty by the end of this.

After only a few minutes of digging, Benji finds his first ring, and with all the slack he has because of how close I am to the middle, he runs to his pole and places the ring around it. He's barely made it back to his spot to dig when I find my first ring and dart to my own pole, sending him flying toward the middle of the circle. Benji probably weighs less than 140 pounds, and I quickly realize that I can drag him wherever I need to without expending that much energy. I feel him tug faintly against the cable, but I won't budge until I'm ready.

After placing my first ring on the pole, I start moving from the center of the ring progressively toward the edges. From the bleachers, the teams are yelling, encouraging us to keep going. I hear Lana screaming my name, while Tris is coaching Benji as much as she can. Over all the voices, I hear a distinctly Australian voice telling me to "get a move on, sunshine," and I bite back a smile.

Benji and I find our second rings at nearly the same time, but he can't get to his pole as I tug him toward mine. I easily place the second one on, and then begin digging on the very outskirts of the circle. From where I am, Benji can't reach his pole, and I realize my plan is working. He is on his stomach, desperately trying to army crawl toward his pole, but there's not enough slack for him to reach it. I'm an immovable stone wall.

Sand is in my eyes, down my sports bra, coating my hair, but I don't stop. I keep methodically scooping sand from the pit, focusing on keeping my breathing steady so I don't gas out. I'm mid-scoop when I feel a cool metal object brush against one of my fingers and nearly squeal in excitement as I grip onto it and pull the black metal ring out of the sand. Benji hasn't stopped trying to get to his pole, but he's clearly exhausted, and I feel a little guilty as I literally drag his limp body with me and reach my pole, placing my third and final ring around it. I hear Lana, Naji, and Joss go crazy, as I give them a triumphant nod toward the bleachers. Blaire and Ivy have scowls on their faces that quickly fade as I make eye contact with them and hurl a cheeky wink at Ivy. My eyes drift to Tris, and I dart them away just as quickly as I see the disappointment seeping into her features.

Before the producers can even unclip me from the cable, I walk over and stand beside Benji, his black hair coated with tan sand.

We say nothing as I extend an arm and help him up off the ground, both of us dusting ourselves off as much as possible, an act that's admittedly futile. I'll be finding sand in every crevice of my body for weeks; of that, I have no doubt.

The producers signal for our teammates to join us, and Lana literally jumps into my arms, squealing with excitement. Tris hugs Benji in an embrace that is full of heart-wrenching sadness before she turns to me, surprising me with a hug of my own.

As she embraces me, she whispers in my ear, "If we had to lose to anybody, we're glad it's you two. You can win this competition, Dani. We're rooting for you."

As she pulls away, I realize tears have appeared at the corners of her eyes, looking out of place against her tough exterior, the shaved sides of her head and the fierce look of her eyes. Before I can say anything, though, Dax is before us, commanding our attention.

"Tris, Benji—it's been a pleasure, but unfortunately, you do *not* have what it takes to face the Gauntlet. Safe travels."

And with that emotionless farewell, the climbers are ushered away, put into a van, and driven off to pack and leave the camp without another word to anyone.

"Dani, I'd say you definitely proved your strength tonight," Dax says, and as he does, a little beam of pride hits me like sun in my eyes. "What inspired you to fight like you did tonight?"

I take a deep breath, letting it out slowly before I begin. "I'm here for my sister, Penny. She has an intellectual disability called Williams syndrome, and she's had a really hard time finding a job because of it. Because people don't see her value. That's what I need my half of the prize money for—to help pay for a college-like program for her to get experience. My family…can't really afford it otherwise."

Dax's typically-intense look softens the slightest bit. The stone cold *American Gauntlet* host may have a heart buried deep beneath that stony exterior after all. "Thank you for sharing that, Dani. You got the job done tonight, so you and Lana can go join the rest of the teams."

"HOW am I supposed to compete against you after that?" Naji asks me as we all climb back into the van. "You need to pay for your sister's program? I've never met Penny, but I don't want to *ruin her future!*" he exclaims with a flail of his arms.

"In that case, you can do us all a favor and just drop out now, mate," Joss jokes.

Naji laughs. "Yeah, no worries there. I've got no problem competing against *you*, Joss."

The van feels vastly emptier without Tris and Benji to fill the seats. Sarge and Junior are silent, as always, in the back. The Twisted Twins are also uncharacteristically silent; it feels odd, since they typically try to be the center of attention, although I'm sure they're already plotting their next ploy to take me and Lana down. The more I get to know them, though, the less they intimidate me. It turns out the "Twisted Twins" aren't twisty at all; they're not as much scary beasts as they are annoying pests beneath my shoes. A nuisance but not a true threat.

When the van pulls back onto the camp grounds, I separate from the teams and take a walk around the compound, trying to decompress and wrap my mind around the fact that I just won the elimination and get to stay in this wild competition. I'm so lost in the labyrinth of my own mind that I don't see Ivy as I walk right into her in the near darkness, the only light coming from the spaced out lights above the walkway.

"Oh, sorry," I blurt.

"It's fine," Ivy says with her signature smile. I'm convinced that will be the entirety of our conversation, but then she adds, "In the dark, I almost thought you were Naji. Your silhouette is so… broad."

A huff of a laugh escapes me. "Thanks, I've been working on it," I toss over my shoulder as I begin to step past her.

The smile falls from her lips. She glances down, and after I get a few steps away, she remarks, "You're a confident thing, aren't you?"

Despite her words, her voice isn't laced with its typical

passive aggressive snark. It's stained with something deeper. Introspection, maybe.

Her tone and the question itself catches me off guard. I mull it over in my mind, practicing a little introspection of my own. *Am I confident?* I want to immediately answer in the affirmative, but there's a voice in the back of my mind that makes me question if that would be the truth. I suppose I'm confident in certain things. My body is one of them. I'm proud of the physique I've built, of how I can deadlift more than half the men in the gym, of how self-reliant I feel when it comes to anything physical. I know I don't need to ask anyone for help to move furniture or heave in heavy shipments at the gym. But I'm not so self-assured when it comes to…other things. I struggle to let people in—guys, especially—because I'm afraid they'll get to the core of who I am and find that I'm not worth sticking around for. That they'll find something just like Justin did. That they'll walk out the door just like my dad did long before Justin. Sometimes I wonder if that's why I've built the physique that I have. It's an intimidating fortress, a reinforced stronghold, intended to keep people out. To keep me safe.

"Yes and no," I reply truthfully to Ivy. I know she posed her question rhetorically, but I answer it nonetheless. "Are *you?*"

I don't know why I turn the tables on her. Maybe it's because I think her question had more to do with her than with me. Maybe it's because I'm curious to hear her answer. Either way, it hangs stiffly in the air between us.

When I look at her, I find her face devoid of its usual fake smile, not an insincere nose crinkle to be seen.

"I—"

Before she can answer, another voice comes from behind her in the darkness.

"There you are," Blaire sighs, exasperated. "Did you get lost or are you just—"

She stops when she finds me standing in front of her sister. "Oh," she says.

I watch Ivy's face intently as her sister approaches, a motley of emotions flashing across her features in quick succession. Dejection. Annoyance. Disdain. Not one of them is happiness or even mild affability at the sight of her sister. Regardless, Ivy smiles at her as she says, "I was just heading back."

As I take in the scene before me, a lot about the Twisted Twins seems to click into place. I'd been wondering why Ivy didn't like me from the get-go, but now I'm wondering if it's because she doesn't really like herself. I imagine it'd be difficult growing up with an identical twin, having another version of you, a perfect mirror image, to compete with on a daily basis, even if you didn't realize it. Since the first day of the competition, it's been obvious that Blaire breathes confidence, while Ivy oozes insecurity. Both of them clearly crave being the center of attention, but I think Blaire does because she's simply always commanded it, while Ivy feels she's never gotten enough of it.

I'm not quite sure what to do with these observations. Whether they're accurate or not, it won't change how either of them feels about me. It certainly won't change how they act toward me, I'm sure. But perhaps I'll find it easier to ignore their overt jabs and loud whispers knowing it has everything to do with them and little to do with me.

WHEN the sidewalk finally wraps back around to my cabin, I'm surprised to find Joss leaning against my door in low-hanging black sweatpants.

He's also not wearing a shirt.

I try to keep my eyes away from the V-shaped muscles that are on full display at the base of his abs. The harsh overhead light posts that illuminate the camp in the dark cast wicked shadows across his chest. They emphasize every finely carved muscle, every chiseled line.

Still, I can't let Joss catch me looking at them after the muddy debacle at the first competition.

"Hate to break it to you, but this isn't Bondi Beach," I say as I approach. "Put a shirt on."

"Are you sure you want me to do that, Dani?" he asks with a knowing grin, and I hate the way that I love the way my name sounds when he says it. I blame the accent.

"What are you doing here?" I ask, trying to not sound as flustered as I feel. "Whatever mind games you're playing, they won't work."

"Maybe I'm playing mind games," he says slowly, as if he's pondering his own response, "or maybe I just came to tell you congratulations on your win tonight."

"I'm touched," I say, casting him a sidelong look, my eyes narrowed in suspicion. I trust him about as far as I could throw him.

"It's a shame, really," he says, his tone playful.

I know he's baiting me, but I don't care. I take the bait anyway. "What is, Joss? Do tell."

"It's a shame you did all that work tonight just for me to eliminate you in the next phase of the competition."

"Menace."

He smiles and bends down to me, a wave of coconut-scented shampoo and spearmint gum washing over me. He puts his lips so close to my ear that they're almost touching, and I feel my breath hitch, even as I try to fight it. I half-feel like he's going to blurt out another random fact about nurdles.

But instead he says, his voice a mere rumble, "Have a good night, sunshine."

PHASE Two is coming. We're not sure when—the producers have kept the date of the next competition a secret—but I feel the Endurance Phase looming, and I'm itching to get a chance at redemption after a less-than-desirable result in the first phase. I'm also itching for a little bit of power.

"Do we *have* to?"

Lana's question pulls me out of wherever I've zoned off to. Here at the camp, my thoughts always seem to be consumed with strategy and tactics and training. And *winning*.

"Yes, we have to," I reply, tugging on a sports bra. It's always a bit of a struggle to get it over my back and shoulder muscles.

"But what if the competition is today and we're just tiring ourselves out by working out beforehand?" she asks, hoping I'll buy the excuse she's selling. Spoiler alert: I'm not.

I drag a dramatic Lana to the gym and give her some dumbbells to curl as we start an upper body session. I know it's her least favorite, and I'm pretty sure she'd rather donate a kidney than lift a weight, but I've noticed that despite all the training she did with Graham leading up to coming here, her upper body strength is still severely lacking. We need to keep working on it. It's only a matter of time before we're hit in the face with an arm strength-focused challenge by the producers.

She barely gets two reps in before she's struggling. Like arms shaking, can't-curl-the-dumbbell type of struggling.

"My arms are rebelling," she says, dropping the weight on the ground.

I bite down on the groan of frustration that is desperately trying to escape from my throat. "This should be a warm-up, Lana. According to the training plan I sent you, you should've been able to do four full sets of curls with this weight, like, months ago."

"Oh," Lana says, turning away from me. "Yeah. I don't know. I guess my arms are just tired from all the stuff we've been doing."

"You haven't competed since the first competition over a week ago, though," I say. I don't want to push too hard, but I'm genuinely confused. This should be easy for her by now.

Even though she's turned away from me, I still catch a glimpse of Lana's face in the gym mirror, and I can see how defeated she looks.

"Just take a rest day then," I say. "You can stay and keep me company, though," I add. It's torturous having to workout without any music, which is our reality since we don't have our phones. I could use the company.

Lana doesn't need to be asked twice. She immediately sprawls on the ground and starts chatting away, as per usual.

"What kind of car should I get with my prize money?" she asks dreamily. "Considering we're definitely going to win, I need to start planning."

"Something reasonable," I say. "A car that will last a long time, one that gets good gas mileage."

"Yeah, yeah," she says, rolling her eyes. "I wish we both got $300K, instead of having to split it. Then we'd *really* be talking."

"Yeah, well we don't, so…" I say, trailing off as I try to breathe through our workout. Well, *my* workout, I suppose.

Lana sits up then, making eye contact with me. "You should keep the money, at least some of it for yourself, Dani. I know you want to pay for Penny's program, but maybe there's some sort of aid she can apply for," Lana says, and her tone indicates just how careful she's being. How she's walking on eggshells that she doesn't want to shatter into a million tiny pieces. "You've… you've already done so much for us. You need to take care of yourself, too."

As gentle as she's being, I still feel sharp emotions poking at me, a hundred needles prodding at my skin, trying to break the tension at its surface. The thing about walking on eggshells is that after they've been shattered, they're impossible to clean up.

"I already looked into financial aid, but she doesn't qualify for it since it's not an 'official' college program. There's no scholarships. There's nothing for her," I say, keeping my tone neutral despite the annoyance stabbing at me.

"Well, let Mom and Dad worry about taking out loans or something. It's not your burden to carry, Dani."

I laugh; actually I *bellow* at what she's proposing. "Dad? The person we haven't heard from in…what? Years? He's not funding one bit of that program, and you know it."

Our father resented all three of us, his daughters that he so desperately wanted to be sons. After Lana and I were born, he simply couldn't fathom the idea that he'd ended up with two girls. *Girls,* he thought. *Emotional, complicated, expensive.* Then when Penny came along, he truly shut us all out, unwilling to try to relate to us. He stayed around for those ten years or so after Penny was born, but he wasn't there, not really. The disdain he felt for all of us, especially Penny, was evident to me, even as a little girl. He didn't *get* Penny, didn't understand her. Not that he tried. Not that he tried with any of us.

And finally, he just walked out. He didn't leave my mom for someone younger, someone prettier; that might've been easier for my thirteen-year-old mind to comprehend.

It turns out, he didn't leave us because he loved someone else more; he left us because he didn't love us in the first place.

I know Lana means well, but she doesn't understand where I'm coming from. She doesn't understand that this is my burden to bear because I've chosen to carry it. I was older than Lana and Penny when Dad left. I understood more; my adolescent brain took in every harsh word, every scornful glance, all of it burned into a pain-filled portrait in my memory. I keenly understood what it felt like to be rejected by someone who was supposed to love you unconditionally, and I never wanted my sisters to feel that same pain. So I decided I'd fight for them the way we should've been fought for by our parents. A parent should go to bat for their child's best interests, and this program is just that for Penny. Since our dad isn't around to do anything about it, I will.

"Luckily," I say, my tone lighter and not portraying even an ounce of the bitterness that I feel, "you get your half and I get mine. And we've got the freedom to do whatever we want with it."

"Yeah" is all Lana replies. "I'm going for a run. I'll catch you at lunch."

I'm grateful to be left alone in the exact silence I was trying to avoid earlier. After Lana leaves, I let myself feel the emotions I always hide away from her. I feel like a parent who doesn't want their kid to see that they feel negative emotions, that they feel angry and sad and irritated and annoyed. I've hid that side from

Lana and Penny ever since I stepped into the mom role for them all those years ago, and even though Lana is an adult now and our actual mom is sober and back to herself…well, you know what they say about old habits.

Even after I've finished shredding apart my muscles from my workout, which usually helps relieve the intensity of my emotions, I still feel them, like crocodiles lurking just below the surface, looming unseen until they explode out of the water. Thinking about Dad does that to me; it brings out this irrational anger that never seems to quell.

As I walk out of the gym pavilion, I'm seeing so much red that I hardly notice as Joss approaches, his usual smirk on his face.

"Getting ready for the next competition, ay, sunshine?"

"Looks that way," I mutter, brushing past him.

"Oh, come on now, Dani. Not in the mood to spar today?"

And that's when I turn on him. If my emotions are a croc beneath the river, he's the unsuspecting gazelle at the watering hole that just became dinner.

"No, I'm not in the mood for whatever game it is you're playing, Joss," I seethe, acid dripping from my tone. "I know this whole competition just seems like one big fun adventure to you—you with your picture-perfect life on Bondi Beach. But *American Gauntlet* isn't just a game to me. It is *everything*, and I don't have time to get distracted with guys like you who are just here to have a good time."

I brace myself for his response, but he doesn't throw acid back in my face like I expect him to. Instead, he tilts his head to the side, as if he's assessing me, evaluating me. I suddenly feel completely naked, like Joss can see straight through me, down to my core.

"Righto," he says, his tone neutral, giving nothing away as to how he feels after I just spat at him. He turns away and heads into the gym as if this were a completely normal conversation

Feeling like I've been dismissed, I turn around and find Ryder has watched our entire exchange, and if I weren't still so jacked up on negative emotions, I'd probably feel embarrassed. But although Joss didn't deserve the tone I used with him, I meant every word that I said. *American Gauntlet* seems to be just another fun vacation for Joss, a vacation where the outcome doesn't make a lasting difference one way or the other. That's not the case for me. I don't have that luxury.

I take a few steps past Ryder before he turns to me, his voice low to where I know Joss can't hear it.

"Take it easy on him, Dani," he says, his voice sounding especially tender beneath his Southern drawl. "He's been through more than he lets on."

Before I can respond, Ryder turns around and joins Joss in the gym. Not wanting to be around anyone else at the moment, I take off to the little lake near the camp and dip my feet in the water until the sun begins to set. I'm exhausted. Physically. Mentally. Emotionally. *American Gauntlet* has begun to take a toll on me that will only grow as we swim into deeper waters, and for the first time since I've been here, I begin to question if all of this is worth it. If I fail to reach the lofty goals I've set for myself—if I do anything short of winning that prize money—I'm not sure I'll be able to recover from it. Or if I'll like the person I become trying to get there.

twenty-one

"GOING casual tonight, I see."

I'm heading back to my cabin after my near existential crisis at the lake, and I snap my head up, finding myself face-to-face with Naji. Night has fallen, but thanks to the camp lighting, I can see he's wearing black jeans and a denim, short-sleeved button-up shirt. His hair looks freshly washed and lightly gelled back into a perfect bun just past the crown of his head.

"Wait, why are you so dressed up?" I ask, and I know the confusion is apparent on my face. The only thing any of us ever wear around the compound is workout gear and lounge wear.

"Didn't you hear from the producers? We're partying tonight!"

I groan. It's happening.

Every season, the producers set up some sort of outing, always involving *lots* of alcohol, to give the competitors a "fun night out" as a reward for the torture we're put through in the competitions. Really, I just think it's so they can film some alcohol-fueled drama or showmance hookups that always seem to take place. This is a TV show, after all, and the viewers love the drama.

"Where are we going? We're, like, a million miles away from civilization."

"Exactly," he says, grinning. "That's why Kelly said they're bringing the party to us. We're supposed to meet at the Commons in an hour."

"An hour. Got it," I say, heading in the direction of my cabin to change. I know this "outing" isn't optional. I imagine if I tried to skip it, production would send Sergey into my room to rip me from my bed and drag me to the party. I shudder at the nightmarish thought.

"And Dani?"

"Yeah?" I ask, pausing.

"Wipe that frown off your face," he teases. "This will be *fun*. You know, fun? Have you heard of it?"

"Nope, never heard of it."

That coaxes a laugh out of him, not that it's particularly hard. Naji always has a laugh at the ready.

"If I don't see you having fun tonight, you will find a spider in your bed this week, a special gift from yours truly."

"Right, because your plastic spider is *so* terrifying."

"Who said anything about a *plastic* spider?"

"YOU look hot, sis."

I check myself in our wardrobe mirror one last time, tilting my head to one side then the next, trying to pull the skin-tight black dress down a little further. The problem is that once I pull it down, it becomes exceedingly low cut. Like, almost scandalously so. I groan. I ordered it online before we came since a "nicer" outfit was on the packing list from Kelly, but I bought it from some bogus website and didn't try it on before we got here. That may have been a mistake, since it's hardly covering anything anywhere.

"I don't know..." My voice drifts. I stare at my reflection as if the longer I look at it, the higher my chances are of getting a different result. I like almost everything about the dress. It's a lovely satiny black material, its bodice held up by two thin spaghetti straps. The fabric drapes at the neckline, making it look nicer than the thirty bucks I paid for it, and it ruches at my natural waistline, perfectly tapering my torso to its most flattering potential. I run my hands over the front of the dress, loving the feeling of the smooth fabric beneath my fingers. The dress is pretty. *Really* pretty. It just needs an extra three inches at the hem to avoid giving Penny a heart attack when she eventually sees it on TV. She'll be scandalized.

"Well, lucky for you, it's all you have," Lana says. "Lucky for *Joss*, more like," I hear her mutter under her breath.

"You did not just say that!" I gasp.

"Sorry, sorry. Not just Joss!" she amends. "Lucky for the world's *American Gauntlet* viewers who get to witness you in that dress. There? That better?"

I deadpan at her through the wardrobe mirror. "No, but thank you for the compliment?" I'm still not sure I want to thank her for what she implied about Joss.

She flashes a self-satisfied grin. "You're welcome."

I help Lana zip her dress, a purple bodycon with long sleeves and a straight-across neckline. She looks flawless, but then again, I think Lana always looks perfect. She has that sort of effortless beauty that requires little maintenance on her part.

Stealing one final glance at the mirror, Lana and I head out of our cabin before I can talk myself into changing. When we arrive at the Commons, we find the other teams waiting outside with the producers.

"Evening, ladies," Sarge says. He's standing with Junior, both of them with their arms crossed and legs shoulder-width apart, wearing clean-cut jeans and crisp white v-necks that contrast beautifully against their ebony skin. They both have gold wedding bands on their left ring fingers.

"Hey there," Lana and I say in unison. "Did y'all plan this ensemble or what?" I ask.

This draws a rare laugh from both of them. "You should see our closets," Junior replies. "All basics."

"I like it," I smile.

The Twisted Twins are, unsurprisingly, dressed to the nines. Ivy is wearing black leather pants with an aqua blue crop top, and Blaire, a tight white skirt with a red halter top. They're currently preoccupied with Naji and AJ, Ryder standing off to the side, listening in on the joke the brothers are in the middle of telling.

I quickly realize Joss is notably missing. A tiny speck of what feels a lot like disappointment drops into the pit of my stomach, but I ignore it as the producers open up the doors to the Commons and usher us all inside.

As we step inside, I feel like I'm stepping into a nightclub in Los Angeles—or, at least, what I imagine a nightclub in Los Angeles is like, although I've never actually been to one. I feel the pound of the bass in my chest, music blaring from a DJ toward the back of the expansive space. The main lights have been turned off, supplemented instead by colorful flashing lights everywhere. A sizable space has been cleared for the dancefloor, and the giant kitchen island has been transformed into a full bar, complete with a bartender with dark, slightly curled hair and a plunging V-neck t-shirt.

"Dang, Kelly, you went all out!" Lana says, as we step past her and journey further into the Commons-turned-club.

"Pretty great, huh?" she says with a glimmer of pride in her eyes. "You girls have fun!"

"Dani! Lana! Come over here," Naji says, beckoning us over to the bar with the rest of the teams. We join them, and I emit a tiresome groan as Naji yells, *"Shots!"*

The bartender immediately starts pouring shots of tequila for each of us, including Sarge and Junior who are surprisingly game for them. The veterans don't strike me as the 'shots' kind of people, but maybe it's what they use to help them loosen up a bit. Come to think of it, I'd actually *love* to see what they're like when they're not on guard twenty-four seven.

While I'm glad Sarge and Junior are in for a shot, that doesn't change my feelings on the matter.

"Absolutely not," I yell to Naji over the pounding bass.

"Hey, remember what I said! If you don't have fun tonight, your bed and a spider have a hot date."

Because I'm actually concerned he will make good on that promise (with an *actual* spider), especially considering all of the pranks he's pulled on everyone so far, I slide the tequila shot over in front of me.

"To *American Gauntlet!*" Naji yells.

"To *America Gauntlet!*" we yell, clinking our glasses together, hitting them on the bar, and downing them in one gulp. I bite into the lime to chase the burn away and hear Ivy over the music, giggling as she says, "Oh my gosh, the look on all of your faces is priceless. I don't even need a chaser!"

I wait for everyone else to order drinks, including Lana who is a notorious lightweight, before I signal to the bartender and lean over, close to his ear.

"I'm going to order 'vodka sodas,' but just give me club soda with lime."

He doesn't ask questions. My kinda guy. "No problem."

I don't want everyone to think I'm not having a good time because now that I'm here, I actually do think we'll all have a lot of fun tonight, but I also don't want to be hungover for the competition, which I have an eerie feeling is tomorrow. Because this is *American Gauntlet* and the producers are cruel, sadistic monsters. (Sorry, Kelly.)

The bartender slides a short glass with a skinny black straw and lime in it over to me and I take a sip. Club soda and lime. Perfect.

Almost everyone has taken to the dancefloor, but I head over to where Sarge is standing on the outskirts. He clearly feels a little out of place among the group, all of us, including his son, a good twenty-plus years younger than him.

"When my wife watches this, she's gonna roast me about how I look like the lame old guy," Sarge jokes. With a laugh, I jump into conversation with him, our voices straining above the music to hear each other.

Despite my best efforts to be fully invested in keeping Sarge company, I can't help but constantly look around, my eyes darting toward the door every few minutes. It's impossible to stop myself. I'm not usually a bad listener, but maybe all of the lights and music have me in sensory overload or something.

Then, like a fresh ocean breeze has blown through the Commons, Joss walks in, casually running his hand through his sandy blonde hair. He's wearing tight light-washed jeans, rolled a little at the ankles, and a navy short-sleeve button-up. The top four or five buttons of his shirt are undone, so his bare chest is on full display, and he's cuffed his sleeves on each arm to where they perfectly fit around the bulge of his delts. I can't help but watch as he confidently strides toward the bar and chats effortlessly with the bartender like they're old friends.

He takes his drink and looks out at the group on the dancefloor, before dragging his eyes across the perimeter; he pauses as they land squarely on mine, and my heart stops right along with it. Our eyes hold for a second, maybe two, before he rakes his gaze down my body and back up. His eyes meet mine again and there's something in his expression that feels… *starved*. No one has ever looked at me the way he's looking at me right now, and it's stirring up something deep inside me, waking it up. Or maybe giving it life for the first time.

"Joss! Come on!" Ryder yells from where he's in a full fist-pump on the dancefloor.

Joss rips his gaze away from mine and joins the group. I dutifully try to turn my attention back to Sarge, but I can't shake the feeling that I need to douse my entire body in ice water.

"Need another drink?" Sarge asks. "I'm getting a refill."

"Oh, yeah, that'd be great," I say, seeing as I've drained my lime water already. "Vodka soda, but make sure he knows it's for me." Sarge gives me a questioning look. "Special way I like it made," I tack on.

Sarge brings me back a vodka soda that I know is only soda water with lime after I take a sip, and we pick up our conversation again, which is mainly me fueling him with questions and him regaling me with stories. I genuinely enjoy hearing about his life, but the thing I love most is the way his eyes sparkle when he talks about his wife. My heart felt like it was going to burst when he told me about the letters she wrote him when they were engaged to be married and he was overseas on assignment. It's the kind of stuff they write books about.

While I'm doing my best to listen to Sarge, my attention

keeps drifting to the dancefloor—to one specific person on the dancefloor—and I hate it. I keep accidentally making eye contact with Joss as he's dancing, and while I shoot my gaze away like you do when you unintentionally make eye contact with someone, he holds it, never being the first to break it.

After a little while, everyone loosened with a few refills on their drinks, Naji and AJ dance over to me and Sarge. "Sorry, Sarge! We're going to steal her," they shout over the music. "You've had a couple drinks. That should be enough for you to dance with us, right?"

I laugh because they're adorable and impossible to turn down, so even though I'm fully sober aside from the tequila shot, I follow them out to the dancefloor, bringing Sarge with us so his wife doesn't give him grief for being the "lame old guy."

When we get to the center of the dancefloor, I can *feel* Joss's eyes on me, searing me like a brand, even though we're on opposite sides of the small space. I try not to look his way, but I can't help the magnetic-like pull he has on me, especially when I see the Twisted Twins surround him, dancing on both sides of him.

Even when they approach him, he keeps his eyes squarely on me, and it's not subtle. Not at all.

I want to be next to him. I want his hands around my waist. I want him to dance with me, not them.

Good grief, what is happening to me? *Get a grip, Dani.* I turn my attention back to Naji and AJ, who are in the middle of the most ridiculous dance battle I've ever seen, before I catch sight of something in my peripheral vision and jerk my head back toward Joss.

I watch as Ivy, swaying her hips in front of Joss, takes her hand and presses it to his chest, the bare patch of chest that is visible because he didn't button his shirt. And it feels so intimate for her to be touching him like that. My mind flashes to when I was pressed against his bare chest, both of us slick with mud and sweat, in that first competition. Ivy snakes her hands up his chest and around his neck, and she's close to him—*so close*—and it feels wrong. Everything about it feels wrong.

"You okay?" Lana asks.

I realize, then, that my mouth is gaping open, but even though Ivy is doing the absolute most to get Joss's attention, his eyes are still locked on mine.

I rip them away and look at Lana, plastering a more normal expression on my face.

"Oh, yeah. I'm fine!" I say, probably a little too enthusiastically. "Just need a refill. Do you need one?"

"You know I'd be wasted if I had more than one of these," she says, laughing and thankfully not picking up on any of the weirdness I'm trying desperately to hide. I've always wondered if Lana is actually a lightweight or if it's something else…if she's scared of alcohol, of taking it too far like mom did. Either way, I'm proud of her for setting boundaries and taking care of herself.

I sneak away from the group and head to the bar.

"One more, please," I tell the bartender. He slides another club soda and lime into my hand, but I don't turn around, not ready to see whatever is happening between Joss and Ivy. Are his hands wrapped around her? Are his eyes locked on hers? Is his mouth locked on hers? And when that thought enters my mind, I seriously consider pouring this ice cold drink over my head since I have absolutely no right whatsoever to feel this way over Joss, especially after what I said to him today. *Holy smokes.* I'm a mess.

I'm still facing the bar when, suddenly, someone is next to me, a long, lean arm leaning against the makeshift bar.

"I'll have another one. Thanks, mate," Joss says to the bartender, and I feel him looking at me, leaning in closer, giving me the opportunity that I've been looking for ever since he walked into the Commons tonight.

"Before you say anything, I want to apologize for how I acted earlier," I say to him. "I shouldn't have said what I said. It's no excuse, but Lana and I had sort of gotten into a conversation that dug up some bad memories, and I snapped at you. I'm sorry. You didn't deserve that."

"No worries, sunshine," he says, his mouth to my ear so I can hear him over the music. I watch as the bartender slides what looks to be an actual vodka soda into his hand. He drains half of it in one gulp and flicks his tongue across his bottom lip to catch an excess drop.

I really need to stop staring at his mouth.

"Are you having fun tonight?" he asks, an edge to his voice that feels dangerous, like we're tip-toeing a fine line.

"Mhmm," I squeak out, and he bends down lower to me again so he can hear me. "You?" I ask.

"I haven't taken my eyes off you, in that dress, all night."

So much for tip-toeing.

His words come out confident, sure of themselves, and as they do, whatever had awakened in me earlier has returned with a vengeance.

But I can't do this here with this guy in the middle of this competition. I'm not at some random bar where it would be fine for me to flirt with a guy I like. *Not that I do much of that anyway,* I think. But this is Joss. He's my rival in this game. And even outside of this secluded camp, he lives on the opposite side of the world.

It's a doomed combination if I've ever heard one.

"You're just saying that because you've been drinking," I say, forcing my words to come out easy and light, like he didn't just cause a wave of heat to rush to my neck, to pool in the depths of my stomach.

"Maybe I'm saying that because I've had a bit to drink," he says, his mouth still to my ear. "Or maybe I'm saying it because it's the truth."

I feel a shiver snake down the length of my arm, and I wonder if he can feel the goosebumps against his skin where it presses against mine.

With Joss still dangerously close to me, the music suddenly dies down. The lights come up, and Ivy is suddenly on the other side of Joss, grabbing onto his shoulder. It makes me want to peel every one of her fingers off of him.

"Time to go, Joss," she says, staring only at him, not glancing in my direction even once. He doesn't immediately relent to her plea, his eyes still firmly on me, before he finally wrenches his gaze away from mine, leaves his drink on the bar, and follows the group out without so much as another word.

I stand there, gathering myself for a moment, before I grab his cup. After the whirlwind that this night has been, I could use an *actual* drink.

I take a giant gulp from Joss's cup and nearly spit it out.

Soda water. He was just drinking water.

PHASE TWO

★★★★

endurance

twenty-two

"SHOPPING cart," Lana and I say with confidence.

"It's definitely called a buggy," says Ryder, his accent instantly transporting all of us to the Deep South.

"Yous must be joking," Joss pipes in. "It's called a trolley."

"Okay, what do you call this?" Naji prompts, holding up his can of Coke. Out of pure boredom, we've been going in circles talking about the different slang terminology we use for various items. My personal favorite so far has been Joss's word for a small child: *ankle biter*. He laughed when I said I call them "tots" because that's funnier than calling them ankle biters, apparently.

"Soft drink," says Joss.

"Pop," Sarge and Junior add.

"That's a Coke," Ryder says.

"Right," Naji replies. "But what do you call this type of drink, like, in general?"

"I already told you," he says. "It's a Coke."

"But what if it's, say, a Sprite?" Ivy asks.

"Still a Coke."

"Ew, no!" the group exclaims in unison.

"*You're a monster!*" Naji screams in the exact same tone as Gingerbread Man in *Shrek*.

The table erupts in laughter, but an explosion of high-pitched sirens throughout the Commons has everyone's laughs morphing into near screams. I'm not sure if my heart will ever recover from the regular intervals of noise-induced abuse. *Maybe I can sue the show for physical and emotional damages if I don't take home the money.* I allow myself to follow that line of thinking, even though I know I practically signed my soul away in the pre-show paperwork. Plus, let's be honest...I love this show way too much to sue it.

Devoid of the luxury of my watch here at the camp, I press two fingers to the soft, hollow area of my neck, confirming what I already knew: my pulse is soaring.

Phase two—Endurance—is here.

The teams immediately disperse like a team of tiny ants to ready ourselves for the competition. Speeding back to our cabin, Lana and I proceed to tug on our purple uniforms and wrangle our hair into their signature styles. Space buns securely in place, I walk into the Commons to make my pre-competition coffee and find it empty except for Naji, who is standing at the kitchen island alone, eating a protein bar.

I keep this coffee ritual for the extra kick of caffeine, yes. But there's something about it that also feels like home. It's the smell of fresh, piping hot coffee, the sound of it streaming into my cup, that instantly transports me to the cramped apartment we call home. I picture Penny sipping orange juice at the scratched wooden dining table we snagged at Goodwill. I see Ford letting himself in through the front door with his own key, eyeing the coffee and asking if it's for him, a smile etched onto his face.

I'm distracted with thoughts of home as I pour the steaming coffee into my to-go cup and add my creamer. I open one of the kitchen drawers to get a spoon to stir it, but when I take a look in the drawer, I suddenly leap back, sending my drink flying everywhere, my heart beating out of my chest. Thankfully, I jump out of the way enough to avoid getting it all over me (and probably acquiring some fresh burns), but the coffee does splash all over my shoes and socks, soaking them completely.

In the meantime, Naji has spewed his protein bar all over the place and is currently doubled over on the floor laughing at me. I take a second glance at the spider I saw in the drawer that looked very real in the moment and realize that it is, in fact, very fake.

"You've *got* to be kidding me," I say, glaring at him. The glare quickly turns into a smile, though, because it's impossible to be mad at someone who's laughing as hard as he is.

My attention is pulled to the Commons door as an upbeat Kelly pops her head in and says, "Come on you two! Time to load up in the van."

"One sec, Kel!" I say to her. I need to run and put on some dry shoes and socks because I definitely don't want squishy foot gear to affect my performance in whatever competition we're in for today.

Naji finally pulls himself off the ground, peering at me with a guilty grin. "I'll make your coffee while you change."

"Thank you," I say, then add, "even though *you* caused this." He winks at me then grabs my cup and presses the button on the coffee maker.

I run back to my cabin, put on a fresh pair of socks and my other pair of trainers and rush back to the Commons to get my coffee. I grab it from where it's sitting on the kitchen island, throw some creamer and a lid on it, and jog to the van. Ivy jumps in right after me, and we take off toward whatever *American Gauntlet* has in store for us today. My mind sprints through the possibilities. *What'll it be today? Scaling a mountain? Racing through some insane obstacle course? Freeing ourselves from a submerged car, praying we don't drown first?* All very real possibilities.

I've grown used to the short van rides to our competitions, but this one takes much longer. We eventually arrive at a rocky hillside, and I realize I haven't even touched my coffee, so lost thinking about everything that happened last night and, more specifically, about what Joss said to me when he was *entirely sober,* it turned out. I shake my head to clear the thought, knowing it's the last thing I need to be focused on as we enter the Endurance Phase of this competition. I chug the coffee in under a minute before we exit the van and approach the cliffside where Dax Philipps is waiting, black Aviators covering his eyes and a stony expression on his face. It appears he won't be dropping his infamous demeanor anytime soon.

As we get closer to the cliff's edge, I realize the cliff is overlooking a giant lake. It's a windy day, which does nothing to ease the afternoon heat; it merely blows the balmy air straight into our faces. The lake's waters look dark, its waves churning so fiercely that the peaks are white and frothy like the foam on a latte. They look so much like ocean waves that I half expect to catch the scent of sea salt in the air, but instead, the earthy smell of the lake fills my nose. It's the same damp smell that permeates a reusable water bottle when you forget to clean it.

In the distance, I see a vessel, of sorts; it's rectangular, almost like a small aircraft carrier, its surface flat on the top. The structure is made of the familiar black and white metal of the camp, and I can see four gold stars spray painted on its side. It's floating toward the middle of the lake, rocking back and forth violently with the waves. There appears to be a thin bar extended horizontally off the side of it with a rope hanging down from the bar, the tip of it skimming the surface of the water.

And even though Dax hasn't given us the competition's instructions yet, I have a feeling we'll be swimming out to that vessel. This swim isn't like the swim on our first day here. That was a tiny lake—more like a pond—compared to this monstrous body of water in front of us. The water that day was extremely calm. I could see the bottom of the pond as I was swimming, and if I was ever in any real danger, I could've made it to where I could walk across the lake bottom with ease.

Today's situation is entirely different. If you're not a strong swimmer, you won't make it to the boat. Period.

Every competitor is leaning over the cliff, taking in the sights that await us below, anxiety with every crashing wave. I'm looking for anything to give me a sign as to how, exactly, we'll be getting down to the water. My first thought was that we might repel down the cliffside, but I don't see any type of equipment, no indicators as to how we'll make our descent. As each competitor watches the waves crash against the rockface, Dax seems to be enjoying the apprehension that's clearly building by the second.

I don't let my mind take over. I don't let the nerves become all-consuming. It's just a swim. I swim all the time. *It's just another swim,* I say again to myself, as if repeating it over and over will help me believe it.

"Hope you're not scared of heights, sunshine," Joss says, drawing my attention toward him. He looks calm and confident, like swimming through waves like the ones below is totally normal. But for him, it probably is. I intend to act like it's just another Tuesday for me, too.

"Are you kidding?" Lana cuts in. "Dani's not scared of anything. You should've seen the way she downed the cockroaches without a second glance on the first day here. She's fearless."

"I'm not surprised," Joss replies, inclining his head toward me. "She's a killer." His accent makes the word come out like *kill-ah.*

I don't know if it's his words, his accent, or the way he catches my eye as he says them, but a thrill shoots through the depths of my stomach. I quickly toss the feeling aside as pre-competition butterflies and not *any other* sort of butterflies.

"Yeah I'm only scared of one thing," Naji cuts in, "and I don't plan on encountering it on the show."

AJ huffs a laugh from where he stands beside his brother. "Don't worry, Naji. Mom won't be showing up at any of these competitions."

We all share in AJ's laughter, as Naji replies, "Oh yeah, I forgot about Mom. So, I guess I'm scared of *two* things."

Dax clears his throat, commanding all of our attention with a single sound. We form our typical semi-circle around him, his back to the cliffside so we have to face the impending challenge before us.

"Welcome, everyone. You've officially made it to phase two of *American Gauntlet:* Endurance. For today's competition, you'll be swimming to that boat." Dax points behind him unceremoniously. "Once you arrive, pull yourself up the rope to the top and traverse across the pole to get on the vessel. Once you're there, you'll wait for the other teams to arrive."

As Dax is explaining the rules, my head begins to feel fuzzy. I'm dizzy, unfocused. My throat is suddenly desert dry, like I've stuffed a handful of cotton balls in my mouth that are now absorbing every bit of saliva.

"You okay, sis?" Lana asks, her brows pinched together in concern.

I nod my head vigorously as if I can physically shake off the fog that has overtaken me. "Yeah, I'm fine."

"The first team to have *both* team members complete the task will have immunity and power this week. The second place team will have immunity this week. And for the rest of you…well, you'll see," Dax says with a wink.

"How are we supposed to get down to the water in the first place?" Blaire asks with a bit of an attitude.

"Oh, I thought that was obvious," Dax says coolly. "You'll jump."

The group is a mixed bag of reactions—some gasps, some groans, some sighs—but I'm having trouble getting my mind straight.

Beside me, Blaire says, "But we're like two stories up!"

"And?" Dax bites. "If you don't want to do it, you can take your chances in the elimination."

"We're fine!" Ivy cuts in shrilly. "Just processing things. We do stuff like this all the time at home!"

After the producers have gone over the safety measures and we ditch our sneakers for water shoes provided by the crew, each team lines up, our toes hanging off the edge of the cliff. A rush of adrenaline at the drop below has helped clear up whatever weird cloud of nausea overtook me moments ago, and I intend on riding this adrenaline wave all the way to the finish line.

Lana stands to my right, and it's clear she's in the zone, ready to compete. I look to my left to see the Twisted Twins beside me, oddly quiet. Ivy and I make eye contact and she looks to be… studying me. I suddenly feel self-conscious, wondering if the other competitors can tell there's something off about me today. Ivy's a shark, and she clearly smells blood in the water.

I look forward—not down, but out—at the vessel awaiting us,

doing my best to focus on the task at hand. As Dax raises the whistle to his lips, time seems to slow. I feel my heart hammer in my chest once, twice, three times. Another beat and the shrill sound of Dax's whistle cuts through the noise of the lake, straight to my ears.

As Naji and AJ start their descent with matching front flips, Lana and I grab hands and plunge into the depths below.

During the plunge, my stomach seems to swirl around itself before my feet finally hit the water. I suck in one last gulp of oxygen, willing my mind to remain calm. To not panic. Lana and I, our hands still interlocked, sink into the water before we begin kicking up, up, up, breaking the surface and wolfing air into our lungs.

With no more than a look, we begin swimming toward our finish line, guided by orange buoys floating along the route. It's a straight shot to the boat, but it's easy to get disoriented in the vast body of water.

I have tunnel vision as we swim. Lana is matching my pace, stroke for stroke, but as we swim and the adrenaline in my system begins to subside, the fog from earlier returns with a vengeance. I struggle to keep up, my endurance quickly dying out like the last beams of light before darkness overtakes the horizon. I smother the urge to throw up, to heave my guts into the water, a violent nausea overwhelming me. I'm not sure what's happening to me, but something is definitely wrong. I say a silent prayer, pleading that I can make it to the boat before I pass out right here in the middle of the lake.

As we swim, Lana and I are continually pounded by waves. Each time I turn my head to the side for air, I'm drowned out by more and more water crashing over my head. I try to focus on the fundamentals. Breathing. Making sure we're moving in the right direction. Conserving energy where I can. But I'm struggling. Badly.

I'm nearly in tears as Lana and I finally reach the rope, its end dipping down into the water, and I'm actually shocked that we are the second team to arrive; I guess the other teams have been struggling with this treacherous swim as much as I have. I look up to see Ryder already on top of the boat and Joss effortlessly pulling himself up the rope, his muscles flexing with every tug. There are knots along the rope to use as footholds, but Joss doesn't even need them; he pulls himself up with only his upper body strength, his hands moving one over the other as he reaches the top. Once there, he swings his body under the pole, pulling himself across by his hands and feet.

I look behind us and see Sarge and Junior quickly approaching.

"Do you want to go first?" Lana asks, quickly.

I want to, but I also want to rest. I suddenly have the urge to lie back and float in the water, letting myself drift away with the waves.

"Dani?" Lana asks again, her tone urgent.

"You go first," I reply, finally.

She begins her ascent, but as she attempts to pull herself up, she doesn't get far. Her hands are slick, and although she takes time to rest on the knotted footholds, she ends up slipping back down almost immediately, unable to heave herself up more than a few feet.

"You go," she says. "I need to rest for a sec."

With Sarge coming up on my tail, I take to the rope and start hoisting myself up, replaying the millions of times I'd climbed the rope in the gym to practice for this very occasion. Even though the wet conditions and whatever sickness I'm battling aren't doing me any favors, I utilize every last bit of strength I have to haul my soaking wet body up, my vision growing blurrier by the second. I wrap my legs around the rope and use the knots to my advantage so I'm not relying entirely on my upper body, which is gassed from the swim. I finally reach the top and mimic Joss's technique, swinging under the pole and inching across it toward the boat.

I'm only a couple feet away, but my hand suddenly slips and I lose my grip. Instinct takes over, and my legs tighten around the pole, leaving me hanging upside down by my legs, the water thrashing below. I'm drained. For a split second, I contemplate letting myself fall and just taking my chances with the elimination, but I muster up my last bit of strength and use whatever abdominal strength I have left to pull myself up toward the pole. I grab on and close the gap to the boat, where Joss helps haul me in.

Ryder and Joss are saying something to me as I stand and walk toward the other side of the boat to rest, but I can't understand them. I can't understand anything.

I'm standing. I'm walking. I'm dizzy. I'm tripping.

And suddenly, I'm plunging into the water below.

twenty-three

A SLAP. My back slapping against the water, head whipping back.

Pain.

And then sinking, sinking, sinking.

I pass out and come to beneath the water's surface. The shock of drowning has kicked my body into survival mode, and suddenly, I'm panicking, thrashing in the water and trying to determine which way is up, bubbles of precious air escaping from my nose with every jerky movement. My lungs are shrieking at me, burning, begging for oxygen, and all I can think about is how much I don't want to drown. The reality of what is happening to me has paralyzed all of my rational brain cells.

Where are the divers? The producers said there would be divers in case of emergency, but no one is here to save me. And for once in my life, I can't save myself. I'm on my own, and it feels absolutely devastating.

The temptation to give in and allow myself to pass out again is suddenly overwhelming. Passing out would be better than *this*. This awareness that my oxygen is running out. This pain. This staggering fear.

Then something crashes into the lake, a torpedo barrelling through the water and coming straight towards me. I feel someone behind me, placing two strong hands beneath my arms and pressing up, propelling me toward the surface.

My head breaks through the water, and a sputter of water escapes me in ragged coughs. Water pours from my nose, and my throat burns as I gasp for precious air, worried that my head will dip below the surface again. The urge to throw up is suddenly immense, and yet, so is the urge to sleep.

I want to give in. Someone is holding me, keeping me above the water, yelling for something, for someone. I don't register a single word of it. I just want to sleep.

I feel a hand on my face, cupping my cheek, stroking my jaw.

"Dani," they say.

My eyelids feel as if they're made of lead, and I can't seem to pry them open, not even for the voice that sounds so soothing as it utters my name like a prayer.

"Sunshine," they say. "Sunshine, are you with me?"

The nickname coaxes my eyes open, and I find myself face-to-face with bright blue eyes and wet blonde hair.

Joss maneuvers himself behind me, his arms underneath my armpits, as he keeps my head above water. I try to speak, but end up coughing instead, the water searing the back of my throat as my body revolts against it.

"Just hold on for me," he says into my ear. "They're almost here."

"I'm fine here," I say, the brain fog back in full force now that I know I'm not drowning. Not dying. "I'll just stay here. With you."

"Okay, sunshine," he says, clutching me close to his chest. "You can stay with me as long as you want."

A few moments later, I'm pulled from the water and placed onto the floor of a boat where I can finally sleep.

THE remainder of the day passed in a blur, like a long-ago memory you're doing your best to remember, but the edges are still fuzzy. In the boat, I remember a sharp pain in my leg that I was too out of it to investigate, before I was taken to a hospital where I was in and out of consciousness all day. I was poked and prodded. Tests were performed. I was given an IV with fluids and who knows what else. I wasn't sure what else was done to me, but I know that Lana and Kelly were by my side the whole time. I have flashes of Kelly's worried face peeking through the hospital room doorway, of Lana's thumb stroking the back of my hand as she held it in hers.

When I was cleared to leave after a couple hours of observation, I was completely exhausted from the day but couldn't find rest. Every movement was labored, heavy. My head felt like a bowling ball, my limbs like sandbags. The journey back to camp was long, and every bump of the road, every sound of passing cars kept me from the sleep I so desperately craved. When we finally arrived back at the camp, I remember making it to my bed before finally being able to rest.

I WAKE up in my bed in our tiny cabin, and I have the distinct feeling that it's the middle of the night. I look over to find Lana sleeping, but as I stir in bed, her eyes shoot open.

"You're awake," she says, jumping out of her bed and coming to sit on the edge of mine. "How are you feeling?"

I sit up halfway, resting my back against the wall behind me. "I feel okay now," I say. "I mean, I have a headache, and I'm still confused as to what exactly happened, but I'm fine."

Lana looks at me, her eyes filled with concern, as she strokes my head, and it feels so odd to have our usual roles reversed like this. I can't think of a time I've ever let Lana worry over me, take care of me. I've always been the one to take care of her.

"So, did they at least figure out what's wrong with me?" I ask, struggling under the weight of her gaze. I drink an insane amount of water every day, so there's no way I was dehydrated. There's (literally) zero possibility I'm secretly pregnant. It wasn't *that* hot outside, so it wasn't heat exhaustion. I'm honestly at a loss. My best guess is I picked up some virus that seriously affected my performance.

Lana takes a deep breath before she says, "Dani, they found dimenhydrinate in your system."

"What? Like, Dramamine?"

The only reason I even know what dimenhydrinate is is because I'm allergic to it. It's my only allergy, actually. A memory of my dad giving me Dramamine on a road trip when I was eight years old grabs hold of me. It's an anti-nausea medication, but I wasn't really that car sick; a huge side effect of the drug is fatigue, so I'm pretty sure my dad was just trying to make me go to sleep so I would stop bothering him with questions. After taking it, I immediately felt overwhelmingly drowsy, which isn't necessarily out of the ordinary for the medicine, but soon after, my tongue started swelling, my vision went blurry, and it quickly became difficult for me to breathe. My mom eventually begged him to pull off to an emergency room where it was determined I had an allergy to the drug. I distinctly remember Dad complaining about how expensive the ER bill was going to be.

"Yes," Lana confirms, nodding her head slowly. "The drug found in Dramamine. The one you're allergic to."

"Did someone stab me with an Epipen? Is that what I felt in

the boat?"

"Yeah. Kelly alerted the team that you had a drug allergy, but we were all confused as to how it got in your system. It could've been something else, like a weird sudden illness or something, but Steph gave you the Epipen just in case. Thank God she did."

My mind feels like one of those carnival rides that not only spins but also tilts back and forth at the same time, creating a dizzying commotion in my brain. My thoughts are chaotic and disjointed, and I don't want them to land on the only way that drug could've ended up in my system before the competition.

"Do you have any idea how you might've ingested it, Dani?" Lana asks.

There's no way around it. The thought lands, and it feels like an atomic bomb has gone off in my mind.

"Naji put it in my coffee."

twenty-four

WHEN morning rolls around, I lay in bed as long as humanly possible, still not ready to face the day and come to terms with the fact that Naji sabotaged me yesterday. I'm mindlessly picking at the split ends of my hair when a knock sounds at the door. Lana, finishing up her makeup in our wardrobe mirror, crosses the short distance to answer it.

From the doorway, Lana looks over her shoulder at me, and I see a subtle grin appear on her face, before she says to our guest, "Yeah, I was actually just running to grab us some breakfast, so you can keep her company while I'm gone."

I assume it's Kelly coming to check on me. Apparently, I assumed wrong.

Before I can protest, Lana skips out of our cabin and Joss peeks his head around the door.

"Can I come in?" he asks.

As he stands there, keeping his distance for the moment, the edges of my memory grow a little clearer. Visions of him holding me, clutching me close to his chest, rapidly surface. Something warm and foreign begins coursing through me as I remember what it felt like to have his arms around me, to have him repeating my name like an oath, a plea.

I snap myself out of whatever trance has overtaken me and fall back on what feels easy. What doesn't terrify me.

"Come to see if I have to pull out of the show?" I ask. With each word, I feel more and more like a coward.

His face is unreadable, but he bites anyway. "I mean, I was hoping you'd be down for the count, but you seem to be doing okay, unfortunately."

I'm relieved to be in more familiar territory, but it quickly fades when Joss sprawls out next to me on my tiny twin bed, our bodies pressed together from the strain of his weight. He faces toward me and rests his head on one arm, giving me a full view of his bicep. My eyes naturally drift there before I quickly glance away, but it's too late. If the smirk on his face is any indication, he knows *exactly* what I was looking at.

The air feels heavy between us, but it feels like the right opportunity to say what I need to.

"Thank you for yesterday," I say, unable to meet his ocean blue eyes. I want to dive into them. Get lost in them.

When I sneak a glance at him, the weight of his gaze feels like too much, and I disseminate the tension. Again.

"I'm surprised you didn't just let me drown," I add. It's my best attempt at nonchalance.

He doesn't take the bait. Not this time.

"Yesterday was bad, Dani. I've saved more people from drowning than I can even count, but I can't explain what it was like watching you fall, watching you sink so quickly. You were so out of it, and I didn't know what was wrong with you, and it was…" his voice trails off, as he runs his other hand over his face. "Terrifying. It was bloody terrifying, Dani."

A pit has formed in my stomach that I can't shake. The conversation feels loaded, and I need to defuse this bomb quickly.

But something Joss said has reminded me of a question I had during the whole ordeal yesterday, and it's the perfect out.

"Where were the divers? I feel like someone should be fired," I say, and it draws a small laugh from him.

"They weren't exactly keeping an eye on you, since you'd already made it up to the boat. There were still seven other people in the water that they had to watch, and you know they keep a little bit of distance so they don't get caught on camera. You fell off the other side of the boat where they couldn't see you. I knew they wouldn't make it to you fast enough, so I—I dove in after you."

"Thank you" I nearly whisper, my mind unable to shake the utter terror and aloneness I felt as I was sinking to the bottom of the lake. What Joss did…I don't know if I'll ever be able to repay that.

The moment feels all too intense, and I take the copout. Again. "It's a shame you just blew your shot at the prize money, though. Should've let me drown when you had the chance."

"Oh, come off it," he groans, rolling his eyes. "You're relentless."

He pauses a moment before he adds, "But so am I."

I SPEND the rest of the day in my cabin with Lana, not ready to face Naji. I know we're competitors, but I feel so betrayed. Naji and I had grown really close since the competition began, and I viewed him as a friend. A *real* friend. One that would maybe even remain even after this show was over. So finding out that he dropped some Dramamine in my coffee to try to slow me down—even though he didn't know I'd have that severe of a reaction to it—is catastrophic. I know betrayal is part of this game, but it doesn't make it sting any less.

Eventually another knock comes at the door, and I answer it to find Dax Philipps on our cabin doorstep.

"Oh!" I exclaim, shocked to see him standing outside our cabin. We never see him around camp. I think it's a tactic to up his intimidation factor. "Sorry—hi. I wasn't expecting you," I fumble.

"Who were you expecting, Dani?" he asks with the raise of an eyebrow. *Gah*, no. He can't be insinuating what I think he is—that I was expecting Joss. Although he doesn't witness what goes down at the camp firsthand, he gets constant updates from the crew, and he's a notorious showmance instigator. I feel like he just enjoys watching them burn to the ground in fiery flames of betrayal.

"Kelly," I shoot back at him.

"Sure," he says coolly. "I came to check on you, and I also wanted to let you know that we're gathering all the teams at the Commons in ten minutes."

"What's going on?" I ask, and the apprehension has already started to build. Do they know what happened? Do they have proof that Naji drugged me?

"You'll see," Dax says, before walking away and heading to the cabin next door.

Classic Dax Phillipps response.

Ten minutes later, Lana and I walk into the Commons and take a seat at the giant black banquet table with the rest of the teams. Crew members have packed the room, squeezed into every available space that won't be caught on camera. I spy Steph, the medic, in one corner and look at her, trying to catch her eye. When I do, I mouth, *"Thank you."*

"You're welcome," she mouths back with a smile. I make a mental note to thank every crew member here a little more. They do so much for us, and I realize I really haven't thanked them enough for their hard work—stocking the kitchen, keeping our bathrooms clean, putting in insane hours to get all the action on camera. I can practically hear Penny in my mind, reminding me to appreciate everyone here every chance I can.

"Look who's alive!" Naji exclaims, pulling me from my thoughts. I say nothing as I take a seat on the complete opposite end of the table from him.

And can I just say—the *audacity*. I don't utter a word as Dax comes to stand at the head of the table, a harsh scowl on his face.

"I'm sure you're all wondering what's happening after yesterday," he begins.

After I got taken away in the boat, they stopped the competition and no one is sure what that means for the game. Will we have to redo it? I hadn't really thought about what it meant for the game; I've been more preoccupied with what's going to happen to Naji. I hope it ends with him on a flight home.

"I think we'll let the footage speak for itself.

Suddenly, a crew member hands a laptop to Dax, and he pulls up what looks to be video from one of the hidden cameras they have all over the compound. The black-and-white video looks like it's coming from a corner of the Commons with a full view of the kitchen, a timestamp in the corner of the frame.

I look at Naji, but he has no reaction, aside from amused interest. He looks like he's settling in at the movie theater; all he needs is a bowl of popcorn. How is he not shaking in his boots? He's about to be put on blast on national television.

Everyone in the room is drawn to the footage playing out over the laptop, and we all watch as I make my coffee, open up the drawer, and spew coffee everywhere thanks to Naji's fake spider. Spectacular. Naji actually has the boldness to *laugh* (along with everyone watching) at the video. Next, we see the conversation between me and Naji, and we watch as I leave and Naji grabs my cup to brew me a fresh cup. I watch intently to see when he adds something to it, but…nothing. He just presses the coffee button, waits for it to fill up, then puts it on the island and leaves, presumably heading to the van.

Less than thirty seconds after Naji leaves, though, we watch as a Twisted Twin enters the Commons, and it's impossible to tell which one it is. She grabs a water from the fridge, before she pauses, eyeing the freshly brewed coffee on the island. There's no question as to whose it is; everyone knows it's mine. Everyone here has talked about my pre-competition coffee addiction countless times; it's been a constant running joke.

The Twisted Twin stares at the coffee another moment before heading to one of the cabinets in the kitchen, and I already know which one it is. The medicine cabinet. The medical crew stocked one of the cabinets with basic over-the-counter meds that we could use if needed. Simple things like ibuprofen, Midol, melatonin, and Dramamine for the eliminated players to take to stave off car sickness on the long van ride back, if needed.

You can feel the tension in the room rising. Everyone's eyes are glued to the laptop screen as we watch the twin get not one, but *four* Dramamine pills and drop them into my coffee one by one. She grabs a spoon, stirs in the pills, and then throws the spoon in the sink, before high tailing it out of the Commons. There are a few gasps in the room before everyone goes silent once again. Less than two minutes later, we watch as I re-enter the Commons, put a splash of cream in my coffee, throw a lid on it and head out to the van.

Dax shuts the laptop with a loud clap that makes everyone jump. The entire room is silent, and even though I knew someone had intentionally sabotaged me, it's still shocking to watch. I feel sick to my stomach that someone could be so cruel, but I also feel completely relieved that it wasn't Naji. Being betrayed by an enemy is one thing; being betrayed by someone you trust is an entirely different monster. I breathe a heavy sigh of relief knowing that Naji hadn't befriended me only for him to stab me in the back.

The real question is: which Twisted Twin did it?

I look at them now, assessing their body language. For some reason, I assume it's the outwardly rude Blaire that drugged my coffee, but I quickly realize that it's Ivy who is hanging her head in shame, her twin shooting daggers at her.

Ivy.

It was Ivy.

The Twisted Twin who's supposed to be so sweet and bubbly. The smooth edge to her twin's sharp corners. The good cop to her sister's bad. It would probably be a smart idea for the crew to remove any and all heavy or sharp objects in the room because I'm pretty sure Blaire is going to murder her sister. It turns out, they are the Twisted Twins after all—or at least one of them is.

Everyone is staring at Ivy as she stares at the floor. The tension in the room is palpable, like you could reach out your hand and touch it, mold it. Finally, as the silence becomes almost too much to bear, Blaire unloads a string of expletives on her sister that would make Penny's ears bleed.

Ivy whips her head up at her sister. "How was I supposed to know she's *allergic* to it? I was just trying to slow her down a little bit!"

"Did you not think they'd see you on one of the, oh I don't know, *million* cameras around this place?"

"Well, they wouldn't have been looking that closely if she didn't almost die from it!"

I see Lana's mouth drop open out of my peripheral vision. Meanwhile, Naji and AJ have giant grins on their faces because this drama is so delicious. Sarge looks like a disappointed father, Ryder is sitting back with his arms crossed and a scowl on his face, and when I finally drag my eyes to where Joss is sitting, I expect to find him looking at the twins, but instead, he's looking directly at me. While everyone has their eyes glued to Ivy, he's looking at me, a question in his eyes.

Are you okay?

I nod. He gives me a clipped smile that looks easygoing enough at first glance, but when I take a closer look at him, I realize his fists are clasped so tightly that his knuckles have turned a bright white. His jaw is clenched, a muscle in his cheek ticking every few moments. I can see his neck vein pulsing, a heat rising up to his ears. It's like finding a dog that looks calm enough at first glance only to realize his hackles are raised.

Joss is angry.

Actually, he's pissed.

I have so many emotions whirling through my mind—shock, hurt, anger—but the fact that Joss is so enraged on my behalf makes me feel…cared for. I have no doubt that if Ford were here, he'd currently be restrained by security to keep from causing physical harm to the person who harmed me. But Joss is different. When everyone was focused on Ivy, he was focused on me, making sure I'm okay, that I'm looked after. But he's still just as angry for me. It feels good to have that type of support here.

Before anyone can say anything else, Dax speaks. And when Dax speaks, everyone listens.

"Teams, we're still determining a plan of action for how the rest of this phase will unfold, but we know one thing for sure." Dax levels his gaze at Ivy. "In all my years on *American Gauntlet*, I've never seen behavior as shameful as this. Ivy, you are a disgrace and you'll be leaving the compound immediately."

Ivy continues to hang her head, before Blaire blurts out, "What about me?"

Dax levels her beneath his angry gaze. "*Both* of you are leaving. You clearly do not have what it takes to face the Gauntlet. Pack your things and get out."

Blaire storms out of the Commons, Ivy dragging behind her. Before Ivy steps out the door, she looks back at me, shame in her eyes.

"For what it's worth," she says, "I tried to take it back. I went back for the coffee, but you'd already taken it." Ivy was the last to get in the van, I remember. She slid in only a few seconds after me. I don't buy this lame apology, though; she still could've told me to not drink the coffee in the van, but she didn't. Her apology is as hollow as her personality.

"How dare you?"

The words come from Lana, seething beside me.

"How dare you even speak to her?" She grips the table, her forehead vein pulsing as it does only when she's exceedingly angry. "You're a coward. Stop trying to save face and just get out."

And while I feel that anger too, there's one emotion that won't give way, won't cede to it.

I pity her.

Everything Ivy does is so clearly motivated by insecurity,

by this need to put others down to lift herself up. It's hard to imagine living a life as empty as that. So while I'm pissed that Ivy could've killed me, that she felt so threatened that she thought drugging me was the only way she could get a leg up, it's also just…sad. And now *both* Twisted Twins are paying the consequences. Can't say I'm sad about that.

I say nothing as the door closes behind her.

twenty-five

MY MIND is wheeling after the drama of Dramamine-Gate. Production let us know that we wouldn't be competing for another couple of days, giving me a few extra days of recovery and providing each of the teams the space to unpack everything that went down with the Twisted Twins. I'm aware that the extra days are a rare gift from the typically ruthless *American Gauntlet* producers, but something tells me they need the additional time as much as I do; they'll be scrambling to come up with a game plan after Ivy and Blaire's unexpected early departure. Either way, I'm grateful.

Just a few hours after the commotion, Lana and I are decompressing in our cabin when a gentle knock comes at the door. Before either of us can jump up to open it, Kelly pokes her head in.

"Hi girls! I hope you both are doing okay after…what happened," she says with the tenderness of a baby kitten. "I figured now would be a good time for you two to take your video call."

Lana and I shoot up out of our beds. *"Penny!"* we shout, our eyes wide with excitement.

Every season, teams are allowed one or two video calls home

to their families, and the timing of this call couldn't have been more perfect. Kelly tells us she already notified Penny that we'd be calling soon, and she leads Lana and I to a crew cabin where a laptop has been set up for us. There are, of course, cameras there to record the entire conversation, and while it feels like an intrusion on what could be an intimate family conversation, I'm also glad that the world will get to meet Penny, if only for a moment.

Lana and I are shaking with anticipation as the video call loads, and suddenly, all I see is Penny's smiling face and rosy cheeks on the laptop screen. I want to reach right through it and hug her as hard as my heart is squeezing itself right now.

"Hello, dears!" she exclaims before immediately bursting into tears.

"Aw, Pen, don't cry," Lana says tenderly.

"Oh, look at me," Penny says with her classic housewife-meets-grandma demeanor. "I know I'm crying, but I'm not sad. I'm happy. So, so happy to see you two." She smiles even wider as she wipes the tears from her cheeks. "Mom is at work, but she wanted me to say how proud she is of you. We both are."

"Aw, we love you, Penny," I say, my heart swelling with every word. "We miss you so much. Are you keeping an eye on Ford for me?" I ask because I know the subject of Ford will immediately clear up the tears.

Penny's face lights up. She looks like sunshine incarnate. "Of course I am! In fact, we've been—"

She cuts off her sentence as she looks beyond the laptop, and that's when I know Ford is in the room with her. Since he's not technically "family," he's not supposed to know that we're here and therefore can't be on the call, but just knowing that he's in the room with Penny eases the guilt I have about leaving her for this long.

But as I look back at Penny and see the mischievous look on her face, I'm wondering why she cut her sentence short in the first place.

I quirk an eyebrow. "What have you and Ford been up to, Penny?"

She smears an innocent look across her face, as she nonchalantly replies, "Oh nothing, nothing. Nothing for you to concern yourself with."

I wish I was in the room with them so I could punch Ford in the chest for keeping whatever this secret is from me.

"Mhmm," I reply. I want to press, but it's Ford we're talking about here, so I'm not too worried about it. They can have their fun, whatever it may be.

"How's the competition going so far?" she asks, changing the subject so she doesn't spill the beans, probably.

I say "Good!" right as Lana says "Hard!"

I give my sister the side eye before we ease into conversation with Penny, but a knock comes at the door all too soon, letting us know we have to wrap up our conversation.

"We've gotta go soon, Pen," Lana says.

"Seeing your faces for even a moment has just made my week," Penny says. "Now, you two just focus on doing your best. If you do your best, you're going to win. I just know it."

"We love you, Penny," Lana and I say. As Penny returns an *"I love you too!"* the call is abruptly cut off, my heart sinking right along with it. Fifteen minutes wasn't nearly enough time with her. A depressing mixture of guilt and sadness engulfs me, making my throat itchy.

Words escape us as Lana and I return to our cabin. The only sound that follows is the depthless dragging of our feet against the wooden sidewalk, our feeble shuffle an outward expression of the hollowness that follows Penny's absence. Our short call with Penny has given me plenty to ponder. Focus on doing your best, Penny had said. Had I been doing my *best*? Truly my best? I couldn't help but think I'd been letting myself get distracted with…other things. One tall, blonde, Australian other thing, in particular.

And truthfully, I need to stop denying whatever this *thing* is that I have for Joss. He and I have some sort of undeniable chemistry—something I've never felt with anyone else—but it's just that, isn't it? It's science. It's some sort of chemical reaction that my brain does when I see him. When my eyes lock with the depths of his. When he says things that send shivers down my spine. When he literally saves my life.

Gah, Dani. Stop it.

That's what it is, though. It's chemistry. But this intense magnetism that I feel when I'm around Joss doesn't mean anything, not really.

He's my competition. He lives on the other side of the world. I'm half-convinced he only flirts with me to distract me from the game. Or because he's bored here at the camp. I'm sure there's no shortage of Australian bombshells on Bondi Beach just waiting for him to return home.

But even if we were to somehow overcome all of those impossible roadblocks, deep down I know I'm not relationship material. I'm scared of commitment. I'm terrified of being left, of being cheated on, of being abandoned. All Joss sees is this fierce, competitive, focused part of me—the strong part. He doesn't know the other parts of me. The damaged ones. It's the reason I've tacked myself onto Ford like a permanent backpack; he makes me feel safe. Secure. He's given me the stability I always craved in my life. Joss is…risky. And I know deep in my soul that he's a risk I'm not willing to take.

So I just need to face that Joss and I will *never* work out. And it's time for me to focus on what *will* work out: three hundred thousand dollars in our bank account after Lana and I win *American Gauntlet*.

twenty-six

A CEASELESS pounding reverberates through my brain as soon as I open my eyes this morning. It's a bowling ball slamming into pins, a hammer beating a nail, a fist pummeling flesh.

The events over the last few days seem to finally be catching up with me. Everything has felt so heavy, so burdensome this week, and I know I've been neglecting my health. I haven't hydrated like I should, haven't fueled myself the way I usually do, sometimes skipping meals altogether. Plus, if the wrecking ball swinging through my lower belly and the tenderness I feel as I pull my sports bra on are any indication, I'll be starting my period in the next couple of days.

I knew it was coming sooner or later, since I fully planned on being on *American Gauntlet* through the final—the actual Gauntlet—which would mean I'd be here over a month.

But I'm not surprised. This is American Gauntlet and nothing comes easy, especially for women.

I begrudgingly wrench on a t-shirt and athletic shorts and drag myself to the pavilion gym. If I can push through the pain this morning, I think I'll be okay. Maybe I can take my mind off my throbbing body for a while if I'm too distracted with lifting heavy freaking weights.

The plan fails miserably. I can hardly make it through a warm up before I nearly keel over on the floor, desperately praying the migraine subsides before our next competition. We haven't been told it's definitely happening today, but I'm preparing myself like it is. It's always better to be prepared than to be surprised here at *American Gauntlet.*

I need to drink some water and try to eat something at the Commons; in truth, I should've done that before I tried to workout, but my judgment this morning has been seriously flawed. I need sustenance, but the thought of walking all the way across camp is too much to think about right now. So instead I lay on the gym floor, curled up in a ball, hoping that no competitors walk by and find me.

If I can just lay here for a minute, I'll—

"Oi!"

I don't need to look up to see who just found me in my most vulnerable position, since only one person on this compound uses the word *oi.*

I hear Joss trot over and kneel beside me, but I don't force my eyes open to look at him. I can't. After the wake up call I had while video chatting with Penny yesterday, Joss is literally the last person I want to see.

"Oi," he says again, and I feel him brush a stray hair out of my face. "You alright there, sunshine?"

I can't bring myself to ignore him outright, especially not when I can hear the concern in his voice.

I open my eyes and find myself face-to-face with him. It's overwhelming.

"Hi," he says. A smile creeps into his features, but it scarcely hides the worry etched across his face.

"Hi," I say, and it sounds breathy and weak, but not for reasons that have anything to do with my migraine.

"Are you…is this…does this have something to do with the other day?" he asks. There's a crinkle that forms between his eyebrows when he's worried, and I can't stop staring at it, knowing that he cares enough to be concerned about me in the first place. The only man who's ever cared so selflessly about me is Ford. Having another man worry about my wellbeing feels foreign and unfamiliar, but as I sit with this feeling, I realize it's not unwelcome. Joss's concern feels entirely different than Ford's, less like the well-meaning dominance of an older brother and more like…an equal.

"I think it's a combination of things," I reply.

"Oh," he says, his brow furrowing deeper. "What's wrong?"

"Splitting headache, awful cramps. I think I'm also dehydrated…" My voice drifts off, but my eyes settle on him intently. The crease in between his eyebrows remains, and he stares back at me, his eyes drifting to different parts of me as if he's studying an equation.

A second later, he wordlessly stands and walks out of the pavilion. I'm not sure if I've scared him off or if he senses I might just want to be alone in my angst, but he's gone. Once he leaves, I make an attempt at standing up that fails miserably. The intensity of this episode will pass. Eventually. I just need to ride it out.

A few minutes later, I hear someone approaching the pavilion, and I pray it's not one of the other competitors, except maybe Naji who would probably crack a joke to lighten the mood. I don't think I could knowingly lay here with Junior or Ryder or Sarge staring at me awkwardly as they try to get their morning workout in. It could very well be another cameraman here to relieve the one who is currently standing beside me, filming my agony in complete and utter silence.

Whether this is a new low for me or the cameraman is up in the air. Probably both of us.

Before I turn around to see whose presence I've been blessed with this morning, I hear Joss's voice in my ear saying, "Sit up for me, sunshine."

Why is he back? I ask myself. But before I can wrap my head around what's happening, he drags a weight bench over to me so I can lean my back against it and puts a bottle of cold water in my hand. "Here, drink this," he says. I do. And after I down half the bottle, I'm already starting to feel better.

He then drops two pills in my hand that he probably grabbed from the medicine cabinet in the kitchen. "Take these."

I give him a sideways look because, you know, fool me once and all that.

He laughs at my expression. "Ibuprofen," he says. "Don't worry, I'm not drugging you."

I take the pills, and then Joss slides a styrofoam cup of coffee in my hand. I look down to find there's a splash of cream in it, just how I like it. *He…he knows how I take my coffee?* Before the fluttering in my stomach can travel too far, I squelch it. It was just a lucky guess, I tell myself because the alternative is too much for my brain to handle. The idea that he had taken note of something so small and committed it to memory because he cares that much. *Surely not.*

As I sip my coffee, lost in this back-and-forth tennis match in my own mind, Joss pulls out a banana and gives it to me. He seats himself behind me on the bench to where his legs are on either side of me. I instinctively collapse into the cave his legs have created around me before I realize what I've done and straighten up a little, trying to put some space between us.

Joss leans down to me, and I feel his sandy blonde hair brush against my temple.

"I'm going to touch you now," he says, and I wonder if he can hear my heart beating triple time at his words. At the low, intimate way he whispered them in my ear. "Promise me you won't, like, put me in a chokehold when I do," he adds, and I feel his cheeks raise in a smile.

I swallow, unable to think clearly. "Promise," I finally say.

Joss places two fingers on each of my temples and gently presses, before he starts moving them in slow, deliberate circles. My mind is immediately taken off the headache that's been pounding in my head since I woke up, and every available brain cell is focused on where his fingers are touching me. He then places his calloused hands—the hands of a brickie—on the back of my neck and begins kneading, just like my mom used to. A whimper slips out of me because *gah, this feels so freaking good.* Joss pauses for a second, and I don't turn around to see the smirk that I know has formed on his face, before he continues, bringing his hands to my shoulders, pressing in all the right places.

I've literally melted into him, relaxing into his legs around me, and when he eventually stops massaging my shoulders, I lean my head back against his chest and look up at him. He looks down at me, and he looks so joyful. Like joy simply radiates out of him at all times. Like he couldn't possibly contain it, even if he wanted to.

"Thank you," I say, still gazing up at him, basking in the glow of him. It feels so much like bathing in the perfect summer sun.

He smiles. "Anytime."

"Where'd you learn all this? How many girls have you pulled this routine on?" I tease, even as I imagine him massaging another girl's shoulders, pressing his fingers against her back in places that send shivers down her spine. I quickly wipe the thought away, not enjoying the thing that feels a little too much like jealousy that came with it.

"I don't know," he says, grinning. "Maybe a dozen…or maybe you're the first."

I nearly blanch at what he says because just as I've resolved to close myself off to Joss completely, he nuzzles his way right back. I rip my eyes away from his, but I don't have the resolve or the energy to get up from where I'm so perfectly nestled into him.

"There's one more thing, though," he says.

"Hmm?" I ask in my half-haze.

He lowers his mouth to where it's nearly brushing my ear. "Did you know," he breathes, "that there's literally twenty-six minutes of brooding silence in the *Twilight* films?"

I burst out laughing, as does one of the cameramen in the gym with us.

"Where did you learn all of these random facts?"

He meets my eyes, then looks up, searching the horizon. "That's a story for another day," he says with an almost wistful smile.

I meet his eyes again. "Okay, well, the water, the banana, the ibuprofen," I say, "all great to cure migraine symptoms. I'm not so sure about the *Twilight* trivia."

He smiles even wider. "Oh that wasn't for you, sunshine. That was for me."

I give him a questioning look. "That was so whenever this show airs, I can hear your laugh again. You have my favorite laugh in the entire world," he says. "I think I'll record it and just listen to it over and over and over again."

Something hitches in my throat, and I don't know how to respond to *this*. To Joss saying these words that both thrill and terrify me.

The air is thick between us, but our attention is yanked elsewhere as the competition sirens begin to blare.

My thoughts contradict themselves. On one hand, I'm grateful this moment has been interrupted, but on the other hand, it feels all too difficult to ease myself from this temporary safe haven that Joss had single-handedly created for me. I don't let him see an ounce of the regret I feel as I separate myself from him; instead, I plaster the fierce look that always comes with the *American Gauntlet* competitions on my face and begin to walk out of the pavilion.

Before I can get too far, though, I turn back to him. "Thank you for…everything. Even the *Twilight* trivia." I smile almost to myself before adding, "Menace."

His eyes light up as the corners of his mouth lift into a grin.

twenty-seven

MY HAND slices through the water, seamlessly cutting through the lake's surface, before the rest of my body follows suit. I feel more focused with each stroke, like my body is generating a well of power and concentration with every movement. It's such a stark contrast from the first time I made this very swim a few days ago.

When the van pulled up to this giant lake earlier today—the same lake that I had nearly drowned in just days ago—it felt just like the nervous breakdown I had on the plane ride to LA all over again.

As I looked out the van window and realized we were indeed headed back to the same spot, my heart immediately began to beat faster. My mind started to race. My foot ceaselessly tapped, and sweat began pooling in the palms of my hands.

"You okay, sis?" Lana had asked from where I was sandwiched between her and Joss in the van. Out of my periphery, I could see her caramel brown doe eyes staring at me, wide-eyed and worried.

But before I could answer her, Joss reached over and placed his hand just above my knee. He squeezed gently, and the incessant tapping of my foot halted, as if he'd hit the pause button on whatever turmoil was beginning to smolder within me.

I observed his hand, unwittingly noting how his golden tan skin perfectly complements my olive-toned complexion. As I drew my eyes up to meet his, it was easy to forget my panic, even for a moment. I used to get distracted by the arresting blue of Joss's eyes, but now I couldn't look past how they held so much more in them—care and concern and something that looked a lot like admiration.

All of these things that were seemingly always directed toward me.

"Tell me a fact," I nearly whispered to him.

His lips formed into a small smile. "Did you know," he said, leaning in close to me like he always does, "that cows moo with regional accents?"

Before the smile could even make its way to my lips, Naji stuck his face in between us from behind, his hair coming close to whipping me in the face. "Did you just say cows moo in accents?"

"They sure do, mate," Joss said with a laugh.

When we all eventually came to stand before Dax (luckily on the lake shore instead of on top of the cliffs this time), the group was abuzz with variations of one lingering question: *Is someone going home, even though the Twisted Twins already exited the competition?* Of course, Dax wasn't in any hurry to answer it.

"Welcome, competitors, to the second part of the Endurance Phase," Dax began. "In light of recent events, we had to switch things up for today's competition. You were supposed to start from our makeshift boat immediately following the first part of the competition, but since we're starting over, I'm going to have you swim out there. Again."

Naji groaned dramatically, eyeing the sizable distance from where we stood to the vessel that awaited us yet again. "You know," he said to Dax, "we could just take one of the crew boats out there?"

Dax laughed, although it sounded more sinister than comical. "But where's the fun in that? This is the Endurance Phase, after all."

AJ leaned over to his brother, shrugging his shoulders as he said, "Hey, it was worth a shot."

"Once you make it out to the vessel," Dax said, pausing for dramatic effect, "you'll haul yourself up the same rope from before. Then you'll jump back in the water and immediately swim back to the shore here." That revelation drew a heavy sigh even from Sarge, Junior standing at attention beside him. For once, Sarge looked tired. "Once all of the competitors make it back to shore, you'll each pick up one of these weights."

With one hand, Dax picked up a spherical weight that had been spray painted gold to match the show's aesthetic. It was about the size of a basketball. "You'll hold this weight with both hands above your head. If you get tired and quit or your elbows drop below ninety degrees, you're out. The last one standing wins the competition.

"And remember, the faster you swim, the more time you have to rest before holding your weight. We'll start when everyone makes it back to shore."

"Seems easy enough," Junior said.

Dax tossed him the sphere, and Junior nearly dropped it to the ground when he caught it.

"Heavier than you thought?" Dax asked him.

"Not at all," Junior said, although his subdued grunt gave his lie away.

"If you two are done," Naji cut in, "I have a question."

Dax raised an eyebrow at him in response. "Fire away."

"You already know what I'm going to ask," Naji countered.

"Try me."

"Is anyone going home?" Naji finally asked.

"No."

The group collectively breathed a sigh of relief, and with it, I felt a weight physically lift from my chest. Another week. Lana and I get at least another week here.

"So what do we get if we win?" Junior asked.

Dax sported a wicked smirk. "Wins are always advantageous in *American Gauntlet.*"

"What does that even mean?" AJ asked with a laugh.

"That means we probably don't get anything," Naji replied, mimicking Dax's tone. "Other than bragging rights, maybe."

"So if I'm the last one standing, does it count as a win for me *and* Naji, or just me?" AJ asked.

Dax said nothing, clearly over our questions, and instead brought his whistle to his lips, sending us running into the water.

IN THE throes of the arduous swim, I continue putting one arm in front of the other, my feet furiously kicking like my own personal motor. Since only one of us needs to win, I passed Lana a while back. If I can get this win for us, it'll redeem my blunder from the first competition—not that she holds it against me; I hold it more against myself. I've always been that way. My own worst critic.

I'm not sure what Dax meant by "Wins are always

advantageous in *American Gauntlet*," but Lana and I don't have a win under our belts yet, aside from my elimination win against Benji, and I'm determined to make that happen. I'm determined to prove we deserve to be here.

I pass Ryder on my left and attempt to close the distance between me and Joss, which is admittedly futile. Joss looks like he was made for the water, like he was born to it. His long, lean limbs glide through the water so easily that he barely takes any breaths. I'm half-convinced he'll sprout fins any minute now. The years and years he's spent surfing the Australian shores have clearly paid off, but I'm satisfied to be following fairly closely behind him, taking advantage of the draft he leaves in his wake.

A few yards ahead of me, Joss reaches the rope and is out of the water in a split second, hauling himself upward before he reaches the top and dives back in. Only a minute or so behind him, I reach the rope and begin the process of climbing up again. I know I'll need every ounce of upper body strength for the next part of the competition, so I try to conserve my energy by using the footholds for assistance. I make it to the top quickly and throw my body back into the water, not stopping for even a moment to take a breath.

When I make it back to shore, Joss is lounging on the rocky sand like he's spending a normal Thursday sunbathing at Bondi. The sun is out in full force today—not a single cloud to be seen—and whereas I'm squinting my eyes and looking for any reprieve from the relentless sunbeams, Joss looks like he can't get enough of it. Like he's some sort of solar-powered human battery soaking in every last bit of it, letting it fuel him.

And that's when I realize that Joss *is* the sun; he's sunshine and warmth and happiness, and for a moment, I wonder what it's like to be like that—to be like Joss. To be so easily adored by everyone. To be daylight incarnate.

He's the Saturday sun on those radiant, cloudless days that you savor, musing with a smile, *"Isn't today perfect? I wish it was always like this."*

That's Joss.

For someone who relates more to rain clouds—cynical and untrusting, emotionally unavailable and utterly terrified of letting people in—it's all too easy to get lost in the overwhelming feeling of basking in the sun.

But I'm also quick to remember how easy it is to get burned.

"What's on your mind, sunshine?" Joss says, lifting his head up, peering at me from where he's lounging. And hearing the stupid nickname he always calls me suddenly grates against me in a way it hasn't before, rubbing against my own insecurities until they're pink and raw. I'm so clearly not the sunshiney, carefree, happy-go-lucky girl; Joss calling me by that nickname is his way of mocking me, of reminding me how much I'm *not* sunshine.

My fists clench together as heat rises to my neck—not from embarrassment, but from anger. I'm going to tell Joss to stop calling me that, to stop jeering at me with this little nickname he seems so fond of, but I don't want to snap at him like I did before. I'm always one to keep my emotions at bay; I feel like I've had to rein them in tightly around Lana and Penny, who have lacked any sort of stability in life. I've grown used to allowing my emotions to boil dangerously beneath the surface before extinguishing them completely, and I intend to do the same now. I unclench my fists, flexing my fingers out, and take a deep breath, the rage that threatened to boil over only moments ago reduced to a mild simmer.

I don't snap at him, but still, I can't bring myself to say

anything to him yet either. Instead, I look past him and that's when I notice Sarge and Junior sitting on the shore, completely dry, not a drop of water on them.

"Wait, what's wrong?" I ask, confused as to why they didn't complete the swim. I was so focused on my own performance that I didn't notice their absence behind me.

"Nothing," Junior replies, his tone even. "We just didn't want to waste our strength when there's nothing really at stake. No one is going home this week, and it doesn't sound like there's much up for grabs with a win, so we're conserving our energy."

"It's because I'm old," Sarge tacks on with a smile, the skin around his eyes gently crinkling along with it.

I let out a soft laugh because Sarge isn't that old, although he may feel that way because he's got a couple decades on the rest of us. "What's your wife going to say about this one, Sarge?"

"Hopefully she'll say it was a smart move when it pays off in the end."

I'm not upset that Junior and Sarge decided to sit this one out; that's two less people I have to worry about beating. Still, I am surprised they aren't competing. In previous seasons when teams or individuals have had to leave the game for medical or other personal reasons, the winners of the competition that week have won various things—money, prizes from sponsors, vacations even. Just because Dax didn't tell us what we get if we win doesn't necessarily mean we don't get anything. I'd rather try my hand at gambling today.

Of course, I wouldn't be surprised if we do, in fact, get nothing. Because this is the most intense season of *American Gauntlet* I've seen, and I'm pretty sure Dax Philipps and the producers are *trying* to crush our souls. I wouldn't be shocked if they put us through this torture just for the fun of it.

"Dani," I hear Ryder say from where he's dragging himself out of the water, soaking wet and huffing for air. "I don't know if Lana's going to make it."

"What?" I ask, whipping my head toward the boat-like structure and the rope dangling from it.

And that's when I see her. Lana's desperately trying to haul herself up the rope but failing over and over and over. I watch as she grips the rope with all her strength and makes it one, maybe two, feet up before splashing back into the water every time.

"She's been at it for a while now…" Ryder says gently. "I'm not sure she's got anything left in the tank."

I keep my eyes trained on Lana, watching as she tries the rope one last time before waving her hand in the air in defeat, signaling to the producers that she's done. She can't do it.

A safety diver is beside her in a matter of seconds before the producers swoop by in their motor boat to pick her up; it's the same boat that they used to transport me only a few days ago. Looks like another Di Laurentis sister has to take it for a spin now, too.

Naji and AJ finish up their swim right as the boat reaches shore. Lana is hanging her head, not making eye contact with anyone—namely, me—as she drags her feet through the rough sand. She comes to stand next to me, but I don't even get a word out before Dax is commanding our attention.

"To everyone remaining in the competition, please stand in front of a weight. Sarge, Junior, and Lana—you'll sit the rest of this competition out. You lose," he tacks on at the end, as if everyone didn't already know it.

Despite her apparent shame, Lana plasters a smile on her face and gives me an encouraging *You got this, sis* as I go to stand in front of a weight. Joss is on my right, while Naji stands to my left.

"Now pick up your weight," Dax instructs.

Joss, Naji, AJ, Ryder, and I pick up the weights from where they have been placed, balancing on a small wooden pillar in the sand.

"Very good," Dax says. "Now stand on the pillar."

"What?" everyone asks together.

"Oh, did I forget that little detail?" Dax asked in a mock apology. "You'll be standing on that pillar the whole time."

twenty-eight

I LOOK at the little piece of wood staked in the ground in front of me. The top of it can't be more than a five inch by five inch square, and it's sticking about a foot out of the ground.

"You heard me," Dax says. "Step on your pillars or forfeit."

Each of us does our best to step up and balance atop the tiny stake of wood. The surface area to stand on is so small that we each have to make a choice: put two feet on the tiny platform and essentially balance all our weight on our big toes or use one foot, balancing on one leg the whole time. I opt for the second tactic. I place my right foot on the pillar and stick my left leg out to the side to help me balance. I can't fit my whole foot on the platform since it's so small, so my toes are clenched over the front, while my heel is hanging precariously over the back. It's extremely uncomfortable. I feel the wood digging into my skin, the skin of my healed wounds peeling back, and I've only been standing on it for a few seconds.

"You fall off, you drop your weight, or you let your elbows fall below ninety degrees and you're out," Dax says. "Weights up…" Each of us lifts the weight above our heads. I feel every stabilizing muscle in my body engage to help me balance, my body nearly trembling from the strain already. "The competition has officially begun."

The words have hardly left Dax's lips before AJ loses his balance and tumbles from his pillar. He throws his weight down to the ground in frustration, sending sand flying in every direction.

I want to look at him, want to give him an encouraging word, but it's taking every ounce of concentration to stay on top of this stake. We're facing the lake, so I keep my eyes trained on the *American Gauntlet* boat in the distance, knowing looking at a stationary object will help me stay balanced. My leg muscles are tense, my core is rigid, and my arms and shoulders are already shaking from the weight. It would've been hard enough to keep this weight above my head longer than the rest of my competitors—but the balancing act along with it? It's nearly impossible.

The more I think about it, though, the more I feel it levels the playing field. Ryder is a Division One college football player. He'd beat me in a strength competition every time. But add in the endurance factor from the swim, coupled with the balancing factor…and I've got a real shot to win this thing.

Sure enough, I manage a glimpse at Ryder, who's stationed on the other side of Naji, and I can see the sweat pouring down his face. His hands, his face, his legs—they're all slicked with rivulets of sweat, and he's hardly staying on top of his platform with the sheer size of his body. I focus my eyes back on the boat before I see him fall off his pillar out of my peripheral vision.

"And then there were three," Naji says.

"I reckon I could hang out here all day," Joss returns coolly.

I don't care to respond—I can't. I can't think about anything over the burn of my shoulders and the searing pain of my foot. I can feel the rough wood cutting into my skin where my heel drops off on the back of the tiny platform, especially under the pressure of all my weight localized to that one spot. I'm suddenly not so sure how long I'll be able to last.

Naji, Joss, and I stand there for five minutes, maybe ten, but it feels like an hour. A grueling, backbreaking hour. Every second that passes is agony, and I can feel my energy depleting by the second. My foot aches. My arms are trembling above my head. I can feel my obliques tensing with every subtle movement I accidentally make to one side or the other. This competition is a special kind of torture cooked up just for us.

The pain of my foot soon overtakes everything. I'm wondering if Naji got it right with his two-foot balancing tactic, but suddenly, Naji cries out in pain, the unexpected outcry nearly throwing me off balance.

"*AGH! No!*" he howls from beside me.

"Bro, what is it?" AJ yells at him from the sidelines.

"*Calf cramp!*"

Because Naji has two feet on his pillar, it has put extra strain on his calves to stay balanced. I carefully spare a glance at him and watch as one of his calf muscles twists in a way that makes my stomach churn.

"I—I can't!" Naji yells as he drops his weight and collapses to the ground, writhing in pain at the charlie horse that has made its home in his meaty calf muscles. He rolls onto his stomach and kicks his legs in pain, sending sand spewing with every kick. When that tactic doesn't work to relieve the pain, he flips back onto his back and brings his knee to his chest, massaging the knot in his calf. Eventually he coaxes it enough to relax.

"It's just you and me now, ay sunshine?" Joss asks casually beside me, as if Naji didn't just crumple in pain and we're not precariously balanced on these tiny pillars, fighting for a win in what will eventually air to millions of people across the country.

I grunt in response; it's all I can manage. My arms are on fire. Every thought in my brain is begging me to just drop it, screaming at me that it's not worth it. But I want a competition win. To be honest, I thought Lana and I would have one at this point already, but these competitions have been brutal, so much more difficult than I expected. And while I'm thrilled I won my elimination against Benji, it's not enough. I want this win more than anything. I need to prove that I deserve to be here. I need to prove it to myself more than anyone.

"Keen to make a deal, love?" Joss asks from beside me.

I whip my head toward him and nearly fall off my stake in the process. *He just called me…no. Don't even think the word. Why did he just call me that?*

I rein in the tangent my brain is about to run down with one thought: He's distracting me. It's just the two of us left, and he'll do anything to win. *Snake*, I think to myself. The tactic nearly worked already when I nearly lost my balance.

"Not interested," I bite out. I'm angry again. So, so angry that he would resort to sneaky tactics to try to win. I channel my thoughts toward my indignation, distracting me from the physical pain searing through my body. If Joss wants a fight, I'll give him one.

"Hear me out, Dani," he says. "If you drop now, I'll split whatever I get with you."

"We don't know that we're getting *anything*, you menace. Or if we do get something, how do you know it's something that can even be split. You can't promise me anything."

Joss laughs and for a moment wiggles off balance, shooting his leg out to the side to help steady himself. A small smile forms on my lips. *Two can play at this game.*

"But if we *do* get something," he says, "I'll share it. Just drop now. There's no need to continue putting our bodies through this hell. We've still got two phases *and* the Gauntlet itself left."

"How about this?" I bite back. "You drop and I'll split the prize with you." I'm not about to let him take this win from me, not if I can help it.

"I don't know, sunshine. By the looks of it, I'm going to outlast you here." He makes a pointed look at my quivering arms, trembling dangerously above my head. "You can either drop now and split the prize. Or you can drop later and lose. Choose wisely," he says with an audacious wink. Still, while his voice doesn't sound like he's struggling, the sweat pouring from his brow betrays him.

Distraction, I think. It's all a diversion. Even if we do win a prize that can be split in two, do I trust Joss enough to make a deal like this? Do I believe he'll hold up his end of the bargain when it's all said and done? He hasn't exactly lied to me before… but he also wasn't forthcoming during our meeting at the airport. The sickening feeling I had when I felt like I'd been lied to, been taken advantage of, has returned with a vengeance. It makes me want to puke.

Or maybe it's the stress my body is under at the moment. Either way, I can't freaking think straight.

"What'll it be, sunshine?" Joss asks.

"I—"

I'm cut off by the shrill sound of Jax's whistle. It makes my ears ring.

"That's it, Dani. Your elbows fell below ninety degrees," Dax says. "You're out."

My mouth drops open. I look above me where I've suspended this stupid gold weight for the past—who even knows how long?—and sure enough, my elbows have fallen a hair too far.

And just like that, I've lost. Again.

I throw the weight to the ground, creating a giant sandy crater in its wake, and storm off to the edge of the lake. I don't want to be around anyone, and I also want to soak my foot in the water. Two birds with one stone, I suppose.

As soon as my foot hits the water, I feel like my whole body has been doused in an ice bath. And although my muscles have finally gotten some reprieve, the devastation I feel doesn't subside any less. I wanted that win so badly. I put my body through all that torment for nothing.

"Oi," Joss says, as he throws his long, lean arm around me.

I shrug it off.

"I need a moment," I grit out, still struggling not to snap. "Alone."

"Listen, Dani—"

"No, *you* listen," I say as calmly as possible; I'm not sure how successful I am in that endeavor. "This isn't just a game to me, Joss. I have so much riding on this whole competition, yet you still keep messing with me. *Distracting* me. I lost concentration for two seconds because of you, and that was all it took. You won, so your plan worked, I guess. Congratulations."

"It was a real offer, I swear—"

Dax calls us over to the group before Joss can finish, but it doesn't matter. I don't really care what he has to say anyway.

I walk toward the teams, leaving Joss in my wake. When Joss joins the group, Dax throws him a congratulatory look, a smile we rarely get to see.

"Well done, Joss. You outlasted the competition. You won," Dax tacks on with an air of finality. It's the thick period at the end of a grueling phase of competition.

Joss smiles, but it looks half-hearted, the crinkles not quite reaching the edges of his eyes. "I reckon you'll tell me what I've won then, hey mate?"

"I already told you," Dax counters. There's a devilish gleam in his eye that makes it seem like he's intentionally hiding something. "Wins are always advantageous in *American Gauntlet*."

"Righto," Joss retorts with a laugh. He clearly knows when a battle is futile. "I guess I'll add it to my résumé."

"Couldn't hurt." The nonchalant tone Dax uses does nothing to hide the ulterior motives he's hoarding. Everything Dax does has purpose, and I don't doubt there's some sort of meaning to what he's been saying—that "wins are always advantageous." I just can't figure out what that meaning is yet.

I sneak a glance at Joss and he's practically glowing in the sunlight, the infinitesimal grains of sand sparkling like a million tiny diamonds on his skin, his chest. I know I should be happy for him, for his win. Joss is my…friend. A competitor, but a friend, too. When we're not in competitions, he's been nothing but kind and encouraging to me this whole time; he's practically been an oasis when time at the camp has seemed unbearable, and yet, I can't shake the frustration I feel. That win should've been mine. I need every advantage I can get. Joss doesn't.

"Joss, you've done exceedingly well in *American Gauntlet* so far," Dax says. Everyone's attention snaps to him, our jaws dropping at the uncommon compliment from Dax. "Tell me, Joss—why are you here? Why did you choose to come on the show?"

Joss takes a deep breath and runs a hand through his hair, collecting himself. As he looks up, our eyes meet for a moment and a small smile that feels like it's packing dynamite works its way into Joss's features; before I can fully register it, he looks back at Dax.

"When I was eleven years old, I was diagnosed with Leukemia."

Oh my gosh.

"As you can imagine, it was an extremely difficult time for me, and for my family, as well. In a matter of months, I went from being a healthy, happy kid—surfing, playing sports, driving my parents insane," he adds with a laugh, "to long stays in the hospital for treatment. I was hardly able to do anything, even eat. I didn't have the energy to do anything I loved anymore. Couldn't surf. Couldn't hang out with my friends...I couldn't be a kid."

In a few short sentences, Joss has commanded the attention of everyone, including the producers and crew around us, although the producers probably already knew this tidbit about him. Regardless, everyone's eyes are on Joss, hanging on his every word.

I feel sick to my stomach.

"Oh, Dax, don't give me the pity look," Joss says with a laugh. Dax cracks a smile in return. "Look at me now, hey? You asked me the reason why I'm here and that's the reason. I want to show all the kids out there battling cancer that there's hope. If I can go from being the poster child for childhood cancer—no hair, rail-thin, on a first-name basis with the entire pediatric hospital staff—to this—being on one of the most physically demanding reality shows out there—they can, too.

"I had to work through the despair, the hopelessness when I was a kid. I didn't know anyone in my life who had cancer as a kid and beat it, so I want to be that person for kids out there. That's why I'm here."

Dax responds, but I don't register it, nor do I register any of the comments coming from the other competitors.

Joss had cancer. Not only did he have cancer, but he had it as a *child*, as an eleven-year-old boy. I can't wrap my head around how difficult that must have been for him.

I feel like absolute scum.

How dare I assume that no one else here has been through difficult times? I've been so caught up in my own circumstances that I presumed no one could possibly need the prize money as much as I do, that no one had a stronger reason to be here than me.

How dare I?

Yes, I need the prize money. Yes, I have a damn good reason to be here. But that doesn't mean the other competitors don't deserve it just as much.

This whole time, I've assumed Joss was just here to have a good time, to have a moment in the limelight, his twenty seconds of fame. But that couldn't be further from the truth. How do I know Joss's family isn't in serious debt from his medical bills or that he doesn't have some other purpose for the prize money? Or even if he doesn't have an absolute *need* for the money, he has a reason to be here. He has a reason to win.

The sick feeling in my stomach only worsens as I replay our interaction a week ago. *"I know this whole competition just seems like one big fun adventure to you—you with your picture-perfect life on Bondi Beach."*

I feel the bile rising up in my throat.

I'm embarrassed. Ashamed. I can't stomach a look at Joss as we're directed back to the van.

Instead, I sit in the very back of the van, avoiding him, like the coward I am.

twenty-nine

LANA sleeps in. I let her.

After what I learned about Joss yesterday, I'm avoiding him like the plague. I'm selfish and gutless and rotten and so supremely humiliated about how I've acted toward him that I can't bring myself to face him. Not yet.

I tossed and turned in my bed for hours last night, replaying every interaction I've had with Joss since we got here. How I've incessantly complained to him about distracting me. How I've told him time and time again how much I need to win this prize money—which, to be fair, is true—but it's how I've insinuated that he *couldn't possibly* need it as much as I do that sickens me to my core. I can't shake the image of rot and decay running through my bones where marrow should be.

And it's not just Joss, of course. Even if Joss didn't go through a huge, life-altering event like cancer, it doesn't give me the right to act this way. When it comes to Penny—and to my whole family, really—I feel like I get tunnel vision. Like I'm so focused on making sure they are loved and cared for that I lose sight of almost everything else. To a fault, no one matters as much as they do. Including myself.

So I let Lana sleep in because I know Joss eats breakfast first thing in the morning. And I know he eats first thing in the morning because he usually eats with me. I routinely drag Lana to the Commons bright and early so we can get a solid start to our day, and when we get there, Joss has two steaming cups of coffee waiting for us. Every morning.

I imagine by the time we get there this morning the cups will be cold, maybe lukewarm at best. They'll be there, though. They'll be there because despite the fact I've acted like a veritable brat to Joss, he's still made them for us every day. He's still been sunshine to me, when all I do is bring clouds to cover it up. To be honest, I don't know why he's put up with me.

When Lana finally wakes, we go about our morning routine, just a couple hours behind our usual schedule. When we finally make it to breakfast (more like a brunch at this point), no one else is there, but there are two cups of coffee waiting for us where they always are.

I'm withdrawn at breakfast. I silently drink my protein shake and eat my oatmeal, completely zoned out, when I realize something's off. Lana is quiet too. And Lana's *never* quiet.

I look up from my pile of mushy oats to see Lana staring at the floor, silently chewing her cuticles into oblivion.

"What's wrong?" I ask suddenly. The cuticles are a dead giveaway that something isn't right with my sister.

She snaps her head up as if she's on the starting block at a track meet and I've just fired the gun.

"What? Nothing!" she says. She throws in a perfunctory laugh. It doesn't work.

I feel my brows knit together as I look at her, noting the nervous energy she's just taken on.

"Lana," I say, not yet using my authoritative voice, but getting close. "Out with it."

I barely have time to pull her bowl of oats out from in front of her before she collapses onto the table in cinematic fashion. Her head is nuzzled in a nest of her arms, her lengthy hair cascading all over the table.

"*Ughhhh*," she groans from deep within her hair cocoon. She lifts her head up slightly, peeking an eye out at me. "I'm sorry, sis."

My heart rate begins to quicken; I can feel the blood racing through my veins. From beneath the table, I place two fingers at my wrist, feeling my pulse as it beats faster and faster.

"Lana," I say calmly, "what are you sorry about?" I have no idea what could be eating at my sister this much. She almost never apologizes. For anything.

She sits up so we're face-to-face, our eyes locked from across the black banquet table that's far too large for just the two of us.

Lana takes one last deep breath and huffs it out quickly.

"I didn't do the training plan you sent me. Not one bit of it."

My spoon clangs against my oatmeal dish, ringing out through the Commons and echoing off the metal walls.

"What do you mean you didn't do it? Graham sent me updates about how well you were doing and—"

She winces. Then it dawns on me.

"He lied for you?"

"Not *exactly*," she replies slowly, drawing out every syllable.

I stare at her, making her uncomfortable enough to continue.

"I, um, took his phone and texted you all those updates…then I deleted them and never told him," she says guiltily. "At least you don't have to be mad at him though!" she adds, and it does nothing to ease the blow. Lana went through great lengths to lie to me. She's *been* lying to me. My eyes twitch toward the camera crew member beside us, and mortification seeps through every inch of me. Not only did Lana lie to me—but everyone will know it, too.

The humiliation I felt earlier at my own actions has turned into fury at Lana's. *How could she do this?* This is a once-in-a-lifetime opportunity for us. She, of all people, knows that. But knowing it and truly understanding it seem to be two different things for her.

"I—" I start, but I don't know where to go from there.

"Dani, I'm so sorry," she juts in quickly. "I was so exhausted from school and track and then finals came up and I just couldn't do it. I'm so sorry for everything. I know I haven't performed like I should at a lot of these competitions. I know I've brought us down."

Lana's bright brown doe eyes are staring up at me. I'm half surprised she's not groveling at my feet with that expression.

But doe eyes aside, I'm furious with her. I never felt like she was taking *American Gauntlet* as seriously as I was, and she's just confirmed that. Tiny, pinpoint pains shoot out from where I've dug my nails into my thighs as I think of every red flag I should've already recognized: how she could hardly haul her suitcase off the belt at the airport. How she's struggled with every upper body workout we've done here at the camp. How she couldn't pull herself up the rope in the last challenge. It was all there, right in front of my face, like a glowing neon sign.

Blinders. Always the blinders with my family.

Lana knows what this competition could mean for Penny. And even if she wasn't doing it for Penny, I thought she'd have done it for herself. How many times has she talked about what she's going to do with her cut of the prize? The car, the traveling…

Furious doesn't even begin to cover what I'm feeling. I feel the rage threatening to erupt from me any moment now.

But I can't let that happen. I don't allow myself to. Not with Lana. I'd seen my dad explode on her too many times before he finally left us. I vowed to never do the same.

So instead, I stop myself.

I pull my nails out from where they've dug into my skin, leaving nasty red crescents in their wake.

I school my face into a mask of placid calm. And finally, I look at my sister.

"It's okay," I say to her. The words feel as robotic as they sound.

Her expression changes, but I don't stick around long enough to read it.

"I'm gonna get a run in real quick. I'll catch you later." I give Lana a gentle squeeze on the shoulder, a peace offering, as I pass her on my way to the door without so much as another word.

I AVOID people for the rest of the day. When I see the other competitors, including Lana, at meals, I sit with them, but I'm not there, not really. I can't get out of my own head enough to contribute to any sort of meaningful conversation.

"What's got you in a funk?" Sarge had asked from beside me at dinner, playfully tugging a little piece of my hair.

I smiled softly. "Just…preparing for the Strategy Phase," I'd lied.

I know that as I now jog lap after lap on the narrow sidewalks throughout the gravelly ground of the camp, I'm procrastinating returning to the less-than-spacious cabin Lana and I share. I'm half-hoping she's asleep when I make it back, but I know that won't be the case. She'll be waiting. I can feel it.

As I finish up my last lap, I feel like I've resolved my highly charged feelings from earlier enough to act normal when I see my sister again. After all, there's literally nothing we can do about her lack of training now. It is what it is.

The little door to our cabin squeaks as I open it. When I step inside, Lana jerks her head up at me.

"Sorry if I scared you," I say easily. She's sitting on her bed, holding a letter from Graham, another one of the letters he'd stowed away in her suitcase. She doesn't respond. She looks as if she's assessing me, probably wondering if I'm still upset with her. I don't want to let any of my frustrated feelings from earlier taint our interactions tonight. The next phase of the competition is likely starting tomorrow, and we need to be in sync if we're going to stay here another week.

I open up my wardrobe casually and grab an old, ragged t-shirt to sleep in, its threads unraveling at every seam. "Have you had a good day?" I ask cheerily.

Lana drops the letter on her bed.

"Are you freaking kidding me, Dani?"

I freeze, my shirt half way off my back, at her words, her tone. I yank it back on and stare at her, my mouth slightly agape.

"What?"

"I said, are you *freaking kidding me*, Dani?"

"Kidding about what?" I'm in a disheveled state somewhere between dismay and utter confusion.

Lana grunts loudly in frustration at me; I just have no idea why. She furiously gets up off her bed and closes the distance between us in three steps.

"What the heck is wrong with you?" she huffs.

"Wrong with *me?*" I ask, aghast. "I have no clue what you're mad about!"

"What I'm mad about?" she yells. "Dani, you should be mad at me! Livid! You should be upset and angry and, at the very least, *disappointed*," she scoffs. "And yet you walk through the door and genuinely ask how my day has been, as if nothing ever happened? I can't with you."

I can feel my mouth hanging open as I stare at her just a few inches in front of me. She looks positively murderous, her arms crossed defiantly in front of her, her forehead creased with anger. Tiny beads of sweat have begun pooling along her hairline, and as I direct my gaze back to her eyes, Lana looks completely foreign to me, like a stranger I've never met before.

"You're mad that I'm *not* mad at you?" I scoff.

"Yes!" she screams, throwing her hands up in the air. Lana has successfully rendered me speechless. I continue staring at her until she realizes I can't respond; I genuinely don't know what to say.

"Dani, you're my sister! We're only two years apart! We're supposed to be best friends who argue and get on each other's nerves and drive each other crazy until we get over it and are best friends again. That's what sisters do! Not…whatever *this* is!"

"But that's what I'm doing," I reply, my voice even. "I was upset with you earlier and now we're cool again? That's literally what you just said."

"No! That's not what happened, Dani," she yells. "You didn't get mad at me. You didn't even seem that upset that I had, one," she holds up a finger, "lied to you; two," she adds another, "impersonated my boyfriend to intentionally mislead you; three, haven't taken this competition nearly as seriously as I should have; and four," she says, waving four fingers in my face, "literally struggled through almost every single competition we've had."

"I—I don't know what you want me to say right now, Lana," I sigh, rubbing my eyes with my hands. I'm exhausted. This whole conversation has drained what little energy I had left today. "Like, obviously I'm not thrilled about any of that, but I just—"

"You're not my mom, Dani!"

Lana's words slice through me like a searing hot knife. It feels like I've been hit by a truck that Lana was driving, flooring it as she smeared my guts across the pavement. I take a few steps back from her, catching a glimpse of my reflection in the wardrobe door mirror. I look like I've just been slapped across the face.

As Lana looks at me, her eyes widen. She knows she's gone too far, but she can't very well reverse the truck she just crashed into me. The damage is done.

She takes both of my trembling hands in hers and guides me to my bed, where we both sit on the edge, our weight causing it to sink.

"Listen," she says to me, her voice soft and tender, the antithesis of what it was only seconds ago. "You're not my mom, Dani—and I don't want you to be. You took care of me and Pen all those years when mom couldn't, and I'll be forever indebted to you for that. But listen, we deserve to be *sisters* now. I know you love us more than anything in this world, but we need our sister now, not a stand-in mother."

I take a deep breath and try to process her words, try to pick my heart off the pavement and shove it back into its cavity.

"I hate to break it to you, sis, but I'm an adult now, even if I'm not very good at it yet," she adds with the barest hint of a laugh. "You don't need to take care of me in the same way you always have. You've got to let me make mistakes and deal with whatever the consequences of those mistakes are. We get to be sisters now—*real* sisters—for the first time since we were preteens, before our lives got flipped upside down. We've got a lot of angsty high school sister fights to make up for."

I robotically stare straight ahead as I attempt to disarm the nuclear bomb Lana has dropped into my chest, but I'm ripped from my stupor as I feel something wet streak down my face. Lana reaches up and gently wipes it away, and that's when I realize I'm crying. The last time I shed a tear was years ago when I found out Justin cheated on me; since then, I haven't shed a single tear. Not one. But just as soon as Lana has wiped the droplet away, the rest come pouring out—years of tears that have refused to fall, all streaking down my face like rain on a car window. But it's not the sad rain. It's like those rare days when it's raining but the sun is out at the same time. It's the kind you don't run inside from; you stay out and enjoy it and wonder at how the sun could still be shining at a time like this.

Lana holds my hands in hers as I cry restorative, healing tears, and when they finally stop, I feel physically lighter, like this experience with my sister was the last weight on the platform and the giant barrel of water just toppled, its floodwaters rushing out, all at once.

I reach out and tug her to me, burying my head in her shoulder. "So what do you want me to do now, then?" I ask her, my voice muffled from where it's nestled into her. "I might need a little help on how to be a normal sister."

She laughs and helps me up off the bed. She positions me to where I'm standing in the middle of our tiny cabin, our faces inches from one another.

"I want you to yell at me," she says, completely serious. "I want you to scream at me and yell at me and tell me how awful I am!"

We both burst into laughter.

"Are you serious?"

"Do I look like I'm kidding, Dani?"

"Okay," I say, still not sure how to go about this. I'll do my best though; I'll do my best for her.

"Lana…" I say, taking a deep breath. As I exhale, I lose my nerve. "I can't do this. I can't yell at you."

"Ugh, Dani. Yes, you can! Remember what I did? I lied to you and manipulated you and have possibly thrown our chance at three hundred grand down the drain. Remember?"

As she recounts her confession this morning, I feel that anger start to build within me. But instead of running from it, I greet it, testing what it feels like to finally let it across the threshold.

"Lana, honestly that was horrible. You're horrible!" I yell.

She laughs. "More, Dani! Louder! Tell me how terrible I am."

"You're a brat! One of the biggest brats I know!"

"Keep going!"

"I can't believe you lied to me! Actually, I can believe it!"

"Yeah? Why is that?" she yells.

"Because you're stubborn and self-centered, and you only think about yourself!"

When I look at Lana, I see the smile has fallen from her face. Her glossy brown eyes are staring back at me. I feel like I just kicked a puppy.

"Wait, was that too far?" I ask nervously. I knew this was a bad idea.

Her facade cracks and a huge, genuine grin emerges. "It was perfect," she says, pulling me into a hug. "And by the way, I do not only think about myself. I think about myself a healthy amount, whereas you never think about yourself…and I think you need to work on that."

Lana and I sit down on the cabin floor, our backs leaned up

against my bed. I let her words sink in. All of them.

"I can't just flip a switch, Lana," I say finally. "It's going to take some time."

"I know," she says, picking up my hairbrush from my nightstand and running it through my hair. It feels good to let her care for me in this small way. "But we've got the rest of our lives to practice."

Despite how close I've always felt to my sister, it feels like we're closer now than ever before. It's…different, disparate to my nature in every way, and I admit it makes me a little uncomfortable, this unfamiliar dynamic that feels almost like I've made a new friend and desperately don't want to mess things up. But in a way, I suppose I have made a new friend.

And in spite of my discomfort, I lean into it, into this new relationship with my sister. It'll be better—healthier—for us in the long run, even if there's a hint of pain, of grief, as I finally lay our old relationship to rest. It feels like a funeral, in a way, but I know new life will grow from this soil. It'll need to be watered. Tended to. But it will grow and flourish. And eventually, we'll thrive.

Lana and I eventually fall asleep, both of us sandwiched together in my tiny twin bed.

We wake up in the middle of the night to screaming.

thirty

SCREAMS jolt me awake.

Although, as I listen, they sound more like groans rather than outright screams. It's the distinct sound someone produces when they're in unmistakable pain.

Incredibly, Lana has slept through the commotion, and she's still sound asleep, even as I stir in bed beside her. As the groaning continues from outside our cabin, I jostle her until she rubs a sleepy hand in her eyes, confusion swallowing her features.

"Oh, sorry," she mumbles, "I'll get in my own bed."

"It's not that, it's—"

The groan sounds again, echoing off the corrugated metal and gravel that covers the camp, amplifying it like a megaphone.

"What is that?" Lana asks, suddenly fully awake, eyes wide.

"I don't know," I mutter. "Let's go see."

We hurry toward our cabin door and throw it open, taking a few steps out onto the sidewalk, the harsh lamplights beaming down on us in the darkness of the night. We're not alone. A slew of people—producers and crew members and medics—are dashing around in an organized sort of pandemonium. It's like watching a colony of ants, frenzied, but with a decided system to the chaos.

I hear the indisputable sound of gravel flying through the air, pelting against our shipping container cabins as someone backs a van up in between the two cabins adjacent to ours, eventually bringing it to a stop near the door of the cabin two units over. My heart drops as I realize whose cabin it is.

It's Joss's.

Naji and AJ, their hair in jumbled disarray, join us where we're stationed on the outskirts of the bedlam.

"What's going on?" AJ asks, squinting against the overhead lights illuminating the sidewalk.

"We don't know yet," Lana responds, but I hardly register their remarks. I haven't taken my eyes off Joss's open cabin door, crew members flying in and out in a fever.

The next second, a team of medics dash past our group with a stretcher in tow. Steph is among them, her auburn braid flying behind her. I feel like vomiting. Someone is obviously sick or injured, and by all accounts, it's serious. While the groaning has ceased, I replay it in my head on a horrifying loop. Was it Joss's voice? Was that the sound of him crying out in pain? My chest abruptly feels too tight, like it'll squeeze itself to death, suffocating me from the inside out.

Seconds creep by torturously slow until I see the edge of the stretcher emerge from Joss's cabin. I'm looking at the feet on the end of it, my brain trying to assess who they belong to, before the answer is clear. Joss rushes out of the doorway, helping carry the stretcher that Ryder is lying on. His body is so large that he hardly fits on the device and requires five people to carry him.

I unwittingly exhale in relief, but guilt begins to creep in before I've even begun to inhale again. I'm not *happy* that something is wrong with Ryder, but the mere moments I stood here, not knowing who was in distress, made me realize how much I couldn't stomach the thought of it being Joss. It's an ugly truth, but a truth nonetheless.

As he's carried out, Ryder clutches his abdomen, his face stricken in pain. He suddenly grunts again, and the sound, without walls to impair it now, is sickening. As Ryder cries out in agony, Joss's eyes become panicked in a way I've never seen before. My body takes a step forward in his direction before I realize what I'm doing and freeze. I can't very well just go to him, in the middle of this crisis, no matter how much I want to take his hand in mine and tell him everything's going to be okay.

Joss helps load the stretcher into the van and climbs in after the medics, but just before the double doors close, Joss looks up, his piercing eyes finding mine in the hazy night. I hold his gaze before the van doors slam shut, severing our connection like a guillotine.

Kelly strides over to where Lana, Naji, AJ, and I are standing, and I wonder how she does it, how she can undoubtedly feel panicked or—at the very least—stressed, over this emergency with Ryder, and yet she exudes an air of calmness and undeniable control. I guess being a mom of four "wild, rowdy" boys (her words, not mine) will do that to you.

"I know you all have questions," she begins, just as Sarge and Junior join us, both of them wearing gray long johns and crisp white t-shirts that are miraculously unwrinkled. They fold their formidable arms over their chests, each subconsciously mimicking the other, as they listen intently to Kelly. "I don't have answers. Clearly, Ryder is experiencing a medical emergency of some sort. He has severe abdominal pain and is being transported to the hospital as we speak. That's all I know.

"I'll let you know when I have an update, but for now," she sighs, rubbing her eyes and revealing the subtlest crack of her armor, "it's best if you try to get some rest."

We mutter our thanks to Kelly as each team shuffles back into our cabins. And while it's been what feels like hours since Lana and I stumbled into our separate beds, I'm lying awake, unable to think of anything but whatever situation is unfolding at the hospital. I desperately hope that Ryder is okay, that whatever is happening to him is a matter of simple medication or quick treatment. But while I want Ryder to be fine, I can't help thinking about Joss, of him sitting alone in a hospital waiting room, awaiting an update on his cousin. I want to sit with him. I want to be next to him in the same way he's been next to me whenever I've needed him since…well, since the day I met him.

Like a ship with a lousy anchor, my mind slowly drifts even further in my state of half-sleep. What if Ryder can't continue in the competition? Does that mean Joss is out too?

The question sends me spiraling, tumbling into the dark recesses of my dream-like state, imagining what it would be like to be here without Joss. I don't need to dwell on the thought long to know that I don't like it.

It's a terrifying concept, really. The idea of Joss leaving is scary, but the fact that I'm so scared of Joss—my competitor—leaving the game is absolutely *terrifying*. I should welcome the thought of him leaving; I should *celebrate* it.

Instead, I fear it.

I DON'T sleep. I finally bit the bullet and dragged myself out of bed and to the pavilion to work out at 5 a.m. It killed all of one hour. I ate breakfast and got ready for the day but have since found myself lying here in the gravel for an indiscriminate amount of time. I take a deep breath, letting the chilly pebbles prod against my skin in a way that isn't entirely uncomfortable.

The other teams seem to be sleeping in this morning thanks to our middle-of-the-night wakeup call, but I wish Naji or Lana were awake to distract me from my thoughts that seem to be entirely consumed by Joss. Joss has been by my side every day for the last—*How many weeks have we been here? They've all begun to blur together*—and knowing he's not two doors down from me has caused me to think of him incessantly. I hate it.

I pick up a wad of rocks in both fists before slamming them back to the ground. I'm frustrated. I can't stop thinking about Joss, and it seems like the more I try to stop thinking about him, the more he devours my every thought. I need to focus on what lies ahead; the third phase is coming, possibly *today*, and yet, I haven't thought of it once this morning.

I jerk up out of the gravel as I hear the pronounced sound of the *American Gauntlet* van in the distance, wheels crunching against the dirt road that leads to camp. Every embittered thought flees my mind at the thought of Joss being back here, at camp, with me. My heart pounds annoyingly as I see the van drawing closer, the small dot in the distance growing larger by the second. Is Joss back? Is Ryder better? Or is the van devoid of the cousin duo, carrying back producers and medical staff only?

My heart sinks as I see two producers, Steph, and several other medics exit the van. He's not here.

But not more than a second later, I see the undeniable silhouette of Joss stepping out of the van, the sun silhouetting him at his back, and I can't help myself. I wait for the crew to disperse before I break into a jog, no one around to witness me running to my competitor. Running to Joss.

He's turned away from me, looking out toward the sun rising

on the hazy, golden horizon, but he hears my feet pounding against the ground and turns around just in time for me to throw my arms around his neck. He wraps his arms around my waist and lifts me up, pulling me tight against him, squeezing until I can hardly breathe. He can't see the smile that has materialized on my face, but something tells me he's wearing one to match.

With my arms wrapped around him, I release a breath, a heavy sigh of relief, before breathing him in the next moment, taking in the smell of coconut and spearmint and savoring the feel of his skin against mine.

"Hi, sunshine," he breathes into my shoulder.

"Hi," I say into his neck. I can't help noticing the goosebumps that appear on his skin as I greet him, my lips mere centimeters from his skin.

He sets me down and hooks his index finger underneath my chin, lifting it toward him.

"Careful," he says, eyes gleaming. "Someone might think you missed me."

"Menace," I say, smiling softly and basking in the glow that always seems to surround him. How could I possibly fight this… *whatever* it is I have for Joss? Why would I push this feeling away when it feels so right when we're together?

Just as suddenly, reality sets in and I remember why I'm here. I remember what winning could mean for my family, for Penny. *That's why you're fighting it, you idiot. He's standing between you and everything you've ever hoped for.*

I take the smallest step back, putting distance between us, and while Joss's smile remains, it doesn't meet his eyes, not anymore.

"How's Ryder?" I ask, shepherding our conversation into safer territory.

Joss's face falls, as if the moment we had distracted him from whatever reality he's facing.

"He's okay. It was his appendix. It ruptured, and they had to perform an open appendectomy," he says, sighing. "He's fine now; he's stable and recovering. But he's out, Dani. He can't continue in the competition."

"Joss, I'm so sorry," I reply, grabbing his hand and squeezing it before quickly dropping it. "Did the producers say what this means for you? Do you have to pull out of the competition?"

I should want him to say "yes," but I can't bring myself to think it.

"I asked them, but they didn't give me an answer. You know how they are," he says, running his hand through his hair. "They're so secretive. I'm sure Dax will give me the news when he's drawn out every bit of drama he can."

"Yeah." I'm trying to process the information and the potential outcomes and my feelings all at the same time. "You should eat something," I finally say.

"Yeah, okay. Will—" he pauses, eyes meeting mine. "Will you come with me?"

"Yes," I say, grabbing his hand and leading him toward the Commons, trying not to give away the mix of butterflies and panic his simple question catapulted into motion.

I don't know what to do with this feeling—this feeling that maybe he wants to be with me as much as I want to be with him.

PHASE THREE

****

strategy

thirty-one

"JUST picture it, sis. Croissants in France. Pasta in Italy. Waffles in Belgium—they actually have good waffles, right? Or is that not a thing?" She pauses before continuing, "Regardless, it'll be the European vacation of our dreams. We can see it all, everything we've ever imagined."

"Are you sure you're not just hungry?" I tease, drawing an eye roll from Lana.

"I'm serious," she says, narrowing her eyes at me.

"It'll be amazing, Lana," I say, the teasing gone from my tone. "Make sure you and Graham send lots of pictures, so I can live vicariously through you two." I laugh, before placing our Greek yogurt bowls on the banquet table in the Commons and taking my seat across from Lana and next to Joss. Sarge is silently eating his eggs at the opposite end of the table. "But make sure you get your car first, and then use whatever you have left over for the trip."

"You know, you could always stash some of our prize money away for yourself and come with us," she replies as casually as possible.

"And third wheel with you and Graham on a romantic European vacation? Yeah, I'll pass." I don't mention the fact that every penny of my half of the prize money will go to Penny. She knows this fact already, yet she's still prying.

Joss chuckles beside me. Even after hearing his laugh for weeks straight, I feel the corners of my lips curling into a grin, the perfect harmony of his laugh instantly sending a shot of serotonin straight to my brain.

"Just bring someone with you!" Lana says, before blurting out, "Joss, you want to come to Europe with us?"

I nearly spew my coffee everywhere, but Joss is entirely unfazed. "I'm in," he says, raising an eyebrow at me. It's a challenge, clear as day.

"You know, it's a shame. You'd have to pay for this vacation out of pocket, since Lana and I will be taking home the prize money."

"Is that so?"

"That *is* so," I reply, my tone matter-of-fact. "It doesn't matter, though, since I won't be going with them."

"You're no fun," Lana says, rolling her eyes.

"I'm—"

I don't have the opportunity to finish my sentence, as a blood-curdling scream cuts me off mid-thought.

Lana, Joss, Sarge, and I all jump up from the table as one.

"Who was that?" Sarge asks, already rounding the corner of the table and taking control of the situation.

"It had to be a woman, right?" Lana asks, judging by the pitch of the scream. "Dani and I are both here, so it had to be a crew member?"

"Oh my gosh," I say, starting to run toward the door. "Kelly!"

The four of us run toward the crew cabins with a wolf pack-like unity. I'm tailing just behind Lana when our group suddenly comes to a grating halt, our feet sliding against the tiny rocks beneath us. Each of us almost slips backward like we would if we'd stepped on a banana peel. It would've been humorous if not for the disconcerting alarm marring our circumstances.

My brain attempts to process the scene unfolding outside of the bathroom, a plethora of emotions ranging from panic to confusion to bewilderment unfolding in quick succession, like snapshots from an old projector.

Our group watches as Junior, wearing only a bath towel knotted around his waist, sprints in jagged zig zags outside of the bathroom cabin, his eyes blown wide in a state of hysteria. At first sight, I can't determine what has overcome him, but as I take a closer look, I notice he's being *chased* by something.

Is…is that a snake?

"Help! Help! Somebody get it away from me!" Junior shrieks in a voice that sounds entirely alien. The pitch is several octaves higher than usual; the look of sheer terror on his face isn't helping matters.

My brain takes in the scene in rapid bursts, and when I look to my left and see Naji rolling on the ground in tears, I understand what's happening. Naji has tethered a fake snake to fishing line and clipped it on the back of Junior's towel so that no matter where he runs, the snake appears to be chasing him. Junior jumps around with high knees, as if he's running on hot coals, trying to shake the snake, and soon enough, his towel drops completely; in a panic, he picks it up and thrusts it onto the snake in a last-ditch effort to outrun it.

"Holy. Smokes." Lana says beside me. "It's…it's like a train wreck. You want to look away, but you just can't," she says, before all of us keel over, clutching our stomachs in laughter.

Junior runs back into the bathroom and soon peeks his head around the corner of the doorway, eyes alert and searching for his adversary. He squints his eyes, investigating, before they land on the (rubber) snake, and in one second flat, his terrified expression transforms into pure, unadulterated rage.

"NAJI!" he screams. *"I'M GOING TO MURDER YOU."*

In between heaving breaths of laughter, Naji yells, "Well, come on then, Junior!"

Junior takes a step outside of the bathroom before remembering he's completely naked, his eyes shooting up to the camera crew around us, and while they've tried to remain professional, every member of the crew is holding their fists to their mouths, struggling to keep in their amusement.

"Pops!" Junior yells. "A little help here!"

Sarge hasn't stopped laughing and can hardly utter a response.

"Sor—sorry, Leslie," he says, cackling. "You're on your own here."

"Leslie?!" AJ shouts from where he's joined the commotion. "That's your real name?"

Junior shoots him a murderous glare. "Why do you think I go by Junior?"

"Is…is Junior supposed to be better?" AJ asks amusedly.

"Be proud of your name, son," Sarge crows. "It's a family name!"

"I, for one, love the name, Leslie and Leslie Junior," Joss says to Sarge and his namesake.

"As soon as I get dressed, you're dead." Junior glowers at Naji in a way that is genuinely terrifying.

"You should have seen him packing his suitcase," AJ muses to us. "Nearly half of it was full of his prank gear."

Naji doesn't respond to Junior's threats. He can't. He's still laughing.

But the merriment comes to a screeching halt, as sirens suddenly blare across the compound, pitching us from our laughter-induced stupor.

Phase Three: Strategy is here.

And it's also time to find out Joss's fate now that Ryder's gone.

MY COMPETITORS and I form our usual semicircle around Dax, who glowers at us behind jet-black sunglasses. As the sun peeks through the clouds, it illuminates the top half of Dax's face, and the numbered scars around his eyebrows and forehead from his lengthy MMA career become even more pronounced. While some people might view scars as unwanted blemishes, Dax wears them like a badge of honor; he paid for them in blood, after all.

We didn't take our typical van ride today; instead, we're standing a football field away from camp, the sun hanging above the mountains surrounding us. If I wasn't anxious to get going with the impending competition, I'd be in awe of how truly beautiful my surroundings are, but I'll allow myself to admire the natural beauty around me when Lana and I have $300K in our bank account.

Dax takes his time before he speaks to us, and every second is misery. I need to know Joss's fate in the game, but as I catch a glimpse of him to my left, he looks every bit the laid back, easygoing surfer that he is. For a moment, I envision a gangly eleven-year-old boy, bald and pale, enduring months of leukemia treatment. I suppose when you've faced death itself and come out of it triumphant, you don't sweat the small things, and while Joss's *American Gauntlet* fate doesn't feel small to me, it pales in comparison to what he's braved in his life.

Selfishly, I want him to stay. Deep in the pit of my stomach, I know I need him here.

What a terrifying thought.

Still, winning this cash for Penny trumps any feelings I may or may not have for Joss, but I'm greedy. I want to have my cake and eat it too. I want Joss to be here as long as possible before Lana and I ultimately beat him in the Gauntlet.

And while we live a world apart and I know there is absolutely no future for Joss and me, I just want to soak in his warmth, his joy, a little while longer. The way I feel when I'm around him… I've never felt it before. I'm not ready to let it go. Not when I've barely had enough time to even try to understand it.

"Welcome, competitors, to Phase Three: Strategy." Each of us hangs on Dax's every word as he addresses us, a group of dedicated parishioners come to hear our weekly homily. Dax's sermons, however, only ever bring challenges, never comfort.

Dax flashes a wolfish smile; it's anything but merciful.

"I'm sure you're curious what today's competition will entail."

Now that he's mentioned it, I *am* eager to learn what today's competition will be since there are absolutely no indicators around us. No equipment. No grand structures or heavy objects. Nothing to hint at what we'll be begging our tired bodies and exhausted minds to do today.

"To take on the Gauntlet, you've got to be strategic. Cunning. Calculated." Dax punctuates every word like a knockout punch, the one that turns the lights out before you even realize you forgot to pay the bill. Dax gives one final raise of his eyebrows before finally saying, "Let's begin."

The group nearly lurches forward in anticipation. It hangs heavy in the hot, dry air, each of us breathing it in with each inhale.

"All you have to do today," Dax declares, "is answer one

simple question. There is no right or wrong answer. No one will be eliminated based on your answer. But there will be consequences."

"Is…is that supposed to be some kind of riddle?" Naji asks, his voice always teetering on the edge of comedy.

"Not a riddle. A question. Simple as that."

"What 'consequences' are you talking about?" AJ follows up, emphasizing the word "consequences" with air quotes.

"Ah, yes. Well, that's for you to determine, isn't it?" The sun hits Dax's eye at just that moment, accentuating the gleam that appears when he delivers his infamously vague statements.

"If you two are done," Junior interjects, glaring at Naji and AJ, "I'd like to hear the question."

Dax obliges.

"Each of you, individually, will have a choice," Dax says, each syllable hefty and deliberate. "Here is the question you must answer: Do you want to continue in this competition as a team with your current partner? Or do you want to…switch things up?" he asks, a hint of mischievousness seeping into his usual menacing demeanor. "You'll have the option to continue in *American Gauntlet* with your current teammate, choose a *different* teammate, or choose to play as an individual. You will not have time to consult your teammate. The time to make your choice is," he glances at his watch, "right now. Let's find out if blood is truly thicker than water."

Naji's eyes go wide at the opportunity before him, but this "strategy move" is simple for Lana and me. Obviously, we'll continue as partners. It's not really even a question for us, and I doubt it will be for any of the other duos either, no matter how much Naji is playing up the drama of the moment. I don't think anyone is about to jump ship on their family member that doubles as a teammate.

While the question isn't up for debate for me, the one facet I hold onto like a lifeline is the fact that Joss can stay. He can continue as an individual. He doesn't have to leave the game. Part of me wonders if the producers invented this option as a ploy for it to make sense for Joss to stay. It wouldn't surprise me, since I have no doubt he'll charm the pants off America when the show airs. Viewers will eat him up, the tall, tan, strikingly handsome, and deeply kind man that he is. I'm sure the accent won't hurt either.

On the other hand, the *American Gauntlet* producers are a special type of cruel, so I wouldn't be surprised if they planned this part of the competition as a way to stir up some chaos. I wonder what the Twisted Twins would have done if they were still here. Something tells me we would've witnessed some family drama firsthand.

"By the way, if you choose another teammate, they'll need to accept. It must be mutual. Got it?" Dax asks.

Each competitor nods before Dax turns to Sarge and Junior standing at one end of the semicircle.

"Sarge," he says. "What'll it be?"

"If he'll stick with this old bag of bones," Sarge says, playfully elbowing Junior beside him. Junior doesn't flinch. "I'd like to stay with my son."

Dax raises a questioning eyebrow at Junior.

Suddenly cracking through his stoicism, Junior takes his dad into a half-headlock, half-hug.

"Wouldn't have it any other way, Pops." Sarge smiles before Junior tacks on, "And you're extremely dramatic for a middle-aged man who can lift more weight than everyone here… combined."

"It sure doesn't seem like it after these weeks here," Sarge jokes.

"Naji," Dax says, turning to the disorderly brothers. "What's your decision?"

"Any takers?" Naji asks, looking around exaggeratedly at the rest of the competitors. "Dani? Joss? Junior, I know you're just dying to team up with me."

We all laugh at Naji's antics—everyone, that is, except for Junior, who is still clearly entertaining murderous thoughts after Naji's shenanigans this morning.

"You're the worst," AJ gripes.

"Kidding, kidding!" Naji says, ignoring Junior's death stare and his brother's annoyance. "Me and AJ gotta see this one through to the bitter end."

"Agreed," AJ adds.

I can only imagine the producers are disappointed at the lack of drama unfolding; they clearly missed their target reaction from each of us.

"Dani," Dax says, meeting my eyes directly. "What'll it be?"

I throw an arm around Lana. "We're sisters," I say, accentuating the word. No one will pick up on the extra emphasis, aside from Lana. It's my offering to her today. I'm working on being a sister, not a mom. For her. "We're in this thing together."

Dax shifts his gaze to Lana, a silent question hanging between them. A formality, really.

Curiously, Lana shimmies from beneath my arm. I figure I've probably trapped her hair beneath the weight of it, pulling it uncomfortably.

But mere moments later, Lana meets Dax's gaze, not giving me a second look.

"I'd like to continue as an individual. Alone."

thirty-two

A GRENADE just exploded into a million tiny bits beside me. At least, that's what it feels like. My ears are ringing at a criminally high pitch. I suddenly feel dizzy, nauseous. My body is rebelling, and my mind has simply turned to scrambled eggs.

I've clearly misheard my sister because there's no way she's serious. She—she can't just *abandon* me. Not after everything we've been through.

"Interesting," Dax replies, a study in nonchalance. He could teach a master class on the art of apathy. "Dani, I'll return to you in a moment. Joss, what—"

"What? No!" I interject, my words coming out much louder than I intended. "No," I add, more quietly this time but none less urgently. "We're not splitting—we're not splitting up. I just need a second to talk to my sister." I can't even breathe her name.

Dax swallows a look that tells me this is exactly the type of juicy stuff the producers were looking for with this fun little twist in the game.

"No time for discussion," Dax says. His tone comes across in a way that feels almost patronizing, instantly rubbing against my patience like coarse sand.

"No need to discuss anything anyway," Lana replies from

beside me, her voice nearly matching his in its condescension.

It feels like…like I'm the butt of the joke. Like no one could possibly want me as their teammate. Lana clearly doesn't; she jumped ship the first opportunity she got. And to put it plainly, I'm confused. I felt like we had made so many strides in our relationship these past few days, but clearly it hadn't been enough for Lana. She's still resentful of me; that much is clear. How long has she felt this way? Like I'm some overbearing wanna-be stepmother on a power trip? How long has she harbored this bitterness, letting it fester until it finally erupted?

Or maybe it's not resentment. Maybe it's greed. Maybe half of the prize money simply won't cut it for her; she wants the whole thing.

So many feelings are soaring through my head at lightspeed. Anger. Frustration. Pure bewilderment. But I refuse to believe that the Lana I know—the sister I've loved and grown up with—could be this cruel. On the other hand, though, she's completely blindsided me on national television without so much as a whisper of warning. Was it due to a lapse of judgment on her part? Or was it malicious intent?

"Joss," Dax says, slashing through my thoughts. I don't even register what Joss says back to him, as I nearly hyperventilate trying to process this betrayal of epic proportions by my rash, unthinking sister.

How thrilling for this breakdown to be filmed for millions of viewers to watch! How exciting to be deserted by one of the only people I truly trust in this world!

I don't register a thing Joss says, not until he says the words, "Whaddya say, sunshine?"

I whip my head so fast that it sounds like I've just had an alignment at the chiropractor.

"What?"

The corners of Joss's mouth curl. "I said, whaddya say? Do you want to be my partner? I think you and I should have a go at it."

If I weren't in the middle of a crisis, I'd let my mind linger on how the word "partner" sounds coming out of Joss's mouth, how he pronounces it like there isn't a single 'r' in the word. I'd dwell on this feeling—this feeling of being chosen. Wanted.

But I don't have that luxury. I need to make a potentially life-altering decision. And I have all of ten seconds to do it.

"What'll it be, Dani?" Dax prompts, as I stand there, my mouth still propped open like a fish.

My eyes fly up to meet Joss's, and as soon as our gazes connect, I know what my answer will be. I'd be an idiot not to accept his offer. He's been dominating the competitions, and with both of our strengths combined, I think we'd give the Gauntlet a run for its money. We probably have a better shot of winning than if I were to still be partnered with Lana.

Gah, even just thinking her name makes my stomach roil.

"Dani. An answer. Now," Dax demands, impatient now with my apparent indecision.

Without a second glance at my sister, I look Dax Philipps straight in the eye.

"I accept."

LANA avoids me the rest of the day, and I avoid everyone else, including Joss. I have no idea what this means now. I have no idea how to act. I have no idea how to feel.

I had grown used to this dynamic that had formed between Joss and I, a clear and easy barrier to hide behind. While the lines between competitor and friend had somewhat blurred during the endless idle hours we'd spent together at the camp, there was a stark, crisp line in the sand when it came to competitions. He was my competition. I needed to beat him in order to get to that prize at the end of the Gauntlet.

But now…

Now I just don't know. Joss and I are on the same team. We're *partners*. And I'm just not sure what that means for us.

Since my last relationship debacle, I've always been self-reliant, never anchoring my happiness or success to another person. I'd learned my lesson with Justin, and after a devastating season, I had come out the other side stronger. Wiser. Even when I was partnered with Lana, I was never truly reliant on her. It was always clear that I was driving the ship, I was calling the shots. I came up with our plan (even if she chose not to follow it).

This dynamic with Joss would be unfamiliar at best, a disaster at worst. Who knew if we would even make good partners?

Only one way to find out, I suppose.

I return to our cabin, and I know the inevitable is coming. When I walk through the door, Lana looks up at me from where she's seated on her bed. For a moment, I think she'll say something, but then she looks down, as if I'm not even there.

"Lana," I say.

She keeps her head down, avoiding me. I'm not sure if it's out of contrition or spite.

"Lana?" I ask, as if she didn't hear me before. "Are we going to talk about what happened earlier?"

She looks up, indifferent.

"What's there to be said?"

I bite back a scoff. "What do you mean what's there to be said?

An explanation would be a great place to start."

She sighs, meeting my eyes again, but her expression is entirely unreadable. In this moment, my sister is a complete stranger to me.

"I don't know what you want me to say, Dani. I don't want to be your partner anymore. I thought that much was clear."

Each word is a slap to the face. Lana knows every crack in my armor, every weakness, every insecurity. She knows being tossed aside like this is my greatest fear. She knows how much her words are hurting me, yet she chose to say them anyway. Rage builds within me, and while I'd usually fight it with every fiber of my being, Lana herself had asked for a sister.

So she'd get one.

"Are you really that greedy? You want the whole thing, don't you? Every last dollar for yourself," I scoff. "I can't believe you'd do that to Penny. I'm starting to think I don't know you at all."

"Maybe you don't, Dani!" she yells. I stifle a wince. "Maybe if you weren't so focused on controlling every aspect of my life, you'd know me better than you do."

"Oh, yeah? So I'd have known you're actually rotten to the core?" I laugh. "I should've never come here with you."

Lana, her face a fortress of granite, meets my eyes. "Maybe so. But now, my best path to the end of *American Gauntlet* is without you."

"Selfish," I mutter, loudly throwing open the wardrobe doors and yanking my shirt off my back.

"I tried to tell you before. You think I'm selfish because you never put yourself first. Don't blame me for doing what you can't," she spits.

I turn to her, scoffing. "You won't last ten seconds in the next competition by yourself."

She stands from her bed, turning her sheets down and sliding under them, as if we weren't having the biggest argument of our lives. She looks smug as she asks me, "You really think that, sis? The strength phase is over. I'm faster than you. I've got just as much endurance. I'm college educated. I think I'll do just fine on my own." She pauses before punctuating the end of our conversation. *"I don't need you, Dani."*

I—I can't handle this side of my sister. The cold side. The cruel one. It's disparate to everything I thought I knew about her, and it's too much for me to comprehend. The cabin suddenly feels too small, as if the metal walls are pushing in on me every second. My breathing grows quick and shallow, and I feel cold sweat prickling at my forehead.

I need to get out of here.

I bolt to the door and slam it behind me, not caring who hears. I'm running, not sure where I'm going, before the building beside me suddenly makes it clear. I rush into the bathroom and shut myself in a stall, knowing it's one of the only places on the compound where cameras can't find me. I suddenly feel wet streaks running down my cheeks, but crying feels entirely different than it did a few days ago. It's not healing. Not cathartic. The tears are miserable and angry and sour, and they only compound every bitter emotion I'm feeling.

I always thought that someone else would be the villain in this cutthroat game, but what the Twisted Twins did pales in comparison to this treachery. Apparently, I didn't need to worry about the other teams; it turns out, my throat would be slit by my own sister.

It's difficult for me to come to terms with the Lana who wiped my tears and brushed my hair and showed me so much love mere days ago to *this* version of Lana. The love she'd given to me was tough love, yes; but it was genuine. It wasn't self-serving. It brought us so much closer together; at least, that's what it seemed like at the time. I think it's why this betrayal is so catastrophic. How had we gone from being in a better place than ever before to this absolute disaster? Is it really that bad being my teammate that Lana thinks her only path to success is without me?

She'd said she can handle herself. She's an adult now. She doesn't need me.

I just didn't think that meant she also doesn't want me.

thirty-three

"WHAT did that poor drawer ever do to you?"

I squint at Naji, his eyes alight with amusement, before looking down at the drawer that had popped open again because of the excessive force I used to close it. I'm clearly still angry after the—fight? discussion? complete and utter disaster?—I had with my sister last night, and I've turned to taking my rage out on inanimate objects. Better than animate objects, I suppose.

I give Naji a look that voicelessly says, *"Ask me another question and you'll find out."* Intelligently, he backs away, both hands in the air in the universal sign for, *"I surrender."*

At that moment, Joss enters the Commons, and it's always as if his presence sucks all the oxygen out of the room. You'd think I'd be used to it by now, but even still, I inhale sharply, my greenish hazel eyes looking up to meet a pair of glacial blue ones.

It's difficult to feel enraged when Joss smiles at you as if you're his favorite person in the world. I'm not sure how he does it—how he makes everyone feel important—but as I catch the wide grin he throws at me, I feel my mood lighten ever so slightly.

"Ah, there's my partner," he grins, striding toward me. "Just the girl I was looking for," he says, his Aussie accent turning "girl" into *"giyl."*

"Proceed at your own risk," Naji tosses over his shoulder.

I glare at the back of Naji's head, his bun bobbing up and down as he walks, but he doesn't glance back. I'm half-convinced if he had, he'd have been turned to stone beneath my glower.

Joss leans down, resting his forearms on the island in front of me, his fingers interlocking together. A strand of blonde hair drifts into his eye before he throws it back with a shake of his head.

"How are we today?" he asks, and while there's still a degree of levity to his voice, I can tell he means the question.

"We're…fine," I finally reply, even though we both know it's a lie.

He frowns, and I suddenly get the urge to rub my finger across it, tracing the curve of his lips under my thumb. It's always been obvious how attractive Joss is, but it's not until this moment, with his long, lean body draped before me and a pair of devastatingly blue eyes piercing holes into mine that I realize Joss is the most attractive man I've ever seen.

His appearance has always drawn me in; from the very first day when I thought he was "airport-hot-guy Kellan," he was alluring. But I've felt myself drawing closer and closer to him as he's revealed more of himself to me. It's like taking a casual dip in the shallows, but then looking down and realizing you're in the deep end. It's simultaneously thrilling and alarming, knowing I'm so far gone and knowing this only ends one way.

Joss and I, our days are numbered. I need to remember that.

Joss suddenly stands up, clapping his hands together. "Righto, you're coming with me. Go get changed."

"Oh yeah?" I ask, raising an eyebrow at him. "And where, exactly, are we going?" Our options are obviously limited here at the camp.

"You'll see," he replies simply. "It's time for a team training exercise with my new partner, I reckon. Consider it *team building*," he adds, his tone edging on playful.

I laugh. "Alright. But what am I supposed to change into?" I ask, glancing down at my running shorts and tight athletic crop.

"You won't need much. Just put on your bathers," he says, before adding, "and your thongs."

"Excuse me?" I blanch, nearly spewing the water I just sipped. I suddenly feel heat rising to my neck, my ears.

Joss chuckles. "Sorry, what do you Americans call them? *Flip flops?* We're going down to the lake, Dani. You just need flip flops to get there."

I exhale fully, letting the relief seep into my skin.

"Right," I finally say.

Joss laughs again, before adding, "I mean, when you think about it, our Aussie term makes the most sense."

I groan. "I'll meet you there, menace."

"See you soon, sunshine."

AFTER splashing some cold water on my face in a desperate attempt to remove the flush that's permanently residing there, I change into my "bathers" and walk to the lake just over the hills to one side of the camp. There, I find Joss waiting for me with a single white and aquamarine blue paddleboard that I assume he pulled from the equipment shed.

I toe off my flip flops—or *thongs*, if you will—and shimmy off the shorts I put on over my bathing suit. Out of my peripheral vision, I watch Joss readying the paddleboard, inspecting it closely. Apparently pleased with its condition, he glances up and catches sight of me for the first time. He stills, freezing his gaze as it settles on me. He lets it linger there before I see him swallow slowly, his Adam's apple bobbing once. I busy myself, setting my clothes aside, before I finally bring my eyes to his. He drops his gaze, suddenly preoccupied with the paddleboard in front of him, but I don't miss the grin that follows or the way his cheeks flush for the first time since I've met him. It's impossible not to feel flattered.

With such a muscular build, I've always felt confident in my skin, knowing the hours and hours of brutal work it took to get here. I'm thankful for my body, my muscles that are capable of lifting excessive amounts of weight and bringing me through this back-breaking competition. I'm grateful for it, for this powerful body of mine. But, like all bodies, not all men are attracted to it. I'm definitely not every guy's "type," and it takes a secure man to see my solid, sinuous muscles and the raised veins running down my arms and not be intimidated by them.

The look Joss gives me tells me he clearly isn't.

As if he could read my thoughts, Joss clears his throat, and I immediately pull my gaze away, taking in the late afternoon sun over the lake. I close my eyes, breathing in the fresh air, listening to the hum of insects and the quiet lapping of the waves as they languidly grace the shore. I squelch the coarse sand in between my toes, relishing the cooling effect it has as I dig deeper.

"You ready?" he asks, his voice huskier than usual.

"Ready," I reply, taking in the moment in one final breath. When I finally bring myself to open my eyes, I'm confused. "Wait, where's your paddleboard?"

Joss grins. "Right here."

"Then where's mine?"

His grin broadens. "Right here."

I feel my eyes go wide, even as Joss's smile grows even larger.

"We're getting on this *together?*"

"We're partners now, Dani. We need to be able to work together—to trust each other. We should probably work on our team dynamic before we're thrown into the next competition together, ay?"

I swallow. He's right, of course.

"Yeah…" I reply, still unsure about how exactly this whole thing is going to work. "Just beware, I've never paddleboarded before. You've been warned."

He laughs, picking up the paddleboard, his muscles flexing and straining as he maneuvers it into the water.

"Something tells me you'll be a natural."

SO IT turns out, I am not, in fact, a natural.

It took me no less than fifteen attempts just to stand on the paddleboard myself, much less with a whole other human being on it. Joss had me practice standing up by myself a few times before we attempt to stand on it together.

Having finally maneuvered myself onto the board, I kneel down, lowering my center of gravity, waiting for Joss to get on behind me, unsure how he'll possibly be able to get on without sending us toppling back into the water.

But just as the doubt has sunk its teeth into the caverns of my mind, Joss seamlessly guides his body onto the paddleboard and stands up behind me, something that could only be done by someone who has done this very action an unquantifiable number of times on a surfboard.

"Your turn," he says. "Up you go."

I feel like my knees are plastered to the board. As I make even the slightest move to stand up, the entire paddleboard rocks precariously.

"I can't," I huff. I enjoy trying new things; I really do. But it's difficult to try something new with someone who's already a pro at it. It's definitely a blow to the ego, but maybe that's not such a bad thing.

"Yes, you can," he says encouragingly. "Don't overthink it. Just stand."

"You have far too much faith in me."

"I have all the faith in the world in you, sunshine," he says with conviction, instantly instilling more confidence within me. And while I used to detest his nickname for me, I admit it's starting to grow on me.

I begin the painfully slow process of standing up on the paddleboard, my legs shaking with every inch, but Joss stabilizes the board, counteracting my motion every time I lean too far to one side. It's actually *easier* with him.

"See?" Joss says from behind me, and although I don't turn around for fear of throwing off my balance, I can hear the smirk on his face.

Standing half a foot in front of Joss, I take the elongated paddle and begin propelling us into deeper water, gliding along the pristine lake, its surface like glass on this windless day. After a few strokes, though, I begin to lose my balance, but Joss acts quickly, wrapping his arm around my waist, pulling my body flush against his.

"I've got you," he says, his breath warm against my ear, sending prickles down my neck. With every movement, I can feel his muscles adjust, his chest hard against my back, his arm tight and secure around my waist. I can feel my pulse quickening, and as I lean into Joss's body behind me, I feel his accelerate too.

We settle into a rhythm, and although I gain my balance back, Joss doesn't let go of me, and in the deep recesses of my heart, I know I don't want him to. In a few minutes, we make it to the middle of the lake and I pull the paddle out of the water, not sure if—or how—we should turn around.

We stand there just *being* for a moment. I empty my head of thoughts, not worrying about *American Gauntlet* or the prize money or Penny or Lana or whatever this is between me and Joss. We just exist for an instant, simply enjoying the moment— our moment—together.

"We make a good team," Joss says, resting his chin on top of my head, right in between my buns.

"We do," I say, nuzzling further into his neck, not caring about the consequences of any of my actions, something I might come to regret later. But out here in the middle of the lake, free of the incessant cameras, it seems like it's just the two of us—Joss and me. For this moment, *American Gauntlet* ceases to exist. The fact that Joss and I live on the other side of the world from each other doesn't matter. The looming competitions with potentially life-changing consequences have been erased. The heavy baggage I always carry with me is nowhere to be found.

It's just us. Joss and me, me and Joss.

"Should we turn around now?" I finally ask, even though I could spend another two hours pressed against Joss's chest on this paddleboard and be perfectly content.

"Hmmm," he murmurs. The sound rolls down my spine, shivers following in its wake. "Not yet."

Suddenly, Joss pulls my body even tighter against his and launches us into the water, the chilly water sending a shock straight through my nervous system. We dunk under the surface for a moment before Joss, his arm wrapped securely around my waist, pulls me up for air. He loses himself in a fit of laughter before I turn to him and spew the mouthful of lake water I nearly ingested in his direction. He laughs and laughs, and the sound is like long summer days, the ones you never want to end.

I swim over to him and put my hands on his shoulders, dunking him under, before he surfaces, and places his arm in the crook of my knees, pulling up and sending me flipping into the water, squealing every second of the way. When I breach the surface again, I shove him, laughing, back under the water before swimming back over to the paddle board for safety. I reach the board, holding onto it as a floatation device, but when I turn around to see where Joss is, I don't see him. He's still under the water.

Slowly at first and then all of a sudden, panic takes over. Joss is an expert swimmer. He's a lifeguard at Bondi Beach, for crying out loud. Surely, he's fine…right?

I pull myself onto the paddleboard, straddling it, so I can get a better vantage point, but I still don't see any sign of him. All of our splashing has disturbed the water, sending bubbles and waves in every direction, so it's not exactly immaculate for viewing what's beneath the surface anymore.

Suddenly, I hear a rush of water behind me, and Joss breaks through the surface, spewing lake water at me. I squeal in surprise, before a laugh breaks through to match Joss's.

"And to think I was actually worried there for a second!" I say, refusing to look down at him as my own act of rebellion.

The next moment, Joss effortlessly launches himself out of the water and onto the paddleboard, immediately stabilizing it as he settles. I don't need to turn around to know he's straddling the board behind me, his feet brushing my ankles as they dangle so close together in the water. I feel the warmth of his body, mere inches separating us, and it feels like the air is somehow thinner, my breath shallow in my lungs. The atmosphere that was filled with lighthearted amusement only seconds ago now feels electric, like I could reach out my hand and feel the current running between us like a live wire. Drops of cool water drip from his hair onto my shoulders as he inches his body closer to mine. He pauses before our bodies touch, but I close the distance myself, relaxing my back into his chest, resting my head in the bend of his neck and shoulder.

We stay there a moment, matching each other's breaths, our chests rising and falling in rhythm. *I could stay here forever.* The thought enters my head, and for once, I don't push it away. I breathe in deeply, trying to understand the sensation of his skin touching mine, how every nerve comes alive when our skin is pressed together. He takes a hand and sweeps the loose, wispy hair away from my neck, goosebumps trailing closely behind his fingers, before he bends his head down toward me, brushing his lips delicately along the back of my neck like the whisper of a kiss.

The urge to kiss Joss—to *really* kiss him—is suddenly overwhelming. I want to bring his mouth to mine, the phantom sensation of his lips brushing my skin still lingering. It's not enough.

I lean to the side and tilt my head up toward him. He looks down at me, his eyes glazing over, his pupils darkening. We remain there a second, maybe two, giving both of us the opportunity to stop what seems inevitable in the next breath. Neither of us does.

Finally, I reach up and clutch the back of his head, drawing his mouth down to mine.

I feel the whisper of his lips again, but before they're fully mine, we pull away sharply, suddenly hearing a distinct noise—a mix between a *buzz* and a *whir*—approaching. We look up to find a drone zooming across the lake, and it soon comes to hover right above us, a camera staring menacingly in our faces.

As Joss and I look at each other again, a few inches between our bodies now, it feels like an icy bucket of water has been poured over our moment in almost cinematic fashion.

"Looks like the camera crew found us," Joss says with a laugh.

Either Joss has recovered insanely quickly from our almost-kiss or he's hiding his disappointment with humor, but either way, I can't even produce a half-hearted laugh in response. My body is still sizzling at the moment Joss and I just shared, and every coherent thought seems to have left my brain.

The moment has clearly passed, and I'm at war with myself over how I feel about it.

On one hand, I wanted that kiss so deeply, desiring Joss in a way I've never wanted anyone before. My blood seems to hum when I'm around him, my skin singing at his every touch. He feels like warmth and sunshine and happiness, and it feels too good to let go of so soon.

But on the other hand…it may be for the best that we didn't cross any physical lines. It's been so long since I've kissed someone, and even the *possibility* of kissing Joss has turned my brain to mush. If we did kiss, I have no idea how it could affect me and my…attachment to him. Over the last few years, my body has felt like one of the only things I have complete control over. Kissing someone feels like giving up a piece of that control, and while I wanted it in the moment, I also want to make sure giving up that little piece is worth it. That Joss is worth it.

So I continue to convince myself that this drone was divine intervention and not simply a poorly timed, nosy camera crew. I tell myself it's for the best that Joss stays my *American Gauntlet* partner and nothing more. I remind myself that I need to stay focused. That I'm not here to find a boyfriend or a fling or a potentially disastrous showmance. I'm here to create a better life for Penny.

As we begin making our way back to shore, I try to empty my head of this excursion with Joss. Of every laugh, every tension-filled second, every warm and fuzzy feeling. Instead, I focus on the ceaseless hum of the drone above us, watching our every move like a hungry hawk.

thirty-four

IN TRUE *American Gauntlet* fashion, the next competition of the Strategy Phase has arrived at the most inopportune time. My mind still hasn't fully recovered from the rollercoaster of emotions that was my paddleboard excursion with Joss yesterday, but nevertheless, he and I will be competing as a team for the very first time today. Perfect.

Not only are my thoughts in complete shambles, but everything about this competition has been abnormal, which has only fueled my anxiety more.

While the competition was signaled by the typical earsplitting sirens, that's where all routine halted, putting every competitor on edge even more than usual. All of the teams were first sequestered in the Commons before production entered and called out Naji and AJ. By themselves, they left the Commons and haven't been seen since.

Sarge and Junior were called next, leaving Lana, Joss, and me in the Commons alone in a painfully uncomfortable situation. Lana and I haven't spoken more than a few mumbles to one another since our argument a couple nights ago. I suppose we don't have anything left to say, each of us disappointing the other in ways we couldn't begin to comprehend until it all started unraveling.

It's difficult to even look at Lana because when I do, all I see is the little sister I thought I knew. My brain simply can't reconcile how she could go from wanting to better our relationship one day to single handedly wrecking it the next. Perhaps she'd simply been trying to make the best of a situation she wasn't thrilled with, but then Dax Philipps presented her with the perfect out. She didn't hesitate to take it.

Thinking about that day makes me sick to my stomach. Dax's nonchalance. Lana's cold indifference. The feeling of being completely blindsided by someone I wholeheartedly trusted. Staring at Lana on the opposite end of the kitchen table now only fuels my rage, and I feel myself bite down on the inside of my cheeks, my fists clenched at my sides. I'm done pushing my anger aside when it comes to my sister.

Lana didn't want me to be her mom? Fine. But I wouldn't be her equal—I'd be her better. And as for *American Gauntlet*, I intend to make sure Lana comes to regret her decision to abandon ship. I'm ready to eliminate Lana from the game entirely, and if her hostile demeanor is any indication, she's just as prepared to do the same to me. Lana had said how confident she is in her ability to win in these last phases of the game, but even if she thinks she's evenly matched with me, I have a glorious leg up on her, one she probably never saw coming: Joss.

I have Joss on my side, and if we make a halfway decent team, I like our chances.

There's always going to be a part of me that loves my sister unconditionally. Lana and I will mend our relationship, but it won't be during our time on *American Gauntlet*. There are innumerable things we need to hash out between the two of us, and I think the one thing we can agree on is the fact that it shouldn't be done on national television. I can't imagine what it would do to Penny, seeing the two of us at each other's throats even more than we already have been. No, the repair will need to wait, as will any sense of camaraderie between us.

After an indeterminate amount of excruciatingly silent minutes with Lana, Kelly pops her ponytailed head in and calls Lana to face her fate, leaving Joss and I alone in the Commons. None of the other competitors return from wherever they've been whisked off to.

While the silence is comfortable with Joss, the waiting has started to wear on me. *Why are they doing the competition like this? Why would they be sequestering us from the other teams? Has the game already begun? Is this part of it?* I rack my brain trying to make sense of my questions and come up empty each time.

Frustrated, I begin chewing at a hangnail on my thumb, biting and pulling at it until it bleeds. As a thin line of red fills the crevice of my nail bed, Joss looks at me, taking my bleeding hand in his.

"You want another fact?" he asks.

Despite my irritation at the unknown circumstances surrounding this competition, I can't help but nod at him, grinning.

"Hmmm," he says, cupping my hand in both of his and bringing it up to rest beneath his chin. "Did you know…" he begins, drifting off while contemplating what random fact he'll pull out of his brain. His eyes light up as he seems to settle on one. "Did you know that falling coconuts are a bigger threat to humanity than sharks?"

Despite myself, I giggle, the sound surprising me as it escapes. "Are you serious?"

"Deadly," he says, winking at his pun. "You're far more likely to be killed by a falling coconut than you are by a shark attack."

"Is this what you tell yourself when you're out surfing the shark-infested Australian waters?" I ask, laughing.

"It's a true fact!" he cries. "But just so you know, yes, it does cross my mind from time to time when I'm in the water."

I grin at how sheepish he looks in his admission, giving me a glimpse at what Joss may have been like as a kid. And then I realize that all at once, I've forgotten why I was anxious in the first place.

"Alright, time to spill," I say.

He quirks an eyebrow at me.

"The facts. The trivia. The random expertise," I list off. "I need to know how you've gained this plethora of knowledge… unless of course, that's what they teach you in school over in Australia?" I tease.

He grins, shaking his head at me. He pauses for a moment, before looking back at me, still grinning, but it's noticeably different. It's reminiscent, like he's gone somewhere else, but I'm still here, witnessing it.

"It was to pass the time, really," he begins. "When I was getting my treatment, I was stuck in the hospital with nothing to do. I hated watching TV—I found it so boring. Still do. I read books and I did puzzles and games and stuff with my parents, but I always eventually got tired of those too.

"One time, my mum found some online trivia game—it was really just her asking questions, and then I'd try to guess the answer. It started off with pretty basic stuff, but we eventually went through every question on it and immediately found more questions online, an endless cache of trivia for me to try and answer. It was a game I never got bored of, learning new things. It just never seemed to get old. Though, I've got to admit I've forgotten a lot of it, mostly anything important or useful," he says, laughing. "It's the funny stuff I remember. And it's a habit that's stuck. Whenever I find myself mulling around with nothing to do, I look up random, funny trivia. I don't know," he drifts off, absently running a hand through his blonde locks, "I like cheering people up with the funny facts. Especially you."

I exhale slowly, taking in Joss's words. I expected him to blurt out some joke or funny story about the origin of his random knowledge, but the truth is so much deeper than I imagined. I shouldn't be surprised, since I feel like I discover a new layer to Joss every day that I'm with him.

"Thank you for sharing that with me," I whisper, squeezing his hand. He tenderly threads his fingers through mine.

I smile at Joss, even as a kernel of sadness wiggles its way into my chest. To think of the things he's been through in his life… it's like finding a kindred spirit, both us having experienced things that kids should never have to go through. The difference was Joss came out of it like a luminescent ray of sunshine and I came out of it like an ominous storm cloud.

"How do you do it?" I murmur, nearly beneath my breath, as if I myself am unsure I should've asked it.

"How do I do what?"

"How are you so joyful, even when you've experienced so much pain?"

Joss doesn't hesitate. "Because I wake up every single day grateful to be here. Grateful to have my health and a body that lets me do the things I love."

"But aren't…aren't you afraid your cancer might come back some day?" I ask, nervously chewing at my lip. As soon as the question comes out, I wonder if I shouldn't have asked it at all.

But Joss just smiles softly, giving me grace even when I'm not sure I deserve it.

"What kind of life is that, Dani? What kind of life is it to be so afraid of what might happen that you don't even live?"

A kaleidoscope of thoughts and emotions courses through my head, countless shapes and colors flashing before me at once that I can't unpack any of them. But I intend to. When I have time and space to myself, I intend to pluck each individual shape out to dissect it fully because this isn't a conversation that should be glossed over.

"I'm sorry I said all those things to you before, Joss," I say quietly. "I…I just got too wrapped up in my own situation. You have such a good reason to be here—to win—but even if you didn't, even if you were here just for the fun of it, it doesn't discount your experience."

Joss squeezes my hand, leaning his head down so I'll look him in the eyes again. I didn't realize I'd dropped my gaze to the floor.

"The way you love your family is something I admire the most about you, sunshine," he says gently. "I hated standing in the way of that. But now I get to help you win—we get to help each other."

Before I can even finish exhaling, a noise jerks our head toward the Commons door and in pops Kelly, her ponytail bobbing with her every step.

"Ready you two?" she squeaks, cheerful as ever, as if we weren't about to compete in a competition that could potentially determine our fate in this game.

"We're ready," Joss says, grasping my hand with conviction. He peers into my eyes, helping me up from the table as he says, "Let's see what the rest of the Strategy Phase has in store for us."

I walk toward the door, cracking my knuckles along the way, a renewed fervor washing over me. The waiting is over. It's time to tackle another tough challenge from the Gauntlet—and do it with Joss by my side.

thirty-five

JOSS and I are driven back to the vast open field from the very first phase of the competition, but instead of being greeted by a mud pit, there seems to be an obstacle course of sorts awaiting us.

Dax wastes no time after we arrive.

"Ah, our newest duo. Welcome. I guess we'll find out if you made the right choice in teammates, won't we?"

It's incredible how Joss towers over Dax by at least half a foot, yet Dax is the one who looks intimidating. I'm not sure if it's the all black attire, the mirrored aviators that make it impossible to see his eyes, or the deep scars carved into his face from so many years of MMA fighting. Probably a mix of all three.

"During this competition in the Strategy Phase, you will be faced with a series of decisions. At each checkpoint, you will have two options of obstacles to complete. You two will determine what choice is best for you as a *team*. You must both complete the same obstacle—you cannot split them between the two of you.

"Some of these options may be better suited for individuals, while others will be faster as a team. Your fate rests in the decisions you make."

What a way to test our connection right off the bat, I think to myself. Not only are we completing obstacles together, but we have to make decisions—together. I'm not sure that either of us would back down if we disagree…but I guess we'll cross that bridge if we get there.

Off camera, the producers explain each obstacle to Joss and me. The viewers won't see that part, but in the spirit of keeping the intensity up when the competition begins, they don't want us to pause and have things explained along the way. We're given the rundown of each obstacle, but they bar us from discussing which option we'll choose, so we won't know what the other is thinking until we get to that set of obstacles.

As we wait for the camera crew to get set, Joss and I wait next to each other at the starting line in anticipation. I smooth my hands over my new uniform that now matches Joss's. When the producers asked us which color we'd opt for as a team, I jumped at the opportunity to wear Joss's blue. Purple reminds me too much of Lana. Plus, it would be a crime to make Joss wear another color when this one so perfectly matches the color of his eyes. You're welcome, America.

I sneak a quick glance at him out of the corner of my eye and am surprised to find he's already looking at me. We both smear matching grins across our faces, before Joss leans over and tucks a stray piece of my hair back into one of my buns. The gesture is so tender that I can't help the honey-sweet warmth that begins to flow through me, filling me up, seeping out to my limbs.

"Not having second thoughts on accepting me as your teammate, are we?" Joss quips.

Of course not, I immediately think, but instead, I say, "I guess we'll find out after this, menace."

Joss's laugh fills my ears, but it's abruptly drowned out by the shrill shriek of Dax's whistle. The sound shuts out all other thoughts like a heavy steel door, and all that's left is sheer focus. One glimpse at Joss tells me he feels the same.

We race toward the first checkpoint where we're met by our first pair of obstacles. The first is a rope and pulley system that straddles a clear plexiglass wall about fifteen feet high. If we choose this option, we'll need to first pull all of the slack out of the rope—and there seems to be *a lot* of rope judging by the huge pile of it on the other side of the wall—and then climb the rope before scaling down the other side of the wall.

The other option is a huge plexiglass climbing wall that looks at least two stories tall. This isn't just any climbing wall, though; instead of hand and foot holds, the wall *only* has dozens of peg holes. We'll need to pull our way up, inch by inch, by sticking wooden pegs into the wall and using that as our leverage.

Looking at our two options, the rope and pulley seems like a better option—for an individual. The producers explained that after one of us got to the other side, we'd have to reset the obstacle, pulling all of the rope back to the other side only for our teammate to pull it *back* over. We'd lose precious time with the extra work for two people.

The peg wall would be absolutely brutal on the upper body, but there are enough pegs to where Joss and I could scale it at the same time. I feel at least semi-confident in my climbing abilities after doing some during my pre-show training, so I'm leaning toward that option.

"What are you thinking, Joss?"

"Peg wall, for the sake of time?"

"You read my mind."

We run to the wall and do an awkward high-knees run over the huge mat at the bottom of the wall that will catch us if we lose our grip and take an instant plunge to the ground. (How sweet of the producers to provide us this luxury, although I'm sure Dax tried to convince them to let us fall to the rock hard ground instead.)

There's a bucket of pegs awaiting us at the bottom of the wall. In the bucket, I count six pegs available for us to use. *Strategy*, I think, before plucking a peg out of the bucket and sticking it as high up on the wall as I can reach.

"For a foothold later," I tell Joss.

"Atta girl," he says, before grabbing two pegs for himself out of the bucket.

I grab two pegs and eyeball the last peg at the bottom of the bucket. I hate to leave it there, unused, but I can't carry it with me.

Think, Dani. This is the Strategy Phase. You have to be clever.

Suddenly, I shove one of the pegs in my mouth, clenching down on it with my teeth, and grab the last one from the bucket in my hand. I have no doubt how ridiculous I look with a peg sticking three or four inches out of my mouth, but I couldn't care less. This is the Strategy Phase, after all, and I might need this peg later. *I hope you get a good laugh when this airs, Ford,* I think to myself.

A hint of a grin materializes on Joss's face when he sees me.

"Hon't you hare," I grit out, my best attempt at "Don't you dare" with a peg shoved in my mouth.

"What was that, love?" he teases, his smile lingering a second before he seemingly remembers we're in a competition for our lives in this game. "You first," he says, all business, signaling to the wall.

Holding onto both pegs, I find holds for them above my head and pull. Instantly, I begin to question if this was a catastrophic mistake. While I'm able to heave my body up with a chin up-like motion, it will be a struggle to remove one of the pegs and place it higher in order to keep moving up the wall. I'm strong, but…this will be a grind. If Tris and Benji were still in the competition, they would put me to shame.

For Penny. You're doing this for Penny.

With no time to waste, I put all my weight into my right arm—the arm that's currently holding my chin up position—and I shimmy my left hand peg out of the wall, placing it higher. While holding onto the peg, I take out my right hand peg and place it near the left and haul my body upward. I do this same routine one more time, my arms already shaking from exhaustion, but I realize I've made it to the spot where I can take advantage of the foothold I'd placed earlier. With both of my arm pegs securely in the wall, I place my foot on the peg and give my upper body a much-needed rest, if only momentarily.

I look down and see Joss begin his climb, and if I weren't so exhausted, I would roll my eyes. Or clap. I'm honestly not sure.

With a feline-like grace, Joss hauls himself effortlessly up the wall. He doesn't even need to use both pegs at the same time like I did; he just pulls himself up in what is basically a one-armed pull-up—*left, right, left, right.* In under a minute he's made it to where I'm resting on my foothold.

Although he's hardly even breathing heavily, I turn over the foothold to him, and begin heaving my body upwards.

It's not long before I taste salt in my mouth, streams of sweat running down my face. My arms violently shake, and I struggle to regulate my breathing. Every heft of my body upwards is agony, but I repeat the same four words in my head like a silent war hymn.

This is for Penny. This is for Penny. This is for Penny.

Over and over again, I chant to myself silently, the words

charging through my mind like a battalion of soldiers marching off to war. They're bloodied. They're exhausted. But they're marching on like the good soldiers they are.

A grunt suddenly shatters my concentration, and I nearly miss the peg hole I'm shooting for with my left hand, but I shove it against the plexiglass, and it finds its mark. That minor lapse in focus suddenly seems to be the least of my problems, as I look beside me where Joss's grunt came from.

Completely engrossed in my own battle with the wall, I didn't notice Joss had caught up with me, but as I look at him next to me now, I blanch. He's hanging from the wall, both arms gripped to one peg. My fears are confirmed as I look to the ground beneath us and see a peg resting against the blue mat at the bottom.

Joss dropped it.

"Your extra peg, Dani," he grunts. "I need it."

The extra peg. I'd nearly forgotten I have it in my mouth, although as I'm suddenly aware of it again, I realize it's practically wet with my breath and saliva, teeth marks etched into it from the force of my bite. It'll have to do though.

But as Joss hangs there, both hands gripped to his one peg, I freeze. *I can't get it to him.* I can't take one of my pegs out of the wall to hand to him because I can't hang on this wall one-handed while also trying to pass the peg to him. I'll fall. There's absolutely no way around it.

Panic rapidly takes over my already flushed features. I can feel my pulse pick up even more, skyrocketing to what I'm sure is an unhealthy rate. Joss, from right beside me on the wall, suddenly leans as far toward me as possible, his grip on the one peg coming precariously close to slipping.

"*Hut are you hooing?*" I grit out, the peg still shoved into my mouth.

And that's when I realize what he's thinking.

He continues leaning as far toward me as possible, but he can't close the distance—I'll need to help. Without time to rethink it, I bring my face as close to his as possible, and he finishes the job. He opens his mouth, closing his lips around the peg and brushing mine in the process.

If possible, my face reddens even more as Joss takes the peg from my mouth *with his mouth*. America will definitely get a show on this episode because it looks like Joss and I just made out mid-competition. Can't wait to see this little number show up on social media.

And despite everything, I still can't get the feeling of his lips brushing against mine out of my head.

Joss makes a dangerous maneuver to unlatch one of his hands and grabs hold of my saliva-ridden peg, and we continue our climb.

After what feels like the most brutal upper body workout of my life, I can see the silver lining. We're nearly at the top. We're almost there. And despite our little bump in the road, I think we've made pretty good time, although my arms beg to differ.

Joss summits the wall first before helping me up over the top. We sit there, each of us straddling the wall, as we look down on the behemoth we just conquered. We give each other a knowing look, letting our gazes linger together for one moment, maybe two, before we grab the ropes waiting for us and repel down.

One down. Two to go.

Once our feet hit the blue mat at the bottom, we race toward the next set of obstacles in a full sprint. We're soon met by two options. The first is an army crawl through thick, sludge-like mud for what looks to be the length of an entire football field. In theory, an army crawl seems easy enough. In practice, though, it's a different story. I know just how tiring it can get, especially in mud as thick as this mud looks. The second option is simple. If we choose the second option, Joss and I would need to traverse a thin, low-to-the-ground slackline that looks to be at least thirty yards long. If either of us fall, we'll *both* need to go back and start over.

"Army crawl?" Joss asks.

I quickly mull the options in my head. While the slackline has the potential to be faster, thirty yards is *a lot* to walk without falling off, meaning it also has the potential to be a huge setback. At least with the army crawl, we know we'll get to the finish line eventually without the risk of starting over.

"Let's get dirty," I say, and I don't miss the quirk of Joss's eyebrow before we take off toward the football field of mud awaiting us. There's a net suspended over the top of the course that'll keep us low to the ground as we crawl through; we need to be careful not to get caught in it in the frenzy.

As we approach the mud, though, something looks off…I can't place it at first, not until we're right in front of it.

The mud—it seems to be *moving*.

thirty-six

THE mud is moving. There's no doubt about it.

But the movement is decidedly…strange. It looks almost like a rumble beneath its surface, as if an earthquake were shaking the mud like loose pudding.

"Do you…?" Joss signals to me, not needing to finish his question. We study the mud and its gelatin-like jiggle before we both knock some sense into ourselves. We don't have time to stop and stare. Instead, we dive head first, side by side, under the net and into the mud.

It's impossible to keep our faces out of the mud. The net is so low that we'll be plowing forward, head first, out of necessity. When I slide into the mud and open my eyes, rubbing them clean like windshield wipers, that's when I realize what the subtle movement of the mud is.

It's not the mud that's moving; it's what's *in* the mud that's moving.

As I peer down at my mud-soaked arms and chest, I realize Joss and I are not alone in the sludge. There are thousands of *creatures* with us. I immediately notice ruddy pink earthworms, slimy and fat, squirming in the sludge. Even worse, though, are the yellowish-white maggots that appear in writhing clumps in every direction.

"Gnarly," Joss remarks, before we dig into the mud even further, army crawling as fast as our bodies will allow.

I was worried my upper body would be too weak for me to move quickly through the thick sludge, but the maggots have solved that problem. I can feel them sliding down my shirt, propelling me faster and faster with each wiggle of their plump bodies. I owe the *American Gauntlet* producers a thank you for this fun little twist, I suppose. I can't even begin to fathom how they got all of these bugs here, but a disturbing image of a truck full of worms and maggots comes to mind. I'll probably see it again in my nightmares.

Joss and I move through the muck like a machine, as if we're two parts of the same body. Side by side, we drive ourselves forward with impressive efficiency. The only time we break our stride is to pull the occasional worm off our face or a maggot out of an ear, a sensation that I pray I never have to experience again. Joss's foot momentarily gets tangled in the net above us, but we eventually drag ourselves out of the bug-ridden mire. As we grab each other's hands and stand together, I can feel the worms wiggling under my skin-tight uniform, but there's no time to go digging around for them in every cavity of my body. I do my best to shake off the mud as we run to our third and final set of obstacles, and I watch as the maggots fall loosely from my hair, which is now poking wildly out of my once-neat buns.

If we weren't in the middle of a competition where the outcome determines my *American Gauntlet* fate, I'd take a moment here to freak out about how absolutely vile it feels to have maggots and worms writhing through my hair and under my clothes and across my skin. But at the moment, I'm a racehorse with blinders on, solely focused on sprinting across that finish line.

I can't wait to see Penny's reaction when this episode eventually airs. I imagine her shaking her head while pressing a hand to her forehead, an *"Oh dear"* escaping her in horror. Ford will make some comment about a maggot digging its way into my brain, but I'll get to shove it in his face that all of the training in the mud was worth it.

Joss and I sprint to our final checkpoint, where we're presented with two simple options: Solve a riddle or solve a puzzle. There are two tables before us, each covered with a sheet concealing the riddle and the puzzle, so we don't know what each one entails. The puzzle could be anything. Sudoku. A Rubik's Cube. A literal jigsaw puzzle. We have no idea.

"What are you thinking?" I ask.

"I do fancy a riddle."

I ponder for a moment. *A riddle.* I mull the thought over in my mind. It could be fast. If we know the answer, it'll be over in seconds. Does Joss's trivia knowledge extend to riddles?

The other side of the coin, though, is if we don't know the answer, we're done. We can throw as many answers out there as we want to, but riddles are notoriously tricky. If we can't come up with the correct answer, we're finished.

A puzzle, though…it could be slower, but there's always the opportunity to get it right. You keep moving the pieces around enough, and you'll get there. Eventually.

"I think we should do the puzzle." My tone is confident, sure of itself. I know this is the best path forward.

Joss's brow furrows, cracking the quickly drying mud on his face. "Are you sure?"

I don't hesitate. "I'm sure."

Joss pauses for a moment, the wrinkle remaining near his forehead, before he subtly nods his head. I take that as his acquiesce.

"Let's do this," I say, ripping off the cloth covering the puzzle. When I see what lies beneath it, I almost burst into tears.

"Oh my gosh."

"What? What's wrong?" Joss asks, the crease returning to his forehead, this time in concern.

"Absolutely nothing," I reply, grinning.

I could cry happy tears staring at this puzzle; I really could. The puzzle awaiting us is a *tangram*. I practiced tangrams nearly every day since learning I would be a contestant on *American Gauntlet,* knowing they love to throw this type of puzzle into the challenges. I had gone through website after website of online tangrams, working from the easiest puzzles to the most difficult ones until I was wholly confident in my tangram abilities.

This puzzle is a gift.

Joss stands before the puzzle, looking at the multicolored pieces in every shape from triangles to trapezoids to rectangles. We'll need to fit each of these pieces into the square frame using every piece and without any pieces overlapping. It'll be a perfect square when it's finished.

Joss looks utterly lost, and I don't doubt he wishes we'd picked the riddle. But I haven't shown him what I can do yet.

I take each piece and begin fitting it into the square frame, making small adjustments as I go. Out of my periphery, I see Joss staring at me, a look of amazement starting to make way to his face. My hands fly over the pieces, flipping them this way and that, upside down and rightside up again, as my brain looks for the perfect pattern, the ideal combination of shapes.

After some maneuvering, I have three pieces left to fit, and at once, I see the ending come together before even placing them. The pink rhombus here. The yellow equilateral triangle there.

And there it is—the perfect space for the aqua blue triangle, the final piece. I fit the piece snugly in the puzzle, and for once, I'm happy to hear Dax's ear-splitting whistle because it signals our competition is over.

I did it. *We did it.* And we didn't kill each other in the process.

I turn to Joss who's staring at me, dumbstruck.

"What…" he drifts off. "What was that? You did that puzzle in, what? Less than two minutes?" Joss's look of pure awe suddenly turns into the widest, toothiest grin I've seen. He suddenly scoops me up, worms and all, and spins me around. "Brilliant," he says into my neck. "Absolutely brilliant."

"We make a good team," I say, as he sets me down. "Except!" I yell, suddenly remembering our earlier obstacle. "You dropped your peg!"

He lifts a hand to his hair, attempting to pull some of the dried mud out of it, and looks down sheepishly. "Yeah, I'll admit—not my finest moment," he replies. "Although, it didn't turn out so bad, if you ask me," he tacks on with a grin.

The sudden feeling of Joss's lips grazing mine returns like a ghost. Subconsciously, I bring my fingers to my lips, before I look up to see Joss looking at me, his eyes trailing down to my mouth. He brushes his tongue over his bottom lip and—

Behind us, someone obnoxiously clears their throat, and Joss and I whip around to see Dax standing before us, an impatient look on his face, although, if I didn't know any better, I'd swear his expression nearly turned to a smile.

"It's time to find out your fate, you two. Shall we?"

WHEN we return to camp, the rest of the competitors are

waiting for us. Sarge and Junior are mud-caked like us, while Naji, AJ, and Lana are decidedly clean, meaning they opted for the slackline over the army crawl. It's no surprise the vets chose the obstacle they did.

The producers don't allow us to speak to each other, giving Dax the task of dramatically delivering the results to us. I look at Lana, but I can't get a read on how she did. She doesn't return my glance.

"Let's cut to the chase," Dax declares once we're all standing at attention before him and the cameras are rolling at every angle. "The top two teams from today's competition were Sarge and Junior and Dani and Joss." Joss leans over and nudges me, a smile on his face. "An interesting note: your times were separated by less than four seconds."

My stomach plummets to my feet. *Four seconds.* Four seconds is *nothing*. Four seconds is sprinting slightly faster between obstacles. It's fitting the tangram puzzle pieces together a hair quicker. It's not stopping to pull a maggot out of your ear. It's nothing. But it could mean everything.

"The team," Dax continues, "with the fastest time of the day was…"

I can hear my heart pounding in my ears. I picture the words "Dani and Joss" coming out of Dax's mouth and feeling the overwhelming joy of an *American Gauntlet* victory in my grasp.

"…Sarge and Junior," Dax finishes. The hope-filled expression on my face plunges, my heart along with it. "Congratulations. Dani and Joss, you are safe from elimination this week as well. Good job out there today. Looks like you didn't make a terrible mistake with your choice of partner," he adds.

Relief instantly floods through my body, but it's soon overshadowed by a cloud of disappointment. I'm thankful that

Joss and I get to stay another week here, but I really wanted that win. Dax's words from the Endurance Phase bounce around in my head. *"Wins are always advantageous in* American Gauntlet." And while I had done well in the competitions so far, I was starkly short on wins.

Another thought bounds into my head like an uninvited guest: Lana will go into an elimination against Naji or AJ, or potentially *both* of them at the same time. While I had prepared myself to eliminate her from *American Gauntlet*, I hadn't prepared to *watch* her be eliminated by another team…I know it's the same result either way, but something about it feels unsettling.

Don't go weak on me now, I think to myself. *She abandoned you. Don't forget that.*

Just thinking the word "abandon" immediately triggers a deep emotional response in me, flaring up the fiery hurt and the searing pain that Lana's choice had stirred in me, and I suddenly don't care who eliminates her. She made her bed. Now she has to lie in it.

"Typically," Dax continues, "the bottom two teams would face each other in an elimination; however, the circumstances in today's competition are…unique." The way Dax has been emphasizing his words throughout his monologue demonstrates how much he clearly lives for these moments, how much he relishes us hanging on his every syllable.

"Lana," Dax says, and my head suddenly whips to my sister. Why is he calling her out? I try to get her to make eye contact with me, but still, I'm met with nothing but her stone-faced profile. "Naji and AJ completed today's competition; you, however, *didn't even make it past the first obstacle.*" Every word is dealt like a blow. The tone. The inflection. The cold, disappointed stare that goes with it. Dax is shooting to kill, and judging by the look on Lana's face, he's done it.

She didn't make it past the first obstacle? While I thought the lack of mud on her clothes meant she had chosen the slackline at the second obstacle, it instead meant she hadn't even cleared the first one. My emotions war within me, battling between compassion and satisfaction, concern and resentment.

My head whips back to Dax when he deals his final blow. "Unfortunately for you, this disqualifies you from the game. You do not have what it takes to face the Gauntlet. Your time here is finished."

My mouth drops open. I didn't—I didn't think they'd send her packing without so much as another word. I thought she'd have to complete another task, prove herself another way, *something*. But instead, Lana nods her head and wordlessly walks toward the producers who will shuttle her into our room for her to gather her things and leave without the luxury of a goodbye to us. To me.

My emotions are all over the place. I'm mad at her, although the word "mad" doesn't seem strong or complex enough for how I feel. My anger is a square, while the emotions supporting it are a prism, each warring emotion feeding its intricacy, its depth. I thought I was ready to watch her leave the show, but now that I'm actually seeing her walk away, I second guess everything. I want to run to her. I want to hug her and tell her everything's fine and I'll figure out a way to get her a car and also pay for Penny to go to school and I'll save up money for the next twenty-five years so I can take her to Europe.

But I can't.

Instead, I watch as she marches away and I wonder if things will ever be the same between us again. *Does she regret it? Does she regret what she's done?* As she gets further and further away, every step feels more final, and it begins to set in that she's really leaving. But just before she rounds the corner to our cabin, she looks up, her eyes finding mine. We hold our stares as if we're holding each other, as if this moment is our goodbye. She gives a small but definitive nod of her head, and then she's gone.

As soon as she's out of sight, I feel a sudden emptiness in my chest. I bring my hand up to my sternum, half expecting to find a vast chasm in it, but instead, all I find is flaky mud and a worm that's smushed under the strap of my sports bra.

"The last phase of *American Gauntlet*—Grit—is coming," Dax says. "I suggest you get some rest. You're going to need it."

Dax walks away and the rest of the competitors—such a small group of us now—begin to disperse, but Joss grabs my hand, holding us there for a moment.

"Are you okay?"

"Yes…No?" I sigh. "Honestly, I don't really know."

I drag my gaze up to Joss, expecting to find some sort of blind pity that I don't want, but instead, he regards me with such empathy that it's almost like looking in a mirror. Like he somehow feels exactly what I feel.

He reaches up and tenderly pulls a clump of cakey mud out of my eyelashes.

"Do—do I have something on my face?" I ask, which draws an immediate chuckle from him. It's exactly what I need to hear, my mood instantly lightening with the sound of his deep rumble of a laugh.

"I'm sorry your sister's gone," he says as we walk back toward the main part of camp. Just before we part, he adds, "But for the record, I'd choose you as my teammate any day."

thirty-seven

AFTER cleaning the maggot remnants from my every body cavity, I begrudgingly return to our cabin—my cabin now, I suppose—dragging my feet with every step.

I know when I cross the threshold, Lana's absence will feel permanent, and it all just feels like so much right now. I never expected *American Gauntlet* to send my mind and emotions through the meat grinder. I expected the physical component, of course, but this competition has affected me in ways I never imagined.

From the beginning, my emotions have been a jumble of chaotic spaghetti in my mind. At home, my life feels simple. I go to work. I provide for my family. I do it all over again the next day. My life is defined by a sense of duty to my loved ones, and I've never questioned it. Come to think of it, it's really all I've ever known.

Here, though, I've been a walking contradiction, my obvious feelings for Joss battling my obligation to winning and my primal instinct to protect myself, my anger at Lana warring with my inherent desire to care for her. Even little aspects of the show have caused me inner turmoil, like how I promised I wouldn't get attached to any of the competitors, and yet, Naji and Sarge and nearly every other person here—Twisted Twins aside—have burrowed their way under my skin and even further, splitting through my chest, into my heart.

American Gauntlet has forced cracks in the armor I spent so long forging that I can't help but feel weak.

In frustration, I finally throw the door open, bursting into my now-empty cabin. Lana's side of the room has been cleared out, which I expected; what I didn't expect, though, was a note waiting for me on my bed. I cross the room in three broad strides and take the letter in my hands. As I hold the piece of paper, scribbled with Lana's telltale messy handwriting, I notice my hands are trembling, and I can't bring them to stop.

Dani,

By the time you read this, I'll be on a plane back home, and you'll still be right where you need to be: winning American Gauntlet. I hope you can forgive me for what I did, but it's important for me to explain why, so before you throw this letter in the trash, hear me out. Please.

I couldn't do it, Dani. I couldn't keep being your partner, knowing that I was holding you back. We both know I wasn't ready for this competition, and it only gets worse from here. When Dax presented the opportunity to go on as an individual, I had to take it—I had to free you from this sinking ship. We weren't going to win together, and no matter how much you try to deny it to protect me, it's the truth. I don't have what it takes to face the Gauntlet. But you do.

I couldn't tell you my reason for breaking up our

partnership—I had to make you hate me, if only for a week. I knew if you were mad at me, you wouldn't hold back for my sake in the competitions. I couldn't let you sacrifice yourself for me, so for once, I sacrificed myself for you. And I'd do it all over again if I had the chance. (And for the record, I tried my hardest with that first obstacle...it clearly wasn't meant to be for me. It was my time to go. I'm at peace with it, and I hope you can be, too.)

I had mere seconds to make my decision. I didn't know if you'd continue on by yourself or if you'd partner with someone else, but I knew that either way, you'd be in a better position to win without me. Little did I know, everything would work out perfectly and you'd end up partnered with one of the strongest competitors here. From the start, I've been betting on you to win this thing, Dani. But now? You and Joss will be unstoppable.

I love you more than I'll ever be able to express within the confines of this letter, but for now, all I can say is thank you for the adventure of a lifetime. Mine is over, but yours is just beginning. Now's your time, sis. Go show that Gauntlet what Dani Di Laurentis is made of.

All my love,
Lana

p.s. Joss is a good one, sis. Don't let the memory of what's-his-face keep you from a good thing. Remember to put yourself first every once in a while. xoxo

MY MIND is as blank as the stark white ceiling I've been staring at for the last two hours, all of the emotions that have been whirring through my mind at lightspeed finally dying out like the last remnants of a shooting star. Two hours. That's how long it's taken me to process Lana's letter.

My brain has worked through its own twelve-step process, beginning at guilt for the resentment I've harbored toward my sister, then flowing to anger at how she made this game-altering decision without consulting me first. There's been a touch of denial, coupled with a tinge of sadness. And that brings me to my final step: gratitude.

Lana's right. We weren't going to win this competition together, no matter how much I tried to dismiss it when we were still partners. Even making it to the Gauntlet would have been a stretch, but winning? It just wasn't going to happen, not with so many solid competitors this season.

With Joss as my partner, though, it's an entirely different story. We not only have a good chance at winning—we have a *great* chance. A *fighting* chance. I'm feeling more confident than ever after our performance yesterday, and even though we didn't win, we're a force to be reckoned with, especially considering how seamlessly we worked together.

My mind drifts to Penny's motto, the words she repeated to me before I came here. *Even when the rainiest day seems to be at its darkest, the sun is always there, even if you can't see it behind the clouds. It'll come back out eventually.* This week, I've felt like I've been at my darkest, Lana's apparent betrayal sending me into a spiraling tornado of anger and sadness. But now…it feels like maybe the sun has finally come out. And it's beautiful.

A knock comes at the door, but I don't need to answer it to know who it is.

"Come in, Joss," I call.

The door opens with a quiet squeak, and Joss, a slight grin on his face, peeks his head through the small opening. His tremendous height makes the entire cabin appear like a dollhouse.

"How'd you know it was me?"

I can't help but smile. "I just had a feeling."

"I came to check on you."

"I know."

He laughs, the sound rolling through the metal cabin in reverberating ripples. I soak it in, letting the sound wash over me like ocean waves. They're not the dirty Galveston waves either; they're the picture perfect, cerulean blue, Bondi Beach waves.

"So how are we then, sunshine?"

"Better."

He dips his chin, giving me a look that says he's not quite buying what I'm selling.

"I'm serious. I'm better. Come look," I say, holding Lana's note up.

I quickly fold the bottom part of the paper under, not wanting Lana's P.S. to meet any eyes other than my own. Joss flops on the bed beside me, the tiny twin bed frame shuddering beneath his weight, his body elongating next to mine as he settles in. It's impossible for our bodies not to naturally gravitate in toward one another, and I can't bring myself to pull away from where our arms touch, from where my knees press against his legs. If I shifted only a few inches toward him, I would fit perfectly into the curve of his body, a key fitting into its lock.

"You know what this means?" Joss asks, handing the letter back to me. I reach across him and tuck it away in the nightstand drawer. As I do, the scent of Joss's spearmint gum hits me; I nearly taste it on my own tongue.

"Hmm?" I ask, settling back beside him, perhaps a little closer this time.

"We *have* to win now. We can't let what she's done go to waste," he says, the rare crease of his forehead illustrating just how serious he is.

"Winning *American Gauntlet* has never been an option for me—it's always been a necessity. I have to win, Joss. I have to win for Penny, for Lana." I haven't yet figured out how I'm going to swing Penny's program fees and Lana's car (a necessity), but I'll get it figured out. I'll recruit more personal training clients, pick up more shifts at the gym. I could save up extra cash, and, coupled with my half of the winnings, it would eventually be enough. I tell Joss none of this. Instead, I say, "We just really need to win."

Beside me, Joss's eyes soften, as if he, too, feels how badly I need this money. He reaches his arm around me, cradling me in the nook of his chest. I let myself sink into him, relishing this feeling of…of comfort. Warmth. Like I've finally found a soft place to land after all this time.

We lay there, our chests rising and falling as one, as I let the exhaustion overtake me.

As I begin to doze, visions of Penny and Lana and my mom flash through my mind like violent streaks of lightning. In my state of half-sleep, I murmur, *"We have to win. We have to win."*

"What's that, sunshine?" Joss asks, his voice deep and rumbly, as he, too, gives into the fatigue.

Joss's voice, coming from just above where I've nuzzled into him, wakes me up enough to understand what I've been mumbling, aloud, in my semi-consciousness.

A quiet laugh escapes me. I probably sound unhinged, repeating how badly Joss and I need to win, even in my sleep.

"Sorry," I murmur, my eyelids already losing their laborious battle to stay open. "This whole thing just means a lot to me…" I say, my voice drifting off as sleep coaxes me further into her grasp. "…in case you were wondering why I sound crazy."

It may have been a dream, a trick of my mind as reality blurred with sleep-induced fantasy, but I could've sworn I heard Joss, his reply a mere whisper, as he said, "The only thing I'm wondering is what it would be like to be loved with that kind of fervor…what it would be like to be loved by you."

SIRENS blare throughout the cabin. My eyes burst open, only to be met with a rock solid wall, which I quickly realize is Joss's chest. The cabin lights are still on, and I can see Joss's impossibly long arms draped over me like a safety blanket, our legs intertwined with each other like ivy.

We fell asleep, I remind myself. Right.

The sirens continue to trumpet loudly. *It must be morning. It must be time for the next competition.*

Joss stirs beside me, incredibly not yet fully awakened by the deafening alarms. I take in Joss's face two inches in front of mine, noting everything about it, committing it to memory. This close, I can see a faint scar just below his eyebrow, a tiny silver sliver above his left eye. I observe the generous curl of his absurdly long eyelashes, the slight pout of his lower lip. Without a second thought, I brush my thumb along his lip, my flesh just barely grazing his.

Joss opens his eyes, a brief look of disorientation crossing his face before understanding overtakes him. He smiles a drunken, lazy smile, before he closes his eyes and tightens his arm around me even more securely, clutching me tighter against his chest.

"Five more minutes," he mumbles. I barely leash the shudder that rolls through my body at the deep rumble of his morning voice.

Shivers aside, I chuckle before pushing against his chest and getting out of bed. He opens his eyes at my absence, his subtly pouty expression while he slept reappearing on his face.

"Get up, menace," I say. "It's time for the next competition."

As he begins hauling his limbs out of the bed—out of *my* bed—I open the door to head to the bathroom and stop cold. I expected to be met by the blinding morning sunlight, but instead, I'm met by darkness, the only light coming from the harsh lights above the sidewalk.

Joss appears behind me in the doorframe, his arm hovering above me on the cabin wall.

"Uh, Joss. What time is it?"

He looks over at the clock on the bedside table, the one I'd ignored in my Joss-induced haze and my siren-activated disorientation.

"It's…it's 3:00 a.m."

From somewhere across camp, I hear the unmistakable voice of Dax Philipps booming through a megaphone.

"Rise and shine, competitors! It's time for Phase Four of *American Gauntlet: Grit.*"

PHASE FOUR

★ ★ ★ ★

grit

thirty-eight

grit (n) – a firmness of mind or spirit; unyielding
courage in the face of hardship or danger

OF ALL the phases of *American Gauntlet*, Grit intimidates me
the most.

The Strength and Endurance Phases are straightforward to
prepare for. They're hard work, yes, but the work is simple. Lift
more. Run faster. Swim further. Do the work. Not necessarily
easy, but simple nonetheless.

Strategy is a bit trickier, but even then, there are tasks to be
done. Practice common puzzles. Evaluate your critical thinking
skills. Watch past seasons to see what strategy moves benefitted
competitors and which ones had them digging their own grave.
Above all, trust your gut.

Grit, however, is a whole other beast. It's in a league of
its own—a *realm* of its own. How does one prepare to face
challenges that are specifically designed to break you? To snap
your will between its iron-clad fingers? To leave you *begging* to
quit?

It's simple to prepare your body for this game. It's something
else entirely to prepare your mind.

And the way my mind has been all over the place lately
doesn't necessarily boost my confidence as I stare at the

corrugated metal warehouse-like structure before us.

In the 3:00 a.m. chaos back at camp, Dax gave us all of four minutes to change into our uniforms and load up in the van. He warned us that if we were late, we'd be disqualified from the game; I wasn't sure if he was serious or not, but I wasn't about to call his bluff. As Joss dashed to his cabin to change, I threw on my uniform and hurled a capful of mouthwash into my mouth, nearly choking on it as I ran to the van, embracing the fiery burn left in its wake. Sure enough, four minutes after Dax's announcement, the van took off, its wheels spinning slightly as it spewed the gravel beneath.

Before we left camp, everyone—especially AJ—was legitimately concerned that Naji would miss the deadline, but he made it with less than two seconds to spare, his long, inky hair spilling wildly over his shoulders. IFlustered, he attempted to tie it into his usual bun, but he kept leaving pieces of hair out (because everything is automatically more difficult in the pre-dawn hours). When he tried to shove the stray pieces back in, his usually sleek, flawless bun ended up as a lawless knot.

Unable to endure his painful struggle anymore, I reached over the seat from where I sat directly behind him and began untangling the bird's nest atop his head, combing out the tangles with my fingers. I then French braided the top part of his hair until it reached the crown of his head, where I twisted it into a neat bun and secured it with the clear elastic hair band he brought with him.

In the time I've known Naji, there have been very few moments when he was truly serious—rare moments when he wasn't hiding behind humor. When I finished his hair, he turned around and looked me square in the eyes, his own looking nearly black in the darkness. "Thank you, Dani."

There was no sarcasm, no alternate comedic meaning to his statement. Just gratitude from a friend. A friend that is also a fierce competitor, one who is directly trying to eliminate me from this game.

What an odd dynamic to be caught up in.

From where he sat beside me, Joss leaned over to me, quietly saying, "You're very good at that, even in the dark." A fresh wave of spearmint gum tingled my nose, the mintiness awakening my senses. Joss had clearly put a new piece of gum in his mouth in the four minutes we had to get ready.

"I've been doing my sisters' hair for years," I replied. "It's basically muscle memory at this point."

Joss smiled softly before tilting his head even more toward me.

"You smell like peppermint," he said. "I love peppermint."

I breathed a subtle sigh of relief, thankful that the mouthwash did its job. There's nothing worse than morning breath.

"You smell like spearmint," I replied.

"Figured it would be a good idea," he said, "just in case we end up in another situation like the last competition."

My mind jolted back to the two of us next to each other on the peg wall, our lips grazing as he took the peg from me, the two of us practically performing mouth-to-mouth.

I unwittingly bit my lip before realizing that Joss was staring at me, his eyes tracking right to my mouth, my lips. He dragged his gaze up to my eyes before a grin materialized on his face. It was flirtatious. It was bold. It was downright dangerous.

And instead of running from it, I leaned into it, my voice, barely more than a whisper. "You know, Joss, I'm beginning to think you dropped that peg on purpose."

He paused a moment, before he said, "You know, sunshine, I wouldn't jeopardize this competition for…selfish reasons."

Despite the sickeningly early wakeup call, the conversation with Joss had fully awakened my brain, just as every nerve of my body activated when he placed his hand just above my knee, his thumb brushing against the inside of my thigh. His callused hands, a reminder of the labor he performs on a daily basis, were coarse but not unpleasantly so. They felt so similar to my own.

As I stand in front of the domineering warehouse before us now, I'm thankful to have an alert mind, even though the Joss-incited butterflies have been displaced by nerves of a different kind.

It's time to find out what awaits us in the Grit Phase, and something tells me it'll be one for the books.

IN THE pre-dawn haze, the three remaining teams face Dax, anxiously awaiting our instructions. Staring at the foreboding warehouse before us, my mind begins to wander down dark, crooked paths, curious as to what could be awaiting us in this next competition. Instinctually, my hand reaches for Joss's, and heat seeps through the cool morning air as he takes my hand in his, gently brushing his thumb across mine.

Beside me, I see Joss *grinning* at the warehouse. Even Sarge and Junior are revealing a touch of fear in their features; Joss, on the other hand, looks like he's about to get his turn in the fun house at a carnival.

"The rules of this competition are simple," Dax begins. "Once inside, follow my instructions. Fail to follow instructions, fail the competition. Simple as that.

"One more thing," he adds. "This competition is pass-fail. If you don't complete the competition, you'll be on a plane back to wherever you came from. Got it?"

The six remaining competitors—me, Joss, Naji, AJ, Sarge, and Junior—each give a clipped nod of our heads.

Even in the dim light, I see the vicious gleam in Dax's eye, one that says how much he'll relish this next phase of the competition.

"Let's begin. Welcome to the Warehouse of Horrors."

Dax throws open the doors behind him, and we enter at his directive. As Joss and I cross the threshold, our hands still linked, we're met by complete darkness. Just as my eyes begin to adjust to the pitch black darkness, lights as bright as stunning streaks of lightning begin to flash across the vast space, immediately disorienting me. If it weren't for Joss's hand anchoring mine, I probably would've fallen over.

Through the rapid beams of the strobe light, I make out three cubicles on the warehouse floor, looking disturbingly close to stand-alone jail cells, complete with metal bars. In each cell stands a box that looks roughly the size of a slim telephone booth. Dax instructs each team to enter a cell, but my mind can't seem to comprehend his words. Luckily, Joss guides me toward the bay closest to us, and I'm thankful he seems to be less affected by the blinding flashes of light. As soon as we enter, we're suddenly hit by the harsh blast of sirens, twice as loud and three times as cruelly piercing as the ones that signal the competitions at camp. Each toll of the sirens reverberates through my head, and an impending headache begins to take shape.

Between the flashing strobe lights and the grating sirens, I find myself in a state of utter disorientation, but Joss grabs my other hand in his, his features flashing in front of me like snapshots of old film. With each brief flicker of his features, his eyes find mine, and they act as a grounding force, rooting me to the present moment despite the chaos surrounding me. *We can do this*, he says to me, wordlessly.

We can do this.

Over the noise, we hear Dax's instructions through his megaphone telling us to enter the phone booth-like box in our cell. As I peer at it through the abrupt strobe flashes, I see it's made of the same corrugated metal that has characterized this whole season of *American Gauntlet*. Joss and I glance at each other and then step into the box, squeezing through its slim opening. As we step in, a crew member closes the door behind us, and I hear a series of *clicks* that sound like levers sliding into place.

As soon as the door closes, Joss and I are in pitch darkness, not a single shred of light piercing through the enclosed walls around us. There's undoubtedly night-vision cameras rigged somewhere in here to catch all the action.

The booth is extremely tight for the two of us, Joss's body pressing flush against mine as we stand face-to-face (although it's more like face-to-chest considering our height discrepancy). I can't imagine how Sarge and Junior fit in the booth together.

As we stand there awaiting further instruction from Dax, I breathe in the smell of Joss's spearmint gum; that's when I notice that Joss is noticeably quiet. He always has a mood-lightening comment at the ready, and I'm shocked he hasn't taken advantage of our...*close* proximity to quip some flirtatious remark.

"What's wrong, menace? Don't tell me you're claustrophobic," I tease.

Joss's breathing quickens, tiny bursts of spearmint whirling toward me faster and faster.

Oh. He actually is *claustrophobic.*

I press my hand to his chest and feel his heart thudding rapidly, sweat beginning to dampen his uniform, bleeding through the spandex-like material. I've never seen him react this way to any of the obstacles we've faced here at *American Gauntlet*, and until this point, I honestly didn't think he feared anything. But although he sometimes seems like some invincible breed, Joss is, in fact, a human, and this very human struggle he's currently experiencing squeezes something in my chest, triggering an instinct within me to somehow make it better. To fix it.

I pull his head down toward mine and press my forehead against his.

"I'm here," I say, an unexpectedly powerful fervor seeping into my voice. "Just breathe."

Our foreheads still pressed together, I take his hand and press it to my heart. *"Breathe,"* I say again. With his hand on my chest, he can feel my slow, deep inhale, and with my other hand pressed against him, I feel him mimic it. I hold my breath for a few seconds before exhaling slowly, feeling his heart rate slow as he does the same. We repeat the process, breathing with a slow, deliberate cadence.

I reach up, cupping his cheek. "You with me, menace?"

I feel his lips curl into a smile. "Always."

"Competitors!" Dax's voice booms, amplified over the shrieking sirens by the megaphone. "There are four levers in your booth that you'll need to pull simultaneously to release yourself."

I instinctively look around before remembering it's impossible to see anything in this black hole. We'll need to feel around the space, finding the levers with our hands, but it seems easy enough. We're bound to find the levers eventually.

Dax's next statement, though, forces a fierce ripple of anxiety to flit through me.

"You have ninety seconds. Starting now."

Joss and I spring into action shooting to the walls to feel for levers. I crouch down toward the lower half of the booth, while Joss stretches his long limbs toward the ceiling where it's easier for him to reach. I immediately feel a lever down toward my left; the only indication that it's there is a miniscule gap between the metal of the wall and the metal of the lever. If you grazed over it too quickly, you'd miss it.

"There's one down here!" I yell.

I commit its location to memory and keep feeling along the bottom, my body crammed into the confined space toward the bottom.

"Top right corner!" he yells.

How many seconds have passed at this point? Thirty? Forty-five? It's nearly impossible to gauge how much time has ticked away, which only increases my intensity. If Joss and I don't complete the task in ninety seconds, we'll be out. Sent home. Done. Just like that.

I reach behind him and run my hand up the wall to his back and find another lever mid-way up.

"Found it!"

Seconds agonizingly tick away, and I can't help but imagine an hourglass precariously close to depositing its last drop of sand.

Drip.

Drip.

Drip.

"Got it!" Joss yells, but I don't breathe a sigh of relief just yet.

I won't until this booth door is open and I know we've beat the time.

"You grab the two at the top—I'll grab the two down here!"

I reach behind Joss, tugging at the small lever behind him, and stretch toward the corner where the other lever is. As I pull it, I hear Joss crank the two that he found above us. With a series of satisfying clicks, the booth door opens, and Joss and I throw our bodies out of the pitch darkness and into the flashing, strobe light-streaked bedlam from before. I'm honestly not sure which one is worse. I look to the cell door and see it's been shut and padlocked.

There's a giant red timer being projected onto the warehouse wall, and I watch as it counts down with six seconds to spare, which means one thing: We made it. We beat the time. We didn't just book ourselves a one-way ticket home.

As the timer hits 0:00, Dax blasts an airhorn, signaling that time is up. As it does, I'm suddenly hit with a wave of frigid water misting throughout our cell. I look up and see a sprinkler at the top, relentlessly raining ice cold water down on us. In less than a minute, I'm completely soaked, glacial tentacles of hair plastering themselves to my face. My hands begin to shake as my extremities turn to ice. Instantly noticing my tremors, Joss brings my hands up to his mouth, creating a little dome around my fingers with his hands, and he blows onto my fingers, warming them with the heat of his breath. It's instant relief, if only temporary.

Huge red numbers are soon projected onto the warehouse wall before us, just below the timer that has reset itself to three minutes. As I stare at the numbers, I realize they're not just numbers and symbols—they're math problems. *Oh boy.*

"Solve the three math problems on the wall," Dax orders

through his megaphone. "The answers to each math problem will open the combination lock in your cell, releasing a key. The key will open your cell door and let you out. Do it in three minutes or you'll be on the next flight home."

As the 3:00 timer ticks away to 2:59, the sirens that haven't ceased since we began this horrible competition suddenly halt, giving us one second of blessed silence. But in the next second, the sirens are replaced by exceedingly loud music…if one could call it that. Voices are shrieking, drums are banging, dissonant sounds are clashing together as one; merely thinking straight—much less solving math problems—is out of the question. I'm pretty sure these conditions are torture tactics used in less-than-legal interrogations. I'm half-convinced we'll be waterboarded next.

Torturous conditions aside, Joss and I don't have time to spare as the seconds on the bloodthirsty timer continue counting down. I take a look at the first problem, doing my best to work through it mentally. There's an unsurprising lack of scratch paper in this torture chamber.

$$(17 - 6 \div 2) + 4 \times 3$$

Order of operations. What is the order of operations? Suddenly, all knowledge of mathematics has simply withdrawn from my brain. I can't think over the flashing lights and the frigid water and the music screaming at me, leaving my skull pounding with the force of a jackhammer.

The parentheses are first, right? 17 minus 6 would be 11, then divide that by 2? Or do you divide 6 by 2 first?

"Twenty-six," Joss yells to me over the blasting screamo music. "The answer is twenty-six."

"How do you even—" I cut myself off mid-question. We don't have time for questions.

"Can you remember the answers for me?" he asks.

"That, I can do." I'm thankful for many things about Joss, but at this moment, I'm particularly grateful he is better at mental math than I am. I'll leave this one to him; I carried my weight with the tangram.

I watch as Joss starts to work out the answer to the next equation in his brain, his mouth moving slightly as if he's talking himself through each step of the problem.

$$18 \div 3 - 7 + 2 \times 5$$

"Nine!" he shouts.

Twenty-six, nine, twenty-six, nine, twenty-six, nine. I repeat the answers in my head over and over like song lyrics.

I glance at the clock. A minute and a half to go.

As Joss works through the last problem, I realize a cloudlike fog has started rolling into our cell.

I see it before I *smell* it.

The rancid odor hits me like a baseball bat to the face, filling my nostrils with the overwhelming smell of rotten eggs and sewage. My mouth drops open as I try to breathe through my mouth, rather than my nose, but it's too late. I dry heave, but suppress the bile down, willing it to return down the back of my throat with a burn.

Joss's face twists as the stink hits him, but he appears to stay focused on the last math problem, which is a relief considering we'll have no time to fix it if he gets any answers wrong. My *American Gauntlet* life is entirely in his hands—and his brain— right now, but I trust him. I'm relying on him, and while the *thought* of relying on someone else has always scared me, it just feels different with Joss. It's like my defense mechanisms are trying to convince myself that I shouldn't trust him, but I simply won't obey. Joss is my partner now. When it comes to this game, I trust him completely.

"Fourteen!" Joss shouts, whipping me back to the task at hand. "The last answer is fourteen!"

Twenty-six, nine, fourteen, twenty-six, nine, fourteen, twenty-six, nine, fourteen.

As I rhythmically repeat the answers to myself, a pressing question moves to the forefront of my mind.

"Wait—where is the combination lock?"

Joss looks at me, then around at our cell. There's a padlock on the door, but we don't see a combination lock. We frantically search the small cell, wall by wall, dragging our hands down the bars and across the floor, the dense, disgusting fog making everything difficult. I have to actively suppress the vomit that would love to make an appearance on our cell floor. I check the clock. One minute to go.

"Where is the bloody thing?" Joss yells, frustrated.

We've checked all the walls. We've checked the floor. We checked the booth. Nothing.

The only place left is the cell ceiling.

I shoot my eyes up and see a small combination lock nearly hidden behind the water sprinkler. *Sneaky producers.*

"Joss! There—by the sprinkler."

We shoot up off the ground like freshly-lit fireworks. Joss— bless his ungodly height—can reach the lock on the ceiling.

"Twenty-six, nine, fourteen!" I scream. "Twenty-six, nine, fourteen!"

Joss begins to fidget with the lock while being sprayed directly in the face with an arctic mist, while I whip around, catching another glimpse of the timer. Forty seconds to go. I watch as Joss twists the combination lock, spinning it to twenty-six, then the other direction toward nine. When he starts spinning back toward fourteen, he overshoots it, messing up the whole combination.

"It's fine, start again," I say into his ear. He gives me a brief appreciative glance before starting the process over. Thirty seconds now.

After another attempt, the fourteen slides into place and the combination opens the small attached lock box, sending a key clamoring to the floor. Twenty seconds left.

We both hit the deck, unable to see where the key went in the strobe-lit darkness and dank, musty fog. Finally, I find the key two inches from us and seize it like my life depends on it.

"I've got it!"

We tumble toward the door. Ten seconds left.

My hands are trembling uncontrollably. Whether it's from the nerves or the polar conditions, I can't tell.

I jam the key into the lock, but it doesn't turn, the moisture making it exceedingly difficult to handle. I take it out and flip it, but still, it doesn't turn. Six seconds now.

"You're fine, love," Joss says with a gentle fervor. "You've got it." He doesn't try to take the key from me and do it himself; instead, he whispers encouragingly, fully trusting me to complete my part of the task.

I flip the key back to my original starting point and slide it in gently, careful not to jam it, careful not to twist it too early. *Three seconds.* I turn it. *Two seconds.* It shoots open. *One second.*

We collapse out of the cell in a heap of tangled limbs.

A whistle. A wave of relief. A chuckle from the man lying in a jumble beneath me.

I can't help but snort as Joss loses himself in laughter as we lie on the "Warehouse of Horrors" floor, our ears numb from the music, our fingers and toes suffering frostbite from the icy water, and our nauseous stomachs in a constant battle of wills against our brains that *demand* they keep their contents inside our bodies.

I flip around and look at Joss lying beneath me. We're in almost the exact same position we were in during that very first competition when I tackled him to the ground in the mud. It feels like a lifetime ago. It feels like I've known Joss so much longer than the length of this competition…it feels like I've known him my whole life.

Through strobe light flickers, I catch glimmers of the broad smile on his face. I smile back.

"That…that was horrible," I say. "But honestly, it could've been worse."

Joss sits up beneath me, bringing me into his lap and wrapping his arms around me. His eyes soften as he says, "I hate to break it to you, sunshine, but I don't think it's over."

thirty-nine

THE Warehouse of Horrors was not, in fact, over.

Dax left us on the main warehouse floor, subjecting us to the obnoxious noise and disorienting flashes and putrid smells for a criminal amount of time before calling each team to a different part of the warehouse individually. Naji and AJ, who had broken out of their cell the fastest, were called first, followed by Sarge and Junior. Joss and I, who had escaped with all of one second to spare, were called last.

"Dani, Joss," Dax yells through his megaphone from the other side of the warehouse floor, "we're ready for you two."

Joss and I meet Dax on the other side of the warehouse, where he slides a giant metal door open and shuffles us through. When the door glides closed behind us with a *clang*, my ears finally get the reprieve they've desperately sought from the horrendous noise. A ringing persists in both ears, but I'd take that over the racket that's been assaulting my ears for the last hour any day.

The first thing I notice in the room is a giant tank of water that looks to be nearly three times as deep as a typical dunk tank, a ladder running up its side to the top. There are three padlocks lined up in a neat row at the very bottom of the tank. The next thing I notice is a plexiglass box that looks disturbingly close to the size of a coffin. The top of the box has holes roughly the size of a fist scattered across its lid. I don't have time to think about what the next part of the competition might entail—Dax chooses to enlighten us immediately.

"Ready to quit yet?" Dax asks.

Joss smirks, a defiant challenge working its way into his features. "Not on your life, mate."

"We'll see about that," Dax retorts, returning Joss's smirk. "Like the first part of our fun little adventure this morning, if you fail to complete this task, your *American Gauntlet* days are over; however, there is an incentive to finish the task quickly. If you finish in a faster time than your other competitors, you'll receive an advantage."

"Let me guess," I deadpan. "You're not going to tell us what that advantage is, are you?"

"Look at you, Dani. Catching on so quickly." Sarcasm drips from his voice like poison-laced honey.

"One of you," he continues, "will get in this box here." He slaps the coffin-like plexiglass box beside him. "Three keys will be placed in the box with you, and you'll hand the keys to your partner, one by one. Your partner will then climb up to the top of the water tank and dive down, using the key to unlock one of the three padlocks, before repeating the process until all three padlocks are unlocked. Finish this task the fastest, and you'll receive an advantage—to be announced," he adds, winking at me.

"Oi, what's the catch, mate?" Joss asks.

Dax quirks an eyebrow. "What do you mean?"

"It seems…too easy," I cut in. "Well, not the diving part, but the box—all one of us has to do is hand keys through the holes in this box? I don't buy it."

"Ah, yes," Dax replies. "I guess we'll find out, won't we?"

Fantastic.

"I'll give you two a minute to decide who will be doing what."

Joss turns to me. "What are you thinking, sunshine?"

"I'm obviously not thrilled about whatever information Dax is keeping from us, but I think I'd be stupid to keep you from doing the water portion."

Joss laughs. "I'll do whichever part you want, love. If you don't want to get in the box, you don't have to."

I bite my lip, pondering our options. Joss's offer is tempting. I hate the unknown. I hate not being able to fully prepare myself for whatever Dax has in store…but I also want to win this freaking competition, so I just need to suck it up. Plus, I can't imagine Joss would do well in such a confined space, considering the fact that he's claustrophobic.

"You do the water. I'll get in the box and hand the keys to you"

Joss grabs my hand, giving it a gentle squeeze. "Are you sure?"

"I'm sure." I don't let a drop of hesitancy trickle into my response. I need to be confident. Whatever Dax and the *American Gauntlet* producers have in store for me, I can handle it.

"It's settled then!" Dax says giddily after we tell him our decision. He claps his hands and crew members spring into action, giving Joss a pair of goggles, so he'll be able to see the padlocks underwater. They guide me over to my plexiglass coffin and to my surprise, they also give *me* a pair of goggles, but they're not the type used for swimming. They're large, oversized clear goggles that you might receive in a science lab when working with dangerous chemicals. To my dismay, they also hand me a tiny flexible plastic piece in the shape of a horseshoe.

"What's thi–"

"Nose plug."

Why would I possibly need a nose plug? My stomach twists in knots.

Finally, the crew presses an ear plug into each of my ears. They plug my ear holes, but I can still hear, although it sounds almost as if I'm underwater. Kelly walks over to me from where she was standing behind the cameras and gives me a squeeze on the shoulder.

"Ready?" she asks. She gives me a look that seems almost… apologetic.

Oh boy.

"Ready," I say with all the feigned confidence in the world. *Fake it 'til you make it, right?*

Just as I'm about to climb in the box, Joss steps beside me and tilts my goggled, nose plugged face up toward his.

"Whatever's in that box with you, you've got it. Okay, sunshine? You're a killer."

"I know," I reply, immediately laughing at how nasally my voice sounds with my nose plugged like it is.

Joss smiles, his finger lingering under my chin for another moment, before he releases me, and I climb into the box, lying down as instructed. Then, a man I've never seen before approaches me, climbing up above the box to speak to me. *Is he a crew member? Producer?* I can recognize almost any crew member at this point, but I've definitely never seen him before.

"Hi there," he says cheerily. "So just a quick tip—no sudden movements. If you need to quit and want out of the box at any point during the competition, just yell, 'STOP' and we'll remove you as soon as possible. Good luck to you!"

The mystery man exits the warehouse through a door on the other side of the room, only to reenter twenty seconds later…

…with a giant snake coiled around him.

No, no, no. Not the giant snake. Anything but the giant snake.

My silent pleas are futile. The man—and the mammoth white and yellow snake—quickly approach my prone body in the see-through plexiglass box. I've never felt more vulnerable in my life.

"This is Bertha," he says affectionately. "No need to worry—she's pretty docile. No sudden movements, though, just to be safe."

Before I can even fully process what's happening, he places Bertha's colossal body on the other side of the box, away from my head. Even though her weight is distributed across my legs, I can tell how heavy she is. Her bright yellow body, which looks to be *at least* ten feet long, slowly begins to uncoil around my legs as she begins sliding up toward my head. I don't move. I don't breathe. Her beady black eyes are tracking my every move. *She could swallow me whole. I'm pretty sure Bertha could literally swallow me in one gulp.* She pauses just in front of my face, her tongue flicking in and out just inches from me. *She can smell the fear.*

"Remember, you're more likely to die from a falling coconut!" I hear Joss shout from beside the box.

"That was sharks!"

"It probably applies to snakes too!" he shouts through a laugh.

Bertha suddenly settles in, resting her head on my sternum and easing my nerves. She almost looks…endearing. *This won't be so bad. He said she's docile. You'll be fine, Dani.*

One moment later, though, the man who had placed Bertha on me suddenly reenters the warehouse with a giant plastic bin in his hands.

Another one. There's another giant snake in there.

He climbs the step ladder to my box and opens the lid of his bin, looking down at me apologetically.

Then he unleashes dozens and dozens of snakes upon me.

It all seems to happen in slow motion. The snakes tumble out of the bin as if they're one being, a writhing, tangled mass that seems to hold its shape like a snowball. But as soon as they hit the box in a jumbled heap of scales and forked tongues, they disperse throughout the box, a snowball exploding, dozens of snakes slithering over every corner of my body. I feel them belly into my hair, burrowing near my scalp. I feel their tongues whipping in and out of their mouths. I feel their scaly bodies meandering over mine, some in quick bursts and others in slow, measured movements.

I realize I've closed my eyes, and when I open them, I instantly regret it. My vision is consumed by snakes in every size and color—blacks and rusted browns, bright oranges and lime greens. Suddenly the nose and ear plugs make sense, as some of the snakes are impossibly skinny, almost resembling a snake-worm hybrid, their bodies writhing back and forth in a sickening manner. I close my mouth as much as possible, while still allowing oxygen to flow through. The last thing I need is a snake slithering down my throat.

A crew member climbs the step ladder to my box and drops three keys in various places around the coffin; they're immediately lost in a sea of snakes. Bertha suddenly catches my eye, and her gaze is almost calming. What I would give to be in this box alone with her now.

The crew closes the lid over my box, sealing me in with a hundred of my new reptilian friends. As soon as the lid shuts and Dax sounds his whistle, my mind surges into competition mode, keeping my nerves and fears at bay. My only thought is to find the first key.

I run my hand along the bottom of the box, doing my best not to anger the mob of reptiles, and I soon feel the cool metal of a key beneath my fingertips. My first instinct is to grab it quickly and shoot it up through the opening in the box lid to Joss, but the snake handler's warning replays in my head: *no sudden movements.* So instead, I grip the key and slowly bring my arm up, displacing many of the squirming serpents as I go. One slithers down my arm precariously close to my face before shooting off toward my hair. I finally slide my hand through one of the holes in the lid, and Joss takes it from me, sprinting off toward the tank. I don't lift my head up enough to watch him as he dives into the water, not wanting to disturb the nest of snakes so close to my face, but I have no doubt he'll get the first padlock taken care of without any issues.

While Joss completes his part of the task, I begin my search for the next key, methodically moving my hands up and down the plexiglass, praying to feel that cool tinge of metal again. Bertha suddenly moves from where she had been resting on my sternum, maneuvering her solid body around the crown of my head. As she settles, I see her beady eyes out of my peripheral vision, her tongue flicking back and forth. *Is she a type of boa constrictor? Should I be worried she'll wrap herself around me, squeezing the living daylights out of me?* My knowledge of snake breeds and their behaviors is clearly lacking.

Instead of wrapping herself around me, though, she settles her head on my shoulder, and it's comforting. Like I've got someone watching my back, offering me silent support. I never thought I'd be seeking comfort from a giant snake, but here we are. This is what *American Gantlet* does to its prey.

Suddenly, my fingers brush the top of a key, and I grab it, but in my excitement, I drop it the next second. My hand instinctively shoots out to catch it, but the fast movement clearly angers a nearby snake, and I immediately feel a sharp pain in my wrist. I've been bitten.

Surely none of these are venomous…right?

Without time to contemplate if I'll lose an arm to snake venom or not, I grasp the key and slowly bring it up to the hole above me. Joss seizes it and races toward the tank while I search for the final key.

The third key is exceedingly difficult to find. It's not anywhere on either side of me, so I maneuver my hands up and around my head, wondering if it somehow worked its way up there, but I come up empty. I'll need to inch my body down toward the other end of the box, an undertaking I'm less than excited about. As soon as I move even a centimeter, the snakes become frenzied, angrily slithering around the container. I can't stop, though. An advantage is on the line, and that could be the difference in making it to the Gauntlet or not. I continue my deliberate move toward the other end like an inchworm, scooting my body down little by little, until finally, my fingers scrape across a key. I grab it and hurl it up through a hole in the lid, rejoicing as Joss plucks it from my fingers. A whistle less than two minutes later signals that Joss has unlocked the final padlock, ending this nightmare of a competition.

As soon as the familiar noise of Dax's whistle hits my ears, still piercing even through the earplugs, one thought takes over every available brain cell: *Get me out of this reptile cage. Now.*

With the assistance of the snake handler and an extra crew member, I step out of the container on shaky legs and fall straight into a soaking wet Joss, the feeling of the hoard of snakes slithering over every inch of my body lingering like a burn.

"You alright there, love?" he asks.

"I'm fine," I say, although the quiver of my voice betrays me. Now that the competition is over, my mind seems to be catching up with the fact that I was covered in dozens upon dozens of snakes, feeling every flick of their tongues, every squirm of their serpentine bodies.

Joss runs his hands up and down my arms as if he's trying to warm me up, and every movement seems to wash the sensation of the snakes away. The heaviness in my chest begins to feel lighter, like I can finally breathe again.

"You are…" Joss says, before pausing. I look up to find him already gazing down at me, a look of wonder in his sparkling blue eyes. "Fearless," he finishes.

"It's all a facade," I laugh, immediately wanting to brush off the compliment.

Joss wraps his arm around me, cool water dripping off his shoulders. "Could've fooled me," he says into my ear.

The next moment, I'm whisked off to Steph who quickly takes a look at my snake bite, assuring me that none of the snakes were venomous. There are two minuscule dots of blood on my wrist, and it doesn't require any extra care from Steph other than a wipe of antiseptic. To be honest, the bite is the least of my worries; I'm more concerned I'll be reliving this nightmare in my dreams every night from now until eternity.

When it's finally time to leave the Warehouse of Horrors, Dax doesn't say whether Joss and I beat the other teams' times or not. We're simply ushered back into a van, alone, and driven back to camp.

When we arrive back at the place we've called home for weeks, I barely feel human. I'm physically tired, but I'm mentally exhausted. The Grit Phase has been every bit as draining as I imagined it would be—if not more—and it's not even over yet.

Joss and I step out of the van and into the pre-dawn morning; it must be around 5:00 a.m. As I begin to head back to my cabin for some much-needed rest, Joss grabs my hand, not willing to let me go just yet.

"Watch the sunrise with me."

Despite my debilitating fatigue, I can't help but feel a new burst of energy at the thought of spending more time with Joss, if even for a little while longer. So while my brain knows I should refuse his request, it's some other soft, squishy part of me that answers, "I'd like that."

forty

PURPLISH-BLUE hues stain the early morning sky as Joss and I amble to the lake I've come to love so much. The water is tranquil this morning, a mirror reflecting the last remnants of the stars above, the moon waving its final farewell as it fades into the light of dawn. The air is thick and dewey, and there's something about the fresh air of the morning that feels like new beginnings.

The lakeside sounds blend together in perfect harmony around us. It's the subtle hum of crickets and the lapping of the lake water as it gently washes ashore; it's the gravelly sand crunching quietly beneath our feet as Joss and I walk hand in hand.

We stand, overlooking the lake, before a sudden shudder causes my whole body to convulse.

"What was that?" Joss asks, concern marring his features.

"I, um—I can't get the feeling of all those snakes slithering over my body out of my system." Even talking about it causes another tremble to roll through my body, giving me the sudden urge to scrub every inch of my skin with metal wool until it's red and raw.

"Well, we need to fix that."

Joss suddenly bends down, putting one arm around my waist

and the other under the crook of my knees, and lifts me off the ground as if I weigh nothing at all.

"What are we—"

Joss doesn't answer my half-question. He simply walks us straight into the lake. The chilly water nips at my toes, and I suppress a squeal.

When Joss is nearly chest deep, he stops, not venturing further into the lake, but he continues holding me securely in his arms, even though I could stand if I wanted to.

I don't want to.

"Better?" he asks.

I smile. "Better."

Despite the brisk water temperature, the warmth that Joss always seems to exude seeps into me, warming me from the inside out. Feeling his gaze boring into me, I turn my head toward him, meeting his eyes, before I shift in the water, wrapping my legs around his waist. I don't miss the subtle sigh he releases at our touch, nor do I miss the way his eyes darken as he runs them across my face, raking them down to my lips. I feel it like a caress.

He takes hold of my hand but pauses as he peers down at it. I track his gaze to my wrist, to the tiny red puncture wounds left there from the snake. As I look down at it now, I note how tiny it is, barely more than a bug bite. Even so, Joss lifts my wrist to his mouth, pressing his lips against the tender skin.

"Dani," he breathes, almost as if he can't help but say my name.

Heat courses through me like wildfire, but my thoughts war within me, my desire for Joss battling the knowledge that we're running on borrowed time. Our time together has an expiration date, and while everything is so simple here, we'll soon be back in the real world—on opposite sides of the world, no less—and everything will be…complicated. I've opened myself up in a multitude of ways to Joss, but he hasn't seen every part of me yet. I've purposely hidden away the ugly parts, the bruised and broken and battered ones.

But I choose not to think of all the reasons why this won't work. Feeling—*knowing*—that Joss wants this just as much as I do, I let myself be selfish, if just for this moment. If just for right now.

I place my hand on his face, cupping his jaw, and I run my thumb along his bottom lip. His lips part ever so slightly, and it takes every ounce of willpower to hold myself back from him; and yet, I hesitate as another thought worms its way into my brain. Maybe I've been generous with what Joss thinks of this— of me. Maybe he doesn't want anything more than wherever this exact moment leads. Maybe we can have our time and part ways when this is over, no strings attached. Maybe that would be… manageable. Maybe it wouldn't leave me absolutely gutted when it was all said and done.

Maybe all we need is this moment.

"What are we doing, Joss?" I breathe. "I need you to…to tell me what you want."

He touches his forehead to mine. "I want whatever you'll give me, sunshine."

"All I can give you is right now."

He tightens his arms around me, pulling me closer to him, eliminating any semblance of space between us.

"Then I'll take it."

With his statement, any pretense of self-control dissolves.

Joss grips my face with his callused hands, taking me gently in his grasp, before our lips finally find each other. I wrap my legs tighter around him, not wanting any part of our kiss to end because kissing Joss…kissing Joss feels like finally coming up for air when you didn't even know you needed it.

And once you get it, you wonder how you lived this long without it—how you'll ever live without it again.

He grips my thighs around him, and I slide my tongue into his mouth, relishing the taste of him, never wanting to forget it. He pulls my lip between his before I return the favor, scraping my teeth gently along his bottom lip, the lip I had gazed at, had thought about, so many times. A sigh escapes him before he pulls my head to the side, pressing his lips along my throat, my cheek, my ear. I run my hands through his hair and gently tug his head back, so I can run my lips along his jawline, our mouths eventually finding each other again like magnets too powerful to be pulled apart.

I don't know how long we trade kisses wrapped in each other's arms or when he walks us back to shore, laying me down in the sand beneath him. I don't know when he pulls away from me just so he can look at me like I'm the most beautiful thing he's ever seen before or when he pauses to trace a finger along the length of my collarbone. I don't know when I press him back against the sand, running my hand down his chest, or when I let my fingers linger along the V-shaped muscles at the base of his stomach, savoring the way his breath grows shallow when I do. I don't know when I realize that kissing Joss is a colossal mistake because I don't know if I'll ever find this type of feeling again. I don't know when I decide to not care that this mistake could ruin me because this—this is worth it.

Joss rolls onto his side, propping his head up with an arm as he presses gentle kisses to my temple, and while it's tender and sweet, it's not enough for me, not right now. I grip the back of his neck, bringing him down to me, and I nearly exhale with relief when he obliges, deepening our kiss even further. But when he pulls back a moment later, it's over all too soon.

"Not yet," I plead. "Please."

"Trust me, love," he says, pressing another kiss to my lips, my neck, "I don't want this to be over either."

"Then why are you—"

And that's when I hear them—the sirens back at camp, signaling another competition.

"So soon?" I ask, sounding nearly like a child.

Joss looks at me, a sadness in his eyes. "Looks that way, sunshine."

He bends down, kissing me one last time, and it feels fraught with emotions too big to disentangle right now. When he pulls away, I stop him so I can take in the moment—so I can take in Joss, beautiful and kind and powerful and warm, as he lays with me, the sunrise peeking over his shoulder and turning the sky the color of tangerines and pink peonies. I paint it, sketching the exact expression on his face, rendering the precise color of his eyes to memory.

I wonder if Joss knows how long his portrait will live rent-free in my mind—how when I think of it, the words "what if…" will always be etched in the background.

It takes every ounce of willpower within me to let him go. To let him stand up and help me off the sand. To leave this little sliver of paradise, one that we'll never get back.

NAJI lifts a knowing eyebrow at Joss and me as we join the teams where the producers directed us outside of the Commons.

We look admittedly guilty—both of our uniforms wet, our backs coated in damp sand, our lips red and slightly puffy.

Instead of shying away from the attention, though, Joss decides to double down on it, wrapping a muscled arm around me.

"You got something to say, mate?" he asks Naji playfully, a grin on his face.

Naji throws his hands up in the air in mock surrender. "Nope, no comment here."

"Now *that's* a first," I quip, drawing a laugh from Sarge who's standing nearby. Even Junior flashes a rare smile.

Naji's lips curl into a smirk. "I'll let that one slide since you helped me out with my hair this morning."

"Oh stop—you know I love you."

"I love you too," he replies, "even though I'll need to take you and Joss-o out of the competition here pretty soon," he adds, placing a hand on Joss's back in a feigned apology.

A laugh circulates through our small group of remaining contestants, but a paper-thin cloak of sadness seems to descend on us, each of us suddenly looking anywhere but at each other. As much as I hate to admit it, it's difficult to think about eliminating any of the remaining competitors since we've all grown so close. We're like our own little dysfunctional family, having spent hour upon idle hour with each other in between the competitions over the last month. We all know how badly each of us wants to win. The thought of crushing their dreams is a bitter pill to swallow, but it's one I'll choke down because I know what waits for my family on the other side of that finish line.

"How did y'all do in the competition?" I ask Naji, wanting to distract myself from less pleasant thoughts. "Not scared of snakes, I hope," I add with a wink.

"I told you before, Dani. I'm scared of one thing—well, two things if you count my mom, who I am most definitely terrified of—but I can't imagine a situation where I would encounter either of those things here."

"You say that, but now the producers are going to fly her in just to give you a tongue lashing on national TV," AJ retorts. "Wait, speaking of snakes—Junior, don't tell me you opted for the snake pit?"

The image of Junior running around in nothing but a towel, desperately trying to get away from Naji's fake snake seems to play simultaneously in everyone's mind, sending a rumble of laughter through the group.

"Now, son," Sarge says to AJ, "if Junior had been the one in the snake box, we'd be on a plane home by now."

"Pops!"

"What? It's true!"

Before Junior can defend himself, a wave of coldness suddenly washes over the group's cheery demeanor like a winter chill, which means one thing.

Dax is here.

"Hello, everyone," he says, all business. "Hope you all made good use of your time since I last saw you an hour and a half ago." Dax suddenly turns his eyes on Joss and me, giving us a pointed look that you might receive from a disappointed teacher. I'm not sure if he gathered what Joss and I had been up to from our appearance or if he gets play-by-plays from the crew who were probably filming the whole thing while hiding behind a rock—which is so unsettling, now that I think about it—but Dax knows. He definitely knows.

Heat rushes to my face, and it's only heightened when Joss

leans down, his lips brushing my ear as he says, "I'd say it was definitely a good use of our time."

"What was that, Joss?" Dax asks, an impish look suddenly appearing on his face. "Care to share with the group?" *And the world,* I think.

I expect Joss to laugh it off, but instead, he clears his throat and loudly declares, "You got it, mate. I said it was *definitely* a good use of our time."

I shoot my eyes up to Joss and can't help but crack a smile. Maybe it's the fact that Joss doesn't cower to Dax…or maybe it's the fact that Joss isn't ashamed of me. This fact does all sorts of things to my heart, which I can feel beating out of my chest. My smile only widens even more as something I never thought I'd witness happens: Dax laughs. And it isn't just any laugh—it's a belly-deep roar, a keeled-over, gasping-for-air fit of laughter. I never thought I'd see the day.

"Sorry guys," he says, reining in the last remnants of his uncharacteristic bout of laughter. "I just didn't expect that."

A wink later, he clears his throat and pastes his classic, emotionless mask back on his face as if nothing happened.

"Anyway," he continues, grunting deeply while clearing his throat again, "welcome to the next competition of the Grit Phase. I'm particularly excited about this one," he says, flashing a wolfish grin.

Oh, goody.

A producer hands Dax a small box, and he quickly takes the lid off and reaches inside. *Please don't pull any snakes out of that box, I silently plead.*

Fortunately for us, Dax doesn't pull any living creatures out of the box; instead, he pulls out a set of clear plastic cups that look like see-through Red Solo cups. Each cup has a red line at the top, just a few centimeters from the top rim. Dax proceeds to hand each of us a cup.

"I'll explain what you'll be doing with these in a moment," Dax says, "but first, about the results from our competition earlier…"

Please be us. Please be us. Please be us.

I repeat the words in my head like a prayer. It's absolutely necessary for Joss and I to win this phase of the competition to avoid going into an elimination round against Naji and AJ or Sarge and Junior. Anything can happen in eliminations, and it's a risk that I'd like to avoid at all costs.

"Congratulations to everyone's favorite *showmance*, Joss and Dani," Dax says, throwing a bold wink in our direction.

I squeal as Joss picks me up and spins me around, too excited to care about the inaccurate showmance moniker; instead, I soak in the pure bliss that is an *American Gauntlet* win, one that tastes even sweeter with Joss by my side. A tinge of sadness suddenly hits me, despite the elation from the results.

It'll hurt when Joss and I go our separate ways at the end of this thing. It'll hurt badly.

So much for *"Maybe we just need this moment."* It may have been enough for Joss, but it's not enough for me.

"Your advantage is in your hands," Dax says, regripping my attention.

Holy smokes. I need to focus.

Joss and I look down at the cups in our hands, and that's when I notice that the red line on our cups is further down than the lines on the rest of the competitors' cups by half an inch or so. I don't wait for Dax to explain what this advantage entails, nor do I indulge him with questions. Instead, I stare back at him with a ferocity that rivals his own. I just got a taste of winning, and boy, does it taste sweet.

With our win, the blaze inside me that had dimmed to a mere kindling was reignited; I'm reinvigorated, I'm refocused. I'm ready to win.

When we follow Dax into the Commons, something smells… *off*. I can't quite place it, but it definitely smells different—and distinctively less pleasant—than usual. Typically, the Commons smells of freshly cooked food or of the cleaning products the crew uses to clean in between meals, always leaving a fresh lemony scent behind, but now, there's an almost musky smell, a mixture of mildew and old fish. It's decidedly off putting.

"Geez, what *is* that?" Naji asks no one in particular.

My nose scrunches slightly as I say, "I'm sure we're about to find out."

The producers direct us to stand on one side of the broad white island, while Dax moves to the other side. He bends below the counter and suddenly pops back up with an oversized blender, which he plugs in immediately. He bends down again, this time bringing a large pitcher up with him. He removes the lid from the pitcher, and the smell it emits is staggering. It's the type of stink that you feel inside of you as you breathe, like it's coating your throat, your nose, your stomach. I'm surprised Dax's nose hairs haven't been singed off from the odor; on second thought, maybe they have been singed off; that's how powerful the smell is.

The disagreeable smell from moments ago was only a hint at the odor coming from the pitcher. It's now a full-on assault to the senses.

As soon as the full force of the odor hits my nose, I place it immediately.

Sour, rotten milk.

There were too many times in high school when we'd try to stretch how far our milk could go, unsure when we could get more, only to open the jug and find it had gone sour. It's a smell you don't easily forget.

"*Ooo-wee*, that'll clear the sinuses," Sarge remarks.

Drawing out his actions in dramatic fashion, Dax takes the pitcher and slowly pours it into the huge blender, and my suspicions are confirmed. As the off-white, almost yellowy substance is poured into the blender, it's clear that it's not entirely liquid. Chunks, large and small, fall from the pitcher into the blender with pronounced *plops*, sending sprays of liquid up the side of the clear blender.

After ensuring every last drop—and lump—is in the blender, Dax puts a large bucket on the counter, and although I didn't think the smell could get worse, good grief, was I wrong. As Dax takes the lid off, the odor of fish inundates my senses. I feel the overwhelming need to gag, but I hold it in, not wanting to show any sign of weakness to my competitors, nor to Dax. Nor to all of America watching, for that matter.

Beside me, Joss must either have the same idea or the smells actually don't affect him at all because he is entirely expressionless. Either way, I'm thankful to have him as a partner. I'm not sure Lana would be able to stomach what is clearly about to go down—literally. I just hope it also doesn't come back up.

Without a word, Dax pours the bucket into the blender with the sour milk, revealing its contents: fish parts. I see fish heads, fish tails, fish *entrails*, all of it swimming in a pool of rotten, lumpy milk.

While the blender is nearly full to the brim, Dax bends down one last time, resurfacing with a giant, raw onion. He throws the whole thing, skin and all, in the blender for good measure, then he blends the concoction together. It produces a sickening grayish, curdled mixture that looks almost as bad as it smells.

Almost.

With a look of pure glee on his face, Dax walks to each of our cups and fills it to the red line. "Made with love," he says endearingly as he passes. I've never been more thankful for an advantage; the half inch less that we have to consume could make all the difference. I notice the crew placing small trash cans next to each team as well. *Here we go.*

"The rules of this competition are simple," Dax begins. "The team that finishes their concoctions first wins. The other two teams will be headed to an elimination competition. Hope you've got the grit—and the stomachs."

While the other competitors gripe to one another, Joss and I look at each other with an unrivaled fierceness that soon gives way to a smile.

"What's your favorite ice cream flavor, sunshine?" Joss asks, grinning.

"Easy," I say. "Mint chocolate chip."

"It looks like it's your lucky day," he says with a wink. "How sweet of Dax to make a mint chocolate chip milkshake, just for you."

As I laugh, Dax blows his whistle—which is entirely unnecessary in the confines of the Commons—signaling the start of the competition.

Joss and I grab our cups, clinking them together.

"Cheers, love."

"Cheers, menace."

And with that, we plug our noses and start chugging.

As soon as the mixture hits the back of my throat, I know I'm going to vomit. Whether it's now or later is up for debate, but it'll happen eventually. The mouthfeel of the spoiled milk, coupled with the gritty texture of blended fish and the burn of raw onion is unlike anything I've ever experienced before. It's an utter abomination. I don't know who thought of this specific potion of foods, but whoever it is needs some serious help. This shouldn't be legal.

I know I need to distract myself between gulps or I'll never stomach the whole cupful.

"You didn't tell me your favorite ice cream flavor," I grit out, nearly gagging again even just opening my mouth.

In between grimaces, Joss smiles, clearly welcoming the distraction.

"Chocolate." He takes a huge swig. "Chocolate milkshakes are my favorite."

"It's your lucky day" I joke, forcing the mixture and the bile down my throat. "That looks like the best chocolate milkshake ever."

Joss takes another swallow and then begins chewing slightly, apparently finding a large chunk of fish…or onion?

"Ah, would you look at that?" he says. "Dax even mixed in some Tim Tams. What a bloke!"

I raise a brow. "What are Tim Tams?"

"You're breaking my heart, Dani," he says, and I relish the way the word *heart* sounds through his accent, not an "r" sound to be heard. It distracts me from the monstrosity I'm currently consuming. "If we win this competition, I'll fly you to Australia just so you can taste Tim Tams for yourself."

I laugh. "Deal."

"Deal," he says, smiling. "Bottoms up, love."

I bring the cup to my mouth one last time and drain its contents. My mouth bulges at the volume, and I'm worried

I'll spew it everywhere, but I force it down, flashing my empty mouth to the producers so they know I've finished. Joss finishes a second after me, and I hear Dax's blessed airhorn.

It's over. Joss and I won. Again.

We had been so distracted with each other that I didn't even notice what was happening with the other competitors. For once, Joss's distraction was a *benefit*; I nearly laugh at the irony. I look to my left and see Sarge and Junior have nearly finished their drinks, but now that the competition is over, Junior is curled over their trash can, clearly sick. To my right, I see Naji has gotten pretty far, but AJ can barely stomach any of his. The death glare Naji gives his brother signals there's clearly some animosity between the two over AJ's less-than-stellar performance.

But none of it matters because Joss and I won, which only means one thing.

"Congratulations, Dani and Joss," Dax says, a scarce smile on his face. "You two have proven yourselves in every phase of this game…"

Holy smokes. It's happening. Here it comes.

"You do have what it takes to face the Gauntlet."

You do have what it takes to face the Gauntlet.

I want to tattoo Dax's words on my forehead for the entire world to see for the rest of my life. I had imagined Dax saying that exact phrase to me ever since I found out I'd be on the show, but actually hearing it come out of his mouth? I'll never forget it. I'll record this part of the show whenever it airs on TV and replay it over and over again, putting it on an endless loop to lull me to sleep at night. I'll knit it into a sweater. I'll paint it on my bedroom wall. I'll shout it from the freaking rooftops. I'm running the Gauntlet, and I'm doing it *with Joss*. And we could freaking win this thing.

The only question is which team we'll be running against.

As he nonchalantly exits the Commons, Dax throws one last word for all of us over his shoulder. "See you all at the elimination—tonight."

forty-one

AS WE walk into the arena in two single-file lines, each teammate walking next to their partner, apprehension dangles in the air. Having already secured our spot in the Gauntlet, Joss and I peel off toward the stands at the direction of producers to take our place as spectators. The other teams watch as we separate from the group, a hint of envy in their eyes.

The brief sorrow brought on by our moment of camaraderie before the last competition has all but vanished, leaving a ferocity in its wake. For Naji, AJ, Sarge and Junior, it's do or die, win or go home, put up or shut up. They've got their backs against the wall, and they *must* take the other team out or kiss their dreams goodbye.

I'll miss whichever team leaves us tonight, but I'll also celebrate it, knowing Joss and I are one step closer to winning. The bonds I've formed with this group of people will remain long after the conclusion of the show, so while I'll be sad for either Naji and AJ or Sarge and Junior to leave, I won't mourn it.

As Joss and I take our place in the stands, it's hard not to think back to the very first week here when I found myself in an elimination against Benji. The stands had been more crowded then; the Twisted Twins had been wishing for my downfall, but even then, I'd heard Joss's voice over the noise, cheering me on. Encouraging me.

I feel his presence next to me, and I want to reach out and tuck my hand into his. I want to nestle into the crook of his shoulder and breathe in the scent of him. I want to crane up on my tiptoes and surprise him with a kiss, just because I can.

But I can't.

I can't because Joss isn't mine. Those are privileges I don't hold the rights to.

While our moment together and subsequent win had left both of us on cloud nine, we spent the remainder of the day apart, both of us heading back to our separate cabins for some much-needed sleep. I spent a solid hour in the bathroom, puking my guts up and brushing my teeth no less than twenty-eight times, restraining myself from chugging the entire bottle of mouthwash to disinfect my insides after consuming the mixture that Dax had cooked up for us. Afterwards, I collapsed into bed, letting sleep take hold of me for hours. Later, I was awoken by a knock at the door that produced a sleepy smile and subtle butterflies in my belly. I hoped it was Joss, but it turns out, it was Kelly, telling me it was time to head to the elimination.

The van was tense, as Sarge, Junior, AJ, and Naji mentally prepared for the elimination, so Joss and I didn't speak. I craved his touch, just a squeeze of his hand or the brush of his fingers over my knee, but it never came. He seemed far away, lost in thought…or maybe just distant from me; it's left me feeling like he just needed to get whatever it was he was feeling this morning out of his system. He just needed that moment. And while I thought I'd prepared myself for this exact situation, I was woefully unprepared for how much I had latched onto Joss, how my roots had started to take hold of him, clinging to every bit of him. Now it feels as if they've been harshly ripped out of the earth, tattered and broken.

"Who do you want to win?" Joss asks, turning toward me from where he's seated in the stands beside me.

It's the first time Joss has spoken to me since the competition this morning, and it wrenches me out of my thoughts. Joss's face gives away nothing of what he's feeling. The question is posed as purely game strategy.

"Um, I'm not sure." It's the truth. I honestly don't know which team would be better to take on in the Gauntlet. "Who do you think would be best?"

Joss sighs and runs a hand over his face. "I don't know, Dani."

I usually love the way my name sounds when Joss says it, but I can't help but notice he didn't call me by my nickname. While I used to hate the mocking "sunshine," I've actually grown quite fond of it because…because it reminds me of him.

It's probably better this way—better that he starts distancing himself now, so it'll be less difficult for me when he goes back to his corner of the world after this is over. Our partnership is purely business; I don't doubt we'll still be able to work seamlessly together when it's time to face the Gauntlet.

In the arena ring before us are two thick ropes, each with a red line in the middle, sitting in the sand parallel to one another. It's one of the simplest setups I've seen, and if I'm correct, it looks like there will be a tug-of-war of sorts going on. While Sarge and Junior, with their intimidating physiques and bloated muscles, appear like they would have an advantage in a game like this, I know better than to underestimate Naji and AJ. They have so much functional strength and an innate ability to manipulate their bodies to their advantage…it really may be a toss up.

"Hello, competitors," Dax says, as he moves to stand before

the two competing teams. "This elimination game is simple, a playground favorite: tug of war. Pull the rope until the red line reaches your hands, and you win. Please go stand opposite your opponent."

Naji moves to one side of a rope, standing opposite of Junior. AJ moves to the other rope, standing opposite of Sarge.

I'm trying to figure out how the game will work if one teammate loses, while the other teammate wins. Will they do best two out of three? Will they—

"Oh, sorry, fellas," Dax says, a sinister look suddenly manifesting on his face. "I left one thing out. You won't be competing against the other team—you'll be competing against *your own teammate.*"

I blanch, my eyeballs nearly popping out of their sockets. They—they have to take out their own teammate? The producers have forced these teams to endure so much through the whole competition together, only to rip them apart in the end.

It's cruel.

"You can't be serious!" Junior shouts. "Only one of us is advancing to the Gauntlet?"

"Looks that way," Dax replies, flicking an invisible piece of dirt off of his shirt sleeve.

Naji, who always has something to say about every situation, is surprisingly quiet. He absently drags his foot through the sand, a look of pure dejection on his face.

"That's…" AJ starts, but trails off without the appropriate word. "That's just messed up."

Dax looks at him with a stark lack of kindness. "Looks like you should've just chugged that smoothie earlier then, huh, AJ?"

Holy smokes.

I whip my head up to Joss and find him already staring at me, a look of almost fear in his eyes. We're both thinking the same thing—what if we had to be the ones to compete against each other? To pulverize the other's dreams? Joss knows how much this prize money means to me. I know how much winning means to him, the message he wants to send to the world. It would be downright devastating to take that from each other.

Joss lifts a hand toward me, as if to cup my cheek or tuck a stray hair back into my buns, but he halts, withdrawing his hand just as quickly as he'd raised it. The little piece of hope that had so quickly bloomed in the pit of my belly suddenly crumples, a wilted flower starved for water.

Joss turns his attention back to the ring, as AJ and Naji position themselves on opposite sides of one rope, Sarge and Junior doing the same on the second rope.

"If any of you try to purposely lose the competition so your partner can move on," Dax says, "you'll both be eliminated. Don't be stupid. Put your full effort into this game or suffer the consequences."

I imagined Sarge might throw the competition for his son's sake, but with a threat like that, I doubt he will.

Each competitor lifts the hefty rope in their hands. Their muscles brace tightly as they anticipate the opposing force on the other side of the rope. Dax's whistle sounds, and just like that, they're each in their own fight for their *American Gauntlet* lives.

Naji and AJ are immediately at an impasse, neither brother giving an inch, but that's not the case for their counterparts. While father and son struggle against each other, Junior begins making slow but steady progress, the red line in the middle of the rope inching toward him with every pull. It's a laborious grind; nearly ten minutes pass, yet the red line is only half way toward Junior's side. Another few minutes pass, but Sarge doesn't make any leeway.

Just as I think Junior has nearly sealed his father's coffin, Junior loses his footing in the sand and goes flying forward. The rope is yanked from his hands, and heeding Dax's word of caution, Sarge doesn't throw the competition to his son, doesn't allow him even a second to gather his bearings. His thickly corded muscles begin pumping as he hauls the rope back toward him. The red line passes the middle where it began, moving quickly toward Sarge. Junior, sand clinging to his sweat-soaked skin, gets back to his feet, but it's too late. The momentum is already moving so quickly in Sarge's direction that despite Junior's best efforts, the red line reaches Sarge. Their battle is over.

Sarge will be running the Gauntlet.

As soon as the pair realizes their struggle is over, they both collapse to the ground.

"I'm sorry, son," Sarge says, hanging his head.

"What are you sorry for?" Junior asks through heaving breaths. "You deserve to face the Gauntlet just as much as I do, if not more."

Meanwhile, Naji and AJ haven't conceded even an inch to the other. In a deadlock, they hold onto the thick girth of the rope for twenty minutes, possibly more. Sweat slithers down both of their faces, the salty drops sliding into their eyes. When the red line moves in the direction of one brother, it's immediately corrected by the other. I begin to wonder if we'll be here all night, simply waiting for one of them to slip up, when the red line begins sliding toward AJ. Sweat has greased the palms of Naji's hands, making it difficult for him to hold his grip. AJ starts pulling and pulling, each heave moving him one step closer to victory, when he slips up. He drops the rope, his fingers fumbling over the others to regain control, and Naji seizes the opportunity. The momentum has swung toward Naji on a dime, and he knows it. I see it on his face; he's gotten a taste of impending victory, and he wants the whole thing now. He tugs the rope toward him in huge, sweeping lugs, and while AJ doesn't give up, his efforts are futile. Minutes later, the red line touches Naji's hands. It's over.

The brothers collapse into the sand, both of their heads hanging. Junior and Sarge walk to them, bracing each of their shoulders in solidarity, a kind gesture from the only other people on the planet who knows what this exact moment feels like. AJ finally stands to his feet and walks toward his brother, Naji's head hanging in sadness and disbelief.

"I'm sorry," Naji says, unable to look his brother in the eye.

"Don't be," AJ says, helping Naji to his feet. "You just got me out of enduring whatever sick, twisted Gauntlet they've come up with this year."

Naji finally cracks a smile, bringing his brother into a sweaty, one-armed hug. The producers then signal for the elimination competitors to be brought before Dax.

"I hate to say it…" Dax begins.

"No, you don't," Junior snipes. "Just get on with it."

Through a flash of a grin and the quirk of an eyebrow, Dax deals his death blow. "Junior, AJ—you do not have what it takes to face the Gauntlet. Your time here on *American Gauntlet* is finished."

"It's been fun, brother," AJ says to Naji as he and Junior are led away out of the arena.

Dax summons Joss and I toward the group. When we join him, he addresses us stoically.

"Well, here we are. Naji, Sarge—you *do* have what it takes to face the Gauntlet. You two will compete as individuals against Joss and Dani, who will compete as a team…unless one of you is ready to jump ship?"

There it is. The dangled carrot.

My mind considers the opportunity in a brief flash, like an abrupt bolt of lightning. The $300,000 prize is tempting. It wouldn't be split in two. I could pay for Penny's program, I could help Lana get a car, I could help my mom out. It would solve a lot of immediate problems. It's alluring; there's no doubt about it.

But it's also a mirage in the desert.

Although I don't know where Joss and I stand personally, I know where we stand in this game. I know, deep in my soul, that we're stronger together than we are apart. And I know we'll need every ounce of that strength to beat Naji and Sarge in the Gauntlet.

For the first time in my life, I feel like the odds are stacked in my favor if I have Joss by my side.

So while the offer is tantalizing, I turn to Joss and ask, "Are you with me?"

His eyes light up as he replies, "Always."

forty-two

SLEEP doesn't find me, despite the late hour. I tell myself my sleep schedule is off because I slept most of the day, but I know that's only a fraction of the problem.

I can't get Joss out of my head.

After hours of tossing and turning to no avail, I decide to get some ice cream at the Commons because it just feels right at the moment. I wish Ford were here to take me through the Wendy's drive thru for a Frosty, but chocolate ice cream will have to do. I walk by the wardrobe mirror on my way out, giving myself a once-over. I absently comb my fingers through my hair before deciding I don't need to change out of my old t-shirt and black spandex for my ice cream run. No one will be out and about the camp at this time of night.

I slide on a pair of shoes, but as I open the door to my cabin, I'm surprised to see Joss on the other side of the threshold, his fist half-raised as if he were about to knock.

"Oh," we both say at the same time, our tones a mixture of surprise coupled with a tinge of embarrassment.

"I—" we both start again, then stop, laughing a little. I shut my mouth and decide to let him speak since he's the one who showed up at *my* doorstep.

"I couldn't sleep," Joss finally says.

"Me neither."

"Care to have a chat?"

"Okay," I say, but I stop him as he begins to walk into my cabin. "Not here," I say, not wanting our conversation to be captured for all of America to witness.

"Lead the way then, sunshine."

Joss follows me as we wind our way through the camp, past the majority of the crew cabins. We come to a stop behind the furthest one, and I realize we're in the exact same spot we were on our very first night here at the *American Gauntlet* camp, when I thought Joss had manipulated me or, at the very least, lied to me. Turns out, it couldn't have been further from the truth.

Joss stands before me, his back to the cabin. I want to reach out to him, to take his hands in mine, but I refrain. He hasn't touched me since this morning, and I don't want to cross any boundaries he may have set.

Joss looks down, then sighs, running a hand through his loose blonde hair, and that's when I get this pit in the bottom of my stomach. His brows are knit together in a way that looks almost apologetic, and I have the distinct feeling he's about to tell me what a horrible mistake we made this morning.

"Listen, Dani. I—"

"We don't have to do this," I say, cutting him off, unable to bear hearing the words come from his mouth. "You don't owe me anything, Joss. What happened this morning can stay there. We don't have to discuss it."

He looks up at me, his eyes wide in alarm. "Is that what you think I was going to say?" Hurt stains his voice.

"I...I don't know," I say, suddenly second guessing my ability to read him.

He laughs, a low, rumbly growl of a thing. "Bloody hell, Dani. That's not what I was going to say."

Relief floods through me like a cool rush of air, but it's quickly tainted by a sudden feeling of…of apprehension. If Joss *doesn't* regret kissing me this morning, that only means one thing. This conversation just took a turn, and the direction it's heading is so unfamiliar for me. The discomfort urges me to erect the stone walls I've become so good at constructing, but another part of me knows that this isn't Justin. This isn't my dad.

This is Joss.

He steps forward, closing the distance between us and bending down to press his forehead to mine. My breath hitches as his skin touches mine, feeling so right and so terrifying at the same time.

"I was going to say," he breathes, "that I can't stop thinking about you. I haven't been able to stop thinking about you all day."

His words are charged. They're a loaded gun, and this feels so different than it did this morning. It's like we were both lying to ourselves then, but now it's time to pay up.

"I wanted to give you some…space today. If you needed it," he says. "But I don't want to stay away from you, Dani. I—I *can't.*"

"Lana was wrong." The words come out of my mouth before I can even think about them.

"Lana was wrong about what?" Joss asks quietly.

"When we were on the cliffs before the first Endurance competition—Lana said I wasn't scared of anything. She was wrong. There's one thing that scares me more than anything."

"And what's that?" he breathes.

"*You.*"

Joss pulls back from me. He places a finger under my chin, tilting it up toward him. Even in the near darkness, his blue eyes—the eyes that I'll never be able to get out of my head—find mine.

"Well if we're making admissions, I need to tell you something too then. I lied to you."

My first response is to pull away from him, but I don't. His gaze, his touch, roots me in place.

"About what?" My voice comes out as barely more than a whisper.

The edges of his mouth quirk into the brief makings of a smile before he replies, "This morning, when I said I wanted whatever you would give me." He tilts my head up more, making sure I look directly in his eyes. "I lied. It's not enough, Dani. I want all of you. Every last piece."

At Joss's words, my heart blooms and breaks at the same time. It's everything I've ever wanted to hear, and yet, it's a lie. An unwitting lie, but a lie nonetheless.

Joss doesn't know all of me. He doesn't know what I've so carefully hidden from him.

So I tell him.

I start at the beginning. With my dad walking out on us when I was thirteen. With my mom plummeting into the dark, poison-fueled hole she tumbled into. With me caring for Penny and Lana as if they were my own kids, even though *I* was just a kid at the time. I tell him about Justin, including every humiliating detail—how desperate I was to be loved. How I begged him to stay with me and blamed myself when he cheated. How all of these things have twisted my perception of love, have made me terrified of being left, of being abandoned. I tell him how I don't know if I'll ever be able to be in a healthy relationship. How I don't even know what that looks like.

I deliver my story as pragmatically as possible, not wanting my emotions to muddy the message. I avoid his eyes as I bring it to a close.

"So what I'm saying is I'm sure there are hundreds of girls back home in Australia who are better for you than I am—who would make you happier than I'll ever be able to. And that's… that's all I want for you, Joss. I want you to be happy." I meet his eyes, needing him to feel the sincerity of my statement. "You deserve all the happiness in the world."

He takes a deep breath before he speaks to me.

"Listen to me carefully," he says, cupping my face with both of his rough, callused hands. "I could search the whole of Australia and never find what I'm looking for, Dani—because I'd be looking for you."

I pull my face from his hands. "You don't know what you're saying. You—you don't know what you'd be getting into with me."

"I see every bit of you, and no matter how hard you try to put me off, I won't let you," he says, his voice raw with unleashed emotion. "I see you, Dani Di Laurentis. You're beautiful. Every part of you."

"I'm not though, Joss. I'm not!" I scream, banging my fists against his chest, tears streaking down my face. "People say they love the rain until all it does is rain. Day after day after day, it pours. It grows tiresome, bleak—it's downright depressing. Suddenly all they wish for is sunshine. You might think you want this, Joss, until it's too much. There's too much baggage, too many complications, too many flaws. Too much rain."

"Is that really all you see, Dani? " He looks at me with a tenderness I've never known. "Do you want to know what

I think of when I think of the rain? I think of a desert, of a drought, of an unquenchable thirst—of things that would beg for just one drop of water because it's not just rain—it's a force that *gives life.* And that's what you are, Dani. You take care of the people you love with a fervor I've never seen before. You helped Tris and Benji finish that first competition because they couldn't finish it on their own. You include Sarge when he feels out of place. You show small kindnesses every day, just like you did with Naji this morning. That's why I call you sunshine, Dani. You are *radiant.* Stunningly bright, as brilliant as the sun itself. But if you want to be the rain, then so be it. You're the rain in the desert, Dani—and I'll beg for you."

I don't have the words to respond to Joss. I'm trying to understand, to grasp, this wholly unfamiliar feeling of being chosen. Fought for. *Begged* for. I don't have the words to tell Joss how I feel.

So I show him instead.

I grip the back of his neck, lacing my fingers through his hair, before I bring my mouth to his, savoring the way his lips open and close over mine. I press my body toward his, walking until his back is pressed against the wall behind him and all I feel is the plane of his chest flush against mine. I savor everything about him—the sigh he makes when I kiss him in the crook of his jaw just below his ear. The way his muscles tighten when I press a hand under his shirt. The throaty sound he makes when I run my hands through his hair, tilting his head back so I can kiss his neck.

Joss brings his mouth back to mine before he pulls away for a moment, both of us breathing heavily. He presses a tender kiss to my forehead, then to the tip of my nose, then to my lips.

He brings his mouth to my ear, kissing it gently, before

he whispers, "You're beautiful, sunshine." Another kiss. "Devastatingly so."

I turn my face toward his, so I can look into his eyes, as I whisper back, "*You're* the sunshine."

A smile. "You can call me whatever you want, love."

I kiss him, even as my lips give way to a grin. "Menace," I breathe.

"Say it again."

"*Menace.*"

Joss brushes his lips against my ear. "Ah," he whispers, "The problem is you've always thought I didn't like it when you called me that. The truth is, sunshine, *I love it.*"

Suddenly, Joss scoops me off the ground in one effortless motion. I wrap my legs around him as he flips us around, pressing me against the wall as he takes my mouth in his. The metal shudders behind us, sending a rumble through the camp.

I laugh through our kiss. "You'll wake the whole camp."

"Are you worried a camera crew is going to come running out here?" he teases. "I don't care one bit. In fact, I hope they do come out here. I'll tell the whole world how keen I am, love. I'll scream it from the bloody rooftops."

I press another kiss to his lips.

"I've never met anyone like you, Kellan Josskowski."

JOSS and I walk back to my cabin hand-in-hand, stealing kisses from each other along the way. I don't know what all this means. I don't know how it's going to work when we leave the show. I don't know a lot of things.

But I do know that I'd be an absolute idiot to let Joss get away.

I'm learning that when you have something this pure, this good, you can't be scared of what might happen. You have to take hold of it. Cherish it. Love it for all its worth.

And one thing's for sure: Lana was right. Joss is a good one.

When we arrive at my cabin, he bends down to kiss me, but I stop him.

"Stay," I say. "Please."

He smiles. "Anything for you, sunshine."

So, together, we climb into the tiny twin bed that I've come to love and fall asleep side by side, permanent smiles plastered to our ridiculously, stupidly, obnoxiously happy faces.

forty-three

THREE days pass, yet it's felt like three hours. While the last month here has seemed to move at half speed here at the *American Gauntlet* camp, it suddenly started ticking triple time just when I wanted it to slow down even more.

The producers and crew members have been preparing for the Gauntlet with an almost voracious hunger, as if they've all morphed into Dax Philipps lookalikes. Many of them have been off-site, prepping Lord knows what for us at various locations, but I've been able to suppress my building nerves with a notably tall, blonde Australian.

The past three days have felt like a honeymoon for Joss and me, giving our new relationship the time and space to bloom like a wildflower in the spring. We're utterly inseparable.

We're also disgustingly happy. It's the kind of gross, over-the-top happiness that I didn't think existed until I got to experience it for myself. Now I never want to imagine life without it.

"*Geez*, get a room," Naji griped as Joss stole a sweaty kiss from me while we were working out together in the gym pavilion yesterday. Comment aside, I was happy Naji was starting to get back to himself; he took AJ's elimination—at his own hand— particularly hard.

All things considered, Sarge was doing well. I'm sure twenty-five plus years in the military helps you handle curveballs better than most, and he's still seemed like his upbeat, mildly self-deprecating self over the last few days. And while he likes to joke about being "an old bag of bones," I won't underestimate him, not for a second. He's the picture of health and has endurance for days. I've seen him up at dawn running sprints up and down the nearby mountains, not to mention all the strength sessions he completes at the gym *twice* a day, plus the mental strength he's developed over his long military career. As endearing as Sarge is, I have to see him for what he truly is: a formidable opponent.

Competitions aside, though, I can't help but love him.

"Ah," he sighed while sitting next to me at the dining table in the Commons one afternoon. I hadn't realized I'd been staring at Joss from across the Commons as he cleaned up our lunch one day. Sarge apparently took notice. "You two remind me of me and my girl back in the day. Couldn't get enough of her. Still can't," he added with a fond smile.

Indeed, the last three days with Joss have been filled with some of the most honey sweet moments of my life, but while our mini-vacation has been the biggest gift for our fledgling relationship, I've still felt a tiny shard of doubt pressing into my mind, a razor-sharp sliver of glass pressing against my skull.

It's that little splinter that worms its way into my head as Joss and I spend our last night together before the Gauntlet tomorrow. We're at our spot by the lake—our lake. Joss sits with his back against a lakeside boulder. I'm nestled between his legs, his arms around me like the security blanket that he is. I lean back into his chest and press my mouth to his neck, pausing to breathe him in. A brief wave of coconut shampoo hits me as he shakes a piece of hair out his eye before I breathe in the familiar smell of his spearmint gum.

"What's on your mind, sunshine?"

I know I should be thinking about the Gauntlet tomorrow, but I can't get my one pressing question out of my head. I sigh, trying to figure out how to phrase it.

Best to rip it off like a Band-Aid, I suppose.

"What happens after the Gauntlet?" I ask. "How do we…how do we do this?" My one and only long distance relationship (which wasn't even *that* long of a distance and was "long distance" for all of three months) went up in a fiery blaze of disaster. How were Joss and I going to handle being in the longest distance relationship you could possibly have? We'll be an entire world apart.

Joss tightens his arms even further around me. He absently strokes a finger across my collarbone sending chills down my arms and a wave of goosebumps across my chest. "I'll do whatever it takes to be with you, Dani. We'll figure it out because what we've got, love," he muses with a smile, "this is worth fighting for."

I crane my head up toward him and press a kiss to the bottom of his jaw, thankful for his assurance. I'm still trying to figure out what being in a healthy relationship looks like. Add in long distance? It's really thrown me for a loop, but somehow Joss makes me less afraid.

"Plus," he adds, "I need this to work out between us. You're it for me, sunshine. You've positively ruined me for everyone else."

I laugh, even as my heart feels like it's going to burst through my chest. Being with Joss is like nothing I've ever experienced before, and everything feels so bright and shiny and pure and… right.

"Are you even real?" I tease. "Honestly, Joss. You're, like, perfect. I'm sort of waiting for the other shoe to drop, like I'll soon find out that you're married or you're a serial killer… or your favorite band is Nickelback," I laugh. "I don't deserve you." It's meant to come off as a joke, but the way my voice tapers betrays my deepest, innermost thoughts, ones that I keep buried deep within me. Some part of me still does believe I don't deserve a love like this. I know the lie's origins—I can trace it back to when I was thirteen-years-old—and yet, even after all these years, it still dwells in me, feeding off me like a parasite.

Joss gently grabs my face, tilting it up toward him.

"You are worthy of love and happiness, Dani. Do you understand me?"

I nod. I understand his words, and yet, I still don't feel like they fully apply to me. It'll take time…but I'm learning. Every day.

I sigh, giving him a soft smile. "To be clear, it's a 'no' to all of the above questions, right?"

Joss lets out his loudest laugh that sounds so much like the first day we met, back when we were causing a disturbance on the plane ride to California. Looking at him, I know there's no one else I'd rather wreak havoc with. He shakes his head as he says, "No to all of the above."

"Just checking," I say, giggling and nuzzling further into his chest. "How are you feeling about tomorrow?"

"I'm stoked," Joss replies with a grin. And the thing is, I think he genuinely is stoked to run the Gauntlet, complete with its laborious tasks and exhausting activities and general misery.

A flutter of nerves suddenly hits me like a cloud of gnats, and while I try to keep my expression neutral, Joss reads me like a book.

"We're going to do everything in our power to win this show, sunshine, but if by some miracle, Sarge or Naji beats us to it, I need you to know this: I'm absolutely mad about you, Dani Di Laurentis. I knew the minute our plane landed in LA. I've been on dozens of flights, but that was the first time I've ever wanted to stay on a plane, the first time I've ever been *sad* for a flight to be over. And it was because of you. So no matter the outcome of the Gauntlet tomorrow, I'll always be grateful for this show— because it brought me to you, love."

Joss and I stay there for hours. I try my best to simply enjoy the moment, to bask in Joss's sunshine and not worry about what happens next. I don't worry about the Gauntlet or whatever may come after it. For now, I'm content to snuggle in Joss's arms as he whispers the names of the stunningly bright constellations above us until I drift off to sleep.

I stir as Joss picks me up and carries me all the way back to my cabin, where he lays me on my bed and settles in behind me. I turn my head back toward him with a sleep-ridden smile. He presses a kiss to my forehead, his eyes gleaming with what looks so much like content.

"Goodnight, sunshine," he says.

"Goodnight, menace," I whisper before drifting off to sleep.

In the morning, we wake to sirens.

The
GAUNTLET

★ ★ ★ ★

forty-four

THE GAUNTLET is here.

She comes for us like the grim reaper, a tattered onyx cloak concealing her face, a shiny silver scythe notched between her boney fingers. She opens her maw to summon us in the form of sirens wailing across the camp.

I didn't think I'd sleep last night, but somehow, I managed. It was a gift, truly. The Gauntlet usually spans two days, and I doubt I'll be able to doze tonight with adrenaline pumping through me like an IV of Red Bull. I take extra care getting ready in the morning, making sure my signature space buns are pristine, each and every piece of wayward hair tucked into its rightful place. I envelope myself a cloud of hairspray, hoping every strand will stay in place for as long as possible. It's the little things like hair in your eyes or a hole in your sock that can make the difference in the Gauntlet, that can make it ever so slightly more difficult, giving your competitors an edge over you. I do everything I possibly can to ensure the things that I can control are locked into place like an impenetrable safe.

Joss, Naji, Sarge, and I eat together in the Commons in companionable silence. It seems each of us is lost in our own heads, mentally preparing ourselves for the journey ahead. I find myself wondering about the tasks before us, particularly about how working as a team will be advantageous. From a psychological perspective, Joss and I possess a gaping advantage. Having a teammate—someone to encourage you, to help you, to keep you from quitting—is a treasure, a luxury that Sarge and Naji don't have. Yet, I'm sure the producers made many of the tasks ahead more advantageous for one person, seeking to level the playing field. Even so, I'm thankful to have Joss in my corner as a teammate, an equal, a partner in this game. Relying on someone other than myself is a feeling that is entirely unfamiliar, but Joss has shown me just how powerful it can be.

I guzzle a hefty mug of coffee as a final ode to my pre-competition ritual. When our quartet has finished up with breakfast, we make our final preparations for the day, clearing away our dishes and chugging water to hydrate before the Gauntlet begins. In these rushed, frenzied moments, Naji strides over, halting a foot in front of me. He stares at me, his deep brown eyes devoid of their usual lighthearted gleam, instead taking on a more serious look that's tinged with a hint of tenderness. In a blink, he throws his arms around me, blanketing me in a suffocating hug. I wrap my arms around him and squeeze, and when we finally pull away, we don't need to exchange words. We both know there's a mutual love and respect between us—between two friends—that will transcend this competition.

The producers summon all of us to the edge of camp, where we await further instructions. Beside me, Joss grabs my hand, and I look over at him, the morning sun brilliantly illuminating his features.

"You with me?" I ask.

He smiles. "Always."

A moment later, a vehicle appears in the distance, growing

ever larger as it approaches. As it gets closer, the gravelly rocks splaying beneath its tires, it's clear that it's a huge semi-truck with a shipping container-like trailer attached. As the semi makes a large turn ahead of us, I see the *American Gauntlet* logo spray painted on the side of the trailer, its four golden stars glinting against the black metal. After it completes its turn, it approaches us in reverse and comes to a stop a few yards ahead of us. The trailer door starts to lift from the bottom up, and that's when we see a familiar figure standing inside.

Dax Philipps is clad in all black, his arms crossed against his chest, pitch black sunglasses covering his eyes. His mouth is pressed into a thin line, his usual grimace. I'm half-surprised the producers didn't put a fog machine in the trailer to make this movie-like moment even more impactful, but then again, Dax is intimidating enough on his own.

Our host stares the four of us down for an elongated moment before hopping out of the trailer with a feline grace. He inhales deeply before finally saying, "Welcome to the Gauntlet."

A thrill races up my spine at those four words. *I'm here. I made it. I have what it takes to face the Gauntlet.* And although I always pictured Lana standing beside me when this moment came, I'm thankful for her sacrifice. If Joss and I come out the other side of this wild journey as winners, I'll spend the rest of my days repaying her for what she did. My buoyant, carefree, impulsive sister who "thinks about herself a healthy amount," yet is entirely selfless when it matters most. She grew up into a stunning woman, yet I seemed to have missed it in my attempts to take care of her. I'll always make sure Lana is taken care of; it's a big sister trait that I'll never shed. Even so, when this whole thing is over, I'm going to focus on being just that—a big sister—and not the maternal figure I had to be for so many years. All things have a season that must eventually come to an end, but that's the beautiful thing about seasons—when they end, they turn into new ones.

"What are you all standing around for?" Dax asks. "Get in the truck."

And with that warm introduction, the Gauntlet begins.

THE four of us load up into the trailer, and Dax slams the door closed behind us with a resounding *bang*. There are no seats in the trailer, so Joss and I fumble our way to the floor, leaning our backs against the sides while we wait to be transported to wherever it is we're headed. It's pitch black in the trailer, a suffocating darkness, and while it's not exactly the tightly-enclosed box from the Grit Phase, it's still a dark, confined space, and I worry it'll trigger Joss's claustrophobia. I place my hand on his thigh, and he covers it with his own, gently brushing his thumb across the top of my hand.

"You okay?" I ask him.

"All good, sunshine," Joss replies, squeezing my hand.

I don't know if it's the truth or not, but nonetheless, I lace my fingers through his, thankful to have someone to face this terrifying Gauntlet with me.

It quickly grows hot and muggy in the trailer, and I suddenly feel as if I'm back in Houston, breathing in the liquid humidity. Sweat drips down my temples, tracing rivulets behind my ears and down my neck. It's wildly uncomfortable in the stifling heat, but I know this is only the beginning.

None of us talk, not even a playful quip from Naji. It's clear the gravity of the situation has hit us all, helping us grasp what's on the line at the end of this game. Sarge had given me one last fatherly squeeze on the shoulder in the Commons before we awaited the semi-truck. As we climbed in, though, all warmth had drained from his expression, leaving only cold ferocity in its wake. The time for camaraderie was over.

We ride along in the bumbling trailer for at least a few hours, every second growing more oppressive than the last. My mind races as I think about what could be awaiting us on the other side, so eventually I give up, instead attempting to empty my mind entirely. I force out all thoughts and try to steady my breathing, something that's made easier as I tune into Joss's deliberate, measured breaths beside me.

Finally, the semi-truck comes to a rest, and a blinding light peeks through the bottom of the trailer door as it's lifted. White spots blot my vision as my eyes attempt to adjust to the harsh contrast of broad daylight against the utter darkness of the trailer. I'm grateful, at least, for fresh air, but as I stumble out of the trailer, I quickly realize how hot it is. Once my struggling pupils adjust, I also realize something else.

We're in the middle of the desert.

For miles, all I see is sand and dirt and the occasional brittle shrub or barbed cactus or uniquely shaped tree. In the distance are rolling, sandy hills that seem to stretch for miles. The sun beats down on us from above, and I quickly realize how thirsty I am. I've already lost a lot of water just from sweating on the ride here, and with the unrelenting sun above us, I'll need to rehydrate soon. Even mild dehydration can cause nasty side effects, usually starting with a headache and quickly leading to fatigue, which are the last things I need today.

"We're in the proper outback, aren't we?" Joss jokes, still sounding as upbeat as ever.

While the camera crew gets into position, a production assistant gives each of us a tiny cup of water. It's the kind of cup the dentist gives you when they're giving you a fluoride rinse, which is to say, there's all of two sips of water in it. *Surely this can't be all they're giving us…right?*

Wrong.

After we've had our measly drink of water, Joss and I are given a GPS to share, while Naji and Sarge, as individuals, get their own. The semi-truck pulls away, and that's when I see the giant logs awaiting us. There are three logs in the sand, two short ones, each about four feet, and one long one that's twice the size of the smaller ones. Joss and I are directed to stand in front of the longer log, while Naji and Sarge each stand by the others.

The instructions Dax delivers are simple. We're to carry our logs while utilizing our GPS trackers to guide our way. We may encounter obstacles in between or we may not—he leaves that little tidbit hanging in the air. While we're allowed to set our log down to take breaks, we're not allowed to sit down; if we do, we'll be immediately eliminated from the Gauntlet. Whoever arrives first at the end of the day will receive a time advantage for the second half of the Gauntlet tomorrow.

"Good luck, competitors," Dax says with a grin. "You'll need it."

Dax's shrill whistle pierces my ears, and Joss and I immediately bend to pick up our log. While it might seem like a disadvantage to have a larger, heavier log to carry, it's actually the opposite. Sarge and Naji have to hoist theirs over their backs or behind their shoulders in uncomfortable ways, while Joss and I simply put it over one shoulder, easily balancing the weight between the two of us. With the GPS at my side, I guide our way as we take off through the desert.

Hauling a huge log through the wilderness is simple but not at all easy. Joss and I move at a quick pace; it's not quite a jog but definitely more than a walk. In an attempt to conserve our energy, we don't say much to each other, but with every step, I feel Joss's presence. We wordlessly share our strength, our energy, with one another. When one of us starts to slack, the other adds a little more pep to their step. When one of us grunts at the effort, the other shoulders more of the weight, if only for an instant.

Joss and I trek for what feels like hours, the sun beating down on our backs and the log growing heavier by the minute. While my upper body grows fatigued from the strain of the log and my lower body grows sluggish, it's the thirst that nips at my sanity. All of my thoughts are consumed by my thirst, and the desire to set the log down and quit in exchange for a gallon of water becomes more and more overwhelming.

"I'm…so thirsty," I grumble, unable to keep myself from saying it.

Even in the midst of this torture, Joss's mouth curls into a smile, his lips dry from the desert conditions, cracking ever so slightly. "What I wouldn't give for some rain right about now." He quirks an eyebrow at me, as if to say, *Do you understand what I meant the other night? Do you get it now?*

My lips fashion into a smile. *I get it, menace. I get it.*

Joss and I stay ahead of Sarge and Naji, but they're always within sight. Sarge chugs along a few minutes behind us, while Naji lumbers even further behind Sarge.

I have to admit, I expected something different out of the first leg of the Gauntlet. I thought it would be chock full of tasks to accomplish and daring feats to tackle, but in many ways, this monotonous grind is worse. Your thoughts are fighting you every tiresome, unvarying step of the way, coaxing you to *quit, quit, quit.* The urge to sit down and rest prods at me over and over again, but every time this thought charges into my brain, it's like Joss can sense it. "Think of Penny" he'd say, followed by a "you're doing great, sunshine." I don't know how Sarge and Naji are surviving on their own.

I keep putting one foot in front of the other, focusing on a finish line that I can't see, when we finally see something other than a cactus in the distance.

We've arrived at our first checkpoint.

forty-five

AS IF there isn't enough dirt in the desert, the *American Gauntlet* producers decided to add some more.

"We made it," I say through heaving breaths as Joss and I reach the first checkpoint ahead of Sarge and Naji.

We immediately toss the bulky log from our shoulders, and it feels as if my skin will be permanently imprinted by it. Joss reaches over to gently massage my shoulders as we take in the scene before us. There are three piles of dirt—one twice the size of the others—with three wheelbarrows beside them. Before we get our instructions for the task, Joss and I receive the same tiny water cups from the crew. I drain it in one gulp, too thirsty to take little sips to make it last longer. Either way, it's still the same amount of water—enough to keep me from passing out, but not enough to quench the insatiable thirst that has overtaken me, body and mind.

About half a football field away from the dirt piles is some sort of rectangular mechanism, as well as a wooden box in front of it. The producers give us our instructions. We are to haul the dirt via wheelbarrow to the rectangular sand sifter awaiting us, where we'll sift through the sand to find a tiny key. The key will unlock the box where, we're told, is our lunch. We'll need to eat whatever's in the box in its entirety before we can move on, but I nearly laugh as the producers tell us that tidbit since my stomach feels so empty, it hurts.

Just like the logs, the pile of dirt is twice the size for Joss and me, even though we only have one wheelbarrow to transport it. The advantage we have, though, is being able to shovel the sandy soil in more quickly with two people—not that the producers gave us a shovel. Tilting the wheelbarrow down, we drop to our knees and begin hauling it in by the armful, swallowing dust and sand with every movement. I quickly begin to feel the gritty bits of sediment in between my teeth, sending involuntary chills through me. I'm not sure what's worse—the feeling of the sand grating against my teeth or the sound of nails scraping down a chalkboard.

Covered in sand and dirt, Joss and I haul the wheelbarrow the fifty yards or so to the sifter, but after our first round, we come up empty. Meanwhile, Sarge arrives at the checkpoint and begins the task, hauling the dirt into his wheelbarrow in huge, graceful sweeps. I'm pretty sure he filled his wheelbarrow in the time it would take three normal men. *So much for that "old bag of bones."*

We dash back to our pile and begin filling it rapidly, not wanting to lose our first place standing, but my heart sinks as I hear Sarge yell *"Yes!"* from his sifter. Incredibly, he's found his key in only one trip and proceeds to unlock his box, just as Naji arrives at the checkpoint. Joss and I continue lugging load after load of dirt to our sifter, coughing up clouds of dust and grit along the way. My throat feels bone dry, only made worse by the sand I can't help but inhale, but my discomfort is momentarily forgotten when the sand from our fourth load drains through the sifter and leaves a key in its wake. Without a second thought, Joss shoves it in the small padlock in front of us, revealing our lunch for the day.

Ah. I see now.

Suddenly, the producers' instructions to "make sure we eat everything" makes sense, and despite my hunger, my stomach roils at the "meal." It's just a giant bowl of what looks to be mayonnaise and a plate of dead crickets. The crickets are fine enough—they'll be great to replenish our protein stores—but I *loathe* mayonnaise, especially when it's been baking in the California sun all day. I'd sooner eat an entire barrel of crickets before I'd consume a bowl of mayonnaise, but even so, the worst part of the "lunch box" is the fact that it's grievously devoid of water.

I'm disappointed but not surprised. Every aspect of the Gauntlet is designed to make us want to quit, and while it's not easy to push through physical exhaustion, it's nearly impossible to overcome your own mind when it's telling you you'll keel over any minute if you don't get another sip of water soon.

Without a word, Joss begins coating the grasshoppers in mayo. I nearly dry heave just watching it.

"Sorry, love. Without water, these crickets will be nearly impossible to swallow. It's all a puzzle," he says, mayo and insects caking his fingers, "and to win, we've got to crack it before they do."

As if on cue, I hear a horrible cough to my left and look over to find Sarge choking, cricket guts spewing out of his mouth. The insects are so miserably dry, and they have so many tiny parts to them—wings and legs and antennae. Joss is right. Without strategically using the mayonnaise, getting the whole plate of crickets down will be nearly impossible.

Shielding our new tactic from Sarge to our left and Naji, who just uncovered his key, to our right, we coat the brittle insects in mayonnaise and eat them with ease. To my surprise, the cricket taste overpowers the mayo entirely, so I don't even struggle to finish my half in under two minutes. After we show our empty mouths to the producers, they give us the green light to continue on.

With our logs left behind at the checkpoint, the second half of the day is simply getting from point A to point B the fastest. So Joss and I run. We run and run and run until my legs feel like they're going to give out and my lungs scream at me, begging for respite. But we don't stop. Sarge is nipping at our heels with Naji close behind him, so we simply can't afford it. The desert sun crushes us beneath its unforgiving rays. The uneven ground begins to wear on my knees and ankles. The arid climate makes my lips desperately dry, and the cracks that form quickly leak blood when I accidentally bite down on them too hard. The harsh metallic taste of my own blood makes me want to vomit.

But worst of all, though, is the thirst. Halfway through the afternoon, the crew gives us another measly cup of water, but it's cruel. It's a tease, giving us a sliver of hope before we realize the couple ounces of water will do almost nothing to quench the implacable thirst that has marred the day. Dax stations himself along our route, yelling at us through a bullhorn. "Just give up now. You'll never make it anyway!"

If I were of sound mind, his words would mean nothing, but amidst the exhaustion and dehydration, his cajoling is almost enough for me to quit. But I can't. The only thing that keeps my legs moving robotically beneath me is the thought of my family…and of Joss. He wants to win just as badly as I do, and while I'm playing for my world, Joss is playing for *the* world. I picture a little eleven-year-old Joss, stuck in a hospital room watching *American Gauntlet* on TV and seeing someone who has overcome his disease not only competing on the show but winning it. What hope might it give someone? How might it inspire them to keep fighting?

Just as I've said since I first got to the *American Gauntlet* camp, losing isn't an option.

As the sun begins to set, delirium coats my mind like thick, syrupy molasses, and I think, *Hey. At least if I die out here, my family will probably get a huge settlement. They'd be set for life.*

Mid-stride, I shake the thought away and a raspy laugh escapes my desert dust-caked lips.

Joss eyes me from the side, breathing heavily, as he huffs, "Everything all right, sunshine?"

This draws an even bigger laugh from me, the hysteria coming on in full effect. As we jog, Joss looks at me with concern that soon gives way to his own laughter, growing bigger by the second. Soon enough, we're both laughing uncontrollably, stitches in our sides, as we attempt to run and laugh at the same time. It feels like Joss and I are on the plane to LA again, giggling and drawing annoyed looks from passengers in the surrounding rows, back when Joss was airport-hot-guy-Kellan and not my competitor and would-be partner and…so much more. Regardless of the outcome tomorrow, this whole journey with Joss has been a gift, an unexpected, unexpected-in-the-best-way surprise that I'll cherish forever.

The golden sky eventually gives way to shades of dark blue with the last of the setting sun, but before we're completely shrouded in darkness, we arrive at our makeshift camp for the night. Joss and I arrive first, sealing in our advantage for tomorrow, with Sarge arriving a few minutes later. The last to make it to camp is Naji.

Again, we're given a tiny cup of water. It's enough to sustain us, but not much else. I don't know if I'll physically be able to continue tomorrow if this is all we're given. I shove the thought aside, as Dax approaches our group.

"Well, you made it," Dax says.

"But at what cost?" Naji asks dryly.

The barest hint of a smile makes its way to Dax's face before he remembers himself and wipes it away. "Your day may be over, but your night is just beginning."

No. No. No. No. There can't be more…I'm pretty sure we just jogged a full marathon in the heat of the desert with almost no water. All I want to do is chug a gallon of water and curl up on this desert floor and sleep.

Clearly over Dax's antics, Sarge moves to sit down, before Dax eyes him. "Uh, uh, uh," he chides. "You won't want to do that… unless you're quitting."

Sarge freezes and straightens back to his full height.

"You'll get your rest…eventually," Dax continues. "But for now, you'll stand here until I tell you otherwise."

And with that, Dax leaves us standing in the desert with nothing but a camera crew around us to document our misery. Before we settle into our standing positions, a set of crew members provides us with our sustenance for the night, which includes energy chews, protein bars, bananas, and beef jerky. After our mayonnaise and cricket lunch, it seems like a gourmet meal, and I savor every bite of it. We're also given another sip of water. I'm almost positive the producers have given us the exact amount needed to keep us alive and functioning while still utterly miserable.

"I could go for some of those Tim Tams right about now," I say to Joss, although I'm still not entirely sure what Tim Tams are.

"I'll make good on our deal, love, not to worry."

After we stuff our faces, we're left to our task: standing here in the middle of the desert until we're told we can rest. The producers separate the three entities, moving Sarge a few yards one way and Naji a few yards the other way. I imagine it's to make us feel alone, so we can't speak to one another to offer a word of encouragement or camaraderie. I'm even more thankful to be on a team with Joss, so we can lean on each other for moral support because as soon as we're left to our task, I realize how excruciating it is to just stand here. Instantly, I wish we were jogging again because at least it's something to *do*. When all we can do is stand in one spot, there's nothing to focus on other than our pain and discomfort. One part of my mind tries to ignore it, while the other part tries to convince me to just lie down and sleep on the sandy desert floor. At least if I'm sleeping, I won't be able to think about my aching body or my insatiable thirst.

Even though it's summer, now that the sun has set, the temperature drops substantially, and I'm suddenly wishing I was wearing more than the scanty uniform I've been provided: Spandex shorts and a tank top that's just as tight and reveals just as much. I shiver involuntarily as a breeze blows over us. In response, Joss steps behind me and wraps his arms around me, leaning me back against his chest.

"Try and rest, if you can," he says into my ear, gently brushing his hands up and down my arms. A new wave of goosebumps that has nothing to do with the cold temperatures prickles against my flesh. I relax further into him as he begins kneading my aching arms and shoulders, working his thumbs across my neck. He moves his hands down the center of my back, eventually hooking his thumbs under the hem of my tank top, drawing lazy circles on top of my skin. I'm acutely aware of every place his skin touches mine, leaving a trail of heat in their wake. And while Joss has made it impossible for me to "rest," at least my body is warming up.

Joss puts his lips to my ear again as he says, "You did brilliantly today, sunshine."

A new warmth engulfs me at Joss's words. Even when his own energy is depleted, he's still pouring into me, gifting me fresh vitality with his encouragement.

"*We* did brilliantly today," I amend, turning my head to the side to press a kiss against his cheek. His skin is salty and sandy, and I don't care one bit.

We stand there for an hour, maybe longer, before I peel myself from where I've been leaning against Joss's body and move myself behind him, allowing him to lean back against me. I wrap my arms around his waist and lean my head against his back, breathing deeply and soaking in the feeling of my arms around him. I know Joss said we'll figure everything out when we leave the *American Gauntlet* camp, but now that the day is nearly upon us, I can't help but feel like this thing with Joss is a dream I'll eventually wake up from. I squeeze my arms tighter around him, as if he'll slip through my fingers like the desert sand if I don't.

"I'm here, sunshine," he whispers. "I'm here."

We stand, holding onto each other, well into the night, and I eventually slip into a sleep-like state. The sound of a semi-truck in the distance draws me out of it like a jarring alarm clock, and my mind, hazy from exhaustion, wonders what else the Gauntlet could possibly have in store.

forty-six

GROGGY and dehydrated and bone-tired, we shuffle over to the familiar semi-truck where Dax has summoned us. We all look worse for the wear, our skin dry, lips cracked, hair unkempt.

Can't wait for the entire world to see me in this state, I joke to myself. At least it'll be worth it if I come out of this with half the winnings.

"If it were up to me, I'd leave you out here all night," Dax says, "but the powers that be seem to think you need some rest and rehydration, so here you go." Dax loudly smacks the trailer once, and the door lifts. I'm expecting an empty container like before, maybe with a sleeping bag for each of us. What I'm not expecting are a medical staff and four IV infusion pumps.

"They're…they're rehydrating us by IV," I muse aloud. "It's sort of genius."

I climb in the back of the truck and sink into a chair, relishing the feeling of pressure coming off my legs. We literally haven't sat down all day, and my swollen ankles and feet finally find some relief in the IV infusion chair. I stick out my arm, and the medic ties a thick band around the top of it before inserting the needle and starting the IV. Precious fluids begin flooding my system, along with a new sense of hope. I wasn't entirely sure the producers were going to let us rehydrate fully, but with an entire IV of fluids, I'll be reenergized for tomorrow. Well, reenergized as much as possible, all things considered.

Joss takes a seat in the chair beside me, and Sarge sits across from me, moving like a sluggish zombie. I quickly notice, though, that Naji is still standing outside of the trailer, peering in at us with wide eyes. He begins pacing back and forth, muttering to himself as if to hype himself up. As I look closer, I see he's begun sweating profusely, and his copper skin has taken on a pale greenish hue.

"Naji," I say. He whips his head toward me, eyes as big as the moon shining above the desert. "Are you okay?"

"I—I'm fine," he mutters.

He steps in the trailer and forces himself to take a seat, but the second his medic brings the IV needle even remotely close to him, he bursts out of his chair, shaking his head violently.

And that's when it hits me. Naji's one infamous fear that he touted he'd never encounter on the show.

It's needles.

"You're alright, mate," Joss says to him encouragingly. "Just breathe. One step at a time."

Naji attempts to receive the IV another time before ripping his arm away from the medic.

"Naji," I say gently. "You've got to do it. You won't make it through the day tomorrow if you don't."

It seems counterintuitive to encourage my competitor to do something that will make it more difficult to beat him, but Naji isn't just my competitor. He's my friend, and I don't want to see him struggle through the day tomorrow in an unhealthy state.

"You don't understand, Dani," he says. "I—I *can't*. I can't with the needles."

"Can you just try one more time?" I plead.

He groans and sits in the chair again. The medic grabs his arm and readies the needle. Naji allows him to come within centimeters of his skin before he shrieks, *"NO!"*

The medic backs away, hands and needle in the air, before Naji rushes out of the chair. How has Naji survived this long as a stuntman with such a phobia of needles? He's either extremely good at his job or simply passes out before they have to stitch him up.

"Do—do I have to do it?" Naji asks Kelly, standing nearby.

Her eyes soften. "No, you don't *have* to," she says gently. "But it's not likely you'll be able to continue tomorrow if you don't. If our medical team determines you can't continue, you'll have to stop. That'll be it for you."

His eyes turn steely with resolve. "I'll be fine. I'll make it. But that needle is not going in my arm."

"That's your choice to make," Kelly replies, her voice saturated with sadness. "These are your sleeping quarters as well."

Naji's medic clears the IV supplies, and Naji sits in his chair, leaning it back as far as possible to make it more comfortable to sleep in. When my IV is finished, exhaustion commandeers my body, forcing it into a fitful rest.

THE sound of an airhorn is already grating. When it's unleashed in a tiny shipping container, it's downright excruciating.

With the objectionable wakeup call by the production team, Joss, Sarge, Naji and I bolt up out of our chairs. For a moment, confusion overhauls every thought in my brain before I realize where we are.

It's the final day of the Gauntlet. And Joss and I could be walking away with $300,000.

"Good morning, sunshine," Joss says as we hop out of the trailer. He presses a kiss to my forehead. "You look beautiful as ever."

"I highly doubt that," I snort. I haven't seen what I look like, but something tells me the first word that comes to mind wouldn't be "beautiful."

He stops me, tilting my chin up toward him. "It's the truth," he says, his voice low and rumbly. He pins me in place with a fierce look that tells me not to argue with him.

"Whatever you say, menace," I reply. I look him over and note just how unfair it is that despite the circumstances, he still looks impossibly handsome. The conditions have made him look a little more rugged than usual, and it's a good look on him. *Every look is probably a good look on him,* I think to myself. What I would give to see him in his natural element, surfing the waters of Bondi Beach. *Maybe one day.*

"Ready to win today, love?" he asks, a spark in his eye.

I grin, still envisioning Joss shirtless and straddling a surfboard, skin glowing under the radiant Australian sun. "Absolutely."

Joss releases me, and the crew directs us to join Sarge in a small line.

"Morning, Sarge," I say with a smile. The day's activities haven't begun, so I think a little harmless fellowship should be allowed.

He returns my smile, crinkles forming at the edges of his eyes. "Good morning," he says, apparently agreeing with my reasoning, though I have no doubt he'll wipe the friendliness from his face as soon as we begin today.

Naji lags behind the group, dragging his feet as he exits the trailer. Despite a few hours of sleep, he doesn't look better. In fact, he looks worse. He appears to be a mere shell of himself; his eyes have taken on a hollow look, his skin devoid of its usual glow. He looks like a ghost.

We're given a bottle of water and the same food as yesterday to refuel. It looks like they won't be rationing our water intake as tightly today, but sixteen ounces of water isn't going to be enough to pull Naji from his dehydrated stupor. He chugs the water so quickly that he chokes, spewing some of it into the dirt.

"You alright there, mate?" Joss asks, placing a hand on his shoulder.

"I'll be fine," Naji says. His tone is riddled with dejection, almost as if he's given up on himself already. I know I should be happy, but still, a barb of sympathy buries itself beneath my skin. Despite his worrisome state, Naji still has it in him to humor us. "What a shame. It looks like Dax couldn't make it today," he says dryly.

When I look around at the crew and producers surrounding us, I realize Dax is notably missing.

"I wonder—"

Sarge doesn't finish his sentence. Instead, all of our heads whip up to the sound of a helicopter overhead, one that looks to be getting closer by the second. It swoops closely above us, sending sand flying in every direction, and that's when we see Dax hanging out of the helicopter with a megaphone in hand.

"Good morning, *American Gauntlet!*"

The helicopter swoops past us, coming to hover a football field away, sand and dust swirling in every direction as it touches down on the ground. When the rotors eventually swing to a stop, Dax hops out, summoning us toward him through the bullhorn.

"What are you all waiting for?" he asks as we approach. "Get in. We're heading to our next location."

"Sick," Joss says as we're handed headsets to wear. We all don the head gear and climb into the helicopter, where we find two rows of seating facing each other. Dax hops in the seat next to the pilot, while we strap into our designated seats behind them. The rotors start to *whoosh* around us, starting slowly and eventually picking up enough speed to lift us into the skies.

Riding in a helicopter will go down as one of the coolest experiences of my life, especially having only been on a plane a handful of times. When we lift off, it feels as if we're being pushed down into our seats by some unseeable force, but once we're in the air, it feels relatively like I'd expected. The views, however, are *insane*, and I can't seem to wipe the smile off my face, even though I know I look ridiculous. I glance over at Joss, who's seated across from me, and I expect him to be taking in the awe-inspiring desert views below, but instead, I catch him looking right at me, a smile just as big as my own plastered onto his face.

I glance at Sarge, and while I imagine he's no stranger to helicopters, he still gazes out the window with a fond smile on his face. When I look at Naji, however, I'm immediately worried. Sweat drips from his brow onto his lap as he plants his head in his hands, his complexion growing paler by the second. He looks like he's going to be—

Before I can even finish the thought, he grabs a barf bag and hurls into it. He's exhausted. He's dehydrated, which was just made worse by the vomiting. He's in bad shape, and we all know it.

The desert sands below eventually give way to slightly greener land and low, rolling mountains, and we soon begin making our descent near a large body of water. As we land (surprisingly gently), I realize it's the same lake from the Endurance Phase. A different set of crew members and producers are already set up here.

Thanking our pilot, we unload from the helicopter and walk to the familiar beach where Joss and I battled it out for the bonus win after the Twisted Twins were sent home. Losing that competition to Joss felt like a thorn in my side for so long, but it didn't matter in the end, since Joss and I became partners. I nearly chuckle at the irony of how everything worked out.

We make it to the beach and are given our task instructions from Dax. Midway through, though, Naji collapses on his knees to the ground, and for a moment, I think he's going to be sick again.

Dax breaks off his spiel and turns to a nearby crew member. "Yeah, let's have Steph check him out."

"No, no. I'll be fine," Naji mutters, futilely attempting to get off the ground. When he tries to stand up, he loses his balance almost immediately and plummets back to the sand. I bend down, placing my hands on his shoulders to guide him into a seated position. He lifts his head to look at me, and chills sweep through my body. As Naji's eyes meet mine, a look of confusion covers his face. He doesn't recognize me; in fact, he looks like he's never seen me before in his life. Something is very, very wrong.

I see familiar auburn hair and a smattering of freckles as Steph pushes her way through the camera crew and kneels in front of Naji. She shines a small light in his eyes, and I shudder as his pupils don't dilate immediately. She checks his pulse and other vital signs, a grimace steadily taking shape on her face.

She gives Naji a sorrow-filled look before craning her head up toward Dax. "He can't continue," she says. "I'm not medically clearing him. We need to get him to a hospital stat."

Naji doesn't even react to her statement. Instead, he asks, "Where's my brother? Where's AJ?"

My heart cracks. Naji is disoriented and confused—he's practically falling apart at the seams—and his time on *American Gauntlet* is over. Just like that.

I know I should be happy; Joss and I are one step closer to winning that cash prize, and yet, I wish it had happened differently. I still want the outcome to be the same, but *this*…this is simply heartbreaking.

Naji is quickly swept into the care of the medical staff, and Joss, Sarge, and I have mere moments to refocus on the task at hand.

When Dax finishes explaining the scope of the task, one thought rings in my ears: I hope all my climbing practice pays off.

forty-seven

JOSS is beautiful.

That's the thought that pops into my head as I swim beside him, always one stroke behind. He has this natural ease to his movements that makes me feel like I'm diving with a manta ray, graceful and fluid. In fact, Joss doesn't swim; he glides.

It's a stark contrast to the way Sarge harshly chops through the water near us, but while his methods aren't as pretty to watch, they're just as effective. As self-deprecating as Sarge is about his age, he sure keeps up with us easily, having already closed the gap from the small thirty-second advantage Joss and I were given for finishing first yesterday. Sarge is a heck of a competitor, and I'd prefer for him to be at least a little behind us, offering us a semblance of a cushion, but he clearly has other plans.

Using buoys as our guide, we make it to the cliffside from the first Endurance Competition, except instead of jumping *off* the cliffs, we'll be climbing *up* them. The crew has placed temporary silver rungs in the cliffside for hand and footholds to help us scale the rockface, but despite the assistance, it won't be an easy task. As I look up the cliffside, wiping the wet hair from my face, I see there's a nasty overhang that awaits us. It'll be all upper body at that point, and the fact that our hands are wet won't help our cause.

It's clearly advantageous to be a party of one here. Sarge doesn't have to worry about a partner making it up for him to advance; he simply has to worry about himself. For me and Joss, though, we'll both need to ascend the cliff before either of us can advance. I tilt my face to the sky, praying I'm not the reason we lose today. To come so close and not win…it would be wholly and completely devastating. I shake my head; I can't let ideas like those invade my headspace. Today is not the day for intrusive thoughts.

The three of us reach the cliffside at the same time, but Sarge maneuvers himself closest to the silver rungs, blocking us so he can go first. *Yeah, the time for camaraderie is definitely over.* Sarge easily makes it up the first part of the cliff, but when he reaches the overhang, his pace slows. With his muscular build, Sarge has a lot of body mass, and despite how fit he is, it won't be easy to haul himself up without the assistance of his legs. He reaches for the first rung of the overhang, and I watch his fingers slip off immediately. He plummets into the water.

"After you, love," Joss says.

I don't hesitate. I grab each tiny silver rung, first hauling myself out of the water and then further and further up the jagged rockface, ascending like my life depends on it. I reach the overhang, and I'm instantly reminded of every bit of climbing training I did in preparation for this very moment. I replay my back thudding hard against the mat over and over again, and for a moment, I know when I reach for that first rung, I'm going to nosedive back into the lake. I look down and see an abyss below me, and fear tiptoes into my mind, an intruder sneaking in through a cracked window.

But then I remember that feeling of pure elation that took over every part of my body when I reached for the overhang handhold and *didn't* fall to the mat. I play the scene out in my head repeatedly, remembering everything I did to hang onto that tiny rock. I brace my body, keeping my biceps flexed and arms bent, and launch myself to the overhang.

I don't expect to crash into the water. Not this time.

I grip my fingers around the silver rung and hang, suspended above the water for a nanosecond, before I know I've made it. My fingers are already aching from the strain, so I don't stick around to celebrate. Like the peg wall from the Strategy Phase all over again, I heave myself up until I'm high enough to utilize the footholds. From there, it's smooth sailing to the top.

I collapse onto the top of the cliff and catch my breath, lying back and letting myself bask in the warmth of the sun before I sit up. In the distance, I see dark, ominous clouds rolling in. A rainstorm, perhaps. I don't have time to think about it; instead, I look down and see Joss quickly scaling the wall below me. When he's almost all the way up, I watch Sarge plunge into the water again. We've got our head start back.

Joss lugs his body onto the ledge, and I'm so exhilarated that we made such easy work of that menacing cliff that I grab his face and kiss him through smiles and heaving breaths. It's a quick kiss, one born from pure excitement, but as I pull away, my mind already focused on what we need to do next, he tugs me back toward him. He grips my face just below my jaw and pulls me in for a kiss—a real one this time. It's brief, just like the first, but it's also fervent and fueled with so much more than thrilling excitement; it's layered with tenderness and joy and every good thing under the sun.

"Did you know no two lip impressions are the same?" Joss asks as he pulls back, running his thumb over my bottom lip.

I can't help but laugh. "That's news to me."

"Want to know another fact?" he asks through another kiss. "Yours are my favorite."

"Focus, menace," I say, even as giddy butterflies take flight in the pit of my belly.

He laughs, kissing me one last time, his lips already curling into a smile. "You ready to win this thing, love?"

A jubilant grin breaks across my face. "Let's do this."

THE remainder of the day passes in an adrenaline-fueled blur. Where the first day of the Gauntlet was characterized by mindless movement, the second day is defined by incessant activity. We bike. We run. We solve puzzles. We repel down cliffs. We traverse harsh terrain. And yet, Sarge eliminates what little advantage we'd gained and keeps pace with us the rest of the way. Gone is the friendly, self-critical Sarge, and in his place is the fierce, confident military veteran who is out to prove he's still got what it takes to beat a bunch of twenty-somethings in this cutthroat competition.

When the afternoon sun begins to hang low in the sky and the adrenaline has long worn off, replaced only by exhaustion and ache, we make it to our final task. Kelly shouts instructions at us through a bullhorn as we approach our final checkpoint, and we learn that all that's left is to conquer one last mountain on foot. At the top, we'll find Dax waiting for us behind a finish line.

When we realize it's the final stretch of the Gauntlet, there's no dramatic pause, no moment to appreciate how far we've come together. We don't waste a second as we take off in a full sprint up the mountain trail. With Joss running beside me, the only thing on my mind is $300,000.

THE sprint doesn't last long. The mountain trail is steep, so after Joss and I regain the slightest advantage over Sarge, we settle into a jogging pace that we'll hopefully be able to keep up for the remainder of the ascent. Our feet strike the gravelly trail in rhythm, loose rocks splaying out from underneath us, but despite the more comfortable pace, my body fights me every grueling step of the way. The muscle aches play in a discordant symphony across my body, each twinge or throb of pain striking an inharmonious, perverse note. My quads burn, while a sharp pain shoots up my shins. My hamstrings cramp, while my traps, tense from stress, spasm wildly. A charlie horse threatens in my calves, while my obliques twinge with the makings of a stitch in my side. Every step is a dissonant note, the Gauntlet its cruel conductor.

The agony must manifest across my face. I notice Joss glance at me to the side, his lips forming into a thin line as he breathes heavily through his nose. He's worried about me, even though he's struggling just as much as I am. His feet drag where they wouldn't before. His head, usually held high with confidence, drops down to the ground, no doubt wondering how long we'll have to keep this up.

Even so, Joss asks, "Want another fact, sunshine?"

"Please," I huff, desperate for any distraction. I know my body will keep going long after I think she'll give out, but although I know my body will soldier on, my mind still tells me I'm going to collapse any second.

For a moment, the only sound is the crunch of the trail beneath us and our heavy breathing as Joss contemplates which trivia fact he'll pluck from his brain.

"Ah," he says, eyes lighting up as he glances over at me. "Did you know the planet Uranus was originally named George?"

A wheezing laugh escapes me, even as my lungs implore me not to. "George? Who names a planet George?"

"William Herschel."

The corners of my mouth crack as I laugh, and fueled by a bright spot on this endless day, Joss continues.

"Teeth are the only part of the human body that can't heal themselves. A jiffy is an actual unit of time—it's one-one hundredth of a second. You can't hum if you hold your nose."

And so it goes on, Joss distracting me with random knowledge, both of us staying a few yards ahead of Sarge as we jog higher and higher, the air getting thinner by the second. I'm thankful for Joss's diversion, his guiding of my thoughts away from the agonizing ache of my body with things like "an ostrich's eye is bigger than its brain."

Joss and I have managed to put a little more distance between ourselves and Sarge, and as I glance back over my shoulder to see how far back he is, I notice Sarge looks markedly tired. Each step seems strained, his breathing labored. We've been pushing nonstop for nearly two days straight, and all of us have clearly seen better days; it just looks like it caught up with Sarge the fastest.

As I turn my head back around, though, I don't see the tree root in front of me until it's too late. My foot catches on the raised root, and I'm sent flying through the air. I sprawl out across the ground, my body skidding forward over the gravel. My shin catches on a sharp rock, and I feel it split clean open, bright red blood surging out of the gash. As I skim across the rocky ground, my shirt slides up, covering the entire left side of my body in road rash. Raw, pink scratches stretch from my leg up to my ribcage and all across my left arm, tiny particles of sediment and sand sticking to it like Velcro.

Joss skids to a stop, rushing back to me, his features flashing from surprise to concern to distress.

"Dani!" He drops to his knees beside me, propping me up so my head doesn't stay on the ground. As his eyes dart from my bloody shin, a chasm splitting the skin wide open, to the chafed and bloodied cuts painting the entire left side of my body red, Sarge sprints past us. Where he looked to be on his last leg only moments ago, he now looks like a soldier on the battlefield, running to safety.

He saw his opening.

And he took it.

"I'm fine, just help me up," I command.

Joss hesitates for a moment as he gets to his feet. "Are you sure?"

"We're not losing this." He grabs onto my forearms, every inch of raw skin burning with his touch, and heaves me up. My shin bellows at me as I put weight on it, but I don't care. Sarge is still in sight, and I don't plan on losing him. With the trees around us, there's no way to tell how much further we have. We can't let him run away with our win—literally.

As soon as we begin our pursuit, I feel a droplet of water on my cheek.

Am—am I crying?

Another one splashes against my forehead, and I realize it's not tears—it's rain.

A few heavy droplets fall sporadically before it all seems to come in sheets. The water soothes my road rash, washing out the sediment with each drop. It mingles with the blood on my shin, turning it to pale pink streams. I let it soak into my skin, washing the dirt and dust and sweat from my body.

Hello, friend. It's only right that we should finish this as we started: together.

I pick up my pace, my feet moving faster beneath me as if the rain has reinvigorated them, too. Joss follows my lead, running a half-step behind me. I hear his voice like an echo in my head. *Lead the way, love.*

It's as we draw closer and closer to Sarge that I realize he made a devastating mistake. He got too excited by the opening I unwittingly presented to him, and he ran too fast for too long, burning himself out. I can see his steps begin to slow, his chest heaving violently with the strain. If the finish line had been any closer, he would've won. But there's still at least a little ways to go, and he's running on fumes.

My lungs are howling, my body shrieking at me to stop, to just hold on for a minute, but my mind doesn't let them. I will them forward, fueled by what lies ahead if Joss and I can just cross that finish line ahead of Sarge. Joss and I close the distance between ourselves and Sarge, and as we round a corner, I see him.

I see Dax Philipps waiting for us a mere hundred yards away.

I don't hesitate. I force my legs to move faster, my arms pumping with each stride. The three of us are sprinting, and for a moment, I worry that Sarge will edge us out. But he can't keep it up all the way to the finish line, having already burned himself out just a few moments ago.

Sarge lags behind, and it's just Joss and me and open trail ahead of us. I look to my side and see a smile breaking out across Joss's face, one that matches the ear-to-ear grin on my own.

I hear Joss's voice in my head again.

It's you and me, sunshine.

My eyes meet his.

You and me, menace.

Our hands reach for each other, tethering us together as we lunge across the finish line, collapsing in a heap at Dax's feet, our bodies too exhausted to stand even a moment longer.

The rain coats us like a blanket as we lay there in a pile of limbs and bodies, our chests heaving as our lungs struggle to recover. Joss rolls on top of me, propping himself up above me with his arms around my head like a tent. He looks down at me, beads of rain dripping from his hair onto my collarbones.

"We did it." I wish I could photograph the smile that rains down on me.

"We did it."

Joss and I peel our bodies off the ground, and I look back to see how far away Sarge is from finishing; he only has a few yards left, but he's noticeably limping. Joss and I wait for him at the finish line, pouring the last of our energy into encouraging words for him. Part of me wants to go to him, to help him hobble to the end, but another part of me feels that it's important for him to do this himself. To finish this Gauntlet on his own strength.

When Sarge finally crosses the finish line, he celebrates with a relieved smile, but there's still a touch of sadness at the corners of his features. When Sarge watches this episode back, I pray he's proud of himself. He was one unfortunate strategy maneuver away from beating us, and I hope he realizes it. Part of me can't help but wonder if Junior had been here with him if the outcome would be different. But I shove the thought away.

Junior's not here.

And Joss and I just won *American Gauntlet.*

"I'm proud of you," Sarge says, squeezing me into a hug.

"I'm proud of *you*," I say. I hang onto our embrace for

probably too long, relishing the way it feels to have Sarge, who feels so much like a cherished uncle, telling me he's proud of me. I wonder if he'll ever know how much he means to me. I make a mental note to tell him when this is all said and done.

When I finally pull away from our hug, I remember Dax is standing there waiting to address me and Joss, the *winners*. I can hardly believe it as the word floats through my mind. I stand next to Joss, and he puts his arm around me, tugging me into his chest. I gaze up at him with a huge smile on my face before I finally meet Dax's eyes, and my smile falters.

It's something about Dax's expression that just doesn't sit right with me, almost like…

Almost like he still has one last trick up his sleeve.

forty-eight

MY WHOLE body shudders at Dax's expression. I don't know if it's in my imagination or if I'm simply being paranoid, but the edge to his smile does nothing to soothe my anxiety.

"Dani, Joss," he says, breaking the silence. "Congratulations. You had what it takes to face the Gauntlet, and you did just that. You should be very proud of yourselves."

Joss gives me a tender squeeze, but anxiety still pools heavily in the pit of my stomach. Dax's tone seems a little too…cheerful. I feel like he's baiting us, hoping we get our spirits up just so he can crush them in his fist.

Stop sabotaging yourself, I think. *You won. Just enjoy the moment.*

"We just have one last order of business to attend to, and then we'll be on our way." I notice the rain has stopped, as if it, too, is holding its breath. "Joss, do you remember what I said to you when you won the second Endurance competition?"

My stomach plummets to the ground.

"Wins are always advantageous here at *American Gauntlet*," I answer for Joss, battling the urge to vomit.

Dax darts his eyes to me, quirking his brow in the process. "Very good, Dani."

Joss pulls his arm off of me. "What's this about, mate?" he

asks.

"Wins are always advantageous at *American Gauntlet*," Dax repeats. "Joss, *you* have more competition wins than your partner here."

While my stomach plummeted to the floor moments ago, it feels like it's in my throat now. I swallow down the bile that has risen up. It burns as it retreats to my stomach.

I look at Joss, I wait for him to reply, to say something—*anything*—but he doesn't even look at me. He stares intently at Dax, his blue eyes piercing holes into our host's forehead.

"I said wins are advantageous, and I'm here to let you know just how advantageous they are," Dax says, his expression darkening. "You have more wins than your partner, Joss. That means, you get to decide if you'd like to split the money with Dani," he says, pausing, "or take it all for yourself."

I can't fight it any longer. My body begins revolting, my breath growing fast and shallow, chills overtaking me in small convulsions. I've just put my body through a literal Gauntlet, and Dax's proposition to Joss is simply too much to handle. I take a few steps backward, trying to get ahold of myself while simultaneously fighting the urge to deck Dax in the face.

I…I know Joss. I know the kind of guy he is. He wouldn't leave me high and dry after everything we've been through… right?

But I can't stop the thoughts worming their way into my brain like maggots. What would stop Joss from taking the money? A brand-new relationship with me? In the grand scheme of things, our time here at *American Gauntlet* has felt like a lifetime but is really only a drop in the bucket. I'm suddenly second guessing everything I know about Joss. It doesn't help that he won't meet my eyes.

Until he does. His gaze finds mine, and it feels…cold. The warmth I can usually find in the corners of his eyes is gone, replaced instead by cool indifference.

"So what'll it be, Joss?" Dax prompts, his tone bordering on gleefully unhinged. He's living for this moment. "Are you going to split the money?"

It's hard for me to comprehend how I've found myself in this position. I won the Gauntlet, but it's not with Lana. I completed two days of this torturous tournament with my partner, and yet, I'm not guaranteed any of the winnings. Everything I had worked for over the last seven months. Everything I planned to do with the prize money. Everything I had endured in this grueling competition, this excruciating Gauntlet. The physical strain. The mental toll. The pain and the struggle and the perseverance.

I never imagined it would come down to seven words with a question mark at the end.

One, simple question.

And the worst part is I'm not the one answering it.

When Joss finally speaks to Dax, he keeps his eyes locked on mine.

"You know, Dax," he says amusedly, like this isn't the single most important moment of my life. "I recall offering to split my advantage with Dani when we were in that Endurance competition. Do you remember?"

"I sure do."

"And she turned my offer down, did she not?"

"She did." Dax's voice has turned downright maniacal.

This can't be happening. This can't be happening. This can't be happening.

How…how could I be so *stupid*? Like a guy is going to put a brand-new relationship ahead of an extra $150K in his bank account? Especially when I turned down his "promise" to split the advantage? I *knew* this was too good to be true. In the back of my mind, I've been waiting for the other shoe to drop, and it looks like it finally has—in *spectacular* fashion.

How on par with my life.

"Now, son…" Sarge says, but he's ignored. My eyes find his, and I see they're filled with shock and sadness.

I drag my gaze back to Joss and wait for the killing blow.

Each word is a punctuated punch to the gut.

He looks me straight in the eyes as he says, "No. I don't want to split the money."

forty-nine

IT FEELS as if the mountain beneath me has crashed to the ground, pinning me beneath its weight, crushing me until it squeezes the last remnants of air from my lungs. I'm suffocating, the thin, mountain air not doing enough to quell the ache in my chest.

And then.

A small sparkle in Joss's eye. A quirk of his lips, the corners pulling up just slightly at the sides.

The hurt that I'm sure is present on my face metamorphoses into confusion, the teeniest bead of hope daring to step forth.

Joss tears his eyes away from me and meets Dax's gaze.

"No, Dax. I don't want to split the prize money," he says, his voice taking on its usual warmth, "because I'd like Dani to have it all."

Dax wipes the delighted expression off his face, replaced instead by pure shock. His mouth hangs agape, as if even the great Dax Philipps, the creator of *American Gauntlet's* most unexpected game twists, didn't see this one coming.

Joss turns to me again, warmth exuding from him like the sun on a perfect spring day. "I accomplished everything I wanted to in this game. I've lived out every dream I've set for myself, and I think it's time that Penny gets that opportunity, too."

My legs feel shaky beneath me, and my brain struggles to process the whirlwind of events that just took place. I look at Dax, his face still full of surprise, then I look at Sarge, tears brimming at the corners of his eyes.

And finally, I look at Joss to find a mile-wide grin on his face.

I run to him and tackle him to the ground using the same maneuver I used during our very first competition. I pin him beneath me, and he dissolves into laughter.

"You absolute *menace!*" I scream at him. "How could you *do* that to me?" Even as the words leave my mouth, they give way to infectious laughter.

In an effortless maneuver, he flips on top of me, holding himself up with one arm. He places his hand on my cheek, brushing the hair from my eyes.

"Dani, how could you possibly think I would keep all of that money for myself? I mean honestly, I'm hurt it even crossed your mind."

"Right," I deadpan. "How could I *possibly* believe it? I don't think you understand what a convincing performance that was."

"It's reality TV, after all. Gotta have some drama somewhere," he confesses with a laugh. "But I mean it. I want you to have it. I don't want a dime."

Liquid pools in my eyes, and I wonder again if it's raining before I quickly realize, the warm, salty drops of water are my own tears this time.

"You—you can't do that, Joss."

"Ah, but I can." He presses a kiss to my forehead. "And I did. And there's nothing you can do about it, love."

The tears stream down my cheeks in violent rivers. "It's too much, Joss."

"Dani, I have everything I've ever wanted. I don't need that money—I have a job. I have a home. I have a girl that I'm crazy about." He gently wipes the tears from my cheek, a permanent smile on his face. "I don't need it, but your family does. So take it. It's a gift, love. One that doesn't have any strings attached. You could dump me this instant, and it wouldn't change a thing because that money? It's yours." He presses another kiss to my forehead before he looks around, his eyes finding Kelly. He hops off the ground as if we didn't just run a torturous marathon of sorts and helps me up.

"You'll make sure she gets it all, right?" he asks Kelly.

She bobs her head furiously. "Absolutely," she replies with a grin.

"Thank you," I say, wrapping my arms around Joss's neck. He lifts me off the ground, nuzzling into my neck with a contented sigh. "Now that I've taken you for all you're worth, you and I, we're done," I say into his hair, unable to contain the laughter that escapes. My performance isn't nearly as convincing as his.

He puts me on the ground and puts a finger under my chin, lifting my face up toward him. "Look who's the menace now."

I take his hand, threading my fingers through his. "Now what?" I ask, grinning. "What will we do now, Kellan Josskowski?"

"We'll figure it all out," he beams. "Together."

fifty

THE Houston airport feels just like home as I bob and weave through the congested airport crowd. I'm nearly bursting at the seams with excitement to see my family, which includes Ford, waiting for me at baggage claim. I hear an airline agent on the intercom calling the last chance for boarding at a nearby gate, while the smell of sizzling fajitas from a nearby restaurant suddenly hits my nose.

Yep. I'm home.

Just as I'm weaving around a slow walker that's taking up the middle of the lane, I'm tugged back by a finger that's been looped through the belt loop of my jeans. I spin around and find myself wound under Joss's arm.

"You know, we're not running the Gauntlet anymore," he teases. "We don't need to cut off every unsuspecting person trying to make their way through the airport."

"I'm sorry," I laugh. "I'm just so excited to see them." I lace my fingers through Joss's, pulling his arm further around me. I love that I'm the ideal height to nestle perfectly into his chest.

He presses a kiss to the top of my head. "I'm stoked to meet them too, sunshine."

Thanks to some last-minute maneuvering by Kelly, she was

able to change Joss's flight to Houston because, well, we just weren't ready to say goodbye. Ryder had been flown back to Georgia after his appendectomy recovery, and I insisted Joss talk to him on the phone about the prize money. Ryder vehemently refused to take any of it and insisted he's already "swimming in NIL deals." So Joss is here, in my city, with me, and we have no idea how long he'll stay. We have no idea what we'll do next. We have absolutely no plan whatsoever. But he's here for a little while, at least, and that's good enough for me.

I continue steering us toward baggage claim, my mind racing faster than my feet through this airport. I can't wait to share the news with them—the fact that I have enough money to cover Penny's program in its entirety. The actual amount I'll take home from the show is really about $160,000, since it's so heavily taxed, but it's enough to pay for the program and buy Lana a great car and maybe even stow a little bit away in my savings. It's only fitting that Joss is with me to deliver the news, considering what he did. I didn't tell my family that I'd be bringing a tall, blonde Australian with me, so it'll be a homecoming full of surprises.

As Joss and I get on the escalator that will bring us down to baggage claim, my heart pounds with anticipation.

"Okay, so it'll be Lana, Penny, my mom, and Ford," I tell him. "They'll probably have—"

"Giant posters and balloons?"

I whip my head toward the bottom of the escalator to see my little family waiting for me with neon pink "WELCOME HOME DANI" posters and enough balloons to draw the attention of every person within a half mile radius.

"Holy smokes," I say, a wide grin quickly spreading across my face.

Joss smiles. "These are my kind of people."

I watch their faces as they find me on the escalator and then glance at Joss posted at my side, his arm securely around me. Lana mouths, "*YESSSS*," while Penny's eyes go wide, her jaw dropping nearly to the airport floor. Ford smiles at me before he turns his attention to Joss, clearly sizing him up. *Oh boy.* I feel like I'm about to introduce Joss to my overprotective brother, and I'm desperately seeking his approval.

We're barely off the escalator before Penny jumps into my arms, engulfing me in a vicious hug.

"Hi, sis," I say to her before setting her down.

"Hello, darling," she says, wiping the stray tears from her eyes. "I've missed you dearly."

"I missed you so much," I say, before I track her eyes to Joss. *Classic.* "Penny, this is Joss."

"It's a pleasure to meet you, love," he says, extending his hand to her. "I've heard so much about you."

Penny melts into the floor, and I leave her to Joss while I turn my attention to Ford. He effortlessly picks me off the floor and spins me around in dramatic fashion.

"How's my Dani?" he asks before he's even set me down again.

"I missed you," I say, clutching onto him, not ready to let him go just yet.

"I'm so glad you're home." He squeezes his arms around me again before I finally relinquish him. "Who's this?" He quirks an eyebrow toward Joss, who is already in a full conversation with the three other Di Laurentis women.

"That's Joss. We like him."

"Yeah, we'll see about that."

"Be nice," I warn.

"I will, I will," Ford snorts. "I'm kidding, Dani. If *you* like him,

I'm sure he's great."

Before I can respond, Lana throws her arms around me from behind, practically climbing onto my back.

"*I MISSED YOU*," she screams right into my ear. I let her nuzzle into me, before I drop her to the ground, turning around to glare at her.

"I can't *believe* you!"

Her smile drops.

"You lied to me. You made me hate you. And then you just left a *note!* Are you kidding me? Do you know how much emotional damage that rollercoaster has caused me?"

She drops her eyes to the ground before she dramatically brings them back up with an ear-to-ear grin on her face. "There you go, sis! That's the kind of sisterly energy we need." She wraps me in another hug. "So proud of you."

I squeeze her back. "Thank you," I say. "For everything."

I give my mom a fierce hug before they all stand before Joss and I, expectantly awaiting the news.

"Dani, you simply mustn't keep us waiting!" Penny says, unable to contain her excitement. "Did you win?"

Joss and I spill the entire story, starting from when Lana left all the way through to the end.

"I *knew* you two would win! I knew it!" Lana squeals.

"Well…there's actually one more thing," I say. Joss looks anywhere but at my family; it appears the ceiling and airport floor are suddenly very fascinating to him. He's being modest, and it's adorable. When I deliver the news that Joss gave the prize money, in its entirety, to us for Penny's program, the three Di Laurentis women in front of me burst into tears.

"I—I can't believe this. Do you know what this means?" Penny muses, her head shaking in disbelief.

I squeeze her shoulder, as if to let her know this is all real. "I know, Penny. I know."

"Actually, I don't think you do," Penny says, and my stomach does a somersault. What more could there possibly be? I can't tell if they're about to deliver good or bad news. "I'm just thrilled you won the show, Dani. But you won't be using that money for my program."

"What are you talking about? You don't want to do the program?" I ask, uncertainty seeping into my features. "I thought that was your dream, Penny." I'm suddenly wondering if this was something I had pushed onto her. Did she only say she wanted to do it to appease her overbearing big sister?

"It is! It really is everything I've ever dreamed of. I'm still doing the program—I got my acceptance letter and everything! But I don't need your prize money. My tuition is…um, it's covered."

"I—*what?* Somebody fill me in please." I can't process a single word coming out of her mouth.

Ford, a huge grin on his face, cuts in. "Penny and I were very busy while you were gone, Dani." Penny is nearly jumping up and down from excitement beside him. "We met with pretty much every philanthropic rich person in Houston while you were gone…and we found a benefactor for Penny. We found someone who wants to pay her tuition. In full."

My mouth gapes open, and I don't have the mind to close it. The room suddenly feels like it's spinning. Joss grips onto me to keep me from falling over.

"Are—are you serious?"

"Absolutely," Ford and Penny say in unison, matching grins on their faces.

I wrap them both in a hug, unable to accurately express how

I feel. Ford…Ford did this. For Penny. For me. For us. That's the secret that Penny was keeping from me on our video chat all those weeks ago.

They say when it rains, it pours, and I've always felt that way about the circumstances in my life. But now it feels like the sun has finally come out…and it hasn't just appeared. It's shining brilliantly upon us.

In an almost dreamlike state, a cloud nine high, Joss and I grab our suitcases off the baggage claim belt, while my family runs to the parking garage to grab the car. Before he follows the Di Laurentis women to get the car, Ford pulls me aside, leveling me with an unreadable look.

"Oh, spit it out," I say.

"You know, Dani. I think I like him," he says, grinning. "In fact, I think he's…*spectacular.*"

Before I can even respond, Ford turns on his heels, following my mom and sisters out to the car. I didn't understand what Ford meant all those months ago when he said whoever I dated would be "spectacular." But I get it now. Because Joss? He's the definition of the word.

As Joss and I have a moment to ourselves while my family brings the car around, I wrap my arms around his neck. He places his hands at my hips, his fingers sliding beneath the hem of my shirt, resting against the bare skin there. He rubs the goosebumps away, his calloused thumbs sliding gently back and forth.

His hands distract me for a moment before I wipe the euphoric grin off my face. I will my face into a solemnity to match the gravity of the conversation we're about to have, but it's difficult when I can't think of anything but where his skin touches mine.

I focus enough to finally get the words out.

"You have to take your half, Joss."

He frowns, his thumbs stilling. "I already told you, love. The money is yours. The fact that Penny's program is paid for doesn't change that."

My mind is working in overdrive. If Penny's program is paid for, that would mean I could use the money to get Lana a car, give a portion to my mom to help her pay off her debt, and even stash a good portion away in my savings account. In no uncertain terms, it would completely change our lives. But for Joss to not take any of it…

He sighs loudly before I can finish the thought. "I can see you're still internally debating this, so I'm going to stop you right there. It's yours, Dani. A gift. And there's nothing you need to do to repay it—that's what a gift is."

"Are you sure?" I ask, nibbling at my bottom lip.

"I'm absolutely positive, sunshine," he says. "Although, actually…there's one thing I'd like to ask of you."

"Anything," I breathe.

"Dani Di Laurentis, will you go on a date with me?"

I laugh, gripping his neck and bringing his mouth to mine. Our kiss is all smiles and playful laughter as we enjoy this moment, a moment that's not a reality TV show moment with cameras watching and producers lurking. It's a real life moment, and it feels just that—*real*.

Before I can answer, Joss amends his question.

"Actually, you know what? I owe you some Tim Tams," he says, grinning. "Will you go on a date with me…in Australia?"

. . .

playlist

THE CHRONOLOGICAL *AMERICAN GAUNTLET* PLAYLIST

A Moment Apart
ODESZA

West Coast
OneRepublic

Midnight Rain
Taylor Swift

Wonder
Shawn Mendes

Cloudy Day
Tones and I

Labyrinth
Taylor Swift

American Money
BØRNS

Until We Go Down
Ruelle

Electric Love
BØRNS

*open your Spotify app, click 'Search' & click the
camera icon to scan*

acknowledgements

AMERICAN GAUNTLET was truly a labor of love, and I owe its completion to many hours of prayer and an overflowing cup of encouragement from some of my favorite people.

Kyle, you are *the* man of all men, real or fictional. Thank you for believing in this dream of mine and sticking with me through many late nights, long weekends, and endless hours spent in my editing cave to get this book across the finish line. I love you and I can't wait to watch Channing fall in love with you, too.

Thank you to my family and close friends who seem to have formed a personal cheer squad for my books. You make this fun and exciting, even when I'm in the throes of self-doubt.

Thank you to my editor and friend, Carleigh. You are truly a ray of sunshine. Thank you for the love and care you've put into my books and for the extra comments in the editing doc that make me smile (and occasionally laugh out loud). I truly couldn't be more grateful for you.

Thank you to Tay Rose who helped make this book what it is. You have a gift for taking something good and making it great, and I'm so happy we were able to reconnect thanks to a little help from Instagram.

Thank you to the Anxiety Book Club for memes and general anxiety support, even if we've been reading the same book for like four months now.

Thank you, thank you, thank you to the many friends I've made on Bookstagram. I never dreamed I'd find such genuine connections on a social media app, but I truly have found some of the sweetest friends. Thank you for all the love and support. You make this writing thing so much fun.

Finally, thank you to everyone who picked up this book. You're making a little girl's dream of one day becoming an author come true. Thank you, thank you, thank you.

xoxo, allie lewis

ALLIE LEWIS has been obsessed with books since she read
Matilda as a little girl and learned that books are pure magic.
After many years browsing the aisles of Barnes & Noble and
dreaming about what it would be like to become an author, she
finally decided to just make it happen. She likes to say all of her
books, present and future, are "exciting stories about love."

@authorallielewis
authorallielewis.com